The Phoenix Legacy

Winter H Rayne

Phi Long Publishing

Dedication

THIS WRITING JOURNEY HAS helped me understand myself more deeply and transformed me in ways I could never imagined. For that, I have so much to be thankful for.

My husband once told me that every book needs a dedication. So, in honor of the growth I've experienced and the love I've been blessed with, I dedicate this book to all the women out there who have dreams and passions. Believe in yourself. Surround yourself with those who believe in you. And never let the flames of your passion go out.

To my beautiful daughters and my amazing niece — I love you, and I believe in you. If ever you need a reminder of how incredible you are, I hope you'll pick up this book and remember all the laughter, love, and even the tears we shared while bringing this dream to life. Without your support, this wouldn't have been possible.

Map

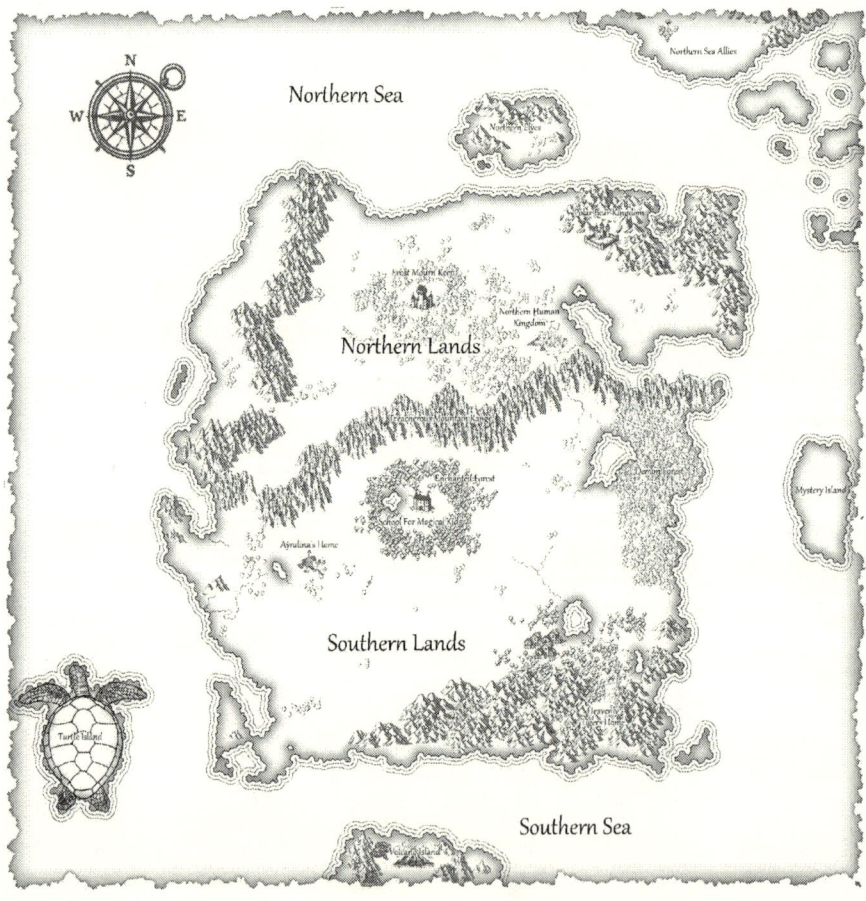

Contents

Prologue I.

WHEN I WAS A little girl, my mother told me countless enchanting stories about princesses and their adventures filled with love and rescue. In her tales, the princess was always saved by her courageous prince. Their journey always began with the phrase "Once upon a time" and would always end with the timeless promise of a "happily ever after." But for me, my story truly began after my "happily ever after."

Like most princesses, I lived what could be described as a very normal princess life growing up in the Phoenix Kingdom. Well at least as normal as life could be for someone of royal blood with a lineage steeped in ancient legend. I was a young 300-year-old phoenix when I met the love of my life, Silvaris. At the time, I was a proud Sunflame Phoenix, radiating the fiery energy of the sun itself, and Silvaris was a 500-year-old Moon Frost Dragon, a being of ice and shadows, embodying the cool serenity of the moon. During that time, he was still fighting his way to the top of the dragon realm. It may seem unusual to imagine a phoenix of fire and a dragon of frost finding love, but in the world of mythical beings, opposites can have a mysterious way of finding balance within one another.

As you can surmise, the lifespan of a phoenix and a dragon are extraordinary, stretching far beyond what most mortals could comprehend—some may even call it eternal. But it isn't just our longevity that defines us. You see, we phoenixes are gifted—or perhaps cursed, depending on how one looks at it—with a unique bond. We only fall in love once throughout our entire existence. That love stretches over from one lifetime to the next, and the next. Our love and our bond once fulfilled becomes eternal. If our beloved passes away, half of our soul follows them into the next life, tethering us to them through every existence. For us, love is not just a fleeting emotion but an unbreakable thread, weaving through time and space, connecting our souls forever. I believe humans call this soulmate.

A Phoenixes journey begins long before we ever draw our first breath. Like humans, we are born from our mothers. However, once born, we are incubated within a cocoon of flame for another 100 years, sometimes longer. Why the variation in incubation time? No one knows for sure, but it is believed that the stronger the lineage, the longer it takes for a phoenix to hatch. When most phoenixes finally emerge from their flame cocoons, they are born in their phoenix form—a magnificent creature of fire and feathers. It then takes another 100 years for them to develop the ability to transform into their human form.

But my family, those from the royal Sunflame lineage, we are different. In the world of the Phoenix, we are considered, unique. Unlike the majestic creatures of legend, born from flame and ash in their full, radiant form, we are born in small, fragile, mortal, and seemingly ordinary human bodies. Our phoenix essence lies dormant within us, like an ember buried deep inside, waiting to be awakened.

Cultivating our phoenix abilities is not a gift we inherit at birth; it is a path we are destined to walk—a sacred journey of self-discovery, discipline, and, often, peril. Every flame we summon, every power we master, comes with struggle and hardship. Our emotions can either ignite our potential or consume us entirely, for the fire within us is both a source of strength and a force of destruction if left unchecked.

The Sunflame lineage, my lineage, carries the purest essence of the first Sunflame. A gift from the sun goddess herself. The original sunflame phoenix, recognized for her light and bravery, was honored as a child of the sun and was bestowed on to her the very first essence. This essence not only gave birth to life but also awakened magic, marking the origin of the Sunflame lineage. Only a true Sunflame Phoenix can cultivate the undying flame of the sun—an essence that sets us apart. Unlike ordinary phoenixes, we alone possess the power to die and rise again from our own ashes.

Our power is more than a birthright, it is also a burden. We are not merely rulers of the Phoenix Kingdom; we are its guardians, living vessels of an ancient fire that has burned since the dawn of time. Through us, the Sunflame has endured for millennia, its power woven into the very fabric of our kingdom's existence.

This connection has made us both revered and hunted. Many have sought to claim our power, believing it can be taken. But the truth is, the flame we carry cannot be stolen—it must be earned. The Sunflame is not a power to be taken lightly. It demands sacrifice, resilience, and an unyielding spirit because each reincarnation carries the weight of every life lived before it.

We are more than a royal family adorned with crowns and titles. We are the last line of defense between light and darkness, protectors of those who cannot protect themselves. The demons that lurk in the shadows, the darkness that spans across the universe—against them, we stand unwavering. It is not just our duty. It is our purpose, etched into our very souls.

So, while others dream of reaching their "happily ever after," it is at this point that my story has only just begun.

II.

"Come quickly. Follow me."

"Where are we going, Father?"

Ayralina struggled to keep up with her father as they sprinted through a brightly lit hallway. Her legs felt like lead, and her eyelids were heavy with exhaustion. The relentless battle that had raged on for three days showed no signs of abating. She didn't know where the demons had come from, but they just kept pouring in.

As they ran, she caught fleeting glimpses of the courtyard where her father had once taught her to fight and harness her powers. It was now a wasteland, littered with bodies and engulfed in flames. Her mother's meticulously tended bushes and flower beds lay crushed and trampled. The castle walls, once a symbol of their kingdom's strength, were riddled with gaping holes.

Ahead, her father, the Phoenix King, kept running. Behind them, Silvaris—her husband—guarded the rear, fending off demons that came too close.

"Father, stop! What's going on?"

The Phoenix King turned, his expression grim, his fiery eyes dulled by fatigue. "This is not the time for explanations, Ayralina," he growled, though his voice carried more sorrow than anger. "You need to get to safety."

Ayralina clenched her fists. "No! I've fought alongside you for three days! You owe me the truth, Father. Why are the demons here? Why is our own family leading them?"

The King hesitated, glancing down the hall where the clamor of battle grew louder. The dragon King–Silvaris, roars of defiance echoed behind them, signaling his struggle to hold the demons at bay. Finally, her father sighed and spoke, his words heavy like the weight of centuries.

"It was your cousin, Saraphina," he admitted. "The one you knew as the gentle phoenix, your mother's niece. She deceived us all. She was not what she seemed."

Ayralina felt the ground tilt beneath her. "Saraphina? That's impossible! She's family! She's—"

She's a demonic phoenix," her father interrupted, his voice heavy with grief. "Born of shadow and flame, the result of forbidden magic. Her mother your aunt Solaraya hid her, hoping to suppress the darkness within, but Saraphina always knew. She came to us with deception in her heart. Your aunt Flora uncovered the truth and warned us, but we believed she could change. We were wrong—she had already embraced the darkness."

Ayralina's heart sank as memories of Saraphina flooded her mind—her cousin's kind smiles, her laughter, and whispered encouragement during training.
"She infiltrated our home," Ayralina whispered. "And we never saw it."

Her father's expression hardened. "She gained our trust—only to betray it. And now, she's bewitched and turned Zepherion the Dragon General against us, using his legions to invade our kingdom. Together, they shattered our defenses and unleashed this hell upon us."
"Ayralina's legs wavered, but she steadied herself. "Why would she do this?"

A sudden roar of flame erupted behind them, and Silvaris stumbled into view, his sword blazing with the frost of the moon. "We don't have time for this!" he yelled. "The demons are closing in!"

Ayralina glanced at her father, then at Silvaris. A fiery determination lit her eyes. "I'm not running," she said, her voice steady. "This is my kingdom too, and I will not abandon it."

"Ayralina, you must go! You must protect your child—our grandchild. This is what it's all about."

Her father's voice softened with urgency as he continued.
"When we learned you were with child," he began, his voice weighted with gravity, "your

mother and I consulted the Divine Astronomer. He prophesied that once every thousand years, when the seven stars align, a golden child would be born to a Dragon-Phoenix family. This child would have the power to either unite or destroy the universe."

Ayralina's breath caught.

Her father pressed on, searching her eyes for understanding. "We didn't want to believe it, so we kept the prophecy a secret. But the stars are about to align now, Ayralina. The astronomer foretold that the child you carry—our grandchild—is that golden child."

Ayralina staggered under the weight of his words.

"This can't be true," she murmured. "How can an unborn child bear such a judgment? This isn't fair!"

She turned to Silvaris, seeking reassurance. Instead, she found guilt etched into his face.

"You knew," she whispered, her voice trembling.

Silvaris stepped closer, cupping her face in his hands. "I didn't want to burden you. I thought we could keep it hidden, but somehow, the demons found out. They want the power that our child will hold."

The balance between good and evil has always been in our favor, and now even more so when the golden child is born. To counter that, in their desperation, the demons decided to steal the ancient Scroll of the Sunflame, convinced that it would grant them unimaginable power and eternal life. Their obsession with the scroll had driven them to sinister measures—they had even bewitched Saraphina, twisting her mind and turning her into their unwilling ally.

Before Ayralina could fully comprehend the weight of these revelations, the ground beneath her feet began to tremble violently. The castle's hallway shuddered, sending small shards of stone and dust cascading from the cracked ceiling. A thunderous roar reverberated through the air, shaking her to her core.

Through the jagged breach in the castle walls, an enormous shadow loomed, casting an ominous darkness across the once-bright corridor. Her heart raced as the fiery glow of red eyes pierced through the gloom—the Right hand Dragon General - Zephiron had arrived. His massive wings beat against the air, creating gusts strong enough to extinguish the torches lining the hall. His armored scales gleamed like molten steel, and his presence radiated an oppressive power that made the very air around him feel heavy.

Before Ayralina could react, a deafening explosion erupted somewhere deep within the castle grounds. The force of the blast sent vibrations rippling through the stone floor, knocking her slightly off balance. The sound snapped her back to reality, her mind racing with the realization that the demons' assault had begun in earnest. Their forces were no longer lurking in the shadows—they had brought war to the very heart of the castle, and the Dragon General was leading the carnage.

"Ayralina," her father said urgently, "the soldiers are giving their lives to protect you. You must survive. Our kingdom's future depends on you."

Ayralina placed a protective hand on her belly, tears welling in her eyes.

"I can't leave without you and Mother," she pleaded.

The Phoenix King's face softened. He stepped forward, wiping her tears and pressing a kiss to her forehead.

"We'll always be with you," he said. "But now, you must go."

Turning to Silvaris, he commanded, "Protect them both with your life."

Silvaris nodded solemnly.

Another explosion shattered the air, and the three of them raced down the corridor. When they reached the royal study, Silvaris quickly barricaded the door, shoving heavy furniture against it while the king activated a hidden mechanism behind his ornate desk. With a low rumble, a concealed passageway opened, revealing a path to the portal and simultaneously triggering the study's defensive traps.

Inside the hidden chamber, the Phoenix Queen stood tall, her silver-blonde hair cascading around her like a shimmering halo, defying the absence of any wind. She looked regal and mighty, her hands glowing with an intense, fiery power as she held the portal open, stabilizing its swirling energy.

Ayralina dashed to her mother, tears streaming down her face as she clung to her desperately. "Please, come with us!" she begged, her voice breaking with emotion.

The queen gazed at her daughter with a sad but resolute smile, gently caressing Ayralina's tear-streaked face. "This is not goodbye, my little flame," she said softly, her voice steady despite the chaos around them. "We will meet again. I promise."

She removed her ruby necklace and placed it around Ayralina's neck. "This will protect you."

The king retrieved an ancient scroll from a hidden box in the chamber and handed it to her.

"This is the Scroll of the Undying Flame," he explained. "Guard it with your life. If it falls into enemy hands, our lineage will be broken."

The queen added, "Seek out your Aunt Flora. She will guide you."

Before Ayralina could protest, her mother raised her hand, sending a gentle force that pushed Silvaris and Ayralina through the portal.

As they drifted away, Ayralina turned back for one last glimpse of her parents. Her heart broke as she saw demons breach the study, her mother and father preparing for their final stand.

"Silvaris, we can't let their sacrifice be in vain," she said, clutching the scroll tightly.

Together, they fled through the swirling dark portal, their forms swallowed by the shimmering void.

When they emerged on the other side, the vast and infinite expanse of space greeted them. Ayralina stumbled slightly, her legs shaky from the disorienting journey. Traveling through portals had always been an unsettling experience, but this one had been hastily conjured, making it even worse. Her battered body felt as if it had been squeezed through a narrow tube, the suffocating pressure leaving her lightheaded. The portal's energy had not yet fully stabilized, and its residual turbulence clung to her, amplifying her discomfort.

She paused to catch her breath, glancing around in awe at the endless, star-studded void. Countless stars sparkled like diamonds against the black canvas of space, their light is both beautiful and overwhelming. The air—or rather, the lack of it—felt strange, as if she were suspended in a dreamlike state.

"Where are we? Ayralina asked, her voice filled with wonder and a hint of unease as she gazed at the starry expanse stretching in every direction.

"We're somewhere between the sun and the Seven Stars," Silvaris replied, his tone steady but laced with urgency. His eyes scanned the void, his dragon senses more attuned to their surroundings. He pointed to a shimmering blue orb in the distance, its vibrant glow standing out against the dark backdrop. "If we head toward that blue planet—Earth—we can hide there."

Ayralina followed his gaze, focusing on the planet he had indicated. It seemed both distant and inviting, a beacon of hope in the cold emptiness of space. She took a deep breath, trying to calm her racing heart, and nodded.

Silvaris extended his midnight-blue dragon wings, their powerful expanse shimmering faintly against the starlit void, while Ayralina's fiery phoenix wings unfurled with a blazing intensity, glowing like the heart of a sun. Together, they launched into flight, hurtling toward Earth with unwavering resolve. The space around them was treacherous, riddled with fiery projectiles and drifting asteroids that threatened to end their escape at any moment. They twisted and veered, narrowly dodging each obstacle, their movements a desperate dance of survival.

But the journey began to take its toll. Ayralina's strength waned, her wings faltering under the weight of exhaustion and pain. A sudden miscalculation brought her dangerously close to a massive asteroid. She twisted sharply, avoiding it by mere inches, but the near-collision jostled her grip on the ancient Scroll of the Sunflame. The scroll, their most precious possession, slipped from her grasp and shattered into two pieces. One half spun violently into the void, drifting far out of reach.

"No!" she screamed, her voice raw with anguish, the sound carrying her heartbreak into the emptiness. She reached out, her fingers clawing at the void, but it was too late.

Silvaris reacted instantly, his massive wings curling protectively around her just as a blazing fireball hurtled toward them. The impact struck with immense force, sending them tumbling uncontrollably toward Earth. The air around them grew hotter as they plummeted through the planet's atmosphere, their bodies encased in a fiery trail of light that streaked across the sky.

As the ground rushed closer, Ayralina's mind was a whirlwind of emotions. Tears streamed down her face, but with each tear came a spark of determination that burned brighter within her. She clung to her purpose; her soul ignited with an unyielding vow.

I will protect my child. I will protect my people. I will protect our legacy—no matter the cost.

The world below loomed larger, and despite the chaos, Ayralina gritted her teeth and braced herself for impact.

III.

"Silvaris. Silvaris!" Ayralina's voice trembled as she knelt beside him, her fiery wings now dim and flickering in the cool, earthy air as it slowly receded. "Wake up! You can't sleep now. You're bleeding too much. I need to heal you first."

Silvaris groaned, his midnight-blue scales dull and streaked with crimson. Slowly, he forced his eyes open, his usually vibrant gaze clouded with pain. "Did we... land on Earth yet?" he rasped, his voice barely audible.

"Yes, I think so," Ayralina replied, her eyes darting around their surroundings. They had landed in a vast, empty field, the horizon stretching endlessly in all directions under the faint glow of moonlight. The tall grass swayed gently in the night breeze; the silence broken only by the soft hum of nocturnal insects. There were no signs of civilization—no roads, no buildings, no lights—just an eerie emptiness that made her uneasy. "We're in an empty field. Nothing but grass for miles. Now sit up. I need to heal you."

Silvaris gritted his teeth, trying to push himself upright but wincing as pain shot through his body. "No, not here," he said, shaking his head weakly. "We need to get to safety first. If they followed us through the portal, this place won't stay empty for long."

Ayralina placed a firm hand on his shoulder, her fiery glow flaring slightly in determination. "No," she insisted, her voice steady despite her fear. "If I don't stop the bleeding now, they'll catch onto your scent and track us. We can't outrun them if you're like this. We at least have to stop the bleeding and mask our trail."

Silvaris hesitated, his instinct to flee warring with his trust in her. Finally, he gave a slight nod, retracting his wings and leaning forward to allow her to work. "Ok," he said gently. "But make it quick."

Ayralina knelt behind him, her breath catching in her throat as her eyes fell on the gruesome wounds that marred Silvaris's back. A jagged gash ran diagonally across his broad shoulders, so deep that shards of his silvery bone glinted faintly beneath torn ligaments and shredded muscle. Blood flowed freely, pooling in the grass beneath him and staining the earth a dark crimson. Her chest tightened with a mix of fear and anguish, but she forced herself to push the emotions aside. Silvaris needed her now, and there was no room for hesitation.

Swallowing hard, she pressed her trembling hands against the edges of the wound. The warmth of his blood seeped into her palms, but she ignored it, closing her eyes to summon the healing energy within her. She let her fiery phoenix spirit flow through her body and into her fingertips, her hands beginning to glow with a golden light.

As the light spread, her essence entered his wounds. She started with the worst damage, focusing on sealing the broken blood vessels to stem the relentless bleeding. The golden light surged, weaving through the ruptured veins like delicate threads, knitting them together until the flow of blood ceased. Next, she turned her attention to the torn ligaments and shredded muscles, her energy coursing through his body like molten fire, coaxing the tissues to regenerate. The process was painstakingly slow; each frayed fiber painstakingly rejoined, and each layer of muscle realigned.

Silvaris groaned softly, his body shuddering under the intense heat of her magic. "Ayralina," he murmured, his voice hoarse with pain, "that's enough. Save your energy. We might need it later."

"No," she whispered, her voice cracking under the weight of her emotions. Tears welled in her eyes, but she refused to let them fall. "I can't stand seeing you like this. It hurts too much."

Her words pierced through his resistance. Silvaris opened his eyes briefly, his gaze softening despite the pain etched across his face. He reached out, his fingers brushing against her cheek before he pressed a gentle kiss to her forehead. "Do what you must," he said quietly, closing his eyes and leaning forward to let her continue.

Encouraged by his trust, Ayralina redoubled her efforts. The golden light intensified, spreading across his back in rippling waves. As the torn muscles mended and the shattered bone reformed, she felt the strain in her own body grow heavier. Healing at this level wasn't without cost, but she didn't care. Each flicker of energy she gave was worth it to see him whole again.

Finally, the wound began to close, the raw edges knitting together seamlessly. Ayralina let out a shaky breath, her hands trembling, she then drew a seed of Sunflame from deep within her core, a piece of her Phoenix essence. She planted it in his spine, letting it take root, winding around his backbone to reinforce it. The seed's power once taken roots would strengthen him and give him the power to regenerate quickly making him more resilient and allowing him to grow stronger with future cultivation.

When she finished, Silvaris's wounds were completely healed, though his energy remained depleted.

Silvaris took a deep breath, the excruciating pain gone. "You're amazing," he murmured, but before he could say more, Ayralina collapsed beside him, utterly drained

"Rest, my love," Silvaris said softly, brushing a strand of her strawberry-blonde hair from her face. His voice carried a soothing calm, a contrast to the chaos they had just escaped. His dark hair, black as midnight, shimmered faintly under the moonlight, and his eyes—deep and clear—reflected the expanse of stars above. Even in his weariness, there was a steadiness to him, an unshakable resolve rooted in his connection to the Earth itself. Silvaris, although he is a Moon Frost Dragon, he has always drawn solace and strength from the embrace of Mother Nature. He was lucky enough to be recognized by her as a son of nature and has a bond with her as timeless as the stars.

Taking a deep breath, he shifted his focus to the ground beneath them. The soft hum of the earth resonated faintly through his fingertips as he plunged his hands into the cool, damp soil. Closing his eyes, he reached out with his spirit, sending a silent call to Mother Nature, a prayer of both desperation and gratitude. The earth responded immediately, as though recognizing the urgency of its ancient ally.

A subtle tremor ran through the ground, rippling outward in waves. Around them, the grasses began to move, not from the wind, but with purpose. The blades thickened and intertwined, creating a living carpet that spread across the field, rolling over their tracks and erasing any sign of their landing. Wildflowers of every color sprang to life, their fragrant blossoms opening in unison, masking the sharp, metallic scent of blood with sweet, earthy aromas.

The air grew heavy, and a dense, silvery fog began to rise from the ground, swirling around them like a living entity. It thickened with every breath Silvaris took, wrapping them in a protective cocoon that shielded them from prying eyes. The fog seemed to carry a life of its own, its cool touch soothing the lingering heat from Ayralina's fiery aura.

Ayralina stirred, her eyes fluttering, but too tired to open. "What... what's happening?" she murmured weakly.

"Mother Earth is answering my call," Silvaris whispered, his voice low and reverent. "She's helping us hide. Rest now, Ayralina. We are safe, at least for the moment." Before he could finish, Ayralina had already nodded off to sleep.

As the fog settled, Silvaris felt the pulse of the earth beneath him slow, its energy grounding him. He pulled his hands from the soil, the connection fading but leaving behind a sense of calm resolve. The field around them was no longer an exposed patch of grass but a sanctuary cloaked in nature's protective embrace.

For a moment, they sat in silence; the only sounds were the soft rustling of the grasses and the faint hum of the earth's heartbeat.

Silvaris glanced at Ayralina, his heart swelling with love and awe. He still couldn't believe how incredible she was—how she had healed him so completely, even in her own exhaustion. Yet a pang of guilt tugged at him. Ayralina was a healer, not a fighter, and the thought of her being forced into battle by his side filled him with anger at himself. He had failed to protect her, and that failure weighed heavily on his soul.

Drawing on the nurturing energy of the earth, Silvaris leaned back and channeled the healing force into Ayralina.

Taking a deep breath, she opened her eyes "Silvaris, I can't see anything!"

He chuckled, his celebrity smile flashing—the same one that had won her heart long ago. "Silly girl. You've got me. Nothing to worry about."

Ayralina rolled her eyes. "That's what I'm worried about. What's the plan now?"

Silvaris hesitated, then smirked. "Here's a thought. Sometimes, the most dangerous place is also the safest."

Ayralina raised an eyebrow. "Go on."

"We'll spread my blood around to confuse them and stay here. You can open a realm big enough to hide us temporarily. The blood will draw them in, but the abundance will make them doubt themselves. They'll assume we've fled elsewhere and leave."

Ayralina considered his plan, biting her lip. "Okay," she said finally. "But if this backfire..."

"It won't," Silvaris reassured her.

As Silvaris carried out his plan, Ayralina directed her remaining energy toward a task that pushed her beyond anything she had attempted before. She was no stranger to creating small realms—pocket spaces designed to store minor objects or conceal fragile items—but this was different. She needed something vast, strong, and stable enough to protect both of them. Closing her eyes, she inhaled deeply, centering herself, and reached into the core of her phoenix magic. Heat surged through her veins as she concentrated, her fiery essence flaring outward. Slowly, the air around her shimmered, rippling like a mirage as she began shaping the boundaries of the new realm.

The strain was immediate and intense. Her flame flickered unsteadily and sweat beaded on her brow. The golden glow of her magic pulsed erratically, threatening to collapse under the weight of her task. Then, a stirring deep within her belly made her pause.

Her unborn child was reaching out.

Ayralina could feel it—an innate, wordless connection—drawing energy from nature itself. In response, Mother Earth answered, sending a surge of raw power through her. Strength flooded her limbs, and the wavering light of her magic steadied.

Gritting her teeth, she pressed on. She envisioned the space with absolute clarity—a sanctuary, a place untouched by the world's chaos—and commanded her magic to shape it into being.

The once-peaceful human village lay shrouded in smoke and ash, its streets soaked in crimson. Broken bodies littered the cobblestone paths, faces frozen in expressions of terror, their final moments stolen by the monstrous fury that had descended upon them. Homes burned, casting flickering shadows that danced with a sinister rhythm as if mocking the lives lost.

Nearby sat a small group of survivors—men, women, and children, they were herded and bound in iron chains in the village square. Their eyes, wide with horror, flickered between the lifeless corpses around them and the demons standing guard. Some whimpered in fear, others sat in silent resignation, their fate uncertain but grim.

At the center of the devastation stood an imposing demon, his grotesque figures born from rage and hatred. Their leader, Valkor, a towering beast with obsidian horns and molten eyes, surveyed the carnage with a twisted grin. His clawed hand gripped a jagged blade, dark as midnight, its edge glistening with a deadly sheen of poison.

They had been chasing him for hours, yet he remained just out of reach, slipping through their grasp time and time again. Worse yet, he had managed to take down several of Valkor's men in the process.

Frustrated, Valkor devised a plan to lure the dragon out.

"This will draw him out," he hissed, his voice a guttural snarl that echoed through the abandoned village. "He cannot resist. His weakness is his humanity."

And so, they waited.

Hours passed. The fires dimmed, leaving only smoldering embers and the acrid stench of death. The prisoners trembled, huddled together as their captors loomed over them, waiting for the inevitable.

Then—a shadow moved at the village's edge.

A figure cloaked in tattered silver and black, eyes burning with quiet fury.

Silvaris.

He stepped into the ruin, his gaze sweeping over the fallen innocents and the terrified hostages. His fists clenched around the hilt of his sword. The demons had succeeded in luring him here, and he will make them pay for it.

With a whisper of frost and steel, his blade, Darkmoon, came to life. The enchanted steel shimmered with an ethereal blue glow, mist curling from its edge as cold as death itself. The air around him chilled, and with a silent vow of vengeance, Silvaris moved.

He struck like a winter storm unleashed. Frost and fury guided his blade as he carved through the demons, each slash leaving trails of ice upon their flesh. Limbs froze and shattered, howls of agony rising into the night. The demons fought back, but they were no match for his speed, his rage, his unrelenting will.

But then—Valkor moved.

From the shadows, the demon lord struck a swift, brutal slash that Silvaris barely deflected. Their blades clashed with a screech of metal and dark magic, sparks flying into the night. Silvaris fought with everything he had, but Valkor was relentless, his strength fueled by dark sorcery.

Then all of a sudden, a feint—a flicker of movement too fast to counter. Valkor's poisoned blade found its mark, sliding into Silvaris's side with a sickening crunch. Pain exploded through him, sharp and blinding. The toxin burned like liquid fire beneath his skin.

Biting back the pain he lashed out, driving Darkmoon deep into Valkor's chest. The blade pulsed with an icy glow, frost spreading from the wound, cracking across the demon's dark hide. Valkor staggered, black ichor spilling from the wound, his body momentarily seized by the creeping cold.

Silvaris couldn't go on—not like this. His vision blurred, muscles stiffening from the poison. The hostages remained bound, demons standing guard.

Adrenaline surged. With Darkmoon, he slashed at their chains, freeing as many as he could. Then, pushing through the agony, he sprinted into the night. The forest swallowed him, leaving the wounded, enraged demons behind.

Valkor snarling through gritted fangs. His molten eyes flickered toward the terrified hostages, his grin returning.

"Run while you still can, Silvaris," Valkor spat, blood dripping from his maw. "The poison will finish what I've started. You cannot escape the poison."

Then, with a cruel grin, he raised his clawed hand, dark magic crackling at his fingertips. Flames erupted, roaring to life as they consumed what remained of the village. The terrified screams of the hostages echoed through the night, swallowed by the inferno. Smoke and embers rose into the sky, a final, merciless act of destruction.

Satisfied, Valkor turned and vanished into the darkness, leaving nothing behind but ash, ruin, and the weight of Silvaris's failure.

Just as the shimmering outline of the realm began to solidify, Silvaris staggered into view. The sight of him nearly shattered her concentration. He was barely upright, his midnight-blue wings dragging limply behind him, battered and torn. His silver armor, once gleaming and unyielding, was shredded in places, streaked with blood and grime. Deep gashes marred his arms and chest, and his face was pale, almost ghostly, from exhaustion and pain. Yet, despite the state of his body, his eyes burned fiercely—a turbulent mix of fury, grief, and regret that took Ayralina's breath away.

"Silvaris!" Her hands trembled as she reached out, steadying him before he could collapse.

"What happened? Why are you hurt?" she demanded, her voice tight with fear as her gaze darted over his injuries. His wounds were deep—jagged claw marks tore across his chest, and scorch marks hinted at the cruel touch of dark magic.

Silvaris swayed slightly, leaning into her touch as he struggled to catch his breath. "They set a trap for me," he said hoarsely, his voice rough and strained. "The demons—Valkor, their commander—were hunting us. In his failed attempt to track us, he made a pilgrimage to a human village."

His fists clenched, knuckles whitening as memories surged back like a tide of regret. "They were stronger than I expected... and they had human hostages." His voice tightened, thick with bitterness. "They used innocent lives to lure me out. I couldn't just stand by and do nothing—I had to try. I had to save them."

His breath hitched; his expression shadowed with grief. "I walked straight into their trap." His voice cracked, and he turned away, shame flickering in his eyes. "But in the end... I still couldn't save them!"

With a sudden, violent motion, his fist crashed against the rock beside him, the sharp thud echoing through the stillness. The impact sent a jolt of pain up his arm, but he welcomed it—anything to drown out the crushing weight of failure that coiled around his chest. His anger, his despair, all of it poured out, raw and uncontained.

Ayralina's heart ached at the sight of him like this, so burdened by guilt and pain. She reached for his arm, her touch gentle but firm, trying to ground him in the present. "Silvaris, you did what you could. You fought for them—you tried—"

"Is it done?" he interrupted, his voice sharp with urgency. He couldn't afford to dwell on his failure—he couldn't save the humans. All that mattered now was ensuring their escape, so he forced his focus elsewhere.

Ayralina hesitated for a moment, her emotions warring within her, but she forced herself to nod. "Yes. It's ready," she said quietly, her voice steady despite the turmoil threatening to overwhelm her.

Silvaris met her gaze briefly, his own filled with exhaustion and regret, but he straightened himself as best he could. "Let's go," he said.

They had no time to mourn, no time to rest—the battle was far from over.

"I can't believe it worked," Ayralina said, looking around. The space was barren, an endless clear sky stretching over flat land.

Silvaris surveyed their surroundings. "Not bad," he murmured before kneeling and pressing his hands into the soil. "Let's make this space more accommodating, shall we?"

The earth responded. A cave rose from the ground, fresh grass spreading across the land. Inside, the cavern soared with high ceilings, its walls glimmering with multicolored crystals that bathed the space in a soft, natural glow. At its center, a serene pool formed, its water clear and inviting. Above it, a red stalactite dripped with the essence of heaven and earth, infusing the pool with power. Off to one side, a jade-carved bed emerged from the stone. The cave stretched wide, with multiple corridors leading to separate chambers, including one with a stone table and chairs.

"How did you do this?"Ayralina asked, awestruck.

"I didn't," Silvaris replied. "I asked Mother Nature to provide, and this is her gift."

Silvaris coughed a harsh, wet sound that sent a shiver of concern through Ayralina. The crimson stain on his sleeve grew darker, a stark reminder of the severity of his wounds. She rushed to his side, her voice trembling with urgency. "Silvaris, sit down. I need to tend to your wounds before it gets worse."

Silvaris waved her off, his expression resolute despite the pain etched into his face. "No, I can still hold on," he said firmly, though his voice faltered slightly. His gaze softened as it met hers. "Ayralina, you're exhausted. If you keep pushing yourself, you'll come to harm yourself... and the baby. I can't take that risk."

Her hand instinctively went to her stomach, and her eyes welled with tears. "Silvaris, please," she whispered, her voice breaking. "Let me check your wounds. I can't bear to see you like this."

But Silvaris shook his head, his resolve unyielding. "No," he said, his tone final. "Heal yourself first. I'll manage on my own for now."

Ayralina hesitated, torn between her duty to protect him and the growing life within her. Deep down, she knew he was right. Although she was reluctant, she did find comfort in the knowledge that she had placed a drop of her phoenix essence into him earlier—a protective flame that should've begun working to heal him already, even if only a little bit at a time. At least for now, his life was not in danger. She nodded slowly, her hands trembling as she lowered herself to the ground.

"Ok but only this one time," she murmured, her voice barely audible. Crossing her legs, she closed her eyes and began to draw upon her inner strength. A soft golden light enveloped her as she entered a meditative state, her energy slowly replenishing.

Silvaris watched her with a mixture of relief and guilt. He let out a quiet, shaky breath, knowing she was safe for now. But his heart clenched with the secret he carried. He knew the demons' blades hadn't just left wounds; they had poisoned him. The venom coursed through his veins, burning like a wildfire. He clenched his teeth, silently bearing the pain. He wouldn't let her risk herself or their child for his sake.

As Ayralina's breathing steadied and her aura strengthened, Silvaris pressed a hand to his side and stepped outside. He found a patch of soft grass beside a moss-covered boulder and sank down, careful to keep his pain hidden from her.

Gritting his teeth, he began cleaning and binding his wounds. His fingers trembled, each movement sending fresh jolts of agony through him, but he endured. The gash in his side pulsed, a relentless burn spreading outward. His vision blurred—the poison was working too fast.

Collapsing against the boulder, he pressed a shaking hand over the jagged wound. Dark veins crept outward, black tendrils spider-webbing beneath his skin. He could feel it—death—coiling inside him like a serpent.

"No," he growled, sweat mixing with blood on his face. "I'm not going to die here."

With a ragged breath, he closed his eyes and reached deep into his Moonfrost heritage. His heartbeat slowed, icy energy rising from within and spreading like a winter storm. Frost crept across his skin, radiating from his fingertips as he pressed them to the wound.

The air turned frigid, mist curling around him as it crystallized beneath his body. A silvery glow pulsed from his chest, his veins gleaming like threads of moonlight. He focused his will, commanding the ice to purge the poison, to freeze the darkness from his blood.

At first, it worked. The burning eased, the black veins retreating—if only for a moment.

Then—something went wrong.

The poison, sluggish at first, seemed to have awoken and fought back. With a sudden, violent surge, the dark toxin reacted to his magic, not retreating but feeding on it. The veins pulsed, expanding like wildfire, the blackness spreading faster than before. Silvaris's eyes snapped open, glowing with icy light—but filled with horror.

"No—NO!" he roared, his voice cracking as the pain exploded inside him.

His powers rebounded violently, backfiring into his system. It felt like shards of glass ripping through his veins, cold and fire colliding in a storm of unbearable agony. His body convulsed, frost and shadow battling beneath his skin in a chaotic dance of life and death.

He tried to scream, but no sound came out—just a ragged gasp, choked by the sheer force of the pain. His strength crumbled. His vision darkened at the edges, narrowing to a tunnel of flickering moonlight and shadow.

With one last, trembling breath, Silvaris collapsed onto the frozen ground. The glow from his powers faded, leaving only the soft crackle of ice spreading around his unconscious form.

A day later, Ayralina finally stirred from her meditative state, her energy partially restored but her body still weak. As she opened her eyes, the dim light of the cave greeted her, flickering shadows dancing along the rough walls. She was alone.

Silvaris must have stepped out for a bit, she thought, pushing herself upright. He's probably feeling better.

But as she stepped outside, a cold, unfamiliar dread crept over her.

There, just beyond the cave's entrance, Silvaris lay crumpled on the ground, motionless. A dark pool of blood stained the earth beneath him, stark against the frost-kissed soil. His face was ashen, lips tinged with blue, and his breaths—if there were any—were shallow, and faint.

A wave of horror crashed over her.

"Silvaris!" she screamed, sprinting to his side. She dropped to her knees, her hands trembling as she cradled his limp body. His skin was cold—too cold—and slick with sweat despite the chill in the air. His face was twisted in silent agony, as though trapped in an unending nightmare.

Ayralina's fingers frantically searched for a pulse, her heart racing faster with every second it eluded her. She finally found it—a faint, erratic flutter beneath her fingertips. Relief clashed with terror.

She propped him up gently, her mind spinning, trying to piece together what had happened. His wounds... they were still there, jagged and angry, seeping dark blood. They hadn't closed. They hadn't even begun to heal.

"No... no, no, no..." she whispered, her voice breaking. She inspected the wounds, her fear growing with each passing second. They weren't fatal—not on their own. They should have started to mend.

Her breath hitched, eyes glistening with desperation as she whispered, "Why... why haven't they healed?"

But Silvaris didn't answer. His body remained limp in her arms, the poison silently claiming more of him with every breath.

Her breath hitched as a terrible realization began to take shape in her mind. "Unless..." Closing her eyes, she reached out with her phoenix energy, letting it flow into Silvaris's body. The moment her power entered him, her worst fears were confirmed. His vitals were faint, and coursing through his veins was a dark, malevolent poison, spreading like wildfire. It clung to his life force with a sickly, unnatural energy—nether energy—so potent it can counteract her own phoenix magic.

Her stomach churned as the full weight of the situation settled over her. She cannot purge the poison, at least not with the power she has right now. She could only hope to seal it, and look for the cure or she has to get stronger in order to completely purge it.

With trembling hands, Ayralina summoned her phoenix flame, the golden light flaring to life as she activated its full power. Carefully, she guided the flames into Silvaris's body, their warmth coursing through him as she focused on shielding his most vital organs. The flames wrapped around his heart, brain, and lungs, creating a protective barrier to keep the poison from reaching them. The golden light shimmered brightly against the dark energy, but the process was painstakingly slow, the nether energy resisting her at every turn.

Beads of sweat formed on her brow as she concentrated, her breath unsteady. With deliberate precision, she corralled the poison, driving it toward his diaphragm. Once it was contained, she used her remaining strength to seal it there, binding it in place with her magic. It wasn't a cure, but it would stop the poison from spreading further and buy her some precious time.

Her body shook with exhaustion as she worked tirelessly, her phoenix flame flickering but holding steady. At last, Silvaris's breathing began to even out, the sickly pallor of his skin giving way to a faint flush of color. His wounds, though still severe, started to close, the edges knitting together under the influence of her magic.

Finally, with a soft groan, Silvaris's eyes fluttered open. His gaze was unfocused at first, but as he saw her, recognition and relief flickered across his face. Ayralina collapsed beside him, her chest heaving as she fought to steady her breathing.

"Ayralina…" he rasped, his voice weak yet filled with relief. Seeing her tears, his heart clenched. He reached for her cheek, wiping away a tear with his bloodstained hand. "I'm so sorry for worrying you, my love. I promise I won't die, okay?" He attempted a weak smile. "I'll even try not to make it a habit."

Ayralina's chest swelled with a mix of anger and overwhelming relief. She punched him lightly in the chest, her tears falling harder. "You idiot!" she cried, her voice trembling. "How can you joke about this? Do you know how scared I was? You're such a jerk!"

Silvaris pulled her into a tight embrace, burying his face in her hair, breathing in her scent. "I'm sorry," he murmured, his voice thick with guilt. "I'm so sorry. I shouldn't have worried you. It's my fault, Ayralina. Please don't cry… it's breaking my heart."

She pulled back; her tear-streaked face contorted with frustration. "You always do this!" she shouted. "Why do you have to play the hero? Why do you always put your life on the line for others? Every time I see you like this, it feels like my world is falling apart. I can't stand it, Silvaris. I'm scared. I'm scared that one day you won't come back to me."

Her words pierced through him, leaving him raw and vulnerable. He cupped her face in his hands and kissed her deeply, pouring all his love and regret into that single moment. When he pulled back, his gaze locked with hers, steady and unwavering.

"I promise," he said, his voice full of conviction. "No matter what happens, I will always come back to you. You are my strength, Ayralina. You're the reason I keep fighting; the reason I have hope. It's because of you that I believe in myself. This promise is etched in my heart—it's my guiding light. I'll always find my way back to you."

Ayralina sniffled, her lips trembling as she tried to suppress another sob. "You promised," she whispered, her voice breaking. "These are your words, Silvaris. And I promise you… no matter what happens, I'll wait for you. And if you ever get lost, I will find you."

Silvaris pulled her close once more, holding her tightly even though the world has crumbled around them, they still have together.

Later, he carried her into the healing pool, the warm, mineral-rich waters soothing their battered bodies and weary souls. Ayralina leaned back against him, eyes closed as relief washed over her. For the first time in days, the world felt a little less cruel. Silvaris kissed her temple, holding her tighter, his silent vow unspoken but unwavering. They had each other—that was enough to face whatever lay ahead.

As days passed, Ayralina made a difficult decision. Silvaris needed rest, and though he resisted, she placed him into a healing sleep. He wanted to stay awake until their child was born, but she feared the poison might break free of her seal, risking permanent damage to his powers. To protect him, she lured him into an enchanted slumber, slowing his blood flow to keep the poison contained.

With Silvaris safe, she turned her focus to the battle still unfinished. Masking their presence, she hunted down the remaining demons, eliminating them one by one. Only then did she finally allow herself to rest, surrendering to her own healing sleep.

IV.

As Ayralina slept, the planet continued its silent rotation, the stars shifting in their eternal dance. At last, seven stars aligned, unleashing a surge of celestial power. The energy pierced through the protective barrier, breaking through the wards that had been carefully erected.

Ayralina jolted awake, pain ripping through her body as a deep, primal instinct took hold. Gasping for air, she clutched her abdomen, her breaths shallow and rapid. The time had come—the baby was ready. Panic gripped her as she turned to Silvaris, who lay motionless beside her, his chest rising and falling in the steady rhythm of deep sleep. She couldn't wake him. Not now. The poison still lingered in his system, and if he tapped into his powers, it could be catastrophic. He had sacrificed too much already, risking him further was unthinkable.

Swallowing her fear, Ayralina carefully slid out of bed. Her legs trembled as a sharp wave of pain coursed through her, but she forced herself forward, each step a battle against her failing strength. A halo of energy flickered around her; she can sense the power of the seven stars' alignment pulsing in time with her ragged breaths. Crawling now, she made her way toward the healing pool nestled deep within their sanctuary.

Moonlight filtered through cracks in the cavern's ceiling, casting a soft glow over the shimmering water. The pool pulsed with an ethereal radiance, imbued with the ancient power of Mother Nature herself—a place of renewal, a lifeline. It beckoned her, its warmth promising relief.

Reaching the edge, Ayralina plunged into the water, her trembling body immediately soothed by its embrace. She whispered a desperate plea, the ancient language flowing from her lips like a prayer. The pool responded at once, its glow intensifying, pulsing in gentle rhythm as though alive and listening.

The earth stirred in response, concealing the massive energy surge, sealing the breach, and channeling healing energy into her. The warmth seeped into her skin, dulling the sharp edges of pain. Ayralina closed her eyes, surrendering to the pool's magic, allowing its ancient power to flow through her like a balm. She braced herself—this battle she had to fight alone.

The water pulsed with energy, its currents kneading her body, soothing the relentless contractions. Ayralina surrendered to the rhythmic embrace of the waves, her bond with nature intensifying. Though alone, she felt the elements converging around her, feeding her strength.

Time dissolved into a haze of pain and raw determination. Then, with one final, shattering effort, a surge of power exploded outward, tearing through her like a storm. The world trembled as she brought life into the world. Not one life—but four.

Ayralina stared in disbelief as tiny cries filled the air, her heart swelling with joy and confusion. Four. The prophecy had spoken of a single golden child destined for greatness, yet here they were—four perfect, tiny beings, each cocooned in the fiery warmth of their Phoenix-Dragon heritage.

A faint smile curved her lips despite her exhaustion. Perhaps, for once, the prophecy was wrong. Maybe this wasn't about her at all. The thought was oddly comforting, a whisper of normalcy in the chaos of their lives.

Summoning the last of her strength, she carefully placed each newborn into their flame-formed cocoons, the fire cradling them in warmth and safety. She gazed at them for a long moment, her heart overflowing with fierce, quiet love. Then, dragging herself back to bed, she curled up beside Silvaris, seeking solace in his presence.

As she drifted into a healing sleep, her thoughts lingered on the tiny miracles she had just brought into the world. Whatever lay ahead, she held tightly to the fragile promise of their future—determined to protect it at all costs.

Elsewhere on Earth, the heavens split apart. Streaks of ethereal light pierced the darkened sky as half of the mystical scroll descended. It did not fall gently. It struck the ground like a meteor, a shockwave tearing through the land, reality itself rippling from the impact.

The scroll landed in the hands of an unsuspecting human.

The moment their fingers touched its sacred parchment, a surge of ancient magic ignited in their veins—wild, chaotic, unrelenting. It wasn't meant for mortal hands, yet its power wove into their very essence, branding them forever.

For a rare few, it was a blessing.

For the rest, a curse.

One percent of those who came into contact with the scroll found their abilities magnified, their minds unlocking the cosmos' deepest secrets, their bodies elevated to near-mythical status. But for the majority, the gift was a cruel mockery—minds shattered, bodies twisted, existence itself warped into something unnatural.

And the corruption didn't stop with them.

The scroll's dark influence seeped into the land, a spreading plague of chaos. Cities crumbled. Friendships turned to betrayal. Alliances dissolved into dust. Order fractured under the weight of its magic.

Worst of all?

The scroll was incomplete.

Its unbalanced, volatile energy twisted fate in unpredictable ways. Reality bent, the fabric of existence warped, and chaos reigned in its wake.

But Earth was not the only one that noticed.

In the depths of the nether realm, a presence stirred.

A dragon's eyes snapped open, pupils narrowing to slits as it sensed the disturbance across dimensions.

Zephiron, the Demonic Dragon King, recognized the power that had fallen to Earth.

It was no ordinary artifact.

It was the Sunflame Phoenix Scroll.

And as long as even half of it remained beyond his grasp, the balance of power was threatened.

A deep, guttural growl rumbled through his throne chamber, summoning his most ruthless assassins.

"Find it."

His voice was a decree of doom.

The demons moved silently, slipping into the mortal world like shadows passing between dimensions.

They were not mere hunters.

They were judges. Executioners. Collectors of souls.

Their mission was simple:

1.Locate the scroll.

2.Eliminate all who stood in their way.

But their methods were far from brute force.

They infiltrated the world's highest circles, watching, waiting. Humans who displayed extraordinary abilities were captured, enslaved, or erased. Those deemed unworthy were discarded. Their presence sowed paranoia, their whispers dissolving into silence.

The scroll became a ghost of history.

Until the world forgot.

But Zephiron never did.

And soon, the hunt would end.

The stench of charred flesh thickened the air. The obsidian walls of the throne room pulsed with molten veins, weeping as though the fortress itself suffered under its master's rule.

Zephiron sat upon his blackened throne, draped in smoke and shadow.

His abyss-black scales gleamed with cracks of molten gold; ancient runes seared into his flesh. His wings, jagged and torn from centuries of war, curled around him like a fortress of death. Their skeletal tips bore trophies of conquest—fragments of armor, shredded banners, the bones of the unworthy.

Beneath him lay the corpse of the previous Demon King, throat torn open, body discarded like refuse. Blood still dripped from Zephiron's fangs—a testament to his rule.

Before him, his court trembled.

Demons knelt in absolute submission, their horned heads pressed to the scorched stone, bodies rigid with fear. None dared breathe too loudly.

The air itself was thick with his presence—dominance, wrath, power unrelenting.

Zephiron flexed his claws, the half-scroll smoldering in his grip. His glowing ruby eyes scanned the room.

Silence.

Then—

CRACK.

The armrest of his throne shattered beneath his grip, molten rock dripping between his claws. The chamber flinched.

"Pathetic."

His voice rumbled like a storm, layered with a thousand tormented screams. His minions quaked.

They had failed him.

Zephiron's wings unfurled, casting the entire hall in his shadow. Slowly, he leaned forward, his talons clicking against the throne as he sneered at the cowering demons.

His gaze shifted to the human prisoners chained before him—frail bodies, hollow eyes, shattered wills.

His lip curled.

"Put them through a trial."

His voice was laced with cruel amusement.

His advisors stiffened. None dared object.

"Keep only the strong. Kill the rest."

One demon, his horns twisted and blackened, hesitated. "M-My lord—"

Zephiron's gaze snapped to him.

The air grew thick. The demon choked, his own shadow tightening around his throat.

Zephiron didn't need to move.

His will alone crushed him.

"Do not question me."

The demon gurgled, clawing at his throat before collapsing into dust.

Zephiron turned away, uninterested in the corpse at his feet. His claws drummed against the throne, his thoughts beyond this trivial display.

His lieutenants stiffened, awaiting his next order.

He gazed down at the half-scroll, its edges still burning in his grip.

"Find the rest." His voice was low, final, merciless.

"Do not return unless you bring me something of value. Or do not return at all."

The demons bowed so low their foreheads nearly cracked against the stone.

"Y-Yes, my lord!"

They fled, vanishing like hunted prey, desperate to escape his wrath.

Zephiron leaned back into his throne, molten stone shifting beneath him. His massive claws drummed against the armrest, his tail curling around the bones of his last victim.

A slow, malicious grin spread across his draconic face.

This kingdom was his.

And soon—

The world would follow.

Chapter 1

IN THE BLINK OF an eye, nearly a century passed. One hundred long years, Silvaris and the children remained in their enchanted slumber, frozen in time, their lives suspended by the magic that shielded them. Yet through it all, Ayralina never faltered in her search for a cure to save him.

Ayralina was a healer by nature, her heart intrinsically tied to mending and nurturing rather than causing harm. Fighting and killing went against every fiber of her being, but for her family, she willingly embraced the burden. She knew the world outside was cruel, and the dangers they faced demanded strength and resilience. Determined to protect them at all costs, she pushed herself to become something she had never envisioned; a warrior capable of standing against any threat.

She trained relentlessly, day and night; her hands, once meant solely for healing now, were strengthened and comfortable wielding weapons and conjuring defensive spells. The soft light of her healing magic began to intertwine with the raw, fierce energy of her newfound combat skills. Each day, she pushed her limits further, her body aching and her spirit weary, yet her resolve never wavered. Ayralina knew she had to grow stronger—far stronger than she had ever imagined possible. The world around her has changed, becoming more perilous with each passing year, but she remains unyielding.

Her years of searching finally bore fruit when she uncovered a long-forgotten legend. In the farthest reaches of the extreme north lay a shard of the Ice Crystal Heart—a mystical artifact born from the union of heaven and earth, it is said to possess the power to strengthen the soul and purify even the most insidious of poisons. It was a beacon of hope for her, even if it's one that is shrouded in peril. The deep north was a land of eternal frost and howling storms, where the icy winds cut like blades and the cold could claim even the strongest in moments. Ayralina knew she wasn't ready. The journey would demand more strength, resilience, and cunning than she possessed. Failure was not an option, for it would mean certain death—and, with it, the end of her hope.

Determined to succeed, Ayralina shifted her focus to acquiring the Heart's Flame Fire Orchid, a rare and fabled flower renowned for its fiery core; it has the power to protect its bearer from the lethal cold of the north. The orchid was also an integral part of the key to repairing the Sunflame Scroll, and unlocking its immense power. Both Ayralina and the demons were locked in a desperate race to obtain it, each driven by their own high stakes.

The Fire Orchid was no ordinary bloom; it was both treasure and trial. It is hidden in a region untouched by time, buried deep within a treacherous landscape of shadowy forests, jagged peaks, and shifting volcanic caverns. Legends whispered of its perilous location, where the air burned hot, and the ground quaked beneath the weight of the earth's restless power.

Guarding the orchid were ancient beasts, creatures born of flame and ash, said to have emerged from the earth's molten core. These guardians, fiercely loyal to their sacred charge, were the embodiments of fire itself, their molten forms radiating heat so intense that it could melt steel. They were rumored to strike down intruders without hesitation, their wrath as unyielding as the volcanic currents that surrounded the orchid's hidden sanctuary.

Complicating her mission further was the unsettling truth that the demons had long since infiltrated human society. They had woven themselves into the very fabric of civilization, with eyes and ears everywhere—lurking in shadowed alleys, sitting in positions of power, and blending seamlessly with the unsuspecting populace. Their spies were masters of deception, manipulating events from behind the scenes, sowing discord, and orchestrating chaos to tighten their grip on both the mortal and supernatural realms. Their influence was subtle yet insidious, a silent infection that had festered for generations.

Over the years, Ayralina had learned this harsh reality through blood, sweat, and narrow escapes. She had survived countless ambushes, traps disguised as chance encounters, and betrayals from those she called friends. Each experience carved her into a sharper weapon, honing her instincts to an almost preternatural edge. She had become adept at masking her presence, blending into crowds, and vanishing without a trace when danger loomed.

Her magic had evolved alongside her wits, not just as a tool of offense but as a shield, a silent guardian that whispered warnings when threats lurked nearby.

Yet, what troubled Ayralina most wasn't just the demons hiding in plain sight—it was the human organizations entwined with them. These groups operated under the guise of mundane institutions, yet there was something off about them. Their agents moved with a precision that felt unnatural, their strength and reflexes beyond human limits. Ayralina sensed a dark familiarity in their presence, an echo of something ancient and demonic pulsing beneath their polished exteriors. It gnawed at her, a connection she couldn't ignore.

She suspected it was the missing half of her Phoenix Inheritance, the Sunflame Phoenix Scroll, which was never meant for mortals. Shattered a hundred years ago, it was said to grant rebirth, cleansing and restoring the soul like a phoenix rising from the ashes. But for humans, its power was a curse.

Once touched by any but a phoenix, its magic corrupted.

With the scroll torn in two, its balance was lost.

The remaining half no longer granted true resurrection. Instead, it bestowed supernatural abilities—strength, speed, heightened senses. But those who died and returned were reborn into darkness, their souls consumed by an unrelenting fire. Tortured endlessly, they became hollow, their minds shattered by suffering with no reprieve.

The only way to save them was to restore the scroll.

Once whole, its power could cleanse the corruption and heal the afflicted.

Ayralina had hidden her half within the protected realm where Silvaris and the children slept. But even as she safeguarded it, she knew she couldn't remain idle. The other half had already fallen into the Demon King's hands.

Under his control, its power twisted and tempted, turning mortals into something beyond redemption. It amplified fear, ambition, and rage, dragging the darkest parts of the soul to the surface until nothing remained of the person they once were. What began as a gift became a curse, turning men into monsters. The corrupted craved more—more power, more control—until they became nothing but hollow vessels feeding the scroll's insatiable hunger.

Yet this dark power had a flaw.

The scroll's unstable magic was both a beacon and a blight. Ayralina could sense its chaotic energy, a faint burning pulse woven through the actions of the corrupted. It became her compass. Every battle with these tainted souls brought her closer to the missing half of her inheritance—and to the heart of the demons' growing dominion.

By tracing the corruption, she could unravel their network of control, expose their puppet masters, and confront the darkness spreading like wildfire across both worlds.

The fate of balance, rebirth, and redemption rested on her shoulders.

This was her birthright. Her burden.

Her Phoenix Inheritance.

The path ahead would test her in ways she had never faced.

The healer who once shied from violence had become a warrior, her resolve hardened by fire. Magic, once used only for mending, had become a weapon as much as a shield. Every step brought her closer—not only to the Fire Orchid, but also the strength she would need to face the unforgiving north.

Simultaneously, Ayralina began tracking her enemies. She had learned to hide her identity, blending seamlessly into human society. By weaving herself into their world under the guise of a doctor, she gathers information and pretends to live a normal life. She became a figure in the background—a healer, a teacher, a quiet presence who moved among humans unnoticed. Through careful observation and calculated risks, she unraveled the movements of those who had poisoned Silvaris and schemed against her family. They were still out there, lurking in the shadows, their plans unfolding over the decades. Ayralina became a master of subtlety, slipping into their circles and gathering fragments of knowledge while ensuring she was never discovered.

Now, after nearly a hundred years of relentless pursuit, The Fire Orchid was within her grasp and, with it, the strength to face the icy wastelands of the deep north. She had spent a century preparing for this moment, and she would stop at nothing to bring Silvaris back to her.

Ayralina stepped through the shimmering portal, her phoenix flame glowing faintly around her as she emerged into the basement of her home. Their home appeared normal from the outside—a modest, two-story suburban house with weathered brick, neatly trimmed hedges, and a quaint garden that is meticulously tended. To any passerby, it was the epitome of domestic tranquility. But beneath its ordinary facade, the house was anything but typical.

Built over a hidden portal forged during the fateful battle that marked her arrival on Earth, the house was designed like a fortress on the inside. Reinforced steel beams were masked behind drywall, enchantments woven into the very foundation to ward off supernatural intrusions. The windows were fitted with shatterproof, magically tempered glass, and the walls were laced with runes for both protection and concealment. Secret passageways connected hidden chambers and escape routes cleverly disguised as closets or basement storage. Every inch of the home was a calculated blend of human engineering and ancient magic, allowing her to travel swiftly between realms to check in on her children and Silvaris on a regular basis.

She hurried up the stairs, taking them two at a time, her urgency palpable. Once on the top floor, she turned towards the back den, a room that doubled as her office. It was her haven during sleepless nights, a space where she could bury herself in research frenzies. The room smelled faintly of old parchment and ink, a testament to the countless hours she had spent poring over ancient texts and deciphering cryptic legends.

Out of habit, she reached for the TV remote and turned it on, craving the comforting noise of the news channel that always played in the background. The familiar stern-faced anchor filled the screen, red words flashing across the bottom: BREAKING NEWS. But Ayralina paid little attention as she sifted through her notes, her thoughts preoccupied with the fragmented visions from her youngest son's dreams.

Her youngest had begun showing signs of telekinetic abilities during this 100-year incubation. It wasn't uncommon for phoenix offspring to develop unique powers, but there was something different about his dreams. They had an ominous edge, filled with flickers of fire and shadow that felt like premonitions.

Ayralina's own dreams had been troubling as well. Phoenixes rarely dream, and when they do, the dreams often carry the weight of prophecy. Her visions had been haunted by the image of her mother, the Phoenix Queen, battling a shadowy demon—a dark reflection of the phoenix flame. At times, Ayralina felt as though she were the demon herself, trapped within its fiery eyes. Other times, she was a distant observer, watching events unfold like a spectator to her own destiny.

Her unease was growing, a foreboding she couldn't shake. Then, out of the corner of her eye, something on the TV caught her attention. An explosion at a cave, the news anchor reported, with images of charred rock and glowing embers. In the background of one of the pictures was a faint glimmer of orange-red—a shape unmistakable to her.

She froze, her heart pounding. Could it really be? The flower she had searched for all these years, hidden away and thought lost to time, had finally revealed itself.

Her fingers flew across her keyboard as she pulled up the news site, zooming into the photograph. There it was, nestled among the rubble—a fiery bloom glowing faintly despite the destruction around it. The Heart's Flame Fire Orchid.

Without hesitation, Ayralina booked the earliest flight to the site of the explosion. As the confirmation email landed in her inbox, she stood, her eyes blazing with resolve. The journey to the north was about to begin, and nothing—neither the biting cold nor the enemies in the shadows—would stop her now.

Chapter 2

STEPPING OFF THE PLANE, Ayralina's body rejoiced at the heatwave that had tourists grumbling. For her, the intense warmth was invigorating, amplifying her powers and serving as a comforting reminder of her Phoenix heritage. She had arrived in Southern Land that morning after an uneventful flight, though her mind lingered on her youngest.

Before she left, Ayralina had quietly checked in on her slumbering children still encased inside their flame cocoon. Their peaceful faces were a stark contrast to the constant turbulence within her heart.

Her gaze had lingered on each child that morning, committing every detail to memory. They all appeared normal—soft breaths, serene faces—but her eyes stayed on her youngest son. In recent days, subtle signs of telekinesis have begun to surface. Small objects shifted near him, their movements tethered to the rise and fall of his emotions. The night before her departure, Ayralina could have sworn she felt him reaching out—not physically, but mentally—as if his burgeoning powers were attempting to bridge the gap between them. Though his abilities were raw and unpredictable, the thought of him trying to connect filled her with both pride and concern. She longed to stay, to decipher the silent message she felt simmering beneath the surface, but she knew she couldn't delay her mission.

Since that fleeting connection, he still hadn't reached out again. Maybe the effort had drained him—or worse, perhaps it had been nothing more than her imagination, wishful thinking born from the ache of leaving them behind. Yet, she couldn't shake the nagging feeling that his message had been important.

Still, the urgency of her quest pressed heavier on her heart. It was the key to enhancing her powers, a necessity for the battles that lay ahead. As much as she yearned to turn back, to wrap her arms around her children and unravel the mystery of these emerging gifts, she steeled her resolve and went on that plane.

Ayralina had packed lightly to avoid delays, bypassing baggage claim and heading straight outside to hail a taxi. She knew time was against her, and traveling unnoticed was essential. Adjusting to human transportation always irritated her. It was slow, crowded, and riddled with inconveniences. But she couldn't risk using her powers frivolously; even the smallest display of magic might leave a trail for her enemies to follow.

Ayralina knows the news of the Heart's Flame Fire Orchid had undoubtedly reached the demons as well. Its location, long hidden in legend, was no longer a well-guarded secret. Worse, Ayralina suspected the explosion that had rocked the region a few days earlier might have been their doing. It reeked of their chaos and possibly a trap—an unsubtle act of destruction meant to destabilize the area and to draw her out. If her suspicions were correct and the demons had caused it, then they were closer than she had anticipated, and the window to secure the orchid was shrinking rapidly.

Ayralina's nerves remained on edge as the taxi rolled to a stop, her gaze scanning the street for anything out of place. Years of being hunted had sharpened her instincts, and she couldn't shake the feeling that she was being watched. If the demons were already here, their agents could be anywhere—blending into the crowds, lurking in the shadows, or disguised as harmless humans going about their daily lives.

She observed the taxi driver closely, scrutinizing him for any signs of danger. He was middle-aged, with a full head of dark hair and a muscular build that suggested he had another job—perhaps as a bouncer or a bodybuilder. The faint bags under his eyes hinted at sleepless nights, adding an air of weariness to his otherwise composed demeanor.

"My apologies, amiga," he said, glancing at her through the rearview mirror. "I fixed my air conditioner last week, but it broke again this morning."

As he spoke, Ayralina felt an odd sense of familiarity that she couldn't quite place, not demonic but comforting. It piqued her curiosity, though she decided to set the feeling aside for now. She needed to stay focused.

"That's okay," Ayralina replied calmly, her tone masking her unease. "The heat doesn't bother me. My hotel is only five minutes away."

"Great," the driver said with a polite nod. "My name is Andre. What is yours, by the way? Are you here for business or pleasure?"

"Ayralina," she answered smoothly, the lie sliding off her tongue with practiced ease. "And a little of both. I haven't taken a vacation in a while and thought I'd visit the ruins. With some extra vacation time, this seemed like the perfect chance."

Andre's expression shifted to concern. "Ah, my lady Ayralina, you're not in luck. The ruins are closed due to an explosion. Officials have declared it unsafe to enter. If I were you, I'd steer clear of the caves—they're especially dangerous."

He looked her in the eyes, his warning sincere.

"I'll keep that in mind," Ayralina said with a polite smile, but her mind remained guarded, her instincts alert. She kept a watchful eye on the road and the driver's subtle movements, unsure if her unease stemmed from paranoia or something more. The demons were masters of infiltration, and trust was a luxury she couldn't afford. For now, all she could do was play her part and stay ready for whatever might come next.

Arriving at the hotel, Andre quickly retrieved her luggage. Ayralina handed him cash—enough to cover the fare and more. His eyes widened as he counted the bills.

"Señorita, this is too much. I cannot accept this."

"It's for your air conditioner," Ayralina said warmly. "And for the kind advice. No need to thank me."

Andre looked overwhelmed. "Thank you, thank you! You're a blessing. My children will have a full meal today, and I'll fix the air conditioner too. I'll never forget this. If you need a ride back, call me—I won't charge you a cent."

Ayralina smiled. "Take care, Andre."

She turned toward the entrance of the hotel, its double doors framed in gleaming gold with two grand columns on each side, the opulent design signaling a high-end establishment. Yet something felt off. The hotel lobby was eerily quiet, the usual hum of activity absent, and the lack of tourists was almost unnerving. As Ayralina stepped inside, the sound of her heels echoed through the vast space, and almost immediately, two bellboys rushed toward her as though they had been waiting. They took her bags and guided her to the front desk, where a receptionist appeared seemingly out of nowhere.

"Welcome to the Mayan de la Ruynes Hotel," he said cheerfully, his polished demeanor betrayed by a slight edge of nervousness. His name tag read Enzo. "You must be Dr. Ayralina Flames. I've taken the liberty of upgrading you to a suite for the duration of your stay."

Ayralina frowned, her instincts prickling with unease. "Wait," she said, her voice steady but sharp. "How do you know who I am?"

Enzo's cheerful expression faltered for a moment, replaced by a flicker of discomfort. He chuckled nervously. "Ms., haven't you noticed? You're the only guest checking in today. In fact..." He paused as if considering his next words carefully. "You're the only one staying here tonight—unless someone happens to drop in unexpectedly."

Ayralina's frown deepened, and she raised an eyebrow. "Why is that?"

Enzo hesitated, the cheerfulness in his tone replaced by a cautious gravity. "You didn't hear?"

Her eyes narrowed, the weight of his words settling like a stone in her chest. "Hear what?" she asked, her voice low, every nerve in her body braced for the answer.

His tone grew serious, the cheerful facade fading entirely. "Since the explosion, people have been disappearing. Mostly locals, but last week some tourists went to investigate the rumors and never returned. Now, people are fleeing the area. They're saying it's something about zombies or demons, but who knows? Either way, it's not safe."

Ayralina leaned against the counter, processing the unsettling news. "So that's why the flights were so cheap," she said, forcing a lighthearted tone in an attempt to mask her unease. "I thought I scored a great last-minute deal!"

Enzo chuckled weakly; skepticism clear in his eyes. "You could probably get your trip refunded. It's really not safe here." His tone carried a quiet warning, as if urging her to leave or testing her resolve.

Ayralina smiled sweetly, but there was a firmness in her tone as she replied, "No, I'm already here. I'll make the best of it."

Enzo smiled and leaned in slightly, his voice dropping to a conspiratorial tone. "Excellent, if you need anything—anything at all during your stay just let me, Enzo know. I'll make sure you are well taken care of. Whatever you need, you name it, I'll arrange it."

Ayralina looked at him suspiciously as she considered his offer. "Actually, I could use a map of the area," she said. "And I'll need you to book me a rental car please."

Enzo straightened, nodding quickly. "Of course. I'll have both ready for you in no time. Is there anything else?"

"For now, that's it," Ayralina replied, her smile returning. "But I'll let you know if I think of anything else."

Enzo gave a short bow as he signaled for the bellboys to escort Ayralina to her room. "Very well, Ms. I'll get on it immediately. Please, don't hesitate to ask if you need anything else," he said, his voice respectful and professional.

Ayralina watched him retreat behind the desk, her sharp eyes catching the slight tremor in his hands as he fumbled with a stack of papers. Her mind was already racing with plans, mapping out her next steps. Despite all the red flags and the growing tension in her chest, she knew she couldn't turn back now. Too much was at stake, and time was slipping through her fingers.

Moments later, she followed the bellboys to her suite. When they opened the door, the luxurious room took her by surprise, if only briefly. The opulent space was bathed in soft golden light from an elegant crystal chandelier that hung from the high ceiling. Rich, cream-colored walls were adorned with intricate gold trim, and plush velvet drapes in deep crimson framed the floor-to-ceiling windows, which offered a breathtaking view of the sprawling city below.

A grand king-sized bed sat at the center of the room, dressed in silken sheets and a thick, inviting duvet embroidered with delicate floral patterns. To the left, a cozy seating area featured a sleek leather sofa, and an ornate coffee table set with a tray of exotic fruits and a bottle of chilled champagne. Across the room, a writing desk crafted from polished mahogany stood near a small library shelf filled with carefully curated books, giving the room an air of refined sophistication.

The ensuite bathroom was equally stunning, with marble floors, a freestanding tub, and a rainfall shower encased in glass. Gold fixtures gleamed under the ambient lighting, and soft, fragrant towels were neatly arranged near a selection of luxury bath products.

Ayralina dismissed the bellboys with a polite nod and tip, allowing the door to close behind them. She stepped further into the room, her fingers brushing over the smooth fabric of the curtains as she approached the window. The afternoon sun began to sink in the sky, illuminating the city in its beauty, but her thoughts were far from the beauty of the scene before her.

She set her bag on the desk and sank into the leather chair, her gaze fixed on the skyline. The comfort and elegance of the room offered little solace. Her mind remained focused on the task ahead, the weight of her mission pressing heavily on her shoulders. The luxurious surroundings were merely a temporary refuge, a brief pause before the storm she knew was coming.

Somewhere in a luxurious private office of the hotel, Enzo knocked softly on the heavy wooden door. "Enter," came a deep, commanding voice from within the room.

Pushing the door open, Enzo stepped inside, bowing slightly. "Our guest has arrived, my lord," he said cautiously.

A man sat at an ornate antique oak table, his piercing gaze locking onto Enzo the moment he entered. Dressed in a finely tailored suit, he radiated both charm and authority. His clean-cut features and effortless poise suggested a man in his mid-thirties, yet there was something ageless about him—an unsettling presence that made it impossible to look away.

A faint smile played on his lips, but it never quite reached his eyes.

On the desk before him sat a polished nameplate.

Damien

Manager

He leaned back in his chair, his fingers tapping lightly on the polished surface of the desk. "Make sure our guest is comfortable," he said smoothly, his tone calm, yet laced with subtle menace. "And shut down the hotel. We are no longer accepting any other guests during her stay."

Enzo hesitated for a brief moment before nodding. "Yes, my lord. And... about the guest?"

The man's smile widened slightly as he leaned forward, his sharp gaze turning icy. "Keep a close watch on her," he instructed, his voice lowering. "Do not lose her. Under any circumstances."

"Yes, my lord," Enzo said quickly, bowing again before retreating from the room. As the door clicked shut, the man turned his gaze toward the window, his smile fading into a pensive expression. His fingers traced the edges of a small, dark artifact resting on the desk, a glimmer of anticipation flickering in his eyes. Their game had begun.

Chapter 3

AYRALINA SHIFTED INTO THIRD gear as she merged onto the main road, her fingers gripping the wheel tightly. The car hummed beneath her as she drove aimlessly through the winding streets of the town, her every turn a calculated attempt to lose the tail she suspected had been following her since she left the hotel. She wasn't entirely sure when it had started—perhaps it had been as early as her arrival in the south or maybe even before that. Either way, she couldn't shake the feeling that eyes were on her, shadowing her every move.

Her heart raced as she glanced in the rearview mirror, scanning the cars behind her. A black sedan had been trailing her for several blocks, and its driver was careful not to follow too closely but still maintained an unnerving consistency. She made a sharp turn onto a quieter street, then another, weaving through town in an attempt to shake her pursuer. If they were demons, they wouldn't be easily deterred, but she couldn't afford to let them follow her to her next destination.

As she drove, her thoughts spiraled. She was heading straight into what could very well be demon territory, her mind buzzing with a mix of dread and determination. Though she often played the part of a carefree blonde, Ayralina was anything but naive. She had studied the rumors of demon activity in the area, and she knew the ever-growing danger that shadowed her steps.

This wasn't her first time confronting demons. She had faced their kind before, often risking exposure while dismantling their lairs. Each encounter had been a calculated gamble, her phoenix powers carefully concealed to avoid detection. But recently, something has shifted. The number of demon lairs was increasing, and their movements had grown bolder. They no longer skulked in the shadows—they were asserting their presence, almost daring someone to stop them.

Ayralina suspected this newfound audacity wasn't random. It felt orchestrated, deliberate, as though they were closing in on something monumental. The rumors she had heard whispered of a grand plan, something that would tip the balance of power irreparably. And if they were true, the demons were dangerously close to achieving it.

Her chest tightened as she glanced at the rearview mirror again. The black sedan was still there, its headlights glowing ominously in the fading light. She clenched her jaw and made another sudden turn, this time onto a narrow alley that opened onto a busier street. The maneuver was risky, but she hoped the added traffic would mask her presence.

Ayralina exhaled slowly, trying to calm her nerves. She couldn't afford to let fear cloud her judgment. Whether or not she was being followed, one thing was clear: she couldn't trust anyone, and she had to stay one step ahead.

This time, the stakes were higher than ever. Both she and the demons were after the same prize—the Heart's Flame Fire Orchid. Worse yet, she had learned of their chilling new ability: the power to create human puppets—people twisted into mindless, shambling servants, mistaken by locals as zombies. It was a tactic designed to sow fear and confusion, and it was working.

Her GPS directed her west, guiding her toward the dense forest Enzo had explicitly warned her to avoid. The further she drove, the more the atmosphere changed. The road ahead grew emptier, the buildings more derelict. Dilapidated houses with boarded windows and sagging roofs lined the streets, their lawns brittle and lifeless. This town had been abandoned long ago, likely consumed by fear of the sinister rumors that surrounded it.

But that desolation worked in Ayralina's favor. No civilians meant no casualties, and that gave her a sliver of reassurance. She glanced at the GPS again, its calm voice contrasting sharply with the tension thrumming in her chest. The last time Ayralina looked back into her rear-view mirrors it seemed she finally managed to lose the tail.

As the trees began to close in around the road, she steeled herself. If the demons reached the Orchid first, the consequences could be catastrophic. She couldn't let that happen. Not this time.

Ayralina pulled her car to a stop at the forest's edge, parking it discreetly behind some thick bushes. After exiting the vehicle, she moved carefully, creeping through dense underbrush until she reached a clearing.

Ahead, she spotted a small group of human puppets. They looked disheveled, their movements awkward and sluggish—likely newly created. The remains of some unfortunate wildlife lay at their feet, their gruesome feast almost complete. Newly created humans meant their leader was nearby.

Ayralina crouched low, her mind racing as she debated her next move. Should she attack to draw out the leader or stay hidden and observe a little longer? Before she could decide, the choice was made for her. From the other side of the bush, a man burst into view, shouting:

"Come play with me, you disgusting-foul creatures! Daddy wants to try out his new toy!"

Her stomach dropped. Andre? The taxi driver?

Her jaw tightened as she watched him wield a flamethrower with alarming skill. He moved with a confidence that seemed almost reckless, his expression a mix of anger and grim determination.

She knew better than to be impressed. Leaders never let their fledglings roam alone, and if this group of puppets was here, their master couldn't be far behind.

For some reason she couldn't leave; she felt a strange pull toward him, a sensation that tightened around her ribs like an invisible tether. It made no sense, but the need to save him was there. Ayralina always believed in her intuition; it had never led her wrong.

So, for now, she remained hidden.

Andre wasn't a novice—his strike was powerful, and deliberate. He managed to take down three of the five puppets with concentrated bursts of flame in the right spots. But Ayralina could see the strain in his movements. The heavy flamethrower was wearing him down, his actions began to falter relying purely on instinct now and precision of someone who's fought in many fights before. Hesitation began to creep into his movements, slowing him further.

"This isn't his first encounter," she thought, narrowing her eyes. Judging by the raw intensity of his attack, it was personal. A blood feud, perhaps?

As Andre began to slow down, Ayralina's sharp gaze caught movement in the distance. A shadowy figure emerged, drawing a bow and aiming an arrow directly at Andre. Her stomach clenched. There was no time to think.

A fireball ignited in her palm almost instinctively. With a flick of her wrist, she launched it into the air, curving its trajectory at the last second to intercept the arrow. Her fireball engulfed its projectile and redirected it, sending it hurtling into another one that had been about to pounce on Andre.

Seizing the moment, Ayralina emerged from her hiding spot, flames dancing in her hands. In a blur of precision and power, she dispatched the remaining puppets with sharp strikes and quick bursts of fire. Ash settled around her as she turned to Andre, brushing her hands off casually.

"Hey, buddy," she said, smirking. "Not bad out there. I take it instead of fixing the AC in your old car, you decided to splurge on a flamethrower?"

Andre stared at her, wide-eyed and stuttering, the flamethrower drooping in his hands. "How... where... What are you? How did this even happen? How did you do that?"

Ayralina's smirk widened as she crossed her arms. "Oh, so you do know fear. That's good to know." She leaned closer, her tone playful but with an edge. "Word of advice: next time you decide to taunt the undead, make sure you're not standing in the crossfire."

Before she could tease him further, six figures emerged from the shadows, moving with inhuman speed and precision. They were small but unnervingly agile, their bodies covered in coarse, bristling fur that shimmered with an unnatural sheen. Their hunched forms resembled oversized raccoons, but their limbs were too long, their clawed fingers too sharp.

Glowing, slitted eyes locked onto Ayralina and Andre, radiating hunger and malice. Their sharp, jagged teeth gnashed together in anticipation, emitting guttural clicks and snarls as they advanced in eerie synchronization. They were fast—too fast—darting forward in sudden bursts, their movements so fluid it was as if they slithered through the air rather than ran.

Ayralina tensed. These weren't mindless beasts. They were hunters.

How did they get here so fast? Ayralina thought, her mind racing.

"No time for chit-chat now," she said casually, her tone slicing through the tension like a blade. Her eyes flicked to Andre, assessing his condition. "What do you think you can handle?"

Andre glanced down at his flamethrower, his hands trembling as he adjusted his grip. His face was pale, sweat glistening on his brow, and his breaths came in short, uneven bursts. "I'm low on fuel, but I still have this," he stated and pulled out his matchet, his voice strained. "Exhausted, too. So maybe... two at most."

"Two, huh?" Ayralina muttered, her lips tightening. She thought quickly, her gaze darting to the advancing demons. It's not ideal, but it'll have to do.

She placed a hand on his shoulder, grounding him for a brief moment. "Alright. That's good enough. Just keep yourself alive. Distract the two on the right—make it count."

Andre nodded hesitantly, his grip on his weapons tightening as he steeled himself.

Ayralina squared her shoulders, her fiery energy beginning to simmer beneath her skin as her eyes locked onto the remaining four demons. "I'll take care of the other four," she said, her voice steady despite the storm brewing within her.

Andre hesitated for a moment before nodding. Despite his exhaustion, something about her calm, commanding presence gave him confidence. He was embarrassed by how much he already relied on her, but he was also grateful for her leadership. "Okay. Stay safe."

"You too," Ayralina said, her lips curling into a brief encouraging smile before she turned to face the demons. Her expression hardened, her stance shifting into one of readiness. She clenched her fists as flames flickered to life in front of her.

Ayralina hit the ground with a shockwave of heat, her presence drawing the demons' attention. The creatures hissed, their blackened claws glinting in the firelight, their grotesque forms shifting as if the shadows themselves coiled around them. One of them lunged at her, its jagged teeth snapping inches from her throat.

With a flick of her wrist, she conjured a wall of fire, the sheer heat forcing the demon back. "You guys really don't learn, do you?" she taunted, stepping forward.

Andre struggled to rise, his flamethrower wheezing, spitting out weak bursts of flame. "I hate to rush you, but I'm running on fumes here," he muttered, swiping a matchet from his belt to fend off the second demon.

Ayralina spun, dodging another claw strike before grabbing the demon by the wrist. With a sudden burst of power, flames erupted from her palms, racing up its arm like hungry serpents. The demon shrieked, its skin cracking and peeling as fire consumed it from the inside out.

The second demon took advantage of the distraction, leaping toward Andre with a guttural snarl. Ayralina reacted instantly. She kicked off the ground, fire trailing in her wake as she intercepted the creature mid-air. A fiery punch to its chest sent it crashing to the ground, but it wasn't finished. It rolled, springing back up, eyes glowing with a malevolent hunger.

Andre, finally catching his breath, forced his flamethrower's nozzle into the demon's mouth and pulled the trigger. A brief, sputtering flame flared from the weapon, barely enough to make the demon flinch.

"Oh, for the love of—" Ayralina groaned. With a snap of her fingers, she ignited the remaining fuel in the tank. A sudden burst of fire roared forth, engulfing the demon entirely. It howled as it crumbled to ash, the infernal light casting grotesque shadows on the cavern walls.

Andre let out a breath, staring at the smoldering remains. "You could've warned me first."

"And miss that....?" Ayralina grinned, stepping past him.

Ayralina turned to the remaining demons, rolling her shoulders as she cracked her knuckles, the smirk on her lips playful, yet lethal.

"Ready for round two?"

The words dripped with mockery, but the demons didn't move.

They had already watched her annihilate their comrades—effortlessly, mercilessly. They had seen the way her fire consumed them, the way her presence alone commanded the battlefield.

And now, with her piercing golden gaze locked onto them, they finally understood.

They didn't stand a chance.

Without warning, panic overtook them.

In a frantic blur, they turned on their heels and vanished into the forest, their forms melting into the shadows like frightened rats.

Ayralina let them go.

She had bigger concerns.

Behind her, Andre collapsed, gasping for breath.

"Why... why didn't you chase them?" he panted, his body sagging with exhaustion.

Ayralina didn't look away from him, her expression shifting from amusement to intense focus. She knelt beside him, her gaze locking onto his, demanding.

"Because I need answers. And you're going to give them to me."

Her voice was firm, and unyielding.

"You've been fighting these things for a while now, haven't you?" She leaned in slightly, her tone pressing. "Tell me everything you know."

Andre's lips parted, a faint, broken whisper escaping.

"I... I..."

His body swayed, his breath coming in shallow gasps, and then—

He crumpled.

Like a puppet with its strings severed, his knees buckled, and he collapsed lifelessly onto the cold ground.

Ayralina's stomach twisted.

She caught him just before his head hit the dirt, pressing her fingers against his pulse.

Still alive.

Her jaw tightened.

"Damn it, Andre!" Ayralina hissed. "No major injuries," she murmured to herself, scanning his body for signs of severe trauma. His shirt was soaked with blood from a deep gash along his side, but it wasn't life-threatening. The real culprits were blood loss and sheer exhaustion.

"Fool," Ayralina muttered under her breath, cutting a strip of fabric from her shirt. Her movements were swift and precise as she tied a makeshift bandage around Andre's wound to stem the bleeding. Her hands worked methodically, but her mind raced. How long had he been fighting? What had he seen that pushed him to this point? She could feel the weight of his struggle and knew there was more to his story than he let on.

Once the bandage was secure, she placed a hand over his forehead, channeling a small burst of energy into him. It wasn't much, just enough to help him regain consciousness. She needed him to wake up—needed answers.

Her gaze flicked to his pale face as his eyes fluttered open. Andre's voice was still weak. "Thank you, Ms. Ayralina... but you should leave me here. Save yourself. More will be coming."

Ayralina rolled her eyes, her tone firm and calm. "Don't worry, I'm not so fragile. With me around, you won't die so easily. No need to play the hero."

Andre gave her a faint, tired smile. "Why are you out here?" he asked, his voice barely above a whisper.

She paused, her expression softening for just a moment. "I'm the one asking the questions," she replied, a hint of steel in her tone. "You're the one who needs to tell me what I want to know."

Ayralina adjusted him into a more comfortable position, propping his head up with her makeshift pillow. The blood-soaked bandage was holding for now, but he needed proper care soon. She scanned the darkened forest clearing, her senses sharp as she listened for any movement. The faint rustling of leaves and the distant howls in the night sent a chill down her spine.

They weren't safe here.

"We need to move," she said, her voice low but resolute. "Can you walk if I help you?"

Andre nodded weakly, his resolve clear despite his condition. "Lead the way," he murmured, his trust in her evident.

Ayralina sighed, steadying him as she helped him to his feet. "My car is just ahead, let's go," she said.

With Andre leaning on her for support, she guided him deeper into the shadows, her sharp eyes scanning for threats as the tension thickened around them.

Chapter 4

WALKING BACK TO HER car, Andre said, "My home is nearby, only five miles to the east."

Ayralina glanced at him, raising an eyebrow. "Do you have a death wish? You need medical attention. We have to get you to a hospital. Why were you out here fighting human puppets with no backup anyway?"

"I can't go to the hospital," Andre replied, his voice firm but tired. "My boys are at home waiting for me. My injuries aren't that bad. I just won't go out for a few days. Please, señorita."

Ayralina sighed, shaking her head. "You're lucky I'm a doctor," she said begrudgingly. "Fine. Lead the way."

"Thank you, Ms. Ayralina, or umm Dr.?" Andre said, his voice filled with gratitude. After a moment, he added, "Puppets? The locals and I thought they were just mindless zombies."

Ayralina sighed again, her expression darkening as they continued walking. "Ayralina is fine, yes puppets, Zombies are reanimated corpses—the walking dead," she explained. "But puppets are far more sinister. They're living people who willingly trade their lives to demons, seduced by promises of power and eternal life. But it's all a lie. The demons trick them."

She glanced at him to make sure he was following before continuing. "They're fed the flesh and blood of lesser demons. At first, it grants them incredible powers—rapid healing, resistance to injury—but it comes at a price. Slowly, their willpower is destroyed, and their humanity erodes. In the end, they become mindless puppets, completely controlled by the demons."

Andre's jaw tightened as he processed her words, his expression a mix of shock and anger. "So, they're not dead... they're also victims."

"Yes," Ayralina said quietly, her tone heavy with regret. "They're victims. And once the transformation begins, there's no way to save them. That's why we have to stop the demons before they claim anyone else."

Andre nodded, determination hardening in his eyes. "Then we have to fight them. No matter what it takes."

"Don't let sympathy cloud your judgment. Once they're turned, there's no saving them."

During the short drive to his home, Andre opened up about his experience. He had been battling these creatures for years, doing everything he could to keep his family safe. The village, once vibrant and full of life, was now a ghost town. Most of its inhabitants had either fled or fallen victim and became puppets, their minds and bodies stolen by the demons' dark influence.

"It's just me and my two boys left Andrew and Alex," he said quietly, his knuckles whitening as he gripped the door handle. "This place used to be home, but now it's... just a battlefield."

"Why don't you leave too?" Ayralina asked, watching him carefully.

"Where would I go?" he replied, his voice tinged with bitterness. "This is the only home I've ever known. These monsters... they took everything from me. They slaughtered my family—my wife included. I can't leave. I have to protect what I have left."

Ayralina was silent for a moment, sensing the depth of his pain. His grief was palpable, his determination raw and unrelenting.

Andre continued, "The money I make as a driver pays for fuel and ammunition to keep them away from our home. It's not much, but it's enough to hold the line. What about you? Why are you here? Where did you learn to fight like that? And those flames—how are you even doing that? Are you... are you human?"

Ayralina studied him, her expression calm but unreadable. After a pause she decided to trust him, she replied, "I won't lie to you, Andre, so I won't answer your questions right now. In time, you'll understand everything. For now, is it enough to know that I won't hurt you?"

Andre searched her eyes, his expression softening. After a long moment, he nodded. "That's enough."

Ayralina smiled faintly and nodded thank you.

When they arrived at Andre's home, that strange feeling she had since she met Andre intensified, like a sense of familiarity that she couldn't explain washed over her. Something about this place or maybe Andre himself, she couldn't quite grasp. For now, she pushed the thought aside. Andre's wounds needed tending, and his boys—if they were anything like their father—likely needed protection as well. As for now, one battle at a time.

Despite Andre's rugged exterior, his home was a surprising contrast—a cozy, well-maintained sanctuary nestled in a peaceful neighborhood. The small, two-bedroom house exuded a soft charm, with its neatly trimmed hedges and a weathered but welcoming front porch. Inside, the air carried a faint scent of cinnamon and wood polish, and the mismatched furniture spoke of a family that valued comfort over appearances. The walls were adorned with photographs, many of them showing Andre and the boys fishing, hiking, or simply laughing together, telling a story of a once happy family with a loving father and mother.

As they entered, Andre called out, "Boys! Come meet our new friend, Dr. Ayralina."

Almost instantly, two boys came barreling into the room. Both were strikingly similar to Andre, with clear brown eyes that sparkled with curiosity and dark hair that fell in slightly unruly waves. The older one, perhaps sixteen, was tall and lanky, his voice carrying a hint of authority as he greeted her. The younger, likely around fourteen, was a touch shorter but brimming with energy, his easy grin hinting at a future as a heartbreaker. Both boys showed the early signs of puberty—deepening voices, a touch of peach fuzz on their upper lips, and a youthful awkwardness that belied their growing.

"Hello, Dr. Ayralina. I'm Alex," the younger boy said with a shy smile. "It's nice to have company. We haven't had visitors in a long time."

"Just call me Ayralina," she replied gently. "Right now, I need to tend to your father before he passes out from blood loss."

The boys' expressions changed instantly, their playful demeanor vanishing as alarm took hold.

"Papa, are you hurt?" the older one asked, stepping forward with concern. "I'm Andrew. I'll carry him—come this way!"

They led her upstairs to the master bedroom, a modest but comfortable space with well-worn furniture that spoke of years of use and care. Ayralina helped Andre onto the bed, his face pale and his breathing labored.

"Your wounds are deeper and more severe than I expected, I don't have the right equipment to stitch you up the traditional way. If I leave you to heal on your own, you will at best, get a few infections and over a prolonged period of time it will eventually heal, or at worst you will bleed out and die." Ayralina said, her tone calm and firm. "So, I will heal you, but the method I'll use is far from traditional—it will heal you completely—but before I proceed, I need your word. You must promise not to expose my secret. By now, you've already guessed that I'm not human. But I can't tell you who or what I am. Knowing too much could put you and your sons in unimaginable danger. So, here are your choices: I can send you to a hospital and ensure you and your boys are relocated to safety, or I can heal you my way, and together, we fight to save your home. What will it be?"

Andre gritted his teeth, his gaze steady despite the pain. "Ms. Ayralina, if it weren't for you, I'd already be dead, and my boys would be left alone in this cruel world. Demons and human puppets have already torn my family and home apart. I owe you everything. If you can destroy those monsters and give my sons a chance at a normal life, I will forever be in your debt. I swear to you; I won't betray your trust. My word is my bond."

Ayralina studied him for a long moment, then nodded. "Very well. I'll begin now."

She closed her eyes, summoning the ancient power of the Phoenix within her. Flames sparked to life in her palms, their golden glow casting dancing shadows across the room. The fire wasn't just fire—it was a lifeforce that cleansed and restored. Ayralina worked methodically, guiding the flames as they sealed Andre's wounds, repairing torn tissue and muscle. Not a single scar remained as the power coursed through him, mending every cell.

As she worked, a strange energy emanated from Andre. Ayralina paused, her senses sharp. Probing deeper, she discovered something embedded within him—a fragment of a moon frost dragon scale. Her breath caught. The scale carried a distinct resonance she recognized instantly. It belonged to her husband, lost during their epic battle a hundred years ago. Somehow, Andre had absorbed it, binding their fates together in an inexplicable twist. No wonder she sensed something about him from the beginning; it's all due to the scale.

When she finished, Andre lay back, his breathing calm and even. His sons, who had watched the entire process in stunned silence, stared at her with wide eyes, their faces etched with a mixture of awe, fear, and wonder.

"Rest for now," Ayralina said softly, adjusting the blanket over him. "You'll feel a little tired, but when you wake up, you'll be as good as new."

"Thank you, doctor," Andre managed to mumble before exhaustion overtook him, and he passed out.

Ayralina turned to the boys, her voice gentle but firm. "Your dad needs to rest now. When he wakes up, he'll be fine."

Alex hesitated, his hands clutching the hem of his shirt as he looked up at her with wide, innocent eyes. After a moment, he whispered, "Are you... an angel?"

Ayralina smiled faintly, her eyes softening, but she didn't answer. Instead, she ruffled the boy's hair lightly and stood, glancing back at Andre before closing the door.

Ayralina stepped outside with the boys, leaving Andre to rest. The warm glow of the setting sunbathed the porch in golden light, casting long, flickering shadows on the wooden boards. She sank into one of the chairs, the weight of the day heavy on her shoulders. Andrew excused himself and went back inside, returning a few moments later with a glass of water and some refreshments for Ayralina.

Ayralina took a slow sip of the cool water, nodding in appreciation before gesturing for the boys to sit beside her.

As they settled, she studied them quietly, a sense of familiarity gnawing at her instincts. There was also something different about them—like their father.

Careful not to alert them, she sent out a subtle pulse of energy, a probe to confirm her suspicions. Keeping the conversation light, she asked them simple questions while her energy brushed against their auras.

Then, she found it.

A flicker of power, ancient and undeniable, buried deep within them.

Each boy also has a dragon scale inside them. Like their father it is also a scale from her husband, the Moon Frost Dragon.

Ayralina's heart skipped with excitement. The Moon Frost Dragon is a legend, a celestial being wielding the power of the moon. Its scales, imbued with eternal ice and lunar energy, were considered sacred, capable of shifting the tides of battle and freezing the entire land in an instant.

The scales hadn't just embedded within them—they had assimilated, chosen them, recognized them as worthy. Ayralina could feel the dormant power stirring beneath their skin, waiting. The scales had already begun shaping them, making them stronger, faster, more resilient. Their perception was heightened, their instincts sharpened, allowing them to react before danger struck.

But more than that—they had the potential to awaken its true power.

If they learned to harness it, they wouldn't just be warriors.

They would be a force to be reckoned with.

Yet the Moon Frost Dragon's power came at a cost.

Its energy was more than ice—it's a cold lunar force, an ethereal presence with a will of its own. If left unchecked, it could freeze their emotions, numb their humanity, and, eventually, consume them entirely.

Ayralina leaned back slightly, her mind racing. These boys are something greater.

Masking her excitement, she turned her attention back to them, her voice gentle, continuing the conversation as if nothing had changed.

"Has anything unusual been happening around here lately? Strange phenomena, odd occurrences?"

Her golden eyes searched their faces.

The boys exchanged a glance, their expressions shifting. Alex smirked mischievously, leaning forward as if to share a secret. "Aside from the zombies and demons, we're not sure what you mean," he said with a shrug. "Oh, and they control tigers too."

"Tigers?" Ayralina asked, raising an eyebrow.

Alex nodded eagerly. "Yeah, and they're really big and white. They're fierce too, and they're not normal. They seem to shoot fire from their mouths. We've never fought them, but we saw them from afar once. They're scary."

Ayralina's gaze narrowed as her mind processed the information. White tigers that could breathe fire were not ordinary—they were likely corrupted and enslaved by the demons to guard their operations. Their presence was troubling, a sign that the demons' influence in the area was stronger than she had anticipated.

She gave the boys a reassuring nod, her expression calm despite the turmoil brewing inside her. "You've done well to avoid them," she said.

"Tell me about the zombies. [not bothering to correct the boys that they're puppets] When did they first appear? What happened before their arrival?"

Andrew hesitated, glancing toward the forest. "Well... there's this story. It's something our dad always talks about—he believes in it, but we've never been sure if it's real."

"Go on," Ayralina urged, her curiosity piqued.

Andrew stood, motioning toward the yard. "Let's walk while we talk. We need to set up the perimeter before nightfall, or the zombies will get too close. Dad taught us how to do it."

Ayralina nodded and followed as the boys led her down a narrow path toward the edge of their property. As they walked, they recounted the fragmented tale that had been passed down through generations.

"Dad says this town was built on cursed land," Andrew began. "A long time ago, there was a battle between good and evil. Legends said that an artifact of immense power—some kind of relic—was hidden here. People say it's what caused the curse, but no one really knows. The zombies and demons didn't show up until recently, though."

Alex chimed in. "Dad thinks the artifact's been disturbed. He believes it's somewhere in a cave deep in the forest, and that's why the monsters are back."

Ayralina listened intently, her mind racing. Could the artifact they mentioned be the Heart's Flame Fire Orchid? Or could it be the missing half of the scroll? If so, its reappearance could explain the chaos. She was deep in thought when a sudden prickle of unease stopped her in her tracks.

Ayralina's senses sharpened as she scanned the surrounding woods, her eyes narrowing at the subtle movements in the shadows. "We're being watched," she said quietly, her voice laced with urgency.

The boys froze, their eyes darting nervously to the darkened forest around them. The once-peaceful air now felt heavy, charged with an ominous energy that prickled at their skin.

Ayralina's mind worked quickly, weighing her options. She needed to protect the boys and, if possible, capture one of their pursuers to interrogate. She turned to them, her tone firm as she addressed them. "Run back inside and barricade the doors," she instructed. "I'll draw them out and lead them away. Quickly."

The boys hesitated, their eyes wide with concern. Alex looked up at her, his voice trembling slightly. "Will you be okay? We can stay and fight with you. We know how."

Ayralina crouched slightly to meet their gazes, her expression softening despite the urgency of the moment. "There aren't many of them," she reassured, keeping her voice calm. "Don't worry about me. I can handle this. You boys need to stay safe. Go now."

She didn't want them taking unnecessary risks, especially since she knew the demons had been tracking her for quite some time now and had finally caught up. There was no doubt in her mind that she was their target, she couldn't let the boys get caught in the crossfire.

The boys exchanged a worried glance but nodded. As instructed, they sprinted toward the house, their footsteps pounding against the wooden porch. Moments later, Ayralina heard the door slam and the heavy thud of furniture being pushed into place.

Once she was certain they were inside, she summoned her powers to create a protective force field around the house. A faint golden shimmer rippled outward, enveloping the structure in a barrier designed to repel any demonic forces. The light pulsed softly, blending into the fading sunlight, invisible to the naked eye.

Satisfied that they were secure, Ayralina turned and strode toward the forest. Her fiery aura flickered faintly around her, drawing attention away from the house. She let her footsteps echo deliberately, baiting the demons lurking in the shadows. Her muscles tensed, every sense on high alert as she prepared to confront the enemies pursuing her. If they thought they could ambush her here, they are sorely mistaken. Ayralina intended to turn the tables and show them that they had underestimated her.

Chapter 5

THE FOREST WAS EERILY silent, save for the occasional rustling of leaves in the wind. Ayralina crouched low behind a cluster of bushes, her fiery aura carefully suppressed to avoid detection. Every one of her senses was on high alert. She was exposed and vulnerable to an ambush, but this was the only place she could intercept the demons before they got too close to the boys.

In the distance, muffled voices drifted toward her, growing clearer with each passing second. Two demons were casually talking to a human; their tone was disturbingly relaxed, given the nature of their hunt.

The larger of the two spoke, his guttural voice rumbling like distant thunder. "Are you sure she went this way? I haven't sensed anything."

The human's reply was steady but laced with frustration. "Of course. Don't question me—especially after you and your useless minions failed to capture her. I've followed her since she left the hotel. What took you so long to catch up? Did you bring reinforcements?"

The raccoon-like demon bristled, lips curling in a silent snarl, but his companions held him back. Hmph... miserable human. I'll let it slide—for now.

Ayralina stiffened. She recognized that voice.

Enzo. The suspicious hotel receptionist who had greeted her.

Now she understands why she didn't quite trust him when she met him. The demons had infiltrated the area faster than she had expected—and they'd been tracking her since she arrived.

Her sharp gaze locked onto the group as they emerged from the shadows, their disguises gone. Their grotesque true forms stood fully revealed in the fading rays of the sun.

The larger demon was a hulking, ox-like beast, its massive frame covered in rough, dark-red hide that gleamed as though slick with blood. Two jagged horns curved from its skull, crackling with dark energy. Its glowing yellow eyes scanned the forest with unsettling precision, and its clawed hands flexed, eager for violence.

Beside it, the smaller demon was no less menacing. It had the form of a raccoon, but its features were grotesquely exaggerated. Its sleek black fur was slashed with glowing crimson streaks, pulsing like veins. A permanent, sharp-toothed grin split its face, while its red eyes darted about with a mix of cunning and malice. It moved with an unsettling twitchiness, shifting unpredictably as if waiting for the perfect moment to strike.

Ayralina stayed quiet, observing them carefully. The ox-like demon let out a low growl, its massive hooves crushing the underbrush beneath it. "If she's here, why don't I sense her?" it asked, its voice a deep rumble vibrated through the air.

Enzo crossed his arms, his tone impatient and angry. "You think a phoenix wouldn't know how to mask her presence? That's why I'm here. I've been keeping tabs on her. You need to trust me if you want to catch her."

They've been watching me since the hotel, maybe even before, she thought, her jaw tightening.

Impressive.

Her fiery magic simmered just beneath the surface as she planned her attack. She couldn't afford a prolonged fight. These demons weren't ordinary—they were hunters, skilled and dangerous in their own ways. If reinforcements arrived, she would be vastly outnumbered. The fight had to be quick, and decisive.

Taking a steadying breath, Ayralina shifted her position, the faintest flicker of fire sparking in her palm. She has to end this before they can call for backup.

Her gaze hardened as she prepared to strike. The element of surprise was the advantage she needed.

Without hesitation, Ayralina moved—swift and lethal. She targeted the raccoon demon first, knowing its reaction speed could put her at a disadvantage. The Ox was larger, likely slower, making it easier to handle second.

As the raccoon demon fell, she turned to the Ox. To her advantage, its reaction was even slower than expected. Seizing the moment, she unleashed a jet of needle-like fire spikes into its eyes, piercing its brain. It died instantly, collapsing before it even hit the ground.

She then turned to Enzo, prepared to take a hostage—but a deep, menacing growl froze her in place. Slowly, she turned, her breath catching as six pairs of glowing yellow-red eyes emerged from the darkness.

Reacting swiftly, she incinerated Enzo with a burst of flames, ensuring no chance of escape or warning. The fire's glow spread through the forest, casting jagged shadows—and revealing a far more dangerous threat.

A pack of tigers emerged from the darkness, their sheer presence exuding menace. At the forefront were two massive white tigers, their fur ghostly pale and streaked with faint, glowing black and red patterns. Their eyes burned like embers, intelligent and filled with malice. Behind them prowled four slightly smaller orange tigers, their coats shimmering unnaturally in the light, their sharp teeth bared in silent snarls. Despite their smaller size, they moved with the same predatory precision, their steps perfectly in sync with the larger tigers.

The male white tiger released a deep, guttural grunt that reverberated through the forest. Instantly, the orange tigers responded, spreading out in perfect formation. Their movements were calculated, encircling her with unnerving coordination, leaving no path of escape.

Ayralina's pulse quickened as she took a step back, her mind racing. Their reinforcements are these tigers. Her throat tightened as the realization hit her. These weren't just ordinary creatures—they were the tigers Andre's boys had described. Big, white, and fire-breathing, and now looking right at her, their presence more terrifying than she could have imagined.

Her fire flickered at her fingertips, but she forced herself to remain still, gauging the situation. The air was thick with tension, the tigers' glowing eyes never leaving her as they stalked closer. The male white tiger let out another low growl, its body lowering as if ready to pounce.

This is worse than I thought, she realized, her jaw tightening. The boys had prayed these creatures wouldn't show up for any reason. These weren't just corrupted beasts—they were demonic predators designed to hunt and kill. And now, they had her surrounded.

Ayralina exhaled slowly, her aura beginning to burn brighter as she braced herself. If I don't take them out now, they'll overrun the house—and the boys won't stand a chance. She squared her stance, preparing for what would undoubtedly be one of the hardest fights of her life.

Before they could fully encircle her, Ayralina bolted, her boots pounding against the forest floor. Fire flared to life in her palms, and she hurled blazing fireballs at the beasts—not to kill, but to throw them off and keep the boys safe. Each explosion illuminated the dark woods, casting wild shadows that danced between the trees.

She spun on her heel, racing deeper into the thicket, but something shocking caught her eye. As she hurled fireballs after fireballs, the white tiger took turn springing into the air with effortless grace and swallowed the blazing orb whole. Each time they would swallow a fireball their fur would lights up in a celestial way. She skidded to a halt, as disbelief took hold.

Heavenly White Tigers.

Her father's stories surged through her mind like a flood. These legendary creatures, revered in myth, were said to wield the power of fire and unmatched intelligence. They were protectors, allies of the righteous, not tools of darkness.

So why were they here, hunting her under the banner of the enemy? Her fists tightened, and her fire burned hotter. She couldn't afford to hesitate now.

Ayralina couldn't dwell on the question for long. A stream of fireballs came hurling toward her, launched from the mouths of the two white tigers. She dodged and sprinted toward the sound of rushing water, knowing that water would be her best ally against their flames.

As she ran, she strategically fired blasts to knock the orange tigers off balance. One by one, she sent them tumbling into the river.

But the white tigers were smarter—and faster. They kept up, evading her flames and coordinating their attacks.

At the edge of the river, Ayralina found herself cornered. There was no escape. The larger male white tiger growled, its body low and coiled to strike.

This was it. She'd have to face them.

Ayralina braced herself, flames igniting fiercely around her fists, their golden-orange glow casting flickering shadows across the forest floor. The growls of the White Tigers reverberated through the air, their luminous, white-striped forms pacing with an unnatural frenzy. Her heart hammered as she took in their predatory movements, their glowing eyes locked on her with unnerving intensity.

The fight began with a thunderous roar, one tiger lunging toward her with claws extended like shimmering blades. Ayralina sidestepped at the last moment, spinning and unleashing a fiery blast that erupted in a dazzling arc. But the tiger surged through the flames, unaffected, its white-striped body glowing brighter as it absorbed the attack. Her eyes widened. These were truly Heavenly Flame Tigers. Ordinary flames would do nothing to stop them. Only the true Phoenix Sunflame could subdue them, but wielding it came at a cost. Every strike would deplete her energy faster, leaving her vulnerable.

She hesitated, weighing her options as the second tiger charged. With no choice, Ayralina summoned the brilliant, searing heat of the Phoenix Sunflame, the air around her rippling with intense energy. Her fists glowed like miniature suns as she struck, sending a concentrated burst of golden fire toward the charging tiger. The flames collided with the creature, not harming it but forcing it to stagger back with a furious growl. The tiger's glow dimmed slightly, proof the Sunflame was working, but her body was already protesting at the energy it consumed.

The male tiger leapt high, its massive form silhouetted against the fading sunlight. Ayralina ducked and rolled, summoning another vortex of Phoenix Sunflame to intercept it midair. The flames engulfed the beast, and this time it yelped, landing heavily and shaking itself as if dazed. Her chest tightened as exhaustion began to creep in. She couldn't keep this up for long—she had to be strategic.

Flames swirled around her in a protective ring as the tigers circled her, their movements deadly. Ayralina switched to using ordinary flames to hold them at bay for now, needing to reserve her true essence for critical moments. One tiger lunged, and she dodged, countering with a burst of dazzling light to disorient it. Another swiped at her, its glowing claws ripping through the air, and she retaliated with a quick strike of her Sunflame, forcing it to retreat once more.

Each use of the Sunflame drained her faster, and her movements grew slower with every passing second. Sweat dripped down her face as she dodged, parried, and struck, her mind racing to formulate a plan. If she could incapacitate them without fully exhausting her strength, she might still uncover the truth behind their corruption.

Her body screamed in protest as she conjured one final, explosive burst of the Sunflame, creating a radiant barrier of heat and light that momentarily drove the tigers back. They hesitated, their glowing eyes flickering as if, for an instant, the flame had shaken whatever dark force controlled them.

Panting, Ayralina steadied herself, her fists still ablaze. The tigers circled her, growling low, their luminous forms still radiating an eerie, golden glow. She knew the Sunflame was her only chance of suppressing them, but her energy was dwindling fast. If she couldn't find a way to end this soon, she'd collapse before the truth could be uncovered.

Finally, after what felt like an eternity, Ayralina managed to maneuver the tigers into a containment spell. The shimmering cage of golden energy hummed softly, its glow casting long, wavering shadows across the forest. The creatures, caught in the spell's unyielding hold, froze in a state of suspended motion. The last tiger collapsed within the binds, its glowing eyes dimming to a faint flicker. Ayralina fell to her knees, her breath raggedy and uneven. She had won, but the toll on her body and spirit was undeniable.

As the adrenaline ebbed, she forced herself to her feet and approached the trapped tigers. Their majestic fur, once pristine, was now matted and dull. Their eyes, once fierce and intelligent, were clouded with a strange, dark sheen that pulsed faintly, like a shadow clinging to their very souls. Ayralina's chest tightened as she stared at them. This wasn't natural—this was vile and malevolent. It burned at her core to see such noble creatures brought to this state. Someone or something had done this to the Heavenly Flame Tigers, and she was going to find out who—and make them pay.

Ayralina sat down on a fallen log to catch her breath, every muscle in her body trembling with exhaustion. Closing her eyes, she concentrated on the wounds scattered across her arms and legs. They weren't deep, but each one burned, a reminder of how close she had come to failing. She summoned a soft glow of healing fire, guiding it across her injuries, the warmth knitting the skin back together until no trace of the cuts remained.

Once her body was whole again, Ayralina turned her attention to erasing all traces of the battle. She stood and methodically began backtracking through the clearing. Scattering ash from her flames, she masked her scent, knowing even the faintest trace could lead her enemies to the scene. With a swipe of her hands, she brushed away footprints, blending them into the natural patterns of the forest floor. Finally, she whispered a cleansing spell, its soft, melodic tones carrying through the air as it swept away lingering magical residue.

This meticulous work had kept her alive for years. Carelessness wasn't an option. Leaving even a hint of evidence behind could bring hunters or dark forces straight to her doorstep. When she was certain the area was clear, she cast one last glance at the shimmering cage containing the tigers.

"Rest for now," she murmured softly, her voice heavy with resolve. "I'll find out who did this to you—and I'll set it right."

With a flick of her wrist, she activated her enchanted ruby necklace—a treasured part of her Phoenix Inheritance, placed upon her by her mother long ago. The containment spell surged to life, pulling the tigers into the necklace's alternate dimension, sealing them away securely within.

Satisfied with her work, Ayralina headed back to the house. As she walked, her thoughts churned with questions. Why had these legendary creatures, once revered as symbols of purity and strength, turned so violent against their nature? What sinister force had changed them? Was this an isolated case, or were other guardians falling victim to the same darkness?

Now that the hotel was compromised, she couldn't go back there. She needed to enlist Andre's help. She had to uncover who or what was behind the power in the hotel—it was likely the same force controlling the tigers. Whatever the truth was, Ayralina was determined to find it. She owed it to the tigers, to Silvaris, and to herself. But for now, she needed rest. The battle had drained her, and the road ahead promised to grow even more perilous.

When she finally reached the house, the boys ran to her, concern etched on their faces.

"Ayralina, are you okay?" they asked, their voices trembling.

"I'm fine," she reassured them, though her exhaustion was evident. "Is your dad up yet?"

"He's not," they replied.

"Okay. Do you mind if I stay the night? I'm exhausted, and I need to make plans with your dad in the morning."

"Yes, of course. You can have my room," Andrew, the older boy, volunteered. "I'll sleep with Alex tonight."

Chapter 6

SITTING DOWN TO BREAKFAST, Andre looked at Ayralina, his voice filled with concern. "Ayralina, thank goodness you're safe! I heard what happened. How did you get away?"

"Just barely," Ayralina replied, exhaustion still evident from the ordeal of the previous night. "But I managed to capture the two white tigers."

Andre's eyes widened as he set down his cup. "Tigers?! What are we supposed to do with them?"

"For now, I need to keep them contained until I figure out what's going on," Ayralina said, her voice heavy with uncertainty. "I'm hoping I can heal them. If not... I'll have to decide what to do."

She glanced at her plate but made no move to eat. "I can sense they're not inherently evil. I've encountered tiger tribes like this before—they usually keep to themselves and don't cause trouble. Something must have happened to make them act this way. I plan to find out why."

She paused, her expression darkening. "The hotel is compromised. I can't go back there until we figure out who's behind this. I suspect it's the demons, and we need to plan what we're going to do next, either get rid of them or at least free ourselves from their control."

Andre leaned forward, his face grim. "And who do you think is pulling the strings? There's always a head honcho."

"That's exactly what we need to know," Ayralina said, her voice firm. "Someone is orchestrating this, and they're powerful enough to manipulate the tiger tribe. Until we figure out who it is, we're flying blind."

With breakfast finished and the tables cleared, Ayralina moved into the living room.

She recalled the ice crystal cage Silvaris had crafted for her long ago—a powerful tool designed to subdue fire-type demons. Without hesitation, she retrieved it from her storage gem and proceeded to release the tigers into the cage, ensuring they remained securely contained.

As expected, the tigers had immediately tried to break free, clawing and slamming against the ice crystal walls. Remaining calm, Ayralina addressed them firmly. "This cage is made from the breath of a thousand-year-old moon frost dragon. Unless you're prepared to risk your lives, you won't be able to break free."

The tigers gradually calmed, their movements slowing. That's when Ayralina had noticed the black gems embedded in their foreheads. The gems blended seamlessly into their black-red stripes; one had to look closely to see any difference. They pulsed with an ominous aura, radiating a cold, dark energy that sent shivers down her spine. The longer she stared at the gems, the more they seemed to call out to her, whispering in her mind, urging her to touch them, to claim them.

Suddenly, from her peripheral vision, Alex reached out toward the gems, his expression vacant. Andre and Andrew had been no less affected. Reacting quickly, she slapped his hand away, snapping the three of them out of the trance.

"What...what just happened?" Andre asked.

"These gems are dangerous," she said firmly. "They're trying to control you. Leave the tigers to me, go out and focus on gathering intel instead. I don't want any of you at risk."

Before the boys left, Ayralina gave them clear instructions. "Go back to the hotel and investigate. See what you can dig up—anything about who's behind this, find out how wide their network of influence is. Be careful, and don't engage unless you absolutely have to."

The boys nodded. "Okay, but you have to be safe. Don't push yourself if you can't save them," Andre had said as he hurried them off, relieved to be getting out of there. The effect of the gems was really disturbing to them, but he also felt a little bit guilty for leaving Ayralina alone with the monumental task of subduing the tigers.

As the boys disappear, Ayralina can finally deal with the tigers in peace. She turned back to face them, her mind racing with questions about the dark power emanating from the gems.

Taking a deep breath, she reached for the first gem. This time, she had prepared herself, flames already igniting around her hand. When her fingers touched the gem, its sinister energy had clawed at her mind, trying to invade her thoughts. The gem's surface had been unnaturally hard, resistant even to her touch.

Ayralina had tried crushing it with sheer strength, but the gem didn't even crack. Frustration simmered as she tightened her grip, feeling the unyielding surface resist her completely. Destroying it would take more than brute force—it would require her phoenix flame.

Closing her eyes, she summoned the full force of her inner fire, channeling it through her palm until the gem glowed white-hot.

The tiger thrashed violently beneath her, muscles coiling in panic, claws scraping against the cage as if trying to break free from an unseen force. A deep, guttural growl tore from its throat, its body convulsing against her hold. The corruption inside it fought back, resisting her, lashing out with invisible tendrils of dark energy that clawed at her senses.

Gritting her teeth, she pressed forward.

With a final surge, the gem shattered, disintegrating into a burst of searing heat. The black shard burned away into nothingness; its dark essence reduced to ash. To ensure no trace of its corruption lingered, she swept another wave of flames over her hand, purging herself completely.

But even with the gem's destruction, the tiger remained slack in the cage, its once-powerful form dulled, its eyes glazed over with an empty, haunted stare.

Ayralina exhaled, pushed past the exhaustion creeping into her limbs. She closed her eyes, extending her mind outward, reaching for the tiger's consciousness. Whatever had taken hold of it ran deeper than the gem.

And she wasn't going to stop until she tore it free.

At first, the tiger panicked. Its voice echoed fiercely in Ayralina's mind. "Puny human! Get out of my mind or I will eat you! Grrrr!"

"You can try," Ayralina replied calmly, her tone unwavering, "but you won't succeed."

The tiger growled in frustration, thrashing slightly within the confines of the ice crystal cage. Ignoring its protests, Ayralina pressed deeper, her mental focus cutting through the layers of its consciousness. She moved cautiously, navigating the tiger's mind until she found it—a shadowy presence, deeply embedded in the far recesses of its thoughts. The darkness pulsed and shifted, resisting her touch.

"There you are," she said telepathically. "There is a shadowed presence lurking at the base of your skull, a poison. It's eating away at you from within."

The tiger snarled defensively, its mind bristling with anger. "You dare invade my mind? My boss will come after you if anything happens to me or my kin. He is powerful beyond your comprehension!"

Ayralina's expression hardened. "Your boss is the one who put this poison in you," she replied, her voice steady. "I can prove it to you if you want to know the truth. Allow me to remove the poison for you, but I can't do it without your help."

The tiger hesitated, its glowing eyes narrowing as it processed her words. Though it growled low, the sound was more uncertain than threatening. "Why should I believe you?" it asked, its tone quieter but still distrustful.

"Because I'm risking my own mind to save yours," Ayralina replied firmly. "This poison isn't just harming you—it's controlling you. If I wanted to harm you, I wouldn't bother with any of this. I'd have left you to your fate."

The tiger remained silent, watching her intently. The anger and fear in its eyes softened slightly, replaced by a flicker of doubt and vulnerability. After a long moment, it lowered its head and let out a deep sigh.

"What must I do?" it asked, its voice quieter now.

"I need you to stop fighting me," Ayralina said. "Let me in fully. This shadow feeds on your spirit. If we work together, we can drive it out—but if you resist me, it'll only grow stronger. You need to trust me."

The tiger's gaze lingered on her, and for a moment, Ayralina thought it might refuse. But then, slowly, it nodded. "I'll give you a chance, human. Don't make me regret it."

Ayralina nodded in return, her flames igniting once again as she prepared to dive deeper into its mind. She felt the connection solidify as she worked. She could sense the tiger's guarded trust, and she understood the risk she was taking. If the tiger decided to turn on her, it could kill her. But she also knew this was a chance to build a lasting impression.

They began the delicate process of cornering and expelling the poison shadow. Slowly but surely, they forced it out of the tiger's mind. The shadow tried to burrow deeper, but Ayralina's persistence left it no escape.

Finally, the poison seeped out of the tiger's ears in dark wisps. Without hesitation, Ayralina incinerated it.

"We can't take any risks with this poison lying around," she said, watching the last of the shadow burn away.

As Ayralina cleansed the first tiger, whom she had learned her name is Ellie, the second tiger—Saber—began to stir. Weak but conscious, he feigned sleep, biding his time in the corner of the cage.

When Ayralina opened the cage to let Ellie out, Saber saw his chance and lunged at her.

It was just before dusk when Andre and his boys found the demons' hideout. The air was thick with the scent of damp earth and decay, the towering trees of the forest casting long, skeletal shadows over the ground. The deeper they ventured, the more the woods seemed to suffocate them, the silence broken only by the distant, guttural growls of unseen creatures.

They had come into town seeking news of the demons, but what they uncovered was far worse than they had imagined. The demons had been luring people into these very woods, drugging them, binding them in darkness, and forcing them to consume the flesh of lesser demons. The tainted meat bestowed unnatural powers but at a terrible cost. Those who consumed it became addicted, their minds unraveling until they were nothing more than human puppets, slaves to their insatiable hunger.

Their prison lay hidden within a cavern that was once home to the white tigers. The cave loomed like a gaping wound in the earth, its jagged entrance draped in thick vines. The air within reeked of blood, damp stone, and something far fouler—the stench of suffering. Faint cries echoed from the depths, barely discernible over the low murmurs of demons standing guard.

Andre and his boys crouched low, listening intently as the demons spoke, their guttural voices weaving a tale of impending war.

The wolf demon's dark fur bristled as it addressed another, an imposing Rhino demon with jagged horns. They carried themselves with authority—commanders, no doubt.

"The damned ox and raccoon—useless fools! And now they've lost the tiger cubs," the wolf snarled. "Damien is furious."

The Rhino demon growled in response. "Gather your ten strongest and fastest trackers. We need to find the Queen Tiger immediately, or Damien will have our heads."

"How many have arrived at the hotel?" the wolf asked.

"Enough," the Rhino replied. "We need to move on the Fire Orchid soon. If we delay, the Tiger King will do something reckless."

Andre stiffened. The Golden Hotel. The Fire Orchid. An ambush for the Queen Tiger. It all connected in a chilling realization—Damien had lost his leverage over the Tiger King. Without the cubs to control him, he was shifting his focus. If he couldn't manipulate the king through his offspring, he would break him through his wife.

Andre exhaled sharply and turned to his boys. "We need to go. Now. Ayralina has to hear this. This is beyond us."

The boys nodded; their faces set with determination as they turned to retreat.

But they weren't alone.

A whisper of movement. A flicker of shadow.

Before they could react, a rat-like demon exploded from the darkness, its eyes glowing with hellish light. It was fast. Too fast.

Claws sliced through the air.

Andre barely managed to parry, steel meeting flesh with a sickening crack. The boys fought beside him, blades flashing in the dim light, but the demon was relentless darting, striking, its twisted grin never faltering.

A clawed hand tore through fabric, drawing a pained grunt from one of the boys. Blood splattered against the bark of an ancient tree. The fight was brutal, chaotic, the demon's strength nearly overwhelming them.

For a moment, Andre feared they wouldn't make it.

With a final, desperate strike, they staggered free, leaving the beast snarling in the shadows, its rage shaking the night.

Breathless and battered, they didn't stop. They couldn't.

Ayralina needed to know what was coming.

Ayralina reacted instinctively, raising her flames, but before the fight could begin, Ellie leapt between them, growling at her brother.

"Stop!" Ellie shouted telepathically, her voice echoing in Saber's mind. "She wasn't hurting me—she healed me! I feel stronger now, and I remember everything. She's one of the good guys, brother. Trust me. Let her help you!"

Saber hesitated, his glowing eyes narrowing as he studied his sister. Confusion clouded his expression, but after a tense moment, he stepped back and nodded reluctantly.

Subduing Saber, however, proved far more challenging than they had anticipated. Sensing his growing agitation, Ellie had to establish a stronger telepathic connection. Her voice was soothing and persistent as she spoke to him directly in his mind. Her influence made him drowsy and disoriented, allowing Ayralina to move quickly.

Using the window of opportunity Ellie provided, Ayralina focused on the black gem embedded in Saber's forehead. It radiated an overwhelming energy, resisting her touch even as flames danced around her hand. She tapped deeper into her phoenix flame, igniting it with full intensity. With a burst of concentrated heat, she incinerated the gem, shattering its hold on Saber and lifting some of the oppressive weight from his mind.

Saber groaned, shaking his head as clarity began to return. Though still weak, he looked at Ellie, his gaze softer. Ayralina stepped back, giving him space as he regained some control.

Working on Saber became easier now that Ellie had vouched for her. Though initially guarded, Saber gradually allowed Ayralina to reach deeper into his mind. The process of removing the poison shadow was just as delicate and exhausting as it had been with Ellie, but with their combined efforts, they managed to purge it completely by sunrise the next day.

Both tigers were finally free, their minds unshackled and clear. Saber lowered his head in gratitude, while Ellie stood by Ayralina's side.

Mission accomplished, Ayralina slumped against the cage, drained but satisfied. Ellie nudged her gently with her nose, a silent gesture of gratitude.

"Rest up," Ayralina said softly. "We have a long fight ahead of us."

Ellie and Saber stood protectively by her side, their strength renewed, and their loyalty forged.

Chapter 7

By LATE AFTERNOON, AYRALINA groggily woke up to frantic calls. "Ayralina! Ayralina, help!" the boys shouted in unison. Blinking the sleep from her eyes, she sat up to a chaotic scene—three boys were perched on the dining table, their faces pale with panic as the two tigers prowled below, trying to get to them.

"Ayralina," one of them stammered, clutching a chair for balance, "can you please call off the tigers? We don't want to become tiger food!"

Ayralina rubbed her temples, still weary from the mental battle earlier. "Mmm, that smells so good. Oh, look what the cat dragged in," she smirked, noticing the bag of food in their hands. "They're probably just attracted to what you brought. They don't eat humans, you know."

The boys looked at each other nervously. "You're sure about that? They sure looked hungry enough to eat us," one of them stated, voice cracking slightly.

With a sigh, Ayralina stood and approached the tigers. "Ellie, Saber," she said firmly, crossing her arms. "Leave them alone. You're not going to eat anyone today, and they are our friends. We especially don't eat our friends. Got it?!"

The tigers eventually backed off, letting out low growls of annoyance. Ayralina reached out and placed a calming hand on each of their heads, reassuring them through a gentle telepathic nudge. Satisfied, the tigers padded off to the corner of the room, still eyeing the food longingly but no longer threatening the boys.

The boys, visibly relieved, climbed down from the table, shaking off the lingering tension.

"Thank goodness," one muttered. "We didn't think you'd actually let us get eaten, but still..."

Ayralina smirked, leaning back with an easy confidence. "Relax. They like you. If they wanted to eat you, you wouldn't be standing here right now."

Ayralina narrowed her eyes at them. "You guys look a little scuffed up. What happened?"

Instead of answering immediately, Andre stepped forward and placed a covered plate on the table before her.

"Eat first, talk later," he said, rubbing the back of his neck. "Figured you'd be hungry after... well, everything."

Ayralina's stomach rumbled in response, and she smiled. "Thanks. That was very thoughtful." She sat down and uncovered the plate, the aroma of warm, hearty food wafting up and reminding her how long it had been since she'd eaten.

As she ate, the boys eagerly recounted their outing, their voices brimming with urgency.

"We went back to the hotel like you asked," one of them started, leaning forward. "But something's off. The whole place is shut down—completely locked down. No one's allowed near the property, and security is everywhere."

"We had to sneak around the back," another boy added. "Almost got caught, too."

Andre nodded grimly. "That's when we saw a demon leave. We followed him and tracked him to the caves."

Ayralina set her utensils down, eyes sharp. "The caves?"

"Yeah," one of the boys continued. "There was a meeting—something about fire and Orchid. They kept talking in circles, but whatever's happening, it's big."

Ayralina's mind raced as she pieced the information together. Between bites, she nodded. "Good work. This gives us a lead. Did you hear when and where this meeting is happening?"

The boys exchanged uneasy glances.

Andre spoke first. "It's at the caves. They're waiting for someone—maybe the top boss named Damien, but we couldn't tell for sure."

Another boy hesitated before adding, "On our way there and back, we ran into some... freshly made human puppets and fought off a rat demon." His voice darkened. "We took them out, but something's changed. The demons are pissed. They're actively hunting for us now."

Ayralina's expression hardened. Suddenly Ellie chimed in "Well, of course they're upset. It's embarrassing for them that they can't even protect their fresh recruits. Anyway, how about Saber and I go back to infiltrate them and keep you informed about what's going on?"

"What?!" Alex exclaimed, his eyes wide. "The tigers can talk?"

Ellie rolled her eyes. "Of course we can talk. We're not just wild animals. We are Heavenly White Flame Tigers, and our family guards the sacred cave."

"Heavenly Tigers? What does that mean?" Alex asked, still in shock.

Ayralina stepped in, her voice calm but firm. "Yes, they're Heavenly Tigers. And no, we will not risk you going back. Now that the demonic aura is gone, there's no way to disguise your powers." She paused and looked at Ellie and Saber thoughtfully. "I sensed something special about them, so I captured them instead of killing them. Their tribe has been cultivating for hundreds of years, developing fire affinity powers. They're just steps away from taking human form." She turned to Ellie and Saber, her expression steady. "So you're the guardians of the cave, correct?"

Both tigers nodded. Ellie spoke first. "We owe you an apology for attacking you earlier. We knew what was happening but couldn't control ourselves. The demons poisoned us while invading our home."

Saber added, his voice heavy with regret. "One day, while guarding the sacred cave, we were ambushed. They captured us and used us to control our parents. Our mom managed to escape with a small group of tigers, but our dad stayed behind to protect us. He's now being held captive and tortured daily."

Ellie's voice trembled as she continued, "They forced our father, King Daxton, to reveal the location of the Fire Orchid. He had no choice but to help them harness its power. Please, can you help us rescue him?"

The room fell silent as Ayralina processed the information.

"Ayralina," said Ellie, "we are very familiar with the cave. Once you come up with a plan, we can lead you in.

"Guard the cave?" Andre finally asked. "What's in the cave that's so important about this orchid, what would the demons do with it, is it the sacred artifacts of legend that we were taught about?"

Ellie hesitated, glancing at Saber before answering. "Yes, it's The Heart's Flame Fire Orchid—with a true fire core. It's a sacred artifact of immense power, and it's our duty to protect it."

Ayralina's suspicions were confirmed. "I came here for the orchid as well," she admitted.

Ellie and Saber exchanged a look before Saber spoke. "If you help us defeat the demons and rescue our family, we'll give you the opportunity to acquire the orchid."

Ayralina nodded in agreement. She understood the nature of sacred artifacts—they could not simply be handed over. She would need to prove herself and tame it on her own.

"Alright, then," Andre said, breaking the tension. "What's the plan?"

All eyes turned to Ayralina.

"We need to gather more information first," she began. "How many demons are there? What kind of defenses do they have? Can you draw us a map of the cave? If King Daxton isn't mind-controlled, he could be a great ally on the inside. We need to find a way to get a message to him so he can coordinate with us. This has to be a careful operation. We can't afford any mistakes."

Ellie nodded. "Our mom is a strong fighter and knows the cave better than anyone. We can find her—she'll help us."

"Any clues on her whereabouts?" Ayralina asked.

"There was a group of demons and human puppets headed towards the north side of the forest with nets and dressed in fire-insulated outfits. They were sent to capture your mom" Andre stated.

"Let's start there first thing tomorrow morning," Ayralina said, her mind already racing through potential strategies. "We'll need to come up with a plan. "

The first order of business was to find the tiger's mother. Her knowledge and insight would be crucial for their next move if she is still alive.

Chapter 8

AT DAWN, AYRALINA'S TEAM set out to find the tiger cubs' mother. The forest greeted them with a serene ambiance, the early morning light filtering through the dense canopy, casting dappled shadows on the forest floor. The air was crisp, filled with the earthy scent of damp moss and the distant calls of awakening birds.

Navigating through the lush undergrowth, they remained vigilant, following the trails the demons had left behind, conscious of the need to avoid drawing attention to themselves. The forest was alive with the sounds of rustling leaves and the occasional snap of a twig underfoot, each noise reminding them to tread carefully. The towering trees stood like silent sentinels, their branches intertwining to form a natural cathedral overhead.

After nearly half a day of cautious searching, they arrived at a secluded clearing bathed in soft sunlight. The queen—a majestic white tiger—was sniffing around, flanked by two orange tigers. Her sleek fur glistened in the light, muscles rippling beneath as she moved with graceful intent, seemingly searching for something.

Not too far from her, hidden in the shadows of the dense forest, were the demons lying in wait, ready to ambush her. Their dark, twisted forms blended unnaturally with the forest, their eyes glowing faintly as they prepared to strike.

The moment the tiger cubs spotted their mother, their joy was palpable. Ellie's tail twitched excitedly as she prepared to shout for her mom and leap toward her, but Ayralina grabbed her shoulder, stopping her.

"Wait!" Ayralina whispered urgently. "Look. We have to deal with the demons first. Let's figure out how many there are and what they're planning. Then, we'll jump in and help when the time is right. We can't let them get away."

Ayralina gestured to the boys. "Andre, you and the boys go! Circle around and figure out how many demons we're up against. Be quick and stay hidden. Report back as soon as you know."

The boys nodded, their faces serious, and silently disappeared, blending into the forest. Meanwhile, Ayralina kept her focus on the tigers and the demons, studying their movements.

Moments later, the boys returned, breathless but efficient. "There are at least a dozen demons, they seem to be fox and wolves type," Andre reported. "They're spread out, but it looks like they're coordinating an ambush."

Ayralina's eyes narrowed. "Good work. Now, stay back and be ready to cover if things get chaotic."

Just as she finished speaking, a large grey wolf lunged from the shadows, its claws reaching for the Queen. The Queen reacted instantly, letting out an earth-shaking roar that echoed through the forest. Her sleek form twisted as she leaped, dodging the demon's strike and landing with grace.

Flames erupted from her maw as she breathed fire, the inferno engulfing two demons and reducing them to ash. The orange tigers flanked her, launching themselves at the other demons, their claws glowing with heat as they slashed through their enemies.

The demons hissed and screeched, their forms shifting unnaturally as they tried to overwhelm her. One managed to grab her hind leg, but she roared again, a wall of flames bursting from her body and sending it flying backward.

Ayralina took the opportunity to leap into action. With a burst of speed, she hurled herself into the fray, her blades flashing as she engaged the demons. One lunged at her, but she sidestepped and drove her flameblade into its chest, twisting as it disintegrated into dark smoke.

Ellie and Saber joined the fight, their fire-infused claws violently slashing through the remaining demons. The Queen roared again, launching a massive fireball that incinerated three more demons instantly.

After an intense battle, the clearing was silent once more, the charred remains of the demons scattered around. The Queen stood tall, her chest heaving, as she surveyed the scene.

After the battle, she finally noticed the cubs. Her ears perked up at the sound of their voices, and she turned toward them, her piercing blue eyes softening as recognition dawned. A low, affectionate rumble emanated from her throat, a sound of relief and love.

The orange tigers, startled by the commotion, immediately moved to shield their queen. Their growls filled the air as they prepared to attack. Their fur bristled, and their claws were ready to strike.

Ayralina, sensing the tension, stepped forward, fireballs forming in her hands as she prepared to defend the cubs. Her stance was firm, her gaze unwavering as she faced the tigers.

"Stop!" commanded the Queen, her voice cutting through the tense atmosphere and ringing through the woods.

The orange tigers hesitated, their growls fading as they backed down, retreating to stand behind her.

The cubs peeked out from behind Ayralina, their eyes wide with emotion. Ellie couldn't contain herself any longer. "Mommy!" she cried, her voice trembling.

The Queen's expression softened further, and she crossed the clearing toward her cubs with a graceful stride. Ellie and Saber ran to her, their small forms colliding into her chest as they buried themselves in her fur.

"My little ones," she murmured, her voice rich with emotion as she nuzzled them. "You're safe... thank the heavens." Her massive frame bent low, her tail curling protectively around them as they clung to her, their joy and relief palpable.

Ayralina watched the reunion, a faint smile tugging at her lips, allowing herself a brief moment of peace. The orange tigers stood back, their tense stances relaxing as they watched the family reunion.

After embracing her cubs, Queen Izzy finally looked up at Ayralina, gratitude shining in her eyes. "You... you brought them back to me, I owe you a debt of gratitude," she said, her voice steady but laced with emotion.

Ayralina nodded, her expression calm but serious. "They're brave, just like their mother. But we're not safe yet. We need to get out of here and find a safe place to talk."

The cubs nuzzled against Queen Izzy, their small forms pressing into her fur as if afraid to let her go again. Izzy wrapped her tail protectively around them, her powerful frame lowering slightly as she reassured them with soft rumbles.

Then, with a subtle nod, "Follow me," she said. "Our hideout is deeper in the forest, where the demons won't dare follow. There, we can speak freely."

As they made their way back to Queen Izzy's hidden sanctuary, the group moved in silence, the weight of recent events lingering in the air. The dense forest around them provided cover, its shadows stretching as the sun began to dip lower in the sky. Finally, Queen Izzy broke the silence, her voice both commanding and curious.

"I am Izzy, by the way. How did you find me?" she asked, her piercing blue eyes narrowing as she glanced back at Ayralina.

Ayralina met her gaze evenly. "My name is Ayralina, and My companions here Andre and his sons Andrew and Alex, while out scouting for information, they discovered that there was a group of elite demons being sent out to capture you. We followed their trail, and sure enough, it led us right to you."

The queen's expression softened at the explanation, but her gaze remained sharp, her protective instincts still heightened.

Andre coughed gently, breaking the tension. "What do we do now? How can we rescue your husband, stop the demons, and retrieve the orchid?"

At the mention of the orchid, Queen Izzy froze mid-step. Her gaze snapped to Andre, her ears twitching. "You know about the orchid?" she demanded, her voice low and dangerous. Her eyes flicked between Ayralina and the others. "Who are you, and what are you doing here?"

Before Ayralina could respond, Ellie stepped forward, her small form trembling but her voice steady. "Mom, wait! Let me explain."

Ellie launched into a heartfelt recount of everything that had happened. She described how Ayralina had found them trapped, how she had fought the demons to free them, and the promise they had made to help her on her quest. Ellie's voice wavered as she recounted Ayralina's courage and the danger they had all faced together.

Queen Izzy listened intently, her sharp gaze softening as her daughter spoke. When Ellie finished, the queen let out a deep sigh, her tail flicking behind her.

"I see," she said, her voice quieter now. She turned to Ayralina, studying her for a long moment before speaking. "You risked your life to save my cubs and now seek to help me save my husband and protect the sacred orchid. That's no small task."

Ayralina inclined her head respectfully. "I couldn't leave them behind. And I couldn't turn away when I learned about what's at stake. We're all in this together."

Queen Izzy nodded slowly, her expression resolute. "Very well. If you're willing to fight beside us, then we'll need to prepare. The orchid isn't just an ordinary flower—it's tied to the power of the phoenix. Its energy can unlock a sacred artifact, though the full details remain a mystery to us. Our tribe was entrusted to guard the orchid, to protect it until the one destined to claim it appears."

"But recently, the demons discovered its location. That's why they invaded our home and took everything from us. They believe the artifact is a key to unlocking a scroll that will grant them ultimate power, and if they succeed, the balance of this world will be shattered. It won't just be my family or this land that suffers—it will be everything, everywhere. The stakes couldn't be higher."

Her piercing gaze swept over Ayralina and her companions as she continued, "However, since the cubs have promised to give you a chance, I will honor that promise. Once we reclaim our home, we will guide you there, giving you the opportunity to prove if you are truly destined to be its rightful owner."

Unaware of Ayralina's true identity as a descendant of the Sunflame Phoenix tribe, the queen remained oblivious. Ayralina, however, chose not to reveal her secret just yet. She nodded respectfully and said, "I understand. Thank you for trusting me with this opportunity. I promise to do my best."

"By the way," Ayralina asked, "what are you doing all the way up here?"

Queen Izzy glanced at the plants around her. "I'm harvesting an antidote, hoping it can cleanse the demons' poison."

"There's an antidote?"

"I'm not sure yet—it's just a theory," the queen admitted. "But I've noticed that when tigers come into contact with these plants, it seems to give them brief moments of clarity. I wanted to test it further. Now that you're here, and you're human, maybe you can figure it out."

"That's great," Ayralina said, her mind racing with possibilities. "But we'll need test subjects..."

"That won't be an issue," Queen Izzy said firmly. "I know where to find them. We can capture a few human puppets to test it on. If it works, we'll spread the antidote throughout their compound."

Ayralina nodded, determination in her eyes as she began formulating a plan. "Let's gather as much of the plant as possible and take it to your hideout. We'll start refining the antidote there."

Queen Izzy gave a sharp nod. "Rest up for tonight. Tomorrow, you and your human companions will harvest the plants, while the tigers and I capture the test subjects for you."

The next morning, Ayralina and the boys set out to the spot Queen Izzy had directed to harvest the plants.

The antidote—a complex blend of Rhodiola Rosea, known for its resilience-building and stress-relieving properties, and Lion's Mane mushrooms, renowned for their neuroprotective effects—holds the potential to reverse the insidious mind-control spell. These ingredients combined could create a potent elixir capable of repairing damaged neural pathways and breaking the magical bond enslaving the human puppets.

They spent the afternoon meticulously harvesting the plants. Ayralina carefully followed Queen Izzy's guidance, ensuring they preserved the most potent parts of the Rhodiola roots, and the delicate, hairy spines of the Lion's Mane mushrooms. Each plant was gently uprooted, cleaned, and stored in woven satchels lined with cooling herbs to preserve its vitality.

As they worked, Ayralina jotted down detailed notes, sketched diagrams of the plants, and recorded observations about their properties. Her mind raced with ideas for extracting and combining the active compounds needed to refine the antidote.

Queen Izzy's voice echoed in her memory, as she had instructed them on ancient techniques for preparing the ingredients. "The Rhodiola must be dried carefully," she had explained, demonstrating with precision. "And the Lion's Mane must be brewed fresh to retain its full potency. Together, their magic and medicinal properties can counteract even the darkest of curses."

By the time the sun dipped below the horizon, casting golden and pink hues across the forest, they had gathered as much as they could carry. Exhausted but hopeful, they made their way back to the hideout, ready to begin the real work of creating the antidote.

When they arrived, they found that the tigers had also returned, dragging several human puppets into the hideout. The captives were knocked out and tied up in a corner, their limp forms a haunting reminder of the curse's power. Queen Izzy stood nearby; her expression unreadable as she watched over them.

Ayralina's gaze shifted from the puppets to the gathered plants in her satchel. Determination flared in her chest. "Let's get to work," she said, her voice steady. She knew that her work had just begun; she was in for a long night.

Chapter 9

"THUMP...UMPH. I THINK THAT'S enough for tonight," Ayralina muttered as she and the boys tossed a few more human puppets into the trunk.

This was their third round of gathering test subjects, and they now had enough to proceed with the next phase of her experiments. Ayralina had just finished refining her first batch of antidote and was preparing to test it further.

Through trial and error, she discovered the antidote was a two-step process. First, the antidote had to be infused into the human puppets. It acted like a tranquilizer, forcing the poison in their bodies to "sleep." The second step required her Phoenix flames to chase the poison out entirely, as she had done with the tigers, before incinerating it.

The process was effective, but it was slow and exhausting. Treating the human puppets one by one drained her energy, and she knew it was unsustainable. By the time she finished detoxing everyone, she'd be vulnerable.

She needed a better solution that didn't rely solely on her physically draining all her powers.

The night was quiet, save for the occasional crackle of the fire and the distant whisper of wind through the trees. The air was crisp, but to Andre, Andrew, and Alex, it felt much colder than it should have.

Andre hesitated before approaching Ayralina. She was focused, absorbed in her work, and he didn't want to disturb her—but she needed to know.

"Something's wrong," he said, his voice low but urgent. "Lately, I've been feeling... off. Cold, even when I shouldn't be. And it's not just me—the boys feel it too."

He exhaled sharply, forcing out the words he had been dreading. "I think we've been infected. I don't know how it happened, but—there. I said it."

Ayralina stopped, her golden eyes darkening with understanding.

He thought it was contamination from the human puppets.

But she knew the truth.

She had put this off for too long.

Taking a deep breath, she rose to her feet and gestured for them to follow.

"We need to talk."

Ayralina sat cross-legged before Andre, Andrew, and Alex, the firelight casting flickering shadows across their faces. The forest stretched into darkness behind them, quiet yet alive with an unseen presence.

The boys watched her warily, their expressions a mix of curiosity and unease.

Ayralina exhaled slowly, centering herself before she spoke.

"There's something inside each of you, something you don't yet understand."

Her piercing gaze locked onto theirs, unwavering.

Andrew shifted. "What do you mean?"

Instead of answering, Ayralina released a pulse of energy—not forceful, but just enough to brush against their auras.

The reaction was immediate.

All three of them flinched, their bodies shivering as if touched by an unnatural cold.

Alex instinctively clutched his chest, his breath hitching. "What... was that?"

Ayralina's expression remained calm.

"That is the presence of a Moon Frost Dragon's Scale inside you."

Silence.

The flames flickered, casting their shock and confusion in sharp relief.

Andre's brows furrowed. "Come again?"

Ayralina folded her hands in her lap, her expression steady, yet tinged with something softer—understanding.

"Each of you carries a dragon scale within you. Not just any dragon, but the Moon Frost Dragon—one of the most powerful celestial beasts to have ever existed."

She watched them carefully, letting the weight of her words settle.

Andrew frowned. "How is that even possible? We're just... normal."

Ayralina shook her head.

"You were never normal. That's why you've survived when others haven't. That's why your instincts are sharper, why your bodies recover faster, why you've always been stronger than most people without ever having to train."

Andre combed a hand through his hair, his breath coming slower, steadier.

"So you're saying this thing has been inside us all this time?"

Ayralina nodded.

"But until now, it has remained dormant. The scales have been strengthening you in the background, keeping you alive, preparing you. But now it's power is waking up. And if you don't integrate with it fully..."

She paused, watching their reactions.

"It will consume you."

Alex swallowed hard. "What happens if we awaken it?"

"If you integrate properly, you'll be able to cultivate its power. Your bodies will become stronger, your reflexes sharper, your perception almost inhuman." She explained.

The flames flickered in her golden eyes.

"But the Moon Frost Dragon's energy is not easy to control. It is powerful, it is also cold. If you fail to balance it, It will strip you of your emotions. You'll lose your sense of self. And eventually...it will consume you."

The weight of her words hung between them.

For the first time, genuine fear flickered in their eyes.

Andre finally broke the silence. His voice was quieter now, more careful.

"So how do we stop that from happening?"

Ayralina's lips curled slightly, though it wasn't a smile of amusement—it was one of determination.

"By learning to cultivate it properly."

She lifted her palm, and a swirl of blue and white energy formed, hovering just above her skin. It danced between her fingers, shifting like a living entity, a perfect balance of ice and life.

The flames around them dimmed as if acknowledging her control.

"I will teach you a cultivation method that will help you harness the scale's power," she said. "But it will take time. It will take discipline."

She let the firelight reflect in her gaze.

"And once my husband wakes up, he will take over your training."

Andre's head snapped up. "Your husband?"

Ayralina nodded, her expression momentarily distant, as if remembering something far away and dangerous.

"He is the most respected ruler of the celestial dragons." Her gaze returned to them, burning with quiet intensity. "And the only one to have ever fully mastered the power of the Moon Frost Dragon. It is his scale that has chosen you."

Her next words were spoken with finality.

"Until then, I will do my best to help you integrate with the scales. But make no mistake—this path will not be easy."

The flames flickered once more, as if whispering of the trials ahead.

Andrew straightened, his fists clenched, and let out a slow breath before giving a firm nod. "Then let's do this."

Ayralina studied them momentarily, searching their faces for doubt and hesitation.

She found none.

A slow, knowing smile touched her lips.

"Alright let's begin."

Leaving the boys to continue absorbing and their newly awakened powers, Ayralina stepped away, letting the cool night air soothe her thoughts.

The sky stretched endlessly above her, the full moon hanging low and luminous, its glow so bright it felt within reach. She lifted her hand slightly, fingers brushing the air, as if she could touch it.

She had come out here to clear her mind, but her body wouldn't let her rest.

Training was second nature to her now—a necessity, not a choice.

She was in the middle of a sequence, channeling her Phoenix energy, when she sensed a familiar presence approaching.

Queen Izzy stepped into the moonlight, her movements as fluid as they were powerful. She observed Ayralina for a moment before speaking.

"Why did you stop?"

Ayralina let out a frustrated breath, pressing a hand against her side.

"It's this stitch. It's been bothering me so much I can't focus properly."

Izzy tilted her head slightly, concerned flickering in her blue eyes. "Do you need my help?"

Ayralina hesitated, then nodded. "Yes, actually. Just sit still and try not to move. That would be most helpful."

Izzy nodded, though curiosity danced in her gaze, then Ayralina placed a hand on her spine.

A warm current of healing energy surged from Ayralina's palm, weaving through Izzy's body like a golden thread, mending unseen wounds from the inside out.

Izzy gasped, eyes widening.

"How did you know I was injured?"

Ayralina smiled softly. "I'm a doctor, remember? And also an empath. I sensed your pain the first time we met, but I knew you wouldn't trust me enough to let me heal you then. Every time you came near me, I could feel it getting worse. If I didn't treat you tonight, you wouldn't be much help in battle. I took a chance, hoping you wouldn't mind."

For a moment, Izzy said nothing.

Then, her expression softened, gratitude shining in her eyes. "Mind? Not at all. Thank you, Ayralina. For all you've done, I truly owe you a great debt. We tigers always keep our promises."

Ayralina chuckled, shaking her head. "There's no need to be so formal. Healing is what I do—it's as natural to me as breathing. Even if you were my enemy, I'd still heal you. But you're my friend now, so it's a no-brainer."

Izzy smiled, standing. "Then, enough rest. Come on, let's train together. Show me what you've got."

They sparred side by side, their movements fluid like a coordinated dance,the night air charged with raw energy. Izzy, ever the warrior, offered insight into fire—its nature, its will, its power.

"For me, fire is a friend," Izzy explained as she moved, flames dancing around her fingertips. "When I ask it for help, it's always there. I let it guide me and flow through me. I don't fight it because I know it won't harm me. When I'm one with my source, it's infinitely more powerful than when I try to control it alone."

She paused, meeting Ayralina's gaze. "Fire is like a river—if you block it, you'll overwhelm yourself. Let it flow."

Ayralina froze, her heart skipping a beat.

Her mother's words echoed in her mind.

She had heard this lesson before—but back then, she had been too headstrong, too stubborn to truly listen.

Now, with Izzy's guidance, she decided to try again.

Taking a deep breath, she reached deep within herself, searching for the core of her Phoenix flame.

At first, it was too much.

The sheer intensity of her power made her hesitate, threatening to consume her.

But then...

She let go.

She surrendered to it.

The moment she did, warmth rushed through her, filling every fiber of her being. The energy no longer fought against her—it moved with her, as if it had always been waiting for her to stop resisting.

She lifted her hands, and flames ignited at her fingertips, but this time, something was different.

She could feel every flicker. Sense every individual spark.

It was as though she had gained sight within the fire.

She could split them apart, control each flame individually, make them dance in harmony, and then merge them again as she pleased.

Her breath caught in awe.

"Amazing! I did it!"

Izzy grinned. "Good. Now do it again—this time, focus. Direct your flames to a target."

Ayralina practiced through the entire night, honing her abilities with relentless determination.

She learned to adjust temperature, intensity, and movement, mastering how to control multiple flames simultaneously.

By the time dawn broke, her powers had evolved to a whole new level.

As the sun's first light painted the sky, Ayralina sat down to meditate, her body and mind absorbing the night's lessons.

And that's when inspiration struck.

Her eyes snapped open, her heart pounding with realization.

She had been approaching the antidote challenge all wrong.

Instead of trying to fight the poison after it had taken hold, she could infuse her flame directly into the antidote, keeping it in a dormant state.

Once inside a human puppet's body, the flame would already be waiting—hidden, unseen, but ready.

Then, at her command, she could activate it remotely, allowing the flame to incinerate the poison instantly without her needing to be physically present.

This new method would revolutionize the treatment process—making it far more efficient and freeing her to focus on the larger battle ahead.

A slow, confident smile crossed her lips.

With renewed purpose, Ayralina opened her eyes, the morning sun reflecting in their golden depths.

She was ready.

It was time to put her plan into action.

Chapter 10

THE WAR ROOM WAS tense, the air thick with urgency.

Ayralina stood in the shadows, her gaze fixed on the tiger warriors as they returned with urgent news. The wind had picked up, carrying with it the weight of something that felt inevitable.

Izzy approached, her eyes dark with concern, her posture rigid.

"What's the situation?" Ayralina asked.

Izzy took a steadying breath "The tigers have returned with news from our allies in the north." Her voice was calm, but a storm of fear and urgency churned beneath it. "When our home was invaded, I warned King Tyrin to be cautious. Now, the demons are making their move—they're after both the Ice Crystal Heart and the Orchid at the same time."

Ayralina's expression tightened. "And the north?"

"They're at war," Izzy said grimly. "Once we finish here, we head north to reinforce them. We can't let the demons take control." She clenched her fists. "For now, we need to deal with the immediate situation ahead. The meeting is at dusk, when the Orchid's power is at its weakest. They plan to force Daxton to subduc it." Her gaze darkened. "But it's too much for him. If he pushes beyond his limits…" She swallowed hard. "He won't survive."

Izzy's expression darkened, the weight of the situation sinking in. "Knowing my husband, he would rather sacrifice himself than let them come near the orchid." She exhaled sharply. "We need to act before they get to him."

Ayralina nodded, a knot forming in her stomach. "So, we strike before they release him to the orchid."

Izzy's gaze sharpened with resolve. "Yes." She pulled out a map, spreading it on the table swiftly. "Here's the plan."

Ayralina leaned forward, her focus razor-sharp.

"We split into two groups." Izzy's eyes met hers. "Ayralina, you stay with the cubs. The tigers and I will lure the human puppets toward your position. Be ready to trap and begin detoxifying them immediately. It's vital we weaken their numbers and break their control. Only then can we move on to the cave."

Ayralina's brow furrowed slightly. "And then?"

Izzy's voice turned colder, sharpening with authority. "Once the puppets are neutralized, the cubs stay behind to ensure no reinforcements arrive. No one can get near the cave. The orchid will burn anyone who tries—except those with an affinity to flame. We'll be the ones to infiltrate."

Ayralina felt her pulse quicken. "And how do we get past the demons guarding King Daxton?"

Izzy's lips pressed into a tight line. "The demons will be stronger than anything we've faced before. Higher-level. Deadly. We'll need to move carefully. Stealth is key, and timing will be everything."

She paused, the gravity of the situation weighing heavily in the air. "Ayralina, conserve your energy. This part will be the most dangerous. You'll need all your strength for the final battle."

Ayralina nodded, her jaw set with determination. "How do we avoid alerting the demons?"

Izzy's eyes flickered with calculation. "The tigers' natural stealth will be crucial. You'll mask your magical energy, and I'll take the lead, drawing the guards away from the entrance. Once we're inside, we move as one. We take out the guards silently, then we'll find Daxton. If we're too late... they'll use the orchid on him, and our chances to save him will disappear."

Ayralina tensed. "What if they unleash the orchid's power while we're inside?"

Izzy's eyes narrowed, her tone unwavering. "We can't retrieve the orchid. Anyone who tries will die. But if, by some chance, it happens, we'll deal with it when the time comes. If we're smart and move quickly, we can turn the orchid's power against them. We can use its energy to destroy the demons."

Ayralina's gaze hardened, determination flaring in her eyes. "I won't let them win. We'll get King Daxton back. We'll stop them."

Izzy placed a paw on her shoulder, the weight of their unspoken bond clear in the gesture. "Good. We move at dusk. Rest now, gather your strength. We'll only have one shot at this."

Ayralina nodded, her heart firm with determination. The team exchanged a silent understanding before moving off to prepare themselves for the critical mission ahead.

The air was electric as Andre, Andrew, and Alex stood at the forest's edge. Raw power thrummed through their bodies as if the land itself recognized their transformation.

They felt the Moon Frost Dragon's Scale fully assimilate into them for the first time. It was no longer dormant—it was a part of them, a living force that coursed through their veins.

Andrew flexed his fingers, feeling the cool energy pulse beneath his skin. "This... this is insane."

Alex grinned, shifting into a battle stance. "I feel incredible. I bet I'm faster than both of you now."

Andre smirked, rolling his shoulders as icy mist curled from his fingertips. "Care to test that theory?"

Andrew lunged before either of them could answer, his body a blur of motion. Alex dodged, twisting midair and landing behind him, the ground freezing beneath his feet.

"Not bad, but you're still slow!" Alex taunted.

Andrew laughed, pivoting sharply before charging at him again, his speed doubling as he pushed his limits.

Andre watched them spar, his heart pounding with exhilaration. He could feel the power surging through them—precise, controlled, and deadly.

The three of them clashed, their blows like thunder, their movements a blur of white streaks and cold mist. They were testing their limits, embracing their newfound abilities.

Andrew spun, launching a palm strike infused with icy force, but Andre deflected it with a simple swipe of his hand, sending shockwaves through the air.

Alex summoned a blade of ice, slashing through the air. Andrew ducked just in time, countering with a blast of frost that sent Alex skidding back.

"Oh, it's on now!" Alex shouted, charging forward again.

The playful battle raged on, their movements effortless—each growing more powerful by the second.

They were no longer just humans.

They were something more—unstoppable.

And they were just getting started.

A sudden clap of hands rang out from the shadows.

"Alright, now that you're done playing—"

The three of them froze mid-motion, turning to see Ayralina standing at the edge of the clearing, her arms crossed, an amused smirk on her lips.

"It's time to go."

They exchanged reluctant glances, the power still thrumming inside them.

Alex whined. "Just five more minutes, please?"

Ayralina's expression hardened, and the air around her rippled with heat.

"Oh, sounds like you want to spar with me instead?"

The challenge hung in the air, thick with tension.

Andrew coughed, breaking the silence. "Uh... yeah. We're ready to go."

Andre chuckled, shaking his head. "Let's move."

As they followed Ayralina toward their next destination, the buzz of energy still coursing through their bodies, they couldn't help but grin.

They had awakened.

They had become something more.

And now, they are ready to truly test their strength.

Under the cover of twilight, the group arrived near the cave's entrance, the moon's eerie glow casting long shadows over the rocky terrain.

Izzy and the tigers led a diversionary assault. Starting a controlled fire in the eastern sector of the forest, they drew the human puppets' attention, forcing them to stagger toward the flames. Meanwhile, Ayralina got to work.

Positioned in a clearing surrounded by tall stones, Ayralina crafted a fire ring using her Phoenix flame. With a flick of her wrist, she released clouds of herbal smoke into the air, the concoction carefully prepared to counteract the poison infecting the human puppets. One by one, they stumbled into her trap.

"Steady," she whispered to herself, weaving delicate threads of flame into their bodies. The fire was alive, a part of her, and it obeyed her commands. The flames searched out the poison coursing through them, burning it out of their systems. Slowly, their snarls and mindless rage faded, replaced by dazed clarity.

The cubs watched with wide eyes, their small forms standing guard as Ayralina worked tirelessly. When the last of the poison was incinerated in the fire ring, she allowed herself a brief moment of relief.

As Ayralina stood among the freed humans, her flame flickering like a second sun, she turned to Andre and the boys, her voice calm but firm. "Stay here and protect them. Keep the cubs safe, and if anything happens, get them as far from here as possible."

Andre nodded, determination in his eyes. "We'll handle it, Ayralina. Go finish this."

Ayralina glanced at the protective circle of cubs and freed humans, then at the glowing entrance of the cave. Following the plan, it was time for her to join the fight inside.

She turned and sprinted toward the cave, her flames flaring to life as she charged in alongside the tigers. The air inside was suffocating, thick with sulfur and decay, and the glow of her flames cast long, flickering shadows on the jagged walls. Where her flames touch, it cleanses away the decay. The tigers moved silently beside her, their predatory grace a stark contrast to the grotesque demons that filled the cavern.

"Stick to the plan!" Izzy shouted from deeper inside, her voice cutting through the chaos. Ayralina spotted her locked in battle with a Rhino-like demon, slashing at its legs with her razor-sharp claws.

The demons were relentless—massive, hulking creatures with gleaming red eyes and fangs that tore through stone as easily as flesh. Ayralina didn't hesitate. She unleashed a torrent of flaming fireballs, the golden-orange flames roaring through the cave and forcing the demons back.

One demon lunged at her, its claws aimed for her throat. She sidestepped and spun, her flames coiling around her like a living shield. With a sharp cry, she sent a blast of fire directly at the demon's eyes, reducing it to ash in seconds.

"Ayralina, over here!" Izzy called, gesturing toward the heart of the cave.

Ayralina pushed forward, the tigers flanking her and striking down demons with deadly efficiency. The closer they got to the center, the stronger the demonic presence. The air grew heavier, almost suffocating, as though the cave was alive with dark energy.

Finally, they reached the glowing pedestal at the center of the cavern. King Daxton was chained to it, his once-bright fur matted and his face gaunt. Despite his weakened state, his eyes burned with unyielding resolve.

"Izzy!" he rasped, his voice hoarse and urgent. "Behind you!"

Izzy spun just in time to block the claws of a massive demon. With a nod to the tigers, she motioned for them to hold off the remaining guards while she worked to free Daxton.

Ayralina moved to assist, her flames burning through demons that attempted to close in on them. Suddenly, a chilling voice echoed through the cave, stopping her in her tracks.

"So, the Phoenix finally comes out to play," the voice drawled, smooth and taunting.

From the shadows emerged a figure unlike any other demon they'd faced—a tall, commanding presence cloaked in darkness, with glowing crimson eyes that radiated intelligence.

"Ayralina, that's their leader," Izzy hissed, her claws still working to break Daxton's chains.

Ayralina squared her shoulders, her flames blazing brighter as she stepped forward. "You must be the coward hiding behind these monsters."

The figure chuckled, a low, chilling sound. "Coward? Hardly. I prefer 'strategist.' Let's see how brightly you burn, Phoenix."

He lunged at her with impossible speed, dark energy crackling in his wake. Ayralina met him head-on, her flames colliding with his shadowy power in an explosion of light and darkness. The battle was fierce, their movements a blur as they exchanged blows.

Ayralina's flames flared brilliantly, scorching the cave walls, but the leader was faster than anything she'd encountered. His strikes were deliberate, as though he could predict her every move. She unleashed a massive wave of fire, finally landing a hit that sent him sprawling.

As the shadows around him dissipated, his face was revealed—and Ayralina froze.

He wasn't a demon. He was human.

Her flames faltered, her amber eyes wide with shock. "You... you're human?"

The man smirked, his expression cold and calculated. "Surprised? You shouldn't be. After all, only a human could have the ambition—and the ruthlessness—to control demons."

Before she could respond, he unleashed a blinding blast of energy. Ayralina raised her flames to shield herself, but when the light faded, he was gone, his presence vanishing into the depths of the cave.

Breathing hard, Ayralina turned back to Izzy, who had just freed Daxton. The King's eyes met hers, his expression grim.

"What happened?" Izzy asked, urgency lacing her voice as she stepped closer.

Ayralina's jaw tightened, her flames dimming slightly. "The leader... he's not a demon. He's human."

"What?!" Izzy exclaimed, her eyes widening in disbelief. But before she could say more, King Daxton's expression grew distant, his mind clearly distracted. Then his eyes widened with clarity "The Phoenix Sunflame," Daxton murmured the words as if they carried the weight of an ancient prophecy. His voice trembled, his mind working to piece together a truth long buried. Stepping forward, his gaze locked onto Ayralina. "It's you... You're the lost Phoenix princess."

Chapter 11

AYRALINA WENT RIGID, FLAMES crackling to life mirroring the storm inside. "What are you talking about?" She denied. "You must be mistaken."

Daxton didn't waver. His expression remained firm. "The fire in your veins, the strength you wield, the way you defy fate itself, only one born to the Phoenix royal bloodline carries such powers. There's no mistake. It's you."

Ayralina's heart pounded. Her fists clenched at her sides.

Izzy's eyes darted between them, realization striking like a thunderclap. "If Daxton's right, this changes everything," she breathed. "If you're the lost Phoenix princess... then you're the one we've been waiting for."

Daxton stepped closer, his tone softening. "You don't have to hide anymore, your majesty. We are your allies." His voice carried the weight of history, an oath passed through generations. "Our ancestors were chosen to guard this place, waiting for the day a true Phoenix—one who carries the Sunflame—would return. Only the rightful heir can claim the Heart's Flame Fire Orchid and break the bond that has kept my family to this duty for centuries." He exhaled, studying her intently. "Now that I see you... there is no doubt. You are the heir."

Ayralina swallowed hard. The truth clawed at her, undeniable. "How did you recognize me? What oath are you talking about? And what do you mean—I can free your family?"

King Daxton regarded her for a long moment, unreadable. Then, to her shock, he dipped his head in reverence, as Izzy followed him. "Your Majesty."

Ayralina stiffened, then reached her hands out to touch them on their heads, "no need for such formality. I haven't been a princess in a long time. Just calling me Ayralina is good enough."

Daxton nodded. "Your reaction tells me you don't know the full truth about the Orchid. You likely assumed it was just an ordinary Fire Orchid."

She said nothing but gestured for him to continue.

"A hundred years ago, one of your ancestors fell to earth," Daxton said. "She was being pursued by an enemy. My mate and I were also being hunted—we were badly injured, and Izzy was pregnant at the time. Instead of running to save herself, your ancestor stayed. She fought with us." His voice grew heavier. "Then, she used the last of her power to heal my mate... and help deliver my cubs."

Ayralina's breath hitched.

"We owed her a debt we could never repay." Daxton's eyes darkened with memory. "In her dying moments, she extracted her Phoenix core and placed it inside an Orchid, entrusting it to us for safekeeping. She made us vow to protect it until her heir came for it." He met Ayralina's gaze. "And now, you're here."

A shiver ran down Ayralina's spine. She had a suspicion—an aching, overwhelming certainty—about this ancestor's identity, but she kept silent. Instead, she forced a faint smile, steadying herself.

"No wonder you were chosen as King," she said, her voice quiet and firm. "Your wisdom is remarkable. Thank you for your loyalty all these years. I'm sorry for the burden this has placed on you."

Daxton shook his head. "No apologies are needed, Your Majesty. It has been an honor." He straightened, his voice resolute. "Now, come with me. I will take you to the Orchid."

Ayralina exhaled, bracing herself. The past was calling, and she was ready to face it.

But before she followed, Ayralina noticed the cuts and bruises marring his body. His stance was strong, but the strain was evident in his breathing.

She knelt beside him, hovering her hands over his injuries as golden light flickered to life, pulsing from her palms. Warmth radiated from her touch, sinking into his torn flesh, knitting wounds together with an ethereal grace.

"Let me heal you first," she said, her voice firm.

Daxton hesitated, glancing at Izzy. She met his gaze and gave a small nod of reassurance.

With a quiet sigh, he relented. "Thank you," he murmured.

As the golden glow of her energy wrapped around him, his pain dulled, his muscles relaxed, and his skin healed before their eyes. The warmth didn't just mend his wounds—it reached deeper, into his very essence, strengthening him from within.

When Ayralina finally withdrew her hands, the injuries were gone, leaving only faint traces of what had once been.

She met his gaze. "Better?"

Daxton flexed his paws, testing his strength. A flicker of something unreadable crossed his face before he finally nodded.

"Much."

They stepped out of the cave, the crisp morning air greeted them, a stark contrast to the damp, shadowed depths they had just emerged from. The people moving about cautiously, still shaken from the chaos of the previous night. Smoke curled from the remains, and scattered groups huddled together, whispering in hushed, wary tones.

Ayralina scanned the scene, relief washing over her at the sight of survivors, but it was quickly tempered by the weight of what still needed to be done. Calling out to Andre she said. "Take them back to their homes, help them settle in," she instructed. "Make sure the wounded are treated and keep an eye out for any aftershocks. The town needs stability before the next wave hits."

Andre gave a sharp nod. "Understood." Without hesitation, he moved into action, calling for others to assist in organizing the townspeople.

Ayralina turned back toward the cave's entrance, her gaze darkening. The Heart's Flame Fire Orchid still awaited her deep within, and she knew time was running out.

With a determined look she said, "Let's go,". Taking a step toward the cave, a sudden chill prickled along her spine. It wasn't from the morning air—it was something else. They were being watched.

Her phoenix energy flared subtly beneath her skin, instincts sharpening as she extended her senses outward. The presence wasn't close, but it wasn't far either. Hidden. Observing. Waiting.

Ayralina didn't react outwardly, keeping her movements steady, her expression unreadable. But inside, she was already recalculating her next move.

The air grew warmer as they descended deeper into the cave, the flickering light of Ayralina's Phoenix flame casting long shadows on the walls. At the heart of the cavern lay a hidden chamber, where the Fire Orchid bloomed in a breathtaking display of crimson and gold. Its petals shimmered like living flames, and at its center, a core pulsed with an intensity that mimicked a heartbeat.

Ayralina approached cautiously, drawn by an unseen force. Her breath caught as realization struck. "It really is a Sunflame phoenix core."

Daxton nodded. "Yes. Her death gave life to the orchid, and her spirit has nourished it ever since. She lingers here, watching... waiting for you."

Ayralina extended her hand toward the orchid, her fingers trembling. The Heart's Flame Fire Orchid pulsed within a shimmering force field, raw energy crackling around it. The moment her fingertips grazed the barrier, a surge of magic lashed out, hurling her backward.

She hit the ground hard, barely catching herself. The lingering burn of magic seared against her skin, her breath coming in sharp gasps. Gritting her teeth, she pushed herself upright, dusting off her robes.

The tigers exchanged knowing glances before Daxton spoke, his voice steady and measured.

"If it were easy, someone would have taken the orchid long ago," he said. "We placed a protective force field around it, and we used a sacred seal of Phoenix's blood. Only one from your lineage can break it. This ensures no one or tigers can claim it, this also prevents infighting amongst my clan." His golden eyes locked onto hers. "To do so, you must awaken your bloodline."

Ayralina frowned. "Awaken my bloodline? How?"

Daxton held her gaze. "Blood," he said simply. "Just a drop will do."

Before she could act, Izzy stepped forward, her tone urgent.

"Before you proceed, stay vigilant," she warned. "The demons may have retreated, but we are still being watched. They cannot claim the orchid themselves, so they wait for you to do it for them. Daxton and I will handle the threat—we will ensure you are not interrupted."

Ayralina gave them both a grateful nod. There was no time to waste.

Without hesitation, she summoned a small dagger and pricked the blade on her fingertip. A sharp sting accompanied the sight of a single drop of crimson blood welling up before falling onto the force field.

The effect was immediate.

The air in the chamber shifted, charged with an ancient energy that pulsed through the cavern walls. The force field trembled, its surface rippling like water disturbed by an unseen force. The golden barrier faded into a deep, molten red, its magic recognizing her blood, acknowledging her lineage.

Then, the temperature spiked.

Heat roared to life, spreading like wildfire. The stone floor beneath her feet warmed, and the cavern itself seemed to breathe, exhaling waves of scorching energy. For anyone without a fire affinity, the unbearable heat would have driven them to their knees. But for them, the inferno felt natural and even welcoming.

The orchid pulsed again, its vibrant petals unfolding slightly as if awakening from a long slumber.

Ayralina clenched her fists, her phoenix energy stirring within her veins.

She felt the energy deep within her, as if a dormant flame had been reignited. She stepped forward, placing her hand on the shimmering barrier. This time, there was no resistance. The force field parted, and she walked through effortlessly.

The moment Ayralina crossed the barrier, the shimmering force field stilled, returning to its unnatural calm as though nothing had disturbed its balance. She took a steadying breath, her fiery amber eyes locked on the glowing orchid before her. The golden light of its core pulsed rhythmically as if it were alive, reflecting in her gaze.

Her hand hovered just above the orchid's delicate, glowing petals, her fingers trembling with the weight of what she was about to do. Closing her eyes, she steadied herself, her voice clear and resolute as she began to chant:

"Ancestors, hear my call. I summon you to imbue me with your powers. I am here to fulfill the vow—a promise made eons ago; one I now release. Let your power flow through me and help me fulfill my destiny."

As her words echoed through the cavern, the orchid seemed to respond. Its golden glow intensified, spreading light across the dark space. The warmth of its energy surged, wrapping around Ayralina like a protective cocoon. The air grew charged with magic, crackling faintly with power.

Suddenly, the light coalesced beside the orchid, taking shape. A female spirit emerged, her form translucent but radiant, her features regal and commanding. Her presence exuded strength and serenity, and her glowing eyes met Ayralina's with pride.

As the tensity of the heat subsided, the cavern settled into an eerie stillness.

A slow, mocking clap echoed through the chamber.

Damien stepped out from the shadows, a smug grin spreading across his face. Flanking him on either side were ten elite demons, their eyes glowing with malevolent energy, their auras thick with dark magic.

"Thank you, my friends, for leading her straight to the orchid for me," Damien said smoothly, his voice dripping with amusement.

A low, guttural growl rumbled from both Izzy and Daxton as they stepped protectively in front of Ayralina, their hackles raised, flames flickering dangerously in their eyes.

"You just couldn't wait, could you?" Daxton snarled.

Damien chuckled, his gaze flicking between them lazily. "If I had waited for her to come out and rejoin you, I might have lost my opportunity to claim the orchid." His expression darkened, the amusement fading. "But if I get rid of you first, then dealing with her alone will be much easier."

His hand flicked forward. "Seize them."

The demons lunged, their speed unnatural, their claws and weapons glinting in the dim light.

With a snarl, Izzy and Daxton launched themselves forward, meeting the onslaught head-on. Claws clashed against steel, flames erupted from the tigers' bodies, and the cavern was instantly thrown into chaos.

Ayralina, oblivious to the others, stared at the spirit before her, recognition dawning in her tear-filled eyes.

The spirit smiled, warmth radiating from her ethereal form. "You have come, child," she said, her voice both otherworldly and rich with emotion. "The blood of the Phoenix flows strong in you. You are the one I have been waiting for."

She tilted her head slightly, studying Ayralina. "Now, tell me—who are you? How are the Phoenix King and Queen? And my niece... ah, my niece! She must have married that good-for-nothing Moon Frost Dragon, didn't she?" The spirit sighed dramatically. "I never liked him. Such a rogue. I hope he's changed his ways and settled down with her."

Ayralina winced at her aunt's bluntness but couldn't suppress the small, bittersweet smile tugging at her lips.

"Aunt Flora," she began hesitantly, "your... good-for-nothing nephew-in-law gave his life to save us all. He's deep in slumber now, and I'm fighting every moment for his life." Her voice softened, her gaze lowering. "And I am that niece."

Flora's teasing expression faltered as Ayralina continued. "I'm doing my best to hold on, given everything. Our parents—the King and Queen—likely perished during the demon war over a century ago." Her voice cracked, but she pressed on. "I'm still searching for a way home... to avenge them. But first, I must wake my husband. He's been trapped in a deep slumber for a hundred years, and the only way to save him is by harnessing the power of the Ice Crystal Heart."

She took a steadying breath, lifting her gaze to the spirit. "But enough about me. How did this happen to you? Mom sent me to find you, but I never could. How did you end up... like this?"

The spirit's fiery glow dimmed, her expression clouding with sorrow. "Oh, Ayralina," she whispered, regret lacing her voice. Her eyes dropped to the ruby necklace resting against Ayralina's chest, and a flicker of recognition passed over her face.

"You wear the ruby necklace..." she murmured, her voice thick with emotion. "You truly are my sister's heir."

The air grew heavy, the warmth of the fire orchids dimming as Flora's ethereal form flickered—a spirit burdened by a century of regret and sorrow.

She sighed heavily, her luminous figure trembling as if the weight of her past threatened to pull her apart.

"A hundred years... It's hard to fathom how much time has passed since the demon invasion."

Her voice faltered, and for a brief moment, a flicker of anger ignited in her glowing eyes.

"I warned them. I warned your mother. I told her they were after the scroll. But no one listened."

Her tone hardened, the bitterness creeping in like a slow poison.

"Your mother—my sister—was too soft-hearted. She refused to believe that her long-lost niece, Saraphina, could be capable of such evil. Without proof, she wouldn't act."

Flora's expression twisted; the raw emotion of betrayal etched into her essence.

"That's why I left—to find the evidence she needed. But they were waiting for me."

Ayralina felt her chest tighten, sensing the pain beneath Flora's words—the weight of a betrayal that had spanned generations.

Flora's voice trembled, anger and sorrow intertwining.

"Saraphina joined hands with the demons. She seduced and poisoned the mind of the dragon general Zephiron, and together, they set a trap. They knew my every move, every step I took. I barely escaped with my life and fled to Earth."

Her glowing form flickered weaker now, but her voice carried the weight of unhealed wounds.

"I was too gravely wounded to return home. I knew I wouldn't last. So, as my final act, I extracted my core and embedded it within the Fire Orchid. I nurtured it with the last of my power and left behind a fragment of my spirit... to wait for you."

Ayralina's breath caught. Her hands curled into fists.

"You gave up everything... Aunt Flora, why?"

Her voice dropped into a whisper.

"What happened to Saraphina? How did my cousin turn into a demon? I didn't even know it was possible for us."

Flora's spirit dimmed, her strength waning as she clung to the last remnants of her energy.

"I don't have much time left, so listen closely."

"Your third aunt—the youngest of our sisters—fell in love with a demon."

Ayralina froze, her mind struggling to process the revelation.

"She became pregnant. But when the truth came to light, she fled, hiding her child from the world. She wanted nothing to do with our family, choosing instead to abandon her Phoenix heritage and live as a mortal." Flora's voice softened, tinged with sorrow. "She thought we had cast her out... but we never did. We never blamed her. She carried guilt that was never hers to bear."

Ayralina's breath caught in her throat.

"But fate was cruel."

Flora's spirit trembled, her voice thick with unspoken pain.

"Her lover—Saraphina's father—found them after she was born. He was overjoyed, thinking he could finally be with them. He renounced his Demon hood, choosing mortality so they could live as a family. But his happiness was short-lived." Flora's glow dimmed. "He didn't realize the demons had been tracking him. He led them straight to their door."

Ayralina's stomach dropped.

"They slaughtered your aunt. They killed her husband. And they took Saraphina."

A suffocating silence fell over them.

"She was raised in their world," Flora continued, her voice tight with anguish. "Raised as one of them. They filled her heart with hatred, told her we abandoned her, left her to die. That we never wanted her."

Ayralina's fists clenched, her pulse hammering in her ears.

Flora's form flickered, her pain manifesting in the unsteady glow of her spirit. "I tried to save her. I tried to bring her back." She let out a ragged breath. "But she was too far gone."

Ayralina felt a chill creep over her skin.

"She lured me into one of her schemes... and I barely escaped with my life."

A tense silence settled between them.

Flora's voice dropped to a whisper, sorrow and rage intertwining. "Your cousin is half-demon, Ayralina. And she despises you. She despises all of us."

"Your mother refused to see the truth. She thought she could save Saraphina, that she could bring her home." Flora's voice wavered, thick with old regret. "But it was too late."

Ayralina swallowed hard. "And now?"

Flora's spirit wavered, her time running out.

"Now, Saraphina seeks vengeance. Not just to destroy us—but to prove that she was never one of us."

Ayralina felt the weight of the revelation sink into her bones.

Her cousin—the one she trusted like a sister, had caused so much pain and destruction was just a child stolen from them.

A child turned into a weapon.

She forced herself to remain composed as Flora's gaze darkened with urgency.

"Don't dwell on her now," the spirit warned. "As Phoenixes, we all face the dark temptation before inheriting the full power of the Sunflame. That's why young Phoenixes are forbidden from leaving our realm—without its protection, the call of darkness grows louder."

Her luminous eyes bore into Ayralina's. "You've felt it too, haven't you?" Flora's voice was firm. "These past hundred years on Earth... Your unstable power is proof. If you don't stabilize it soon, it will consume you."

Ayralina's throat tightened. She knew Flora was right. The fire inside her had always been wild, unpredictable—a force of creation and destruction that she struggled to control.

Flora's spirit dimmed further; her energy nearly spent.

"I will use what little I have left to help you absorb my flame core, hidden within the orchid." Her voice softened but carried the weight of finality. "But you must take it to the volcano—the place where the densest fire energy resides. Only there can you fully integrate its power without losing yourself."

Ayralina tensed. The volcano... The place where fire either tempered—or consumed.

Before she could respond, Flora reached out.

A wave of warmth engulfed Ayralina.

The fire orchid's core awakened, its raw energy pouring into her like a raging inferno. Ayralina gasped, her veins burning with searing intensity, her body trembling as the ancient power threatened to devour her from the inside out.

"Endure, Ayralina," Flora whispered, her voice barely audible over the roaring fire. "You are the Phoenix heir."

Ayralina clenched her jaw, her entire being alight with untamed energy. She would not falter. She could not falter.

Through the haze of heat and emotion, her voice shook as she spoke.

"Aunt Flora... You gave up everything—to protect this orchid, to protect me, to protect our family's legacy."

Flora's form softened; her expression gentler now.

"And I would do it all again, Ayralina."

Ayralina's chest tightened, her breath shallow as her aunt's words wrapped around her like a farewell.

"You are the last spark of the Phoenix flame, the hope of our bloodline. You carry the strength of our ancestors, and now, it is time for you to fulfill the destiny I and so many others sacrificed for."

Ayralina steadied herself, her flames growing steady, her resolve hardening.

"I won't let you down." Her voice was stronger now. "I'll honor our legacy. And I'll bring justice to those who betrayed us."

Flora's eyes gleamed with pride as her spirit faded, dissolving into the flickering embers of light.

"Good. You have the strength of the Phoenix within you, Ayralina. remember—you are never truly alone. Our ancestors walk with you."

Ayralina's eyes burned with unshed tears. "Auntie... what about you? Can't I save you?"

Flora's smile was soft, filled with love, but marked with the acceptance of fate.

"My time is over, child. But the Fire Orchid holds hope. Plant it with care, and one day, it may nourish and revive me."

Her voice faded; a whisper carried away by the wind.

"Until then, use its power wisely. The Phoenix bloodline depends on you."

The last of her essence disappeared, leaving only the soft glow of the orchid and the weight of her sacrifice.

Ayralina knelt, gently gathering the orchid, her tears falling onto the scorched soil. She placed a flame seed within its dormant state—a promise to her aunt, a vow that one day, she would return.

Her fingers brushed over the orchid's delicate petals, Flora's final words echoing in her soul.

"You have awakened your bloodline, Ayralina. You are ready to wield the power of the Fire Orchid. Use it wisely, for its flame is both creation and destruction."

Ayralina clutched it against her chest, her heart swelling with emotion.

Carefully, she placed the orchid inside her ruby necklace, vowing to restore its power and return it to the Phoenix realm one day.

With a final, lingering glance at the fading embers of her aunt's presence, she rose to her feet.

Chapter 12

WHEN AYRALINA EMERGED FROM the force field, she was met with chaos. The battlefield was a maelstrom of fire, claws, and blood. The white tigers fought with unmatched ferocity, their muscular forms weaving through the carnage and tearing through the demonic horde. Their claws sliced through flesh, and their fangs crushed bones, but the creatures were relentless. Dark magic crackled through the air, tendrils of black energy lashing out, warping the battlefield into something twisted and unnatural.

Ayralina didn't hesitate.

She launched herself into the fray, golden flames bursting from her hands as she struck the first demon in her path. A surge of radiant energy erupted, searing through the creature's corrupted flesh. It screeched, its form disintegrating into ash.

Spinning on her heel, she ducked beneath a clawed swipe, the wind from the attack brushing against her skin. With a swift counter-strike, her flame-coated fist drove into the demon's chest, the burning heat melting through its ribcage. The creature let out a blood curdling shriek before collapsing into embers.

Across the battlefield, Queen Izzy fought like a storm incarnate.

Her movements were fluid, every strike was calculated and lethal. She danced through the fray, her sleek white fur streaked with blood and her claws slicing with conviction.

A demon lunged for her throat, but Izzy twisted mid-air, landing behind it in a blur of speed. Her razor-sharp fangs clamped onto its spine, and with a savage jerk, she ripped it apart.

King Daxton was a force of nature.

Where Izzy was quick and graceful, Daxton was pure destruction.

His massive form crashed through the enemy ranks, his claws glowing with divine energy. He ripped through demon after demon, his strength tearing them apart as if they were nothing.

A group of demons tried to overwhelm him.

Daxton reared up on his hind legs with a deep, thunderous roar, then slammed his paws into the ground.

The earth split apart beneath him. A massive shockwave of energy erupted, sending the demons flying into the air. Before they could react, Daxton lunged, his fangs sinking into the enemy's throat. The others barely had time to scream before he shredded through them, leaving nothing but scorched remains.But the demons kept coming.

Ayralina's chest heaved, her golden flames blazing around her like a living inferno.

Then—a spear of dark energy shot toward her from the shadows.

She barely had time to react, twisting at the last second, but the attack still grazed her shoulder. A searing burn of corruption spread through her skin.

She hissed through clenched teeth, forcing herself to stay upright.

Her eyes flickered toward the treeline—where Damien stood, watching.

He remained at the edge of the battle, his expression a mask of frustration.

His forces were falling apart. His minions were dying like insects.

He clenched his jaw, his dark eyes narrowing.

Ayralina locked eyes with him, her breath heavy but her stance unwavering. She could see it—the moment he realized he had lost.

Coward.

Damien took a step back with a sneer of frustration, his form melting into the darkness.

Before she could react, he was gone like smoke in the wind.

Ayralina exhaled sharply, her fists clenching.

He had escaped again.

"This isn't over!" She shouted.

And next time—she would be ready.

Turning to the Tigers, Ayralina began, "Thank you, my friends," her voice tinged with emotion. "You have kept your promise and guarded her for 100 years. I cannot begin to express my gratitude. You and your kin will always have a friend in me."

Daxton stepped forward, bowing his majestic head. "Your Majesty, your ancestors once saved my mate and unborn child, and now once again you have saved us. Between us, there is no need for words of gratitude. If a debt is owed, it is from us to you. You will forever have our alliance."

"What's next for you, Your Majesty?" Izzy asked. "It seems you already know where you're headed."

Ayralina nodded, her expression resolute. "I must enter seclusion at the volcano. My aunt told me its fiery energy will allow me to fully absorb the flame core. Without it, I cannot stabilize the Phoenix within me, and if I fail... it will consume me."

The tigers exchanged knowing glances, their eyes gleaming with understanding. Daxton spoke again, his deep voice carrying a sense of purpose. "Then we will accompany you. The volcano is sacred to us as well. Its energy will aid our healing and strengthen us after centuries of guarding the orchid. We will see you safely to its heart."

Ayralina placed a hand on Daxton's great mane, with gratitude evident in her eyes. "Alright then, let's go."

Before embarking on her next journey, Ayralina, the tigers, and André returned to Mayan de la Ruyns—a grand, luxurious hotel that once served as a stronghold for the demons.

Towering golden pillars gleamed beneath the glow of magnificent crystal chandeliers, casting a warm radiance across the polished marble floors. Intricate gold filigree adorned the high-vaulted ceilings, while heavy velvet drapes framed massive windows, offering a breathtaking view of the cityscape below. Unlike the war-ravaged world outside, this place stood in defiant splendor—a remnant of the past and a symbol of what could be reclaimed.

Yet, beneath its pristine surface, Ayralina could sense a lingering darkness. The demons had not destroyed the structure, but they had corrupted its energy, coiling in unseen corners, poisoning the very essence of the space. It was an invisible infestation—one that had to be purged before this sanctuary could become their base of operations.

Ayralina stepped forward, her eyes glowing with determination. The tigers prowled ahead, their keen senses picking up subtle traces of demonic presence. Suddenly, Daxton, the largest of the heavenly white tigers, let out a low growl. In an instant, a shadowy figure slithered out from beneath the grand staircase, lunging toward them. But Daxton was faster—his claws tore through the darkness, ripping the creature apart before it could fully manifest.

Then, as if sensing their fallen kin, the demons stirred. They emerged from behind the golden-framed mirrors, slithered from the deep shadows of the lavish halls, and unfurled themselves from the folds of the heavy velvet curtains. Twisted remnants of dark magic screeched and howled, their formless bodies writhing in agony as the golden glow of the hotel's light bore down on them.

The sound of hurried footsteps echoed through the grand chamber as Damien swiftly packed his most valuable possessions. His movements were quick and efficient, his eyes flickered with urgency.

Without knocking, one of his subordinates burst through the doors, panting heavily.

Damien shot him a furious glare. "This better be important, or I'll have your head served on a silver platter."

"My lord," the demon gasped, "we are under attack! Ayralina has led the heavenly white tigers here—with an army of humans. They are tearing through our forces!"

Damien's lips curled into a snarl, and he cursed under his breath. Then, with growing fury, he slammed a fist against his desk.

"Damn it all..." he seethed. "Tell everyone to abandon their posts and regroup in the north. We are already behind schedule and cannot afford any more delays." His red eyes gleamed with malice. "Once our task is complete, I will call for reinforcements from Arian. And then... I will return for my revenge." His voice dropped to a menacing whisper. "They will regret ever stepping foot in my domain."

Ayralina wasted no time. Raising her hands, she summoned a wave of radiant golden fire. It surged forward like a cleansing storm, sweeping through the grand hallways, coiling around the elegant furnishings, and cascading staircases. Yet, not a single piece of the hotel was harmed. The flames were pure—designed only to burn away corruption.

The chandeliers flared with renewed brilliance, their golden chains shimmering as dark energy was stripped away. The demons screeched as they were consumed, their wretched forms dissolving into wisps of nothingness.

Meanwhile, André and his sons fought fiercely alongside the tigers, cutting down any lingering entities that dared resist. Swords clashed, claws struck, and the scent of burning shadows filled the air. Within minutes, the battle was over.

Silence fell over the golden halls. But this time, it was a victorious silence.

Ayralina exhaled deeply, scanning the now-immaculate beauty of Mayan de la Ruyns. It was no longer tainted by the demons' presence. Now, it stood as a beacon of light—a sanctuary carved from the shadows of war.

She turned to André, her expression contemplative.

"What do you think of this place?"

André blinked, caught off guard. "Me?"

"Yes, you." Ayralina nodded. "What if you made this your new home? Run it yourself?"

André hesitated only briefly before stepping forward, his mind already racing with the possibilities.

"Dad, I think it's a great idea," a younger voice chimed in.

Ayralina turned to see Andrew, stepping forward with conviction. His eyes gleamed with newfound purpose.

"With the fortune left behind—the wealth the demons amassed—we won't have to worry about finances for a long time," Andrew continued. "And more than that... we can build an intelligence network here. Train the men we rescued. They have strength, but they need purpose. Under proper leadership, they could become a formidable force."

Ayralina studied them both, then nodded.

"Then it's settled," she declared. "This place is yours now. Protect it. Protect the people who will seek refuge here."

André squared his shoulders, determination settling over him. "We will keep it safe, Ayralina. You have my word." His lips curled into a knowing smile. "And when you need us... we will be ready."

Ayralina nodded. For too long, she had fought alone, believing the burden was hers alone to bear. But this alliance proved that power was not enough—she needed allies, a united force.

The heavenly white tigers, too, understood the gravity of this moment. The Tiger King stepped forward, lowering his head in solemn loyalty.

"We, the Heavenly White Tigers Tribe, stand with you, Ayralina."

With Mayan de la Ruyns now secure and an unbreakable alliance forged, the war against the darkness had truly begun.

Far from the battle, Damien stood at the edge of the ruins, looking back at the grand fortress he was forced to abandon. His fists clenched, his body trembling with rage.

One of the lesser demons at his side scoffed. "I hope you live long enough to return for your revenge." The creature sneered. "If I know Arian, you'd better pray he's in a forgiving mood when you tell him we lost one of our strongholds."

Damien's fiery eyes flashed as he turned on the demon, grabbing him by the throat.

"How dare you!" he snarled. "I will return—and when I do, I will repay this humiliation in blood!"

With that, he tossed the creature aside and turned toward the north, where his forces awaited.

This war was far from over.

Chapter 13

THE SKIES STRETCHED ENDLESSLY before them, a vast expanse of soft blues and wisps of white. The sun painted golden streaks across the clouds, casting a warm glow over the group as they soared through the heavens.

Above the endless sea of clouds, the air was crisp and unburdened by the chaos below. The wind hummed in Ayralina's ears, weaving through her hair as she glided effortlessly alongside Daxton and Izzy.

The cubs, wild with joy, bounced from cloud to cloud, their laughter a melody carried by the wind. Their small forms darted between the soft tufts of vapor, their excitement uncontainable.

Ayralina smiled, watching them play. It was a rare and wonderful sight, one she hadn't seen often during these perilous times.

"Stay close, please!" Queen Izzy called out, her protective instincts on full display. "If you can't see me, you've gone too far!"

The cubs giggled but obeyed, circling back toward their mother, their movements graceful and full of life.

Ayralina admired Izzy's natural maternal vigilance, staying close to the cubs while ensuring they had their moment of freedom.

She turned her attention to Daxton, who flew alongside her, his powerful form slicing through the sky with effortless precision. His sharp eyes swept across the horizon before turning back to her.

"The volcano lies in the middle of the ocean," Daxton explained, his deep voice carrying easily over the wind. "It's a dangerous journey, but flying is our best option. Land routes are infested with predators, and the waters subdue our powers too much, so they are not any safer."

Ayralina nodded, her gaze dropping to the earth below. The landscape unfolded like an intricate map—rolling valleys, vast forests, and jagged cliffs leading to deep sapphire waters. Even from this height, she could see how treacherous the terrain was.

They soared forward, gliding through towering clouds that felt like cotton beneath their fingertips. The sky shimmered with scattered rays of sunlight, the golden light shifting as the clouds moved.

Yet, despite the breathtaking beauty, Ayralina remained alert. She knew better than to let herself grow too comfortable.

The ocean loomed ahead, a vast, unending abyss stretching as far as the eye could see. It was both mesmerizing and ominous—a reminder of the dangers that awaited them.

Even at their speed, the journey took two days.

Along the way, they stopped twice to rest.

During these moments, they found shelter in floating islands, their surfaces hidden within the clouds. Ayralina found herself growing closer to the cubs, their playful nature breaking down whatever remained of her guarded heart.

They asked her countless questions about her flames, her past, and even her favorite foods. In return, she listened to their stories, their dreams, and their innocent hopes for a world beyond war.

She trained with Daxton, learning to sharpen her aerial combat skills, while Izzy shared tales of past battles, victories, and losses. They laughed around small, crackling fires, their bonds strengthening.

For the first time in a long while, Ayralina felt something close to peace.

A brief welcomed reprieve in their chaotic world.

As the second night passed and dawn painted the sky in hues of lavender and gold, the silhouette of the volcanic island appeared on the horizon.

Ayralina inhaled deeply, feeling the shift in the air.

The volcano loomed ahead, an imposing structure rising from the ocean. Its molten glow was visible even from miles away, casting an ominous red hue across the sky. As they approached, Daxton began detailing the challenges ahead.

"You'll have to deal with the python," he said nonchalantly.

Ayralina raised a brow. "Python? You mean a harmless snake?"

Daxton chuckled nervously. "Well... harmless might not be the right word. He's more of an 80-foot-long toothless giant with a temper."

Ayralina's eyes widened. "You failed to mention that part!" she hissed, glaring at him.

Before Daxton could respond, a loud hiss echoed through the air. A massive form appeared so quickly that Ayralina didn't see where it came from. The python's scales shimmered like molten gold, and its slit eyes glowed with intelligence and irritation.

"Hissss! Who dares call me toothless? And who dares to intrude upon my volcano?"

Daxton stepped forward, smirking. "You're getting old my friend; it took you this far before you could even detect our presence. Don't tell me you've forgotten me already."

The python's eyes narrowed. "Daxton? Is that you? No wonder I didn't feel a threat coming. Are you here for another beating? Or has the Queen thrown you out again, and now you're here to annoy me?"

"Beating? The last time we fought, you were the one running for your life!"

Before the exchange could escalate further, Queen Izzy's commanding voice rang out. "BOYS! Enough of this nonsense, or I'll give you both a beating. We're here on official business!"

Embarrassed, both the Daxton and the python retreated like chastised children.

Izzy turned to Ayralina and nodded. "Go ahead, my dear."

Ayralina took a deep breath and addressed the python respectfully. "I've come to this volcano to stabilize my powers. From the moment I entered, I could feel its energy helping me. I request permission to remain here temporarily to rest and cultivate."

The python's massive head tilted, his eyes narrowing. "Where did you find this measly human, Daxton? Do you think just anyone can enter my domain?"

"She's no ordinary human," Daxton snapped. "If you're so sure of yourself, test her. But I'll warn you—you won't last three moves against her."

The python hissed in annoyance. "Very well. If she can withstand ten moves, I'll allow her to stay. Let's see if she's as capable as you claim."

Ayralina stepped forward. "Let's begin."

The python coiled, its massive body undulating with quiet power. Each ripple beneath its gleaming scales, a predator whose every movement was calculated, deliberate.

Ayralina stood firm, exhaling slowly, grounding herself in the moment. She recalled Daxton's words from their journey—patience, awareness, control. Let the battle come to you.

The python struck like lightning, its powerful body launching forward with terrifying speed. A blur of muscle and fangs.

But Ayralina was faster.

With a fluid motion, she sidestepped, golden flames bursting from her palm in a beautiful arc. The fire struck the python's thick hide, forcing it to jerk back with a hiss.

"Hmph. A Phoenix flame," the python murmured, his slitted eyes narrowing.

His tone held more than recognition—there was wariness, uncertainty.

He lunged again, snapping his massive jaws, but this time, his movements were off. Slightly slower. Less precise. Ayralina caught the shift instantly—her noble Phoenix bloodline was suppressing his power.

He can't fight her properly, she realized. Her presence alone weakens him.

A small smile tugged at her lips. She could end this fight easily. But humiliating him would serve no purpose.

Instead, she let the battle unfold naturally.

She danced around his attacks, weaving through his strikes, meeting each one with just enough force to prove her strength without crushing him completely.

The python's frustration grew, his powerful coils whipping through the air, barely missing her. Each failed strike seemed to weigh him down further, his confidence unraveling.

Finally, after another futile attempt to strike her down, he slumped back, his immense body coiling into submission.

"Enough." His voice was edged with resignation. "You pass."

Ayralina offered a respectful bow, her flames dimming as she stepped back. "Thank you for allowing me this chance."

The python watched her with sharp, calculating eyes. "Who are you, really?"

Before she could answer, Daxton and Izzy stepped forward.

"It's best you don't know," Daxton rumbled, his tone leaving no room for argument.

The python remained silent, but Ayralina could tell—his curiosity had just begun to peak.

Turning away, moving toward the volcano's fiery maw, she felt his gaze lingering on them.

Suspicious. Watchful.

Long after they disappeared, the python remained coiled in the shadows, his golden eyes gleaming.

Something about their presence unsettled him. The power they carried... the way they moved... It was too deliberate. Too familiar.

Once they were out of sight, he uncoiled, his sleek body gliding effortlessly over the rocky terrain.

But he wasn't retreating.

He was searching.

A growing unease wrapped around him like a second skin, pushing him forward. His journey led him through, past whispered legends, and into ruins swallowed by time. Ancient scrolls, buried deep in dust and secrecy, revealed fragments of a history long erased.

Then, at last—he found it.

A name.

A kingdom.

A war that had once torn the realms apart.

The Phoenix Kingdom.

But his discoveries had not gone unnoticed.

The demon realm, ever watchful, caught wind of his movements. The Phoenix kingdom, wary of betrayal, sensed the disturbance. And the Dragon kingdom, haunted by wounds that had never fully healed, felt old scars begin to reopen.

The python had stirred something dangerous.

Unbeknownst to Ayralina, his curiosity had unearthed more than just her location.

Long ago, before the war, the Phoenix Kingdom and the Dragon King were betrayed   not by an enemy but by their own.

Two traitors had orchestrated their downfall:

Saraphina a royal sunflame phoenix that has turned demonic—her heart blackened by greed and vengeance.

Zephiron. The former right-hand of the Dragon King–Bewitched by the phoenix and turned Demon.

Together, they had infiltrated the highest ranks of their kingdoms, spreading lies, manipulating alliances, and feeding intelligence to the demon realm. However, conquest was never their true goal.

They sought immortality. They covet the Undying Flame—the sacred power of the Sunflame Phoenix. A fire that could never be extinguished. Never be killed.

Their betrayal had ignited a war so devastating it had fractured the balance of the realms.

The Dragon Kingdom collapsed into civil unrest, its once-mighty forces shattered by treachery, its King missing in action.

The Phoenix Kingdom, blinded by deception, had been caught unprepared. Their losses had been catastrophic.

And the demon realm?

They had watched. Waited. And reveled in the destruction.

Now, after a century of tenuous peace, the python's search had set an avalanche in motion.

The Phoenix Kingdom stirred, their trust—already fragile—shattered at the revelation of Ayralina's survival.

The Dragon Realm, haunted by its ghosts, began to mobilize, searching for their long-lost king.

And in the demon realm, where shadows whispered and blood pacts ran deep, a plan was set into motion.

The past was no longer buried. The war was coming.

Chapter 14

Travelling toward the heart of the volcano, following the glowing river of molten lava it snaked through the cavernous space. The air grew hotter, shimmering with heat waves, until they finally arrived at a vast lake of glowing red-orange lava, its surface bubbling and shifting ominously.

"Now what? Which way?" Ayralina asked, looking to the Tigers for advice.

King Daxton gestured to her. "Take out the orchid. It will guide you like a compass."

Ayralina withdrew the fire orchid from her necklace. As soon as it was exposed to the heat of the lava lake, it began to glow brightly and floated out of her hands. The orchid drifted toward the center of the lake and hovered there, as if calling her to follow.

Ayralina watched, mesmerized. "It wants me to go after it," she said, a mix of awe and hesitation in her voice.

Calling upon her Phoenix fire, she enveloped herself in a protective cocoon of flames. The tigers gathered close, and she extended the fiery shield around them. Taking a deep breath, she took to the air, flying toward the floating orchid.

Reaching the center of the lake, the orchid began to descend into the lava lake, its glow visible even beneath the surface.

"It looks like we're going for a swim," Ayralina muttered. Without hesitation, she guided her Phoenix into the lava.

The transition was seamless. Instead of being overwhelmed by the intense heat, Ayralina glided effortlessly through the molten liquid.

"Wow," she whispered, marveling at her surroundings. Her Phoenix had grown, now standing an impressive nine feet tall with wings spanning nearly 18 feet. Its majestic form shimmered in the molten environment, exuding power and grace.

Trusting her Phoenix's instincts, Ayralina allowed it to lead the way. It swam through the lava with ease, navigating the lake's depths. After a while, the Phoenix came to a sudden stop. Ahead, a cluster of glowing crystals pulsed with vibrant energy, their light piercing through the thick, molten surroundings.

The Phoenix squawked excitedly, urging her forward. Ayralina reached out and carefully collected the crystals, feeling the raw power emanating from them.

"These are incredible," she murmured. "But what are they for?"

The Phoenix tilted its head, then let out a series of melodic squawks.

"Ah, I see," Ayralina said with a smile. "You want me to forge my true weapon with these. Do you think I'm ready?"

The firebird nodded solemnly, its eyes gleaming with approval.

"Alright, my friend. I'll try it."

With the flame crystals in hand, the Phoenix continued to guide Ayralina deeper into the lava lake. Not far from the glowing crystals, they discovered another treasure—a cache of flame seeds. Dozens of them were scattered across the lakebed, their fiery cores pulsating faintly.

"How much should I take?" Ayralina wondered aloud.

The Phoenix squawked again, and Ayralina smiled. "All of them? Alright then, let's not waste any of this opportunity."

She collected every flame seed she could find, their warmth radiating even through her fire cocoon.

The Phoenix then turned and began swimming even deeper. The lava grew darker and denser, and Ayralina could sense the volcano's raw, primal energy intensifying.

"Where are we going now?" she wondered. "Aunt Flora did say I'd need time to stabilize my powers. Maybe this is a safe place to rest and grow stronger."

As if understanding her thoughts, the Phoenix glanced back and nodded.

At the bottom of the lava lake, an opening revealed itself—a dark, winding tunnel just wide enough for five people to walk side by side. The Phoenix swam through effortlessly, its fiery form illuminating the narrow passage. Ayralina followed, her body adapting to the intense heat, but the twists and turns of the tunnel blurred together, making it impossible to keep track of the path.

Just as the disorientation threatened to overwhelm her, the tunnel opened into an enormous underground cavern.

The lava gave way to solid ground, and they landed on a smooth obsidian platform, the surface cool despite the molten heat surrounding them.

Ayralina's breath caught as she took in the sight before her.

The cavern stretched as high as a three-story building; its vast expanse dotted with glowing fissures that pulsed like the heartbeat of the earth itself. Dozens of smaller caves and tunnels branched off in different directions, and veins of ember-like light flickered within the walls, as though the very rock held the remnants of ancient flames.

The Phoenix stretched its wings, its majestic form shimmering as it slowly shifted back into its smaller, dormant state, perching gracefully on Ayralina's shoulder.

"It's safe here," Phoenix's voice echoed in her mind, warm and reassuring. "Nothing can harm you. When you are ready to leave, call upon me, and I will guide you out."

Ayralina nodded, her senses tingling as she absorbed the energy of the cavern. The air was thick with fire essence, raw and unrestrained, its power weaving through her very bones. The fire orchid pulsed softly against her chest, resonating with the volcanic energy around her.

She had found her sanctuary.

Days blurred into weeks as Ayralina immersed herself in cultivation and training.

The cavern, once an unknown abyss, became a sacred ground—a place where she could hone her strength without limits. The volcanic energy fueled her, its raw power stabilizing the fire core within her.

She spent hours refining her control, deepening her bond with the Phoenix. Each meditation and each sparring session drew her closer to true mastery. The once-wild flames she wielded became an extension of her will, bending fluidly to her commands.

But it was not just her power that had evolved. The Tigers were also thriving in this environment.

With the fire crystals she had gathered, Ayralina began forging her true phoenix weapon. The process was grueling, testing not just her skill but her patience and resolve. Every strike, every infusion of fire essence, pushed her closer to creating something truly hers.

She could feel her transformation unfolding, her knowledge broadening.

For the first time, she wasn't just wielding fire.

She was becoming one with it. As the days passed, so too did her doubts. The flames that once burned wild and uncontrollable now moved with purpose. The Phoenix within her was no longer a separate entity but a part of her.

Though she knew the path ahead would be treacherous, Ayralina no longer felt uncertain.

She was not the same woman who had entered the cavern weeks ago.

Her body was stronger. Her mind was sharper. Her spirit was unbreakable.

As she stood upon the obsidian platform, the lava pulsing around her like an ancient force, she closed her eyes, feeling the energy surging through her veins.

The time was coming.

She would leave the cavern soon.

And when she did—

Nothing in this world, or the next, would stand in her way.

Chapter 15

DEEP WITHIN THE HEART of the volcano, Ayralina sat before the glowing heart of the flame crystal. Its fiery core pulsed with energy, radiating a heat that felt alive. She took a deep breath, steadying herself. This was her moment to forge a weapon worthy of her lineage.

Around her, the tigers trained with unwavering focus. The fire seeds that Ayralina and her Phoenix had gathered worked wonders, enhancing their strength, speed, and resilience. Their movements had grown sharper, their strikes more precise, and they exuded an almost tangible confidence. Each day, they pushed their limits, testing their newfound abilities in ways they never had before.

The Phoenix, never idle, continued to bring more fire seeds for the tigers to absorb, ensuring the tigers' cultivation progressed without interruption. Its feathers shimmered with an ethereal glow as it soared above them, watching over their growth like a silent guardian.

Amidst the rigorous training, Ayralina occasionally sat in on Izzy and Daxton's lessons with the cubs. She found a quiet joy in these moments—watching the younger generation learn not just how to fight but also how to think, strategize, and control their instincts. Izzy's patience and Daxton's sharp wit made for an effective teaching pair, their lessons blending discipline with wisdom.

The cubs, eager and full of energy, soaked up every bit of knowledge. Sometimes they fumbled their techniques, other times they showed surprising promise, but they shared the same determination burning in their eyes. Ayralina knew that one day, they too would become warriors, protectors of the stronghold and the legacy they were building.

For now, she simply watched, a rare moment of peace amid the storm that always seemed to follow her.

Every Phoenix, for as long as Ayralina could remember, all wield a sacred weapon—a creation forged from their own essence, a reflection of their soul. This weapon was not just an extension of their power but a living thing, growing and evolving alongside its wielder. It would burn with them, fight with them, and ultimately perish with them.

While her allies thrived, Ayralina struggled. She had spent weeks attempting to forge her weapon, yet nothing seemed to work. Her ancestors had wielded legendary arms—flaming swords, whips that cracked like lightning, bows that shot arrows of pure fire, and axes capable of cleaving through stone. Their weapons had become myth, symbols of their might. But Ayralina? She couldn't even form a hilt.

Her first attempt was a sword. She believed it would be the simplest choice, a straightforward channel for her flames. But the essence of fire refused to take shape. The flame crystal, the heart of her weapon, flickered weakly in her grasp, refusing to solidify. Frustration gnawed at her as she moved on to a bow and arrow, thinking perhaps distance would be her strength. The results were laughable. The bow barely held its form, its limbs warping and twisting unpredictably, while her arrows fizzled into harmless embers before they could even take flight.

Day after day, she worked away, willing her essence's flame to cooperate. Weapon after weapon, attempt after attempt, yet nothing came to her. Her hands, once sure and steady, trembled with uncertainty. Despite the fire orchid strengthening her body and the tigers pushing her to new heights in combat, this one challenge remained insurmountable. Once a sacred space for her, now felt like a prison of failure.

By the end of the month, she was at her breaking point. Ayralina stood staring at the unformed flame crystal. "Why won't this work?" she muttered, anger and defeat warring within her.

The crystal pulsed dimly in response, but no shape emerged. No sword, no bow, no weapon of her own. Just silence.

Exhausted, disheartened, and no closer to her answer, Ayralina knew it was time to leave. Her retreat had strengthened her body and spirit, but without a weapon—without this missing piece of herself—she felt incomplete.

Just as Ayralina prepared to leave, a sudden surge of energy rippled through her bond with the Phoenix. The fiery bird let out a sharp, excited cry, darting toward the edge of the lava lake with an urgency that sent a chill down her spine.

"What is it now?" Ayralina muttered, uncertainty creeping into her tone.

But the Phoenix ignored her, its form glowing brighter as it plunged into the molten abyss, disappearing beneath the surface.

Ayralina's breath hitched as she felt their connection hum with an unfamiliar force—something ancient, raw, and overwhelming. Whatever the Phoenix had sensed, it was powerful beyond comprehension.

Without hesitation, she followed.

'I'm going to see what's her excitement about, once I come back we will leave alright, ' she called to the tigers. "Be Careful, there is more to this place that meets the eye," Izzy warned. Nodding as she summoned her Phoenix fire, she wrapped herself in a protective aura before diving into the lava. The heat embraced her, a familiar yet suffocating force, as she descended deeper than ever before.

The tunnels twisted and turned, pulsing with an eerie red glow, the pressure increasing with every movement. Ayralina pushed forward, her heartbeat pounding in sync with the volcanic energy churning around her.

Then, she saw it.

The tunnel opened into a colossal hidden chamber, its walls glowing with embers that pulsed like a living, breathing entity. And at the center of it all—

A massive golden essence crystal.

It pulsed with unimaginable power, radiating energy so potent that even the surrounding lava seemed to bow before it, swirling reverently around its base.

Ayralina's breath caught in her throat. This is the heart of the volcano, the very source of its strength.

For the first time, she understood the python's purpose. He hadn't been guarding the volcano itself—he had been guarding this.

This crystal was a raw, untamed force of nature, an energy that, if harnessed, could reshape the world.

Her awe was short-lived.

The Phoenix screeched in triumph and dove toward the crystal.

"Wait—!" Ayralina lunged forward, reaching out instinctively. But it was too late.

The Phoenix landed on the crystal, wings outstretched, its body glowing fiercely.

Ayralina felt the shift instantly.

The Phoenix was trying to devour it completely.

The golden essence flooded into its being, and its flames turned from brilliant gold to an almost blinding white. Sparks of wild, untamed magic crackled around its form as its hunger grew.

The volcano trembled.

The once-fluid lava lake thickened, darkened, and slowed to a sluggish crawl before solidifying into jagged obsidian.

The volcano, once a pulsing, living force, was dying.

Ayralina's pulse pounded in panic.

"Stop!" she yelled, her voice frantic. "You're taking too much!"

But the Phoenix didn't listen.

It shuddered, its form flickering between solid and ethereal, its hunger insatiable.

A deep rumbling echoed through the chamber.

The tigers burst into the cavern, their flames roaring to life as they took their battle stances. Their bodies pulsed with flaming energy.

Daxton's eyes widened as he took in the scene.

"We have to stop it before it destroys itself!" he roared.

The tigers surged forward, their combined flames coiling around the Phoenix like blazing chains.

But the Phoenix had become too powerful.

With a single burst of energy, it sent them all sprawling, their flames snuffed out by the sheer force of its raw might.

Ayralina's heart slammed against her chest.

She couldn't lose them—not the Phoenix, not the tigers.

Desperation ignited her resolve.

"Together!" she shouted.

The tigers regrouped, determination blazing in their eyes.

Izzy was the first to lunge, her claws sinking into the Phoenix's wing, dragging it downward.

Daxton followed, his fire wrapping around the other wing, muscles straining as he tried to hold it in place.

The others moved in sync, their combined energy pressing down, forcing the Phoenix back.

The chamber trembled violently. The Phoenix screeched, its golden body convulsing as it fought against them.

But Ayralina felt something more profound—not just power, but desperation. The Phoenix's hunger was an echo of its deepest fear.

It didn't want to be weak. It didn't want to be caged.

She clenched her fists, summoning everything she had left.

She reached out, with everything she has, solidifying their soul connection.

Come back to me, she commanded

The Phoenix shrieked one last time.

And then, all of a sudden, it collapsed inward, the power was too much for the phoenix. It couldn't control it, and in its dazed state Ayralina took control and was finally able to force it to return to her.

Ayralina collapsed to her knees, but before she could relax, a strangled gasp tearing from her throat as a wave of unbearable heat exploded within her. Her vision blurred, her lungs burned, every nerve in her body igniting with searing agony.

Her Phoenix's uncontained power crashed through her like a raging inferno, a force far beyond anything she had ever endured.

Her veins felt like liquid fire, the heat searing through muscle and bone, threatening to rip her apart from the inside.

She clutched at her chest, her fingers trembling, her body violently rejecting the overwhelming surge of energy.

It had taken too much.

Her breath came in short, sharp gasps, her heartbeat erratic, pounding like a war drum inside her skull.

Her skin cracked, glowing with flickering golden light as raw, unstable magic tore at her very essence.

The volcano had fallen silent; its fire drained, its lifeblood stolen.

The chamber itself trembled, groaning as if it mourned its own death, the air thick with energy that had no place to go.

Ayralina was suffocating in it.

Her body spasmed, her bones aching under the strain, her very soul fracturing under the weight of the power she was never meant to hold.

Her vision swam, dark edges creeping in.

Ayralina's lips parted, but no sound came out.

She was dying.

The Phoenix, still brimming with stolen power, let out a defiant cry, but Ayralina barely heard it over the roaring chaos inside her.

It wasn't just the Phoenix's hunger.

It was hers now, too.

The all-consuming need for more.

She clutched at the ruby necklace around her throat, her last tether to herself, fighting against the tide of power that threatened to obliterate who she was.

Somewhere in the haze of pain, she heard Daxton's voice, urgent and sharp.

"Get her under control! She's burning out!"

The tigers moved instantly, forming a protective circle around her, their paws pressing against her searing skin.

They tried to channel the excess energy, to siphon what they could before it destroyed her.

But the flames weren't just fire anymore.

It seemed to have a consciousness; it was wild, primal, chaotic, a force that refused to be tamed.

Izzy gritted her teeth, her muscles straining as she fought to contain the surging power. "She's going to explode if we don't suppress this now!"

Ayralina bit down on a scream, her body convulsing as flames burst from her skin, her fire no longer her own.

The pain was beyond anything she had ever known—

Like dying and being reborn at the same time.

Daxton, voice grim, pushed harder. "Hold on, Ayralina."

Izzy growled through clenched teeth. "We can only buy you time— but if you can't contain this soon, it's going to consume you and us with it."

They began channeling her overwhelming energy, absorbing what they could.

But something shifted.

As the Phoenix's power mixed with their own, their flames changed—growing stronger, sharper, infused with a new essence.

They had evolved.

But the power was too great to absorb entirely.

Ayralina fought to stay conscious, fought to breathe through the agony, through the fire clawing at her insides.

She didn't just feel like she was dying.

She felt like she was being rewritten.

Ayralina sucked in a shuddering breath, forcing herself to focus.

She had survived too much to let it end like this.

Through sheer will, she reached deep within herself, into the core of her flames, into the soul of the Phoenix.

And she did the only thing she could.

She commanded it to bow.

The Phoenix inside her screamed, thrashing against the restraint, but Ayralina held on, pouring every ounce of her soul, her will, her fury into containing it.

Her body shook violently, her breath a ragged whisper.

But she would not break.

With a final, shattering exhale, she felt the Phoenix shrink back, its overwhelming force finally, barely contained.

The power still burned inside her, too much to wield, but no longer threatening to consume her alive.

Ayralina swayed, her body weak but intact.

Daxton let out a long breath of relief, shaking his head. "That was too close."

The cubs fainted beside her.

Izzy, panting, studied Ayralina carefully. "You're stable—for now. But you're still carrying too much power. If you don't find a way to refine and control it soon..."

Her golden eyes met Ayralina's deadly seriousness.

"...it will destroy you from the inside out."

Ayralina nodded weakly, swallowing hard.

She exhaled shakily, feeling the strain ease slightly. There wasn't much time—but it was enough.

They had to leave.

She glanced at the now-dormant flame crystal, the once-radiant heart of the volcano reduced to silence.

And she still didn't have a weapon.

Ayralina took a deep breath, steadying herself.

"I will find a way to control this power." Her voice was firm. Resolute.

Chapter 16

EMERGING FROM THE HOLLOWED volcano, they spotted the orange tigers pacing back and forth, their restless movements suggesting they had been waiting for some time. When they noticed them, they hurried to King Daxton, their expressions shadowed with concern.

"We've got trouble," one of them began urgently. "That fool of a snake ran straight back to the Phoenix realm. He's been asking around about you and managed to spread news about your return."

Ayralina let out a weary sigh, pinching the bridge of her nose in frustration. "Of course he did," she muttered under her breath. Her gaze darkened, and she exhaled slowly.

"There's nothing we can change now, how are Andre and the others faring?" She asked.

"They are doing well," the tigers responded. They're keeping vigilance and training every day."

"Good, let's head back."

Ayralina made her way back to the hotel to check on André and the townspeople, ensuring there were no lingering effects of the poison. Over time, she had grown fond of the small community, feeling a deep sense of responsibility for their safety and well-being.

As she approached the Mayan de la Ruyns, she was met with a sight that filled her with pride. The grand hotel had been fully transformed under André's leadership. Its golden pillars gleamed in the sunlight, no longer a symbol of tyranny but of resilience and renewal. The once-haunted halls now buzzed with life—merchants set up stalls in the lavish corridors, selling rare goods and supplies. Skilled artisans had taken residence, crafting weapons, armor, and tools for the growing stronghold.

The hotel had become more than just a sanctuary; it was thriving as a well-defended, self-sustaining community. The people who had once lived in fear were now flourishing under André's guidance. The guards patrolling the perimeter carried themselves with confidence, and Ayralina could sense the shift in the air—this was no longer just a refuge but a home.

Determined to strengthen their defenses further, Ayralina decided to use the fire seeds she had collected to craft fire weapons for André and his people. Each weapon was carefully forged and imbued with the seeds' powerful energy, turning them into a formidable tool of protection. With these weapons, even the weakest would have a means to defend themselves.

As she explored the stronghold, she was pleasantly surprised to find Andrew leading a rigorous combat training session in the courtyard with Alex as his assistant. His moves fluid with purpose, demonstrating self-defense techniques and tactical maneuvers, his voice steady and authoritative. The trainees followed his lead with unwavering focus, their movements growing sharper with each drill.

Ayralina watched quietly for a moment, her arms crossed as she took in the scene. The transformation was remarkable. These were the same people who had once cowered in the face of danger, and now they stood as warriors in their own right.

After the session, she approached Andrew as he wiped the sweat from his brow. "You've done well," she told him, her tone filled with genuine approval. "You're a natural leader."

He gave a modest shrug but couldn't hide the pride in his expression. "They've come a long way," he admitted. "And they're willing to learn, and that makes all the difference."

Ayralina glanced at the fighters still practicing in the courtyard, her heart swelling with admiration.

And under André's leadership, it was only just the beginning.

She stayed for a while, refining their training and introducing the newly forged weapons. The townspeople embraced them eagerly, and Ayralina worked closely with them, ensuring they understood not only how to wield the weapons but how to maintain them.

Before she departed, the entire town gathered, their faces filled with determination.

Andre stepped forward, his voice unwavering. "We pledge our loyalty to you, Ayralina. We are training to be your backup. Should you ever need us, we will be ready."

Ayralina met his gaze, a flicker of gratitude passing through her. These people weren't just survivors—they were warriors in the making.

But there was no more time to linger.

Silvaris's condition was worsening with each passing day. Every moment she delayed brought him closer to the brink of death. The North is facing an impending war, and Ayralina still has to deal with the overflowing powers inside of her.

It was time.

The journey to the north was relentless. Every step over the rugged terrain felt heavier, not just from exhaustion with the unshakable sense of being watched. The wind, once merely scorching, now carried a tension that crawled under Ayralina's skin like unseen claws.

Something was wrong.

"We can't continue like this, we need to lose the tail. They've been following us since we left the volcano," Daxton murmured, his golden eyes scanning the shadows. His voice was calm, but the caution laced within it was unmistakable. "They're waiting for an opportunity."

Ayralina's jaw tightened. She swept her gaze across the horizon, her senses reaching beyond sight and sound. The presence stalking them was patient and calculating—predators.

"We need to find the perfect opportunity and eliminate them all at once."

They moved swiftly to adjust their formation. Izzy and Daxton, their raw strength unmatched, would slip into the darkness, unseen weapons at the ready. From the shadows, they would eliminate threats before they could strike. The cubs, still not ready to fight at full strength, would stay close to Ayralina, keeping their formation tight.

But caution alone wouldn't be enough.

The Phoenix fire raged within Ayralina, burning hotter each day, forcing her to slow down when she couldn't afford to. Every flare of uncontrolled energy is like a beacon, a blazing signal to their unseen enemies. She needed to throw them off her trail.

She veered eastward, away from the direct path to the North.

The detour led them towards a human kingdom deep in the northern lands. The shift in landscape was brutal—jagged cliffs threatened to swallow them whole, winds sharp enough to slice through flesh, and an ever-present sense of danger lingering just beyond sight.

But she welcomed it. The biting cold suppressed her phoenix and kept it under control.

The further they traveled, the more the suffocating heat lifted. The northern chill settled into her bones, invigorating and sharpening her focus. It was a sign—she was getting closer.

Yet with every step forward, the weight on her shoulders felt heavier.

Chapter 17

"Phew, we finally made it." Ayralina exhaled, brushing the dirt from her travel-worn clothes. She cast a glance at the tigers, their once-powerful strides now sluggish, their fur matted with dust and exhaustion. "Days of traveling, being chased, fighting off enemies—this has been anything but fun."

Saber let out a deep sigh, rolling his shoulders as if trying to shake off the weight of the journey. "At least it's over for now." His tail flicked, his ears twitching against the sharp northern wind. "Hopefully, we can finally rest, maybe even enjoy a nice, long, hot bath." He groaned, shivering dramatically. "I don't know about you, but the north is no place for us fire tigers."

Ayralina smirked. "Oh? I thought you were this mighty, unstoppable warrior. And now you're complaining about a little cold?"

Saber narrowed his eyes on her. "A little cold? My paws feel like they've been dipped in ice! My fur is not made for this. We are not made for this. The moment we stepped into these lands, I swear my soul tried to abandon my body."

Ellie chuckled, shaking off a layer of frost from her coat. "We get it, Saber. You're suffering." She nudged him playfully. "But if you complain any louder, the enemy might hear and put you out of your misery."

Saber huffed. "At this rate, that might be a mercy."

Izzy rolled her eyes but let out a small laugh. "Alright, alright. We'll find shelter soon, get warmed up, and figure out our next move. We're not out of danger yet."

Saber groaned but nodded. "Fine. But if I turn into an icicle, someone better carry me."

Ayralina smirked. "I'll consider it. But only if you stop whining."

As they rounded the final bend, their steps quickened, anticipation rising—until they saw it.

The gates of the northern kingdom loomed ahead, an imposing sight of iron and stone. Towering walls, weathered by time but unyielding, stretched high into the sky. Elaborate carvings of mythical beasts and intertwined vines adorned the gate, their artistry dulled but not forgotten. Guards stood like statues, their polished armor glinting under the faint sunlight, their gazes sharp and unyielding as they scanned the gathering masses.

But the scene beyond the gate crushed away their hopes of a swift entry.

A massive line of people stretched before them, huddled together in the biting wind. Families clutched their meager belongings, children buried their faces against shivering parents, and weary travelers slumped against their carts—all with the same haunted expressions of desperation and fear.

A heavy sigh broke the silence.

"Oh no," Saber groaned, his ears flattening.

"Looks like we're still a long way from that hot bath." Ellie stated.

Saber scowled. "This is ridiculous. We should be inside already, not stuck in line with—" he stopped, eyeing the ragged crowd. His tail flicked uncomfortably. "—mortals who wouldn't last a second against a real enemy."

Ayralina shot him a warning look. "Careful, Saber. These people have suffered enough without your complaints."

Her sharp eyes scan the scene, and Izzy lets out a low hum. "Something's not right. Look at their faces. They're not just tired—they're afraid."

Ayralina followed her gaze. She saw it now: the people whispering anxiously, casting glances over their shoulders, and the guards clutching their weapons a little tighter, their eyes lingering on the road behind them rather than the crowd before them.

Something was wrong.

"Izzy, you and Daxton circle around back and sneak in first. We will meet up with you once we're in." Ayralina's voice was firm, leaving no room for argument.

Saber groaned dramatically. "You mean we just traveled all this way, nearly froze to death, and now we have to wait in line?"

Izzy smirked. "You say that like it's a bad thing, see you on the inside, happy waiting."

Ayralina sighed, her expression tense as her eyes moved over the endless sea of faces. The low murmur of the crowd reached her ears—a mix of whispers, coughs, and the occasional raised voice pleading with a guard. "Let's find out what's going on," she said, her voice heavy with concern. "It looks like it could've been a plague just hit here... I haven't exactly been keeping up with the latest from the medical community."

As they inched closer to the line, she quietly conversed with the few people nearby. The stories they shared were deeply troubling, casting an uneasy shadow over those gatherings. A mysterious illness had been spreading like wildfire throughout the region, leaving panic and despair in its wake. According to the hushed whispers, the disease struck without warning. Its victims showed no initial symptoms, and no one could determine how it spread until it was far too late. When the sickness took hold, those afflicted would grow unbearably cold, as if the chill emanated from deep within their bones. No amount of heat or fire could warm them, and within days, they would succumb, their bodies frozen solid like statues of ice.

The rumor mill churned even darker tales, weaving a tapestry of fear and uncertainty. It was said that the Queen herself, along with her newborn prince, had fallen victim to the illness, leaving the kingdom teetering on the brink of despair. The King, consumed by desperation, had issued a royal decree: anyone who could uncover a cure for the enigmatic disease would be rewarded beyond imagination. Their request—no matter how great—would be granted without question. This tantalizing promise had drawn a flood of opportunists, healers, and charlatans from across the land, each eager to stake their claim and test their luck at the royal court. Yet beneath the air of hope lingered a shared unease, for no one truly understood the source of the disease or the toll it might yet take.

Ayralina's gaze lingered on the imposing gates ahead, their iron bars twisting like blackened vines, an unyielding barrier to the city beyond. Guards stood in unusually large numbers, their sharp eyes darting over every person in the line. Their stiff postures and hands hovering near their weapons betrayed an undeniable tension. It was clear they weren't merely checking for entry passes—they were searching for something. Or someone.

As the line inched forward, Saber sidled up to her, keeping his voice low. "Ayralina, this way," he said, motioning to the left. "There's a separate line for doctors—and it's much shorter too."

Ayralina hesitated for a moment before nodding and following him. As they drew closer to the front of the line, her ears caught snippets of hushed, heated conversations among those waiting. "Did you hear about the fire affinity requirement?" one man muttered to the woman beside him, his voice tinged with frustration. "The King's only looking for people with a strong connection to fire magic and some medical expertise. If you can't meet both, you might as well not even bother."

"Fire affinity," Ayralina murmured under her breath, her mind racing. She clenched her fists, the leather of her gloves creaking softly as the weight of the situation settled heavily in her chest. This illness wasn't ordinary. It wasn't something that couldn't be solved with herbs, tonics, or even the most skilled healers. It was something unnatural, something possibly demonic. Something seems off to Ayralina, for now she kept to herself.

The line shuffled forward again, and Ayralina found herself face-to-face with the imposing guards. The lead guard stepped toward her, his armor glinting dully in the faint sunlight. His expression was stern, his eyes sharp with suspicion as they scanned her from head to toe. "State your purpose," he barked, his tone clipped and unwavering.

Ayralina straightened her shoulders, standing tall. She met his piercing gaze without flinching, her voice firm with authority. "Dr. Ayralina, a surgeon and alchemist," she said. "I've come to offer my skills in the fight against the illness plaguing this land."

The guard narrowed his eyes, his expression unreadable. For a moment, she thought he might dismiss her outright, but then he gestured to another guard. "Search her," he ordered, his tone brooking no argument. "No one passes through without inspection."

Ayralina stood still as a female guard stepped forward, patting her down methodically and inspecting her belongings. When they found nothing out of the ordinary, the lead guard nodded sharply. He handed her a blue badge, the polished surface glinting in the sunlight. "This badge grants you access to the finest hotels and restaurants in the city. Don't lose it. Good luck," he added with a faint smile.

Ayralina gave a polite nod, tucking the badge into her coat pocket. She wasn't one to indulge in luxury while people around her suffered. Before taking advantage of any privileges, she needed to get a better sense of the city and the extent of the crisis.

As she passed the gates and entered the city, the air seemed to thicken with unease. The streets were eerily silent, the usual hum of city life was replaced by whispers and hurried footsteps.

Ayralina sat in the dim corner of the tavern, her fingers absentmindedly tracing the rim of her cup. The warm glow from the gas lamps flickered across the scuffed oak tables and timeworn chairs, their surfaces marked by years of whispered secrets and hushed dealings. The scent of roasted meat and fresh bread mingled with the faint smokiness of the fire crackling in the stone hearth, wrapping the room in a deceptive sense of comfort.

Ellie climbed onto Ayralina's lap, her voice barely above a whisper. "What's on your mind, Ayralina?" Wide eyes searched her face, brimming with curiosity.

Ayralina hesitated, still running her fingers over the smooth edge of her ceramic mug. Finally, she spoke, keeping her voice low. "Doesn't this illness feel... deliberate?" She met Ellie's gaze; her golden eyes darken with suspicion. "It's like they've turned the entire kingdom into a net—one I'm about to get caught in. Everyone is searching for something. They just don't realize it's me they're looking for."

Ellie frowned, her tiny paws gripping Ayralina's cloak. "You think the demons are behind this?"

Ayralina exhaled slowly. "I don't believe in coincidences, Ellie. And this? This reeks of something planned." She glanced around the tavern, lowering her voice. "One wrong move, and we'll be exposed."

Ellie nodded, her expression shifting from concern to determination. "Then we wait and lay low."

Earlier, when they had entered the city, Ayralina had felt it—the weight of unease pressing against her like a suffocating shroud. The streets had been far too quiet, whispers floating like ghosts in the air. Fear clung to the people, thick and inescapable. The city's outskirts were near-deserted, life drawn toward the bustling inner districts where safety—or the illusion of it—remained.

To blend in, Ayralina had chosen this tavern—a dimly lit sanctuary where she could blend in, observe, and listen.

Her companions, their true nature hidden beneath the guise of harmless tiger cubs, moved unseen through the room. They wove between tables, ears pricked, listening for anything of value.

Ayralina had ordered a meal, instructing the server to delay its arrival. It wasn't hunger that had brought her here—it was information. The longer she sat, the more she learned.

Snippets of hushed conversation drifted through the tavern, each whispering a puzzle piece fitting into a picture she was beginning to see.

A mysterious illness, spreading faster than anyone could contain.

The Queen grows weaker by the day, while the King slips into desperation.

Fear was running rampant. But fear didn't just cripple people—it made them reckless. And reckless people were easy to manipulate.

She couldn't afford to get caught in their hysteria. Any misplaced word, any subtle misstep, could draw attention to her. And right now, attention was the last thing she needed.

Then, she sensed it, a sharp, pricking sensation at the edge of her awareness.

She was being watched.

Her fingers stilled on the cup, but her pulse remained steady. She resisted the urge to turn her head, forcing herself to stay still. Then, she yawned and shifted slightly in her seat, adjusting her position as if getting comfortable.

Through the corner of her eye, she scanned the room.

Nothing.

No lingering eyes. No obvious threats.

Yet, the feeling remained.

A shadow without form. A presence without a trace.

And then—just as quickly as it had come—it vanished.

Ayralina exhaled, taking a slow sip of her drink. The warmth did little to ease the tension coiling beneath her skin.

Whoever—or whatever—had been watching her was skilled. Too skilled.

She tightened her grip around the cup, her mind working through the possibilities.

Something was moving against her.

And she couldn't afford to be caught unprepared.

Three men seated at the bar had been watching Ayralina for a while, their sharp eyes noting her solitary presence. Rugged yet well-dressed, they carried themselves with a swagger that spoke of confidence—or perhaps arrogance. The first was tall and broad-shouldered, his dark hair slicked back, and his coat tailored and dusted with the faint grime of the road. The second had a neatly trimmed beard and a weathered face that suggested years of experience, his fitted vest hinting at an air of respectability. The third, shorter but wiry, wore a sly grin, his hands constantly fidgeting with the rings on his fingers.

After exchanging glances, the trio approached her. Deep in thought, Ayralina didn't notice them until Saber, sitting loyally at her feet, let out a low, warning growl that made the shortest of the men pause for a moment.

"It's okay, Saber," Ayralina murmured, her fingers lightly brushing the tiger's fur in reassurance. "I've got this."

The tallest of the men stepped forward, a smirk curling his lips as he leaned casually against the edge of the table. "Hey there, pretty lady, my name is Gorrin" he said, his voice smooth carrying a hint of cockiness. "You look like you're new in town. Need someone to show you around?"

Ayralina looked up, her expression calm, her eyes studying each of them. She could feel their intentions even before they spoke, their feigned charm barely masking their interest. She allowed a small, polite smile to form on her lips, deciding to play along. "That's so sweet of you," she replied, her voice light and measured. "I just arrived. Maybe you can tell me what all the commotion at the gate is about?"

The second man, the one with the beard, leaned closer, resting his hands on the back of the chair across from her. "Ah, you noticed that did you?" he said, his tone almost conspiratorial. "The whole kingdom is in an uproar. There's some kind of illness sweeping through, freezing folks solid. We guards are instructed to be on high alert, and they're not letting just anyone in."

The wiry man snorted, spinning one of his rings absentmindedly. "Not unless you've got something to offer," he added, his grin widening. "Or you've got deep enough pockets to grease a few palms."

"Or both," Gorrin, the tallest man chimed in with a chuckle, crossing his arms as he leaned in slightly. "You don't look like you've come for the sights, though. You got business here, miss?"

Ayralina tilted her head slightly, her smile fading as she met their gazes one by one. "I suppose you could say that," she said, her tone cool now, the faintest edge creeping into her voice. "I just got lucky and was one of the first few in line, so I got in earlier than most, that's all."

"Well, today seems to be your lucky day. We're exactly the right ones to ask— let me introduce them to you. This one with the beard is my brother Garrison and shorty here, is our friend Daffy. We are soldiers of the front line, so we got the inside scoop," Gorrin said, leaning in closer with an overly confident smirk. His voice dropped as if he were about to share some great secret. "But how about a drink first? And why don't you tell us your name while you're at it?"

Saber growled again, louder this time, the deep, guttural sound reverberating through the air like a warning bell. His sharp teeth glinted under the dim lights, bared in a clear display of aggression. The tiger's golden eyes burned with an intense glare, leaving no doubt about his displeasure. Ayralina smirked subtly, feeling the faint, familiar tug of their mental bond.

Good boy, she sent silently, her expression remaining composed despite the tension crackling around them like static.

"Whoa, relax, kitty," Gorrin sneered, raising his hands in mock surrender. His smirk widened, dripping with condescension, his bravado a thin mask barely hiding the flicker of fear in his eyes. "Waiter! Get this cat a piece of steak, will you? Make it quick—he looks hungry."

The waiter, clearly unnerved, hurried to comply without protest. Ayralina noted the quickness of his response, her sharp gaze flickering to Gorrin and his entourage. Seems these boys have enough influence to scare the staff, she thought, her smirk lingering, now tinged with something colder.

Ayralina's eyes narrowed, her grip tightening on the edge of the table. She knew exactly what kind of game he was playing—mocking dominance, thinly veiled intimidation—but before she could say anything, the steak arrived. The waiter, hands trembling, set the plate down with a quick nod and retreated without looking back.

Without hesitation, Daffy grabbed the plate, laughing as he carelessly tossed the meat toward Saber, as though mocking his ferocity. The slab of meat landed with a wet thud on the floor, a deliberate insult.

The sound of Saber's low, furious snarl filled the air, vibrating with pure, primal rage. He lunged forward, muscles coiling like a spring, claws scraping against the wooden floor with a sharp, grating screech. Ellie darted close behind him; her smaller, equally fierce frame ready to back him up without question. Gasps erupted from nearby tables, and chairs scraped loudly against the floor as patrons scrambled to get out of the way, their faces pale with fear.

Ayralina didn't move. She didn't flinch.

"Enough!" Ayralina's voice rang out, sharp and commanding. Her words cut through the tension like a blade, and Saber halted mid-step, his body still taut with restrained fury. Ellie skidded to a stop beside him, her tail lashing in irritation.

Ayralina rose to her feet, her expression dark with anger as she glared at the tall man. "What do you think you're doing?" she demanded, her voice low, laced with venom.

Gorrin had the audacity to chuckle, though his confidence wavered under her piercing gaze. "What?" he said with a shrug. "Just trying to be friendly. Thought your pet might appreciate a little snack."

Ayralina's eyes narrowed, her fury barely contained. "Saber is not just a pet, and he doesn't need your scraps," she snapped, her voice like ice. "And if you ever pull a stunt like that again, I'll let him have you for dinner."

The bearded man, Garrison, stepped forward, his hands raised in an attempt to diffuse the situation. "Now, now," he said cautiously. "No need to get all worked up. It was just a bit of fun."

"Fun?" Ayralina shot back, her voice rising. "Antagonizing a tiger and tossing food around like a fool? You call that fun? If you have something useful to say, then say it. Otherwise, get out of my sight."

Daffy, the shortest of the trio muttered something under his breath and tugged on Gorrin's sleeve, urging him to back away. Gorrin hesitated, his smirk faltering as Saber let out another warning growl, the sound deep and menacing.

"Fine, fine," he grumbled, taking a step back. "No need to be so touchy."

The trio retreated toward the bar, Ayralina exhaled slowly, running a hand through her hair to calm herself. She glanced at Saber, who was still glaring in the men's direction, his muscles rippling with barely suppressed tension.

"You did well," she murmured, reaching down to scratch behind his ears. "But let's not give them the satisfaction of rattling us any further."

Ellie gave a low growl and kept her gaze fixed on them. "We should've let Saber scare them a little more. They deserved it."

Ayralina sighed, her lips curving into a faint, wry smile. "Maybe," she said. "But we have bigger things to deal with than idiots at a bar. I didn't sense anything demonic about them, hopefully they won't do anything stupid for now." She sat back down, her sharp gaze drifting back toward the three men, who were whispering amongst themselves. One way or another, she knew their paths might cross again—and not in a way she'd enjoy.

Finishing their drinks the men turned to leave, Gorrin suddenly stumbled and collapsed to the floor, his knees buckling under him. His friends caught him just before he hit the ground, their expressions shifting from smug confidence to raw panic. They looked at Ayralina with wide, fearful eyes, their fingers trembling as they pointed at her.

"What did you do?" Garrison shouted, his voice cracking with hysteria. "You brought the plague!"

The bar fell silent, every patron turning toward the scene. Saber let out a deep growl and stepped protectively in front of Ayralina, his sleek muscles tightened like a spring ready to strike. Ellie mirrored his movements, her sharp teeth bared, standing shoulder to shoulder with her brother.

Ayralina's heart raced, but before she could speak, a calm, authoritative voice broke the tension. "You boys need to back off now. Stop spreading rumors. And learn some respect."

A newcomer stepped forward from the shadows of the pub, his presence commanding instant attention. He was tall and well-built, his broad shoulders and confident stride radiating quiet strength. His dark blue eyes held a calm intensity, and his chestnut hair framed his fair, angular face. Something about him felt strangely familiar to Ayralina, her sharp gaze catching a faint shimmer beneath his skin, like scales glinting faintly in the dim light. Interesting, she thought. I wonder if he also absorbed one of Silvaris's dragon scales. If that's true, he could be a strong ally. Her thoughts flicked briefly to Andre and the others, wondering if his condition mirrored theirs.

Garrison, still brimming with false bravado, snapped, "Mind your own business if you know what's good for you, she's the one causing harm to my brother.'

The man ignored the taunt entirely, keeping his focus on Ayralina. He inclined his head slightly in greeting. "I'm Simon, an off-duty Captain," he said, his tone even but firm. "I witnessed everything that just happened. If you'll allow me, I'd like to help you settle this, Ms....?"

"Ayralina," she said simply, her voice steady.

"Well then, Ms. Ayralina," Simon continued, his gaze flicking briefly to Saber and Ellie. "Could you kindly call off your tigers? Let's keep the bloodshed to a minimum, shall we?"

Ayralina nodded, grateful for the intervention. "Alright, Saber, Ellie—stand down," she said, her voice carrying the weight of authority. Both creatures hesitated for a moment, but then they stepped back, still watching the men with wary eyes.

Simon turned to the drunkards, his calm demeanor hardening as he reached into his coat and flashed a palace badge. The insignia gleamed under the light, drawing audible gasps from the surrounding crowd. "Take your friend and leave, there's already enough going on, there's no need for more," he ordered sharply. "Or would you prefer to spend the night in a cell?"

Daffy, lunged forward with a sloppy punch. Simon moved with practiced ease, sidestepping the blow as if it were nothing. In one swift motion, he grabbed the man's arm, twisted it behind his back, and drove him to his knees. With a well-placed kick, he swept his legs out from under him, leaving him crumpled on the floor.

"Your choice," Simon said, his voice cool and unyielding. "Leave peacefully or face the consequences."

Before the man could respond, Gorrin, who had collapsed earlier, began to shiver violently. His lips turned an alarming shade of blue, and his eyes rolled back as his breathing grew shallow. His friends rushed to his side; their earlier bravado replaced with sheer terror.

"W-what's happening to him?" one of them stammered, his voice trembling.

Simon crouched down beside the man, his sharp eyes scanning him for signs of deceit. "What's going on here?" he demanded.

Ayralina stepped forward, pulling out the blue medical badge from her inside pocket. "Let me see," she said, brushing past Simon. She knelt beside the man, her fingers carefully checking his pulse. Her expression darkened. "He's not faking—he's freezing. His body temperature is plummeting, and he's barely breathing."

Her tone was urgent as she straightened and addressed the group. "Where's the nearest medical facility?"

The drunkards snapped finally out of their stupor, nodding frantically. "We'll take him! Please, help him!" Garrison pleaded; his hands clasped as though in prayer.

Simon stood, his presence towering over them. "You're lucky Dr. Ayralina is willing to help," he said coldly. "If it were up to me, you'd be answering to the King for harassing a doctor during a crisis. Now move!"

Chapter 18

THEY RUSHED INTO THE hospital, their panicked shouts cutting through the cacophony of the bustling emergency ward. The hospital was a stark contrast to the chaotic streets outside—clean, modern, and fully equipped with the latest medical technology. Bright fluorescent lights illuminated the space, gleaming off the stainless steel equipment and polished floors. Nurses darted between rooms, pushing carts loaded with medical supplies, while monitors beeped and whirred in an endless rhythm. The air smelled of antiseptic and urgency, a palpable sense of controlled chaos pervading the atmosphere.

In the middle of it all stood the attending doctor, an older man whose age was betrayed by the deep lines etched into his face and the gray streaks running through his disheveled hair. His shoulders slumped slightly, as though weighed down by the countless lives he had fought to save and the many more he had lost. His once-crisp white coat hung loosely over his frame, now wrinkled and faintly stained—evidence of long, grueling hours. His name tag says Dr. Amuchau. Dark circles framed his weary eyes, and his voice carried the flat tone of someone who had seen far too much.

The moment he saw the man being carried in, the doctor approached, his lips pressing into a grim line. He gave the patient a quick but thorough once-over, his expression unreadable until he shook his head with a deep sigh. "There's nothing we can do," he said, his voice tinged with resignation. "He's dying. It's the same as all the others."

Just as the words left his mouth, Ayralina felt it again—that same prickle at the back of her neck, sharp and intrusive, like invisible fingers brushing against her mind. The sensation of being watched returned, stronger this time, threading through the sterile air like an unseen predator lurking just out of sight. Her instincts screamed to react, scan the room, and find the source.

Out of the corner of her eye, she saw Simon stiffen slightly, his jaw tightening as his gaze swept the room with subtlety. His hand hovered near his concealed weapon at his side, fingers flexing just once before he forced them to relax. He felt it too.

Their eyes met briefly; no words were needed. The flicker of tension in his expression mirrored her own unease. We're not alone.

But there was no time.

The dying man's shallow gasps were growing weaker by the second, and every heartbeat mattered. Whatever—or whoever—was watching them would have to wait. Ayralina pushed the feeling aside, shoving it into the far corners of her mind, locking it away with all the other threats she couldn't afford to face yet.

Her focus snapped back to Gorrin lying on the stretcher. His life was slipping through their fingers, and answers were dying with him.

Ayralina stepped forward, her tone calm but unyielding. "I'd like you to run some tests, please."

The doctor turned to her, his tired eyes narrowing in skepticism. "Tests?" he repeated, almost incredulous. "It's pointless. We've seen this before. We've tried everything we can think of. He's going to die frozen, just like the rest."

"Die frozen?" Ayralina echoed, her brow furrowing as her mind began to race. "Let me examine him myself," she insisted while flashing the blue badge, her voice gaining an edge of authority. "I'm also a doctor, and I've dealt with something similar before."

The older man sighed again, rubbing his temple as though bracing himself for another futile effort. "Look," he said, his tone weary yet firm, "we don't have time to waste chasing miracles. We've been working day and night, and nothing—not medicine, not magic, not even the king's finest healers—has worked. If you want to try, go ahead, but don't get your hopes up."

Ayralina stepped past him without hesitation, her sharp gaze fixed on the patient. She could feel the doctor's eyes lingering on her, doubt and curiosity mingling in his exhausted expression. She knelt beside the man, her hands moving to check his vitals. His skin was like ice, and his breath came in shallow, ragged gasps. Frost crept along the edges of his lips, and his pulse was faint—barely there.

As she worked, the older doctor watched silently, his arms crossed and his exhaustion momentarily replaced by a flicker of interest. "You say you've dealt with something similar before," he said after a moment. "What makes you think this time will be different?"

Ayralina didn't look up; she focused entirely on the man before her. "I know there's more to this illness than what's on the surface. If you've tried everything else, maybe it's time to try something new."

The doctor raised an eyebrow but didn't argue further.

Ignoring his dismissal, Ayralina approached the man on the stretcher. "You're not doing well," she said softly. "The attending doctor has already given up on you. Would you be willing to let me treat you? You might have a chance to live."

The man, barely able to speak, nodded faintly, his trust ignited by the confidence in her voice.

Garrison clasped his hands together, pleading. "Please, doctor, if you can save him, we'll be forever indebted to you. We've heard that everyone who gets this illness dies. Please, help him."

Ayralina nodded. "I'll try."

She turned to the other doctor. "Since he's dying anyway, let me try something. I'll take full responsibility."

The doctor shrugged, clearly unconvinced but too busy to argue. "Suit yourself. You can have that room, but don't expect any help from me or my staff. As you can see, the emergency room is overflowing."

"That's fine," Ayralina said firmly. "Just this room is enough. I'll handle the rest."

The doctor waved her off and told the man's brothers to sign a release form. Simon, standing nearby, clenched his fists. "He's bullying you. Let me handle this."

"It's fine," Ayralina said, her focus unwavering. "Saving a life is more important than arguing over politics."

Simon exhaled sharply, then said, "I'll stay and be your witness in case anything happens to him."

Ayralina gave him a faint smile. "You have so little faith in me. Don't worry—nothing will happen to him."

Once the brothers returned with the signed form, Ayralina turned to Simon. "You'll be my nurse for now. I need the others to wait outside."

Simon carefully positioned the man on the bed while Ayralina readied herself to work. She placed her hands over the man's stomach, closing her eyes to focus. A soft, golden glow emanated from her palms as she channeled her energy, sending a gentle warmth into his body to locate the source of the problem.

"What are you doing?" Simon asked, his tone a mix of curiosity and unease.

Ayralina opened her eyes briefly, her voice calm and firm. "Since I don't have any equipment or tools, I'll need to examine him the old-fashioned way—using energy. I can see that his veins are beginning to freeze over, and ice is blocking the flow of blood. If I can melt the blockages and burn away the poison, he'll survive. But the process is excruciating without anything to dull the pain, and it's risky—if his willpower isn't strong enough, it could kill him."

Simon frowned, concerned flickering in his eyes, but he remained silent.

Ayralina fixed her gaze on Simon, her expression unwavering. "Before I start, I need your trust. You've probably realized by now that I'm not an ordinary human. My healing method is... unconventional, and not everyone can accept it. But I swear to you, I'm not a demon—just someone with a unique ability to help. However, what I'm about to do comes with a grave risk. The flame I wield isn't ordinary—it's a power that's as rare as it is dangerous. Anyone who knows about it becomes a target. If this secret gets out, it could put not only me but you and everyone around us in danger. So, I need to know—do you trust me enough to protect this secret?"

Simon met her eyes, his jaw tightening as he absorbed her words. After a moment, he gave a firm nod. "You're right—I've sensed something different about you since we met. But I feel you are someone I can trust, and I won't let your secret slip. What do you need me to do?"

"Have his brothers stand guard outside the door. With the tigers here, I should be relatively safe," Ayralina instructed, her tone sharp and focused. "I know you sensed a threat earlier. I need you to investigate the source without alerting them. Then come back and stay with the cubs until I'm done."

She stepped closer, her gaze hardening. "Make sure no one interrupts us. If anyone comes close, stop them—no matter what."

Simon nodded; determination etched into every line of his face. "You have my word, no one will get through."

Ayralina allowed herself a faint smile, her voice softened. "Thank you. I appreciate that very much."

She hesitated briefly, her eyes lingering on him, the weight of his trust settling over her like an unexpected warmth. No wonder the Scale chose him, she thought. He is a worthy human, deserving of its power.

But there was no time to dwell on sentiment. She pushed the thought aside, her focus snapping back to the task at hand.

Simon stepped out and approached the brothers, his expression stern and commanding. "Listen carefully," he said, his voice low and commanding. "If you want to save your brother, you cannot leave this door until I return. No one is to come close—no exceptions."

The brothers exchanged tense glances but nodded, the desperation in their eyes outweighing any urge to question his authority.

Without another word, Simon turned and disappeared down the corridor, his steps swift and silent. He moved through the hospital with stealth, blending in with the flow of staff and patients, his senses sharp and on high alert. Every shadow and every flicker of movement was scrutinized as he searched for the source of the unseen threat, careful not to draw attention or alert the enemy to his presence.

Inside the room, Ayralina turned back to the patient, her focus narrowing to the icy blockage constricting his bloodstream. Channeling the searing intensity of her Phoenix fire, she directed it with surgical precision, the golden flames flickering faintly just above her palms. Slowly, the blockage began to melt away, allowing blood to flow freely once more. She expanded her efforts, tracing every frozen vein, carefully burning out the insidious poison without harming the delicate tissues around it.

The process was grueling, both physically and mentally exhausting, demanding every ounce of her concentration. Beads of sweat formed along her brow as the hours stretched on, the room bathed in the dim, artificial glow of flickering fluorescent lights. Outside, night slowly surrendered to the soft hues of dawn, the faint light creeping through the blinds like a silent witness to her work.

When the final trace of poison was gone, Ayralina exhaled deeply, her body aching with fatigue. The patient stirred and then slowly sat up, his complexion noticeably brighter, the color returning to his once-pale face. Now sharp and clear, his eyes held a mixture of disbelief and gratitude.

"This is amazing, I feel great!" he exclaimed, stretching his arms as if shaking off the remnants of death itself. "Doctor, thank you so much. I can't believe I was harassing the right person today. You're incredible."

Ayralina managed a warm, weary smile. "No need to thank me. Just tell me—how did you get this cold poison?"

Before the man could answer, a familiar voice cut through the quiet.

"Cold poison?" Simon's voice was low, tinged with curiosity.

Ayralina's eyes snapped up, her heart skipping slightly—not from surprise but from the realization that Simon had returned unnoticed at some point during her treatment. He stood by the door, silent and vigilant, his sharp gaze scanning the room. His presence was steady and grounding, and he had been guarding her without making his presence known.

Despite her exhaustion, a flicker of warmth stirred in her chest. He's good, she thought, both impressed and reassured.

Simon's brow was slightly furrowed, his arms crossed as he stepped forward, his attention shifting between Ayralina and the now-recovered Gorrin. "Ayralina, do you know what we are dealing with here?"

Ayralina nodded. "Yes, it's a poison often used by frost demons. I've seen it before—that's why I was able to cure him. Did you hear about what happened in the Southern Land?"

Gorrin's eyes widened. "You're that doctor? The one who cured the entire town of human puppets?"

Ayralina nodded again.

"Forgive me for not recognizing you sooner," he said. "You're a miracle worker."

Ayralina chuckled. "It's no miracle. The tigers with me here had lent me their firepower, and it was also them who found the cure, I just had to find the right formula for it. Without them, I wouldn't have been able to help."

Ayralina turned back to the soldier, her gaze sharp. "Now, tell us—how did you get poisoned?"

The man took a steadying breath. "My brothers and I are front-line soldiers. A few nights ago, we were patrolling when we encountered a frost demon. We fought it off, but I didn't realize I'd it then, but now that I think about it, that was probably when I was poisoned." He shook his head, frustration flickering in his eyes. "At first, I just felt cold—nothing serious. But over the next three days, the weakness set in. No matter what I did, I couldn't get warm. It was like a normal fever at first, but then I couldn't sleep. My brothers thought a few drinks might help, so they brought me to the bar. That's where we ran into you."

Before anyone could respond, a firm knock at the door interrupted them.

Dr. Amuchau entered, looking surprisingly refreshed. His once-disheveled coat was now neatly pressed, and though faint shadows remained under his eyes, the exhaustion that had burdened him earlier seemed lighter. He took a step forward—then stopped.

His breath hitched as his eyes locked onto the soldier.

A man who, mere moments ago, had been dying was now sitting upright, his color restored, and his breathing steady. The frost that had lined his lips had vanished, replaced by a flush of warmth.

The doctor's jaw clenched, disbelief flickering across his face. His gaze snapped to Ayralina. "I... I don't understand." He took a hesitant step closer, still staring at the miraculous recovery. "This is impossible. He was nearly gone. How...?"

Ayralina wiped her hands on a cloth, her expression composed. Before she could answer, Dr. Amuchau abruptly bowed his head.

"Dr. Ayralina," he said, his voice thick with regret. "I owe you an apology. I was wrong to dismiss you earlier. I should have listened. You've done what none of us could." He exhaled, shaking his head. "Thank you—for saving him."

Ayralina inclined her head slightly, accepting the apology without unnecessary words. "The important thing is that he's alive," she said evenly. "But this illness... it's not ordinary. You and your staff need to stay vigilant."

Dr. Amuchau nodded, his awe fading into concern. Then, as if recalling something urgent, his expression changed. A flicker of desperation entered his voice.

"Dr. Ayralina," he said, stepping closer, his tone hushed but filled with urgency. "If you've truly cured this poison before, you may be the only one who can help the prince and the Queen.

The doctor nodded gravely. "They've been battling the same affliction for days—barely clinging to life. The fire-affinity healers are doing everything they can, but it's only delaying the inevitable. Their energy is running low, and the symptoms are worsening." He hesitated. "If we don't find a cure soon, they won't survive."

"I heard something about it when I entered the city today. I had originally planned to investigate the illness first before visiting the palace, but if they have the same symptoms, they might not have much time left." Ayralina stated.

A heavy silence settled in the room.

Simon stepped forward, his expression grim. "You must come with me to the palace at once," he said, his voice resolute. "If you can save the prince, the king will grant you anything you ask, if it is as you say, we cannot delay this any further."

Ayralina's jaw tightened. She could already feel the weight of the decision pressing against her. The city was on edge, the illness spreading like wildfire, and now the royal family itself was on the brink.

"We can leave immediately," she said, her tone steady. "But I need to inform my companion of my whereabouts."

Simon nodded without hesitation. "That won't be a problem. Tell me who they are, and I'll ensure they're brought to you. The palace has eyes everywhere—they'll be found."

Ayralina met his gaze, her mind already mapping out the next steps.

"Then let's not waste any more time."

Somewhere in a lavishly decorated room, the air was thick with the scent of exotic incense, and the glow of golden lanterns cast flickering shadows against the silk-draped walls.

A young woman knelt low on the marble floor; her head bowed in deference. Her voice was steady, but there was a trace of unease beneath the surface.

"I was in town today, investigating as you ordered," she began carefully. "A suspicious doctor arrived—she was traveling with two young tigers, and she matches the description we received."

She paused, gauging her lady's reaction, but the woman standing before her remained poised, expression unreadable. Taking a deep breath, she continued.

"I followed them discreetly. They made their way through the marketplace and all the way to the hospital. I kept my distance, but I believe I may have been discovered—Simon, the head guard of the palace, seemed to take notice of me." Her fingers clenched slightly against the cold marble. "What should I do, my lady?"

A long silence stretched between them before a soft, velvety voice cut through the air.

"Resume your normal duties for now. Do not draw any more attention to yourself," the lady instructed, her tone cool and measured. "I will have someone else take over the surveillance."

The young maid hesitated momentarily before nodding, pressing her forehead to the floor in submission. "Yes, my lady."

The woman turned gracefully, the soft rustle of her silk robes the only sound in the quiet chamber. She was breathtaking—elegantly dressed in a flowing crimson gown, adorned with delicate golden embroidery that shimmered in the dim light. A cascade of dark, perfectly arranged curls framed her sharp yet beautiful features, her piercing eyes betraying a mind that was always calculating, always one step ahead.

She moved toward the window, gazing out over the cityscape beyond. "So... she's finally here," she murmured, a slow, knowing smile curving her lips.

Chapter 19

AYRALINA AND THE CUBS traveled immediately to the palace, escorted by Simon, the doctor, and the guards. The palace loomed like a fortress, its high walls and spires a testament to the kingdom's power. Inside, the mood was grim, the halls filled with whispers of worry and tension.

The dimly lit corridor outside the royal chamber was heavy with silence, broken only by the muffled sounds of distant footsteps and the occasional clink of armor. Shadows stretched long against the stone walls, flickering under the torchlight.

Simon seized the moment, pulling Ayralina aside with a firm grip on her arm. His expression was grave, his gaze darting to ensure they were alone.

"Ayralina," he murmured, keeping his voice at a whisper, "there's something I need to tell you before we meet the king."

She stilled, sensing the urgency beneath his tone.

Simon took a breath. "Earlier, at the hospital—we didn't get a chance to talk, but while I was investigating, I ran into a palace maid."

Ayralina's brow arched slightly, her instincts flaring.

"I don't know if she's involved, but something about her felt... off. She claimed she was visiting a relative in the hospital, but I had the distinct feeling she was lying." His voice dropped even further. "She serves the king's favorite concubine."

Ayralina's expression sharpened.

Simon continued, his fingers curling slightly as he spoke. "That woman is not pleased about the queen's pregnancy. When the news broke, she was furious. And when the queen gave birth to the prince—her rage turned cold and quiet." His jaw tightened. "The child solidified the queen's position. His very existence threatened everything the concubine had worked for."

Ayralina inhaled slowly, the weight of his words sinking in.

"If you run into that maid—be careful," Simon warned. "We don't know how far the concubine would go, but if resentment can kill, then in a place like this, it already has."

A pause. A flicker of something darker passed over Simon's face.

"There's more," he said grimly. "Before the prince was born, the queen was attacked—by a frost demon."

Ayralina's breath hitched.

Simon nodded, his voice turning colder. "It nearly caused her to miscarry. The healers had to perform an emergency C-section to save the child. He was born premature,weak... but it wasn't just that." He hesitated. "The prince was poisoned before he even took his first breath."

A chill ran down Ayralina's spine. "Poisoned?" she echoed, the word like a blade against her tongue.

"Yes. While still in the womb. That's why his condition has always been so severe."

She exhaled sharply, the implications unraveling fast.

"Frost demons don't act without purpose," she said, her voice turning hard. "They manipulate from the shadows. They don't strike directly unless there's something—or someone—they need eliminated."

"Exactly." Simon's expression darkened. "We've been investigating, but every lead has led to a dead end. Until now." He glanced around once more before adding, "This stays between us. The king has kept this tightly controlled—if word got out, it would send the entire palace into panic."

Silence hung between them, taut as a bowstring.

"Ayralina... the prince is the king's only heir. If he dies, the royal bloodline dies with him." His words carried the weight of an entire kingdom. "This isn't just about saving a child. It's about the survival of the throne itself."

The words settled heavily in her chest.

Simon continued. "If you can save the prince, his Majesty will grant you anything you ask. But be prepared—this isn't just politics. There is something much, much bigger at play."

Ayralina stood still, her mind racing as she fit the pieces together.

The poison.

The demon.

The concubine.

Everything was converging toward a single, sinister truth.

Her eyes steeled with resolve.

"This is more complicated than I thought," she murmured. "But I'll save him. No matter the cost."

Simon studied her for a long moment. Then, with a slight nod, a flicker of something—relief, perhaps—crossed his face.

"I knew I could count on you."

Before her audience with the king, Ayralina was led to a private chamber to freshen up. After days of travel, battle, and exhaustion, she hardly looked presentable for an audience with royalty. Dust clung to her clothes, her hair was slightly disheveled, and fatigue weighed heavily in her eyes.

Simon motioned to a waiting maid, who quickly stepped forward with a basin of warm water, fresh linens, and a set of clean clothes—an elegant ruby red dress with gold embroidery, simple yet refined, fitting for the occasion.

Meanwhile, the cubs were treated to a more indulgent experience.

Luxurious hot water. Herbal oils. Thick, fluffy towels.

Saber groaned in sheer bliss as warm water soaked into his fur. "Ahhhhhh... finally."

Ellie stretched lazily in the bath, her ears twitching. "Yeah, this is nice."

Ayralina cast them a dry look, unable to hide her amusement. "You two look far too comfortable."

Saber cracked one eye open. "We earned this."

Despite herself, she smirked before turning to her own preparations. The envy was real, but she had little time to dwell on it.

She washed away the journey's grime, brushed her hair into a neat braid, and fastened the dress, adjusting the cuffs with practiced ease. She took a steadying breath as she caught her reflection in a nearby mirror.

Simon's words echoed in her mind.

"Bear with it, Ayralina. I know it's ridiculous, but if you don't dress accordingly, you won't be allowed to appear before the king. This part is all politics."

With her composure restored and her appearance polished, she felt ready.

When she was finally escorted to the throne room, Ayralina was impressed by the grandeur of the space. The room was cavernous, with high vaulted ceilings supported by massive marble pillars. Stained glass windows stretched from floor to ceiling, casting vibrant light patterns onto the polished stone floor. Intricate carvings adorned the walls, depicting the kingdom's storied history—dragons, knights, and long-forgotten battles. At the far end of the room, the King's throne stood on a white and gold platform. The throne was a masterpiece, carved from ebony wood and inlaid with golden filigree, the backrest rising high into an ornate crest crowned with the kingdom's insignia. Torches flickered in their sconces, their flames dancing with an almost unnatural steadiness as though even the fire dared not falter in the King's presence.

Ayralina was brought before the King, an imposing figure seated on the throne. His sharp eyes bore into her, scrutinizing her every move as though he could discern her worth simply by looking at her. King Cedrick, looked younger than she expected, but his regal bearing was undeniable—broad shoulders cloaked in deep crimson robes trimmed with gold and a crown resting atop his dark hair, its gems glinting in the light. Silence fell over the room as Simon stepped forward to speak.

Simon and Dr Amuchau recounted the events leading up to this moment, omitting the more magical elements of Ayralina's methods. He described how she had cured the afflicted soldier, emphasizing her expertise as a healer and vouching for her skill. His voice was steady and respectful but firm, as if daring anyone to doubt her capabilities.

King Cedrick listened intently, his expression unreadable, until Simon finished. His gaze shifted to Ayralina, and his voice was deep and commanding when he finally spoke. "Ayralina, if you can save my son and my wife, I will grant you anything you wish. Gold, land, power—name it, and it shall be yours. But if you fail..." His voice trailed off, heavy with implication. The silence that followed was deafening, the weight of the unspoken consequences pressing down on the room.

Ayralina met his gaze steadily, her own voice unwavering. "Your Majesty, I will do everything in my power to save them. But we must not delay any longer. Please show me to them."

King Cedrick regarded her for a long moment, his piercing eyes searching her face. Finally, he nodded and gestured to a servant. "Take her to the royal wing, provide her everything she needs," he commanded. "Do not delay."

When Ayralina saw the newborn prince, her heart clenched. The child lay bundled in blankets, but that wasn't enough to hide his frailness. His tiny body was unnaturally cold, his breathing shallow and labored. His lips were tinged a deep blue, and his almost translucent skin seemed to glow faintly in the dim light. Ayralina's chest tightened, and unbidden, thoughts of her own children filled her mind. The comparison was unbearable. She clenched her fists, steeling herself. I won't let this child suffer, she thought. I'll do everything I can to save him.

The prince's treatment would need to be exceedingly gentle. Anything too forceful could overwhelm his fragile body. Ayralina placed her hands lightly on his chest, carefully channeling just enough of her Phoenix flame to bring a subtle warmth to his body. The glow of her flame flickered softly, like a candlelight in the dark. Her goal for now was simple: keep him comfortable, stabilize him, and give herself time to determine the best course of action.

After stabilizing the prince, Ayralina wasted no time making her way to the Queen's quarters.

The chamber was elegant and fitting for a queen, but its grandeur dimmed by the suffocating presence of illness. A crystal chandelier hung from the high ceiling, scattering fractured rainbows of light across the room, though its beauty did little to warm the icy air. Deep purple and gold tapestries lined the walls, but even their regal presence couldn't mask the faint, metallic tang of sickness that clung to the air. A roaring fire blazed in the hearth, yet the room felt unnaturally cold as if the illness had seeped into the walls.

Queen Anaya laid motionless in the grand canopy bed; her frail frame propped up by a mountain of silk pillows. Despite the chill, beads of sweat glistened on her brow, her once-vibrant blue eyes now dulled and distant. Each breath she took was shallow and labored, as if every inhale was a battle against the poison spreading through her veins. Frost-like patterns had begun creeping along her pale hands, the unmistakable signature of cold poison.

Ayralina stepped forward, bowing slightly. "Your Majesty," she greeted, her tone gentle. "My apologies for the intrusion, I am Ayralina and with the permission of King Cedrick, I've come to examine your illness."

Queen Anaya tilted her head weakly, her voice barely above a whisper. "That's fine, he did inform me in advance of you coming. You may do what you must," she murmured.

Ayralina nodded, pulling a chair closer to the bedside. She unfastened her bag, setting out her tools and remedies with quiet efficiency.

She could feel the Queen's gaze on her, filled with exhaustion but also something else—hope.

As she lit a lantern, its soft glow cast long shadows over the bed, illuminating the Queen's frail form. Ayralina's hands moved with practiced precision as she conducted her examination, her fingers brushing lightly over frostbitten patches of skin.

She checked the queen's pulse, as expected it was weak and irregular.

Her touch traced the cold, branching veins, confirming what she feared—the poison was spreading through the bloodstream, threading through Queen Anaya's arteries like an insidious vine.

Queen Anaya shivered beneath the thick blankets, the tremors in her body a silent war against the relentless chill. Even with the fire blazing, her core temperature remained dangerously low.

Ayralina sat back slightly, her expression grave but resolute. "Your Majesty," she said carefully, "The cold poison is spreading—you don't have much time, as of now it hasn't yet reached your vital organs. That gives us a small window to act."

Queen Anaya's lips curved into a faint, tired smile. "Then what will the treatment be, are you able to cure me? Dr. Ayralina," she asked.

Ayralina exhaled, nodding. "I can and I will, but I need you to trust me. Can you do that?" The Queen looked at Simon for reassurance. When he gave her a subtle nod, she turned to Ayralina. "I'm willing to take this chance. You may proceed." The Queen stated. "Thank you, before I proceed I'll need everyone to leave the room," she instructed. "Only my companions, the tiger, and I can stay. Simon will guard the door."

Simon stiffened slightly at her words but nodded in understanding. The guards and attendants hesitated, their concern evident, but Queen Anaya raised a frail hand. "You heard her. Leave us."

Reluctantly, they filed out, leaving the room eerily silent.

Once alone, Ayralina reached into her bag, pulling out a small, white pill. She held it out in front of her. "Take this, Your Majesty. It will ease the pain during the treatment."

Anaya's brows furrowed slightly at the suggestion. "Is it truly necessary?"

Ayralina met her gaze steadily. "Yes. The process will be difficult, but this will make it bearable."

A moment passed, heavy with unspoken understanding. Then, with a small nod, she accepted the pill, placing it on her tongue before taking a sip of water. Her trembling hand steadied, reassured by the calm certainty in Ayralina's eyes.

It took a moment for her to pass out.

Standing near the bed, Simon crossed his arms and raised an eyebrow. "What did you give her?" he asked, his tone a mix of curiosity and suspicion.

"A sedative," Ayralina replied simply, not looking up as she sat down and got prepared. "This way, I don't have to explain myself or the process—and I can still guard my secret."

Simon studied her for a moment, then gave a small nod. "Fair enough," he said.

"Thank you. Now, help me guard the door and make sure no one comes in until I'm finished."

Simon moved to the doorway, his tall frame filling the entrance as he took up his post. "Don't worry, no one will get past me tonight," he said, his voice low and final.

Ayralina placed her hands on Queen Anaya's diaphragm, channeling her Phoenix flame into her frail body. Beads of sweat had formed on the Queen's brow as her body trembled violently, the cold poison resisting, clinging to her like a malevolent force unwilling to be exorcised. An eerie mist had seeped from her skin, curling into the air like wisps of ghostly fingers, reluctant to release their grasp.

The process had been agonizingly slow. The Queen's body convulsed with every wave of magic that drew the venom from her veins, her breath shallow and labored. Ayralina had remained steadfast, her hands unwavering, her every movement deliberate to ensure no harm came to the woman beneath her touch. The toll on her own body had been immense, but she had pushed aside her exhaustion, focusing only on purging the poison, on preserving the fragile thread of life that still tethered the Queen to this world.

Hour after hour had passed. The warm light of day had faded, swallowed by the creeping darkness of night, yet Ayralina had not faltered. She had worked through the shifting shadows, her power burning steadily, her will unyielding. Finally, as the moon reached its peak, the icy mist began to thin. The malevolent chill that had gripped the Queen's body had lost its strength. With one final surge of energy, the last remnants of the poison had dissipated completely, vanishing like frost under the rising sun.

The room had felt lighter, the oppressive weight that had loomed over it lifting at last. The Queen's pallid skin had flushed with warmth, color returning to her once lifeless cheeks. Her breathing was steady, no longer strained by the frigid toxin. The frost-like patterns that had marred her skin had melted away, leaving behind only smooth, unblemished flesh.

"It's done," Ayralina murmured, her voice raw with exhaustion as she slowly withdrew her hands. Queen Anaya slowly came through: "The poison is gone. You'll need to rest to regain your strength. You're healed now."

Queen Anaya stirred, her lashes fluttering weakly before her eyes finally opened. They had held a clarity that had been absent for far too long, a renewed vitality that seemed almost impossible. She had looked more alive than she had in years, her face free of the haunted shadows that had lingered beneath her eyes. Her lips had parted in a trembling breath, her fingers clenching at the blankets as if grounding herself in this moment of salvation.

Tears welled in her eyes as she turned to Ayralina, her gaze shining with profound gratitude. "Thank you," she whispered, her voice trembling with emotion. "You've given me a chance to stay by my son's side."

Ayralina offered her a small, tired smile. "You're stronger than you think, Your Majesty. Rest now. There's still much to do, and your kingdom is in need."

Queen Anaya nodded faintly, her eyes closing as she let the relief wash over her. Ayralina sat back, taking a deep breath as she wiped her damp forehead.

Exhausted, Simon led Ayralina to a luxurious room, more ornate and comfortable than anywhere she had stayed in a long time. As they reached the doorway, he turned to her, his expression kind.

"Get some rest," he told her. "If you need anything, don't hesitate to contact me."

She nodded wearily, too drained to say much more. Once inside, she quickly washed up, barely able to keep her eyes open as the warm water soothed her aching body. She collapsed onto the plush bed the moment she finished, sinking into its softness.

The cubs had nestled beside her, their bodies radiating warmth as their gentle purring filled the quiet room. Within moments, the exhaustion had overtaken her completely, and she drifted into a deep, dreamless sleep.

Chapter 20

THE NEXT MORNING, AYRALINA was startled awake by a soft knock at the door. Groggy and still half-asleep, she rubbed her eyes and climbed out of bed. With slow, sluggish steps, she shuffled to the door and opened it, only to find Simon standing there, flanked by Queen Izzy and King Daxton, the majestic white heavenly tigers. Seeing them immediately made her smile, and she quickly opened the door wider to let them in.

But Simon hesitated at the threshold, shifting awkwardly and avoiding her gaze. He coughed lightly and cleared his throat.

"I... uh, sorry to disturb you so early; your friends are here" he stammered. "I'll, uh, let you freshen up first. I'll send someone up with breakfast."

Without waiting for a response, he turned abruptly and hurried down the hall, almost tripping over his feet in haste.

Ayralina blinked, confused. "That was... weird. What's gotten into him?" she asked aloud, turning to Izzy, who had been watching Simon's retreat with an amused expression.

Izzy looked at Ayralina, her icy blue eyes sparkling with mischief. "Maybe it has something to do with the way you're dressed," she said with a sly grin.

Ayralina glanced down at herself and gasped. She had been standing there in her nightgown—a soft, slightly rumpled garment that clung to her sleep-disheveled figure. Her hair had been a wild mess, tumbling in untamed waves around her face. A groan of embarrassment escaped her as her cheeks flushed crimson.

"Oh no!" she exclaimed. "I hope I didn't scare him too much!"

Despite herself, laughter bubbled up, the sound light and genuine.

Izzy chuckled, her elegant demeanor unshaken. "You certainly made an impression. But don't worry, Simon will survive. I'm just glad to see you're well. We have much to discuss."

Ayralina nodded, her embarrassment fading as she shifted her focus to the urgent matters at hand. "We do," she agreed, "but let me freshen up and get changed first. I'd rather not scare off anyone else." With that, she shooed the tigers further into the room and closed the door behind them.

After quickly washing up and dressing in more suitable attire, Ayralina rejoined Izzy and Daxton and sat down to a hearty breakfast. The warm scent of fresh bread and spiced tea filled the air, yet she could barely touch her plate, her appetite overshadowed by the weight of their conversation.

"The situation seems quite dire," Izzy began, her voice laced with concern. "The demons have been here for some time now. They're gathering here, their mission is two-fold. The first is to take over this human kingdom and make it one of their fortresses. And then prepare to invade the North for the Ice Crystal Heart. And the second, you probably already guessed, is to flush you out.

Ayralina's stomach had churned. The Ice Crystal Heart. Her thoughts raced. She needed it to save her husband, yet the demons sought it to unleash unimaginable destruction. Once again, she found herself locked in a race against time, competing with forces that would stop at nothing to claim it first.

"How close are they to getting it?" she asked, her tone edged with urgency.

Daxton, the white heavenly tiger, responded with a low growl. "They've been in the North for some time now, but the Ice Crystal Heart is under the protection of the Polar Bear King Tyrin. So far, every attempt they've made to seize it has failed. King Tyrin's forces are formidable, and they've managed to repel the demons' advances."

"That's a relief," Ayralina murmured, though her relief had been fleeting.

"But" Daxton continued, his deep voice rumbling like distant thunder, "the demons are regrouping. They're waiting for reinforcements. Once they're ready, they plan to launch an all-out war on the North, but before that happens you are still their main target.

Izzy nodded solemnly. "The demons concocted the cold poison plot to draw you out. They knew you wouldn't ignore the sick and dying, not when you had the power to help them. This entire kingdom was infected as bait—to flush you out of hiding."

Ayralina clenched her hands—this confirmed the suspicions she had harbored since first arriving at this kingdom. The heat of her Phoenix flame flickered faintly at her fingertips, a physical manifestation of the fury simmering within her. Taking a slow, steady breath, she forced herself to suppress the fire before it blazed out of control. She had to remain composed, no matter how fiercely anger surged through her veins.

"So, what do I do?" she murmured, more to herself than anyone else.

Izzy tilted her head, her sharp blue eyes watching Ayralina closely. "What will you do? Since this is a trap, curing this poison could be exactly what they want."

Ayralina straightened, her golden eyes burning with determination. "It doesn't matter if it's a trap," she said firmly. "I still have to save these people, no matter the risk. But at least now, we're not flying blind. The demons don't know I'm here yet, and for now, my identity is still hidden. Only Simon has a hint about who I truly am."

Daxton gave an approving nod. "That gives us an advantage—for now. But once you act, they'll know you're here. We need to be ready."

Ayralina's mind worked quickly, analyzing the paths before her. Taking a deep breath, she rose to her feet, her resolve solidifying like steel. "First, we save the prince," she declared. "Then, we deal with the poison and demons. One step at a time."

Each day, Ayralina visited the prince, carefully channeling small bursts of Phoenix fire into his frail body, trying to keep him warm—trying to keep him alive. But despite her efforts, his condition barely improved. The slow progress gnawed at her, and frustration crept in like a shadow.

She had done everything she could think of.

Yet nothing was working.

One evening, as she sat with Queen Izzy, exhaustion weighing on her, she finally spoke her fears aloud.

"I'm struggling," Ayralina admitted, rubbing her temples. "It's been a week already, and there's still no real improvement." She let out a slow, shaky breath. "He's so small, and my Phoenix fire is too potent. No matter how much I try to control it, I fear I'm doing more harm than good."

Izzy frowned, thoughtful. Her sharp mind is already working through the problem.

"Phoenix fire is powerful, but brute strength isn't always the answer." Her voice was calm and contemplative. "Sometimes, a gentler approach is needed." She hesitated momentarily before suggesting, "What about the Fire Orchid?"

Ayralina froze.

"The Fire Orchid?" she echoed, barely above a whisper.

Izzy nodded. "It's connected to your energy, and its healing properties are unparalleled. Perhaps it could help."

Ayralina's fingers curled into fists in her lap.

The Fire Orchid was recently entrusted to her by Aunt Flora before she died. She had guarded it fiercely, keeping its existence hidden, knowing exactly what would happen if the demons ever discovered it.

She had already absorbed the Phoenix Core, meaning the Orchid was no longer necessary for her own survival.

But the demons could still use it to break the seal on the scroll.

If they found out it was here, they would stop at nothing to seize it.

She had always intended to return it to the Phoenix Realm to keep it safe.

But now...

Now, she was faced with an impossible choice.

If she used the Orchid, her location would be exposed.

The kingdom would be in danger.

But if she didn't...

The prince could die.

Her heart pounded. What should I do?

Izzy studied her in silence, sensing the war raging inside her. After a moment, she rose to her feet.

"Let us know what you decide," she said gently. "I'll inform the others to wait on your response."

And with that, she left Ayralina alone with her thoughts.

A soft knock echoed at her door the next evening. Ayralina rose, already knowing who it was before she even reached for the handle.

As expected, Simon stood there, his posture rigid, his expression unreadable. Behind him, Izzy and Daxton loomed, their eyes sharp even in the dim candlelight.

Saber and Ellie lounged lazily by the fireplace, flicking their tails and playfully swatting at each other. The peaceful moment starkly contrasted the tension hanging heavy in the air.

Simon stepped inside, closing the door behind him with a quiet click.

Ayralina gestured to the table, and they all gathered around. The flickering candlelight cast elongated shadows against the walls, their presence grounding her in the moment.

She didn't waste time. "Any updates?"

Simon exhaled sharply, running a hand through his tousled hair. "Nothing concrete yet," he admitted, his voice tight with frustration. "The concubine, Saffayah, is careful. Too careful. She covers her tracks so well that it's almost unnatural."

Ayralina's brow furrowed. "You think she's involved?"

Simon leaned forward slightly. "I don't have proof yet, but there's something suspicious. Her personal maid frequently leaves the palace." His jaw tensed. "We've tailed her multiple times, but every time, she slips away. Either she's incredibly skilled, or she's something else entirely."

Ayralina's gaze sharpened. "You think she's a demon?"

Simon nodded slowly. "It's a strong possibility. No ordinary human can evade trained trackers so consistently."

Izzy exchanged a glance with Daxton. "A demon hiding in plain sight?" she mused. "It wouldn't be the first time."

Ayralina tapped a finger against the table, her mind already spinning through strategies. "I'll find an opportunity to approach her here in the palace. If she's hiding something, I'll sense it."

She paused, her expression hardening. "In the meantime, shift your focus to the frost demon. Track its movements, its patterns—anything we can use. If we can't find it directly, we'll set a trap."

Simon nodded. "Understood. I'll put our best on it."

Ayralina hesitated only a moment before speaking again, her voice lower, heavier. "There's one more thing."

Simon tilted his head, sensing the shift in tone.

"I plan to use the Heart's Flame Orchid to save the prince. Two nights from now."

Simon's eyes widened slightly, but he didn't interrupt.

"I'll need protection while I perform the ritual," she continued. "The demons are after me because of the Orchid. If they realize it's here, they'll come fast, with all the forces they could muster, to stop us from using it."

Simon's jaw tightened, the weight of her words settling heavily between them.

"You'll have it," he said without hesitation. "I'll make sure no one gets through."

Ayralina met his gaze. No hesitation. No doubt.

Ayralina offered a small, approving nod, but instead of moving on, she studied Simon briefly before speaking again. "Before I do this, I must help you become stronger."

Simon's brows furrowed slightly. "Stronger? What do you mean?"

"You probably haven't fully realized it yet," Ayralina stated, "but you are different from normal humans. You're faster, stronger, and sometimes you sense things before they happen, right?"

Simon stiffened. He had experienced these things his entire life but never questioned them deeply. They had always just been a part of him. "Yes," he admitted. "That's been true for as long as I can remember. How did you know this?"

Ayralina's expression softened slightly, but something weighted in her gaze spoke of a long-kept secret. "Because when I first met you, I recognized you right away. That's why I chose to trust you from the very beginning."

Simon frowned. "Recognized me? What do you mean?"

Ayralina took a slow breath before revealing the truth. "Because there is a dragon scale inside you. It has assimilated with you, bonding with your very essence."

Simon's breath caught, confusion and disbelief flickering in his eyes. "A dragon scale...?" He turned and looked at Izzy and Daxton, they also nodded in agreement. "We also recognize this, that's why we also trusted you right away."

A heavy silence filled the room. The weight of her words pressed down on Simon, his mind racing to comprehend what she was saying. Dragons were beings of legend, creatures of immense power. And yet, one of them had left something inside him? Something that had shaped his very being?

"And not just any dragon scale. It came from Silvaris—the Moon Frost Dragon. My husband. For a dragon scale to choose a human is a sign of worthiness," Ayralina continued. "It means you were deemed worthy of its noble lineage. It bestowed upon you some of its abilities. That speed, that strength, those instincts—you've been carrying a fragment of Silvaris's power all along."

Simon swallowed, trying to steady himself. "Then... Why have I never known it? Why now?"

Ayralina's eyes darkened slightly. "Because while the scale grants you power, you are still human. Your body can only absorb so much before it consumes you. If left unchecked, the energy will eventually overwhelm you. That is why I must help you fully assimilate with it—to ensure it doesn't harm you."

Simon clenched his fists. He had always been aware of his abilities, but the idea that they stemmed from something so ancient and powerful unsettled him. Yet, there was no fear, only a burning curiosity, a hunger to understand.

"And once I do?" he asked.

"Once you fully absorb its power," Ayralina said, "you will become stronger. And you will be able to cultivate in the way of the dragon. But I can only guide you so far. Your true teacher will be Silvaris himself—once he wakes."

Simon's mind reeled at the implications, but deep down, something inside him already knew she was right. He had always felt like he didn't quite belong, like something was inside him waiting to awaken.

Shocked but resolute, he met Ayralina's gaze and nodded. "What do I need to do?"

Ayralina's lips curved into a small smile. "Come with me," she said. "We will begin now."

Leaving Simon to absorb the Dragon Scale, Ayralina cast a glance at Izzy and Daxton. Their sharp eyes reflected the firelight as they stood guard while Saber and Ellie continued their lazy play by the hearth, oblivious to the storm brewing beyond these walls.

Chapter 21

THE CORRIDOR OUTSIDE THE prince's chamber was dimly lit, the flickering torches casting long, restless shadows across the stone walls. The faint scent of burning oil mixed with the sterile tang of medicinal herbs seeped through the heavy wooden doors. Ayralina approached silently, her steps purposeful, her heart steady despite the storm of anticipation brewing beneath the surface.

Simon waited for her just outside the chamber, his stance rigid, a soldier's discipline etched into every line of his posture. His sharp eyes met hers as she approached, and for a brief moment, the weight of what they were about to do hung heavily between them.

"Is everyone prepared?" Ayralina asked quietly, her voice calm but carrying the unmistakable edge of authority.

Simon gave a firm nod. "Yes. My trusted guards are patrolling the perimeter," he replied, his tone firm. "They've been instructed to remain alert for even the slightest disturbance. Izzy and Daxton will be stationed right outside this door. If you need us, we'll be able to provide support immediately. No hesitation, no delay."

"And inside Saber and Ellie will be with you," Simon continued. "They're positioned to stay by your side the entire time. All of them—my guards, Izzy, Daxton, Saber, and Ellie—have been given strict orders: they are not to leave their positions, no matter what happens. No distractions, no deviations. Even if the walls are falling down around us, they hold their ground."

Ayralina gave a slight nod, absorbing his words. The layers of protection were meticulously planned, but she knew no plans were ever foolproof . Still, it was enough. She could feel the tension in the air and the readiness of the warriors who stood for her and the prince.

"You'll be able to treat the prince in peace," Simon added, his voice softening just slightly, as if offering not just assurance, but a thread of comfort. "We've got you covered."

Ayralina's gaze lingered on him for a heartbeat longer, appreciating his competence and unwavering loyalty. She then took a deep breath, steadying herself. "Good," she said, her voice now resolute. "Because once I start, I can't afford any interruptions. The demons will sense the orchid's power when I unleash it. They will come."

Simon's jaw clenched slightly, but he gave another firm nod. "Let them."

Without another word, Ayralina turned toward the heavy doors of the prince's chamber. Saber and Ellie silently padded in after her, their eyes glowing faintly in the dim light, ever watchful, ever ready. Izzy and Daxton took their positions outside, their bodies tense, muscles coiled like springs as they stood like sentinel.

As the doors closed behind her with a soft final thud, Ayralina felt the shift in the air—the weight pressing down. This wasn't just about saving the prince. It was about holding the fragile line between life and death, between light and the encroaching darkness.

She approached the frail infant lying on the ornate bed, his shallow breaths barely disturbing the silken sheets.

Bringing the Fire Orchid out in the prince's room, she watched as the delicate petals began to glow the moment they neared the child. The flower reacted as though it recognized the frost poison within him.

Intrigued, Ayralina placed the orchid beside the prince, and to her astonishment, it began to draw out the poison slowly, gently, and without the intensity of her Phoenix fire.

"It's working," she whispered, hope flickering in her heart.

While the orchid's healing powers had been undeniable, its effect was slow. The prince had begun to show signs of improvement—his breathing steadied, and the bluish tint of his lips had faded—but at this rate, it would take months, maybe even years, to completely rid his body of the frost poison.

After days of contemplation and sleepless nights, Ayralina made this bold decision that carried immense risk but offered the only real chance of saving the prince. She would integrate the Fire Orchid directly into his heart. It was a dangerous procedure, something never attempted before, but she knew that without it, the healing process would be too slow. The frost poison would continue threatening his life, and time was not on their side.

With unwavering resolve, she set to work. The process required more than just her Phoenix energy—it needed a connection, a binding force between the orchid and the prince. To achieve this, she carefully extracted a single drop of blood from his fragile heart, cradling it in her trembling hands. The deep crimson drop pulsed with his life essence, weak yet persistent.

Next, she summoned a seed of flame from her Sunflame, the purest and most potent fire within her. The tiny ember floated above her palm, radiating warmth and power, a fragment of the divine energy that coursed through her veins. With painstaking care, she then placed the blood onto the orchid's petals, watching as the delicate flower absorbed it eagerly. The golden veins of the plant pulsed, reacting to the prince's essence as if recognizing him, as if accepting him as its own.

Then, with a steady breath, Ayralina guided the Sunflame's ember into the orchid, merging it with the flower's essence. The glow flared briefly, an intense burst of golden-red light, before settling into a steady shimmer. The orchid changed before her eyes—its energy now intertwined with both the prince's blood and her Phoenix fire.

The scent of the Heart's Flame Orchid filled the room like a soft, golden mist, rich and intoxicating. Its fragrance was unlike anything earthly—sweet yet fierce, carrying an undercurrent of warmth that pulsed with life itself. As Ayralina channeled its energy into the prince, the orchid's magic began to seep beyond the chamber walls, drifting out into the dimly lit hallways like an invisible beacon.

Outside the room, Simon and the guards caught the faint, drifting tendrils of its aroma. The effect was immediate. A surge of vitality rushed through Simon's veins, sharpening his senses and quickening his pulse. His fatigue from long hours of vigilance vanished instantly, replaced by an almost overwhelming sense of clarity and strength. Even Izzy and Daxton, standing like statues beside the door, straightened slightly, their sharp eyes glowing faintly in the dim torchlight.

Simon inhaled deeply, feeling the energy course through him. "Is this the power of the orchid?" he muttered, glancing at Izzy. "No wonder the demons want it so badly."

Izzy's golden eyes flickered toward him, her voice low and tense. "We have to be vigilant. This scent isn't just invigorating—it's a siren's call. It will draw them here. The demons will attack soon."

Simon's hand instinctively went to the hilt of his sword, his muscles coiling with readiness. The corridor was too quiet, and the air was too still.

Then, out of the corner of his eye, he saw her—the concubine's maid, emerging from the shadows like a viper poised to strike. Her face was twisted with unnatural hunger, her eyes no longer human but glowing crimson with feral desire. She moved with jerky, frantic motions, as if fighting an invisible force pulling her toward the orchid. But she wasn't alone.

Behind her, shadows shifted and morphed, revealing the dark, twisted forms of demons—their grotesque features flickering in and out of view as they slipped through the veil between realms. Their black claws gleamed under the torchlight, and their mouths stretched into unnatural grins, sharp teeth glinting like shards of glass.

Simon didn't hesitate. "Archers, ready!" he barked, drawing his blade in one fluid motion as the demons surged forward like a tidal wave of darkness. "Fire!"

The courtyard erupted into chaos. The guards, invigorated by the orchid's lingering power, fought with renewed ferocity, after the volleys of arrows they charged forward. Their swords clashing against the demons' dark, sinewy forms. But it was Izzy and Daxton who truly transformed the battlefield.

With a deafening roar, Izzy launched into the fray, her body igniting in a blaze of heavenly flames—brilliant gold and fierce white, the fire crackling with divine energy. The flames didn't burn like ordinary fire; they shimmered with an ethereal brilliance, scorching through demonic flesh as though it were paper.

Right beside her, Daxton followed, his massive form engulfed in the same radiant blaze, his claws glowing white-hot. Every swipe of his powerful paws sent arcs of flame slicing through the darkness, leaving trails of ash and scorched stone in their wake. The ground trembled under their combined fury, their roars mingling with the screams of the demons as they were reduced to nothing more than blackened remnants.

Simon's blade met the first demon with a sickening crunch, black ichor spraying as he twisted and drove the steel deeper. The creature let out a gurgled snarl before collapsing into dust, but Simon was already moving—faster than he ever had before.

Something was different.

And then it hit him.

The Moon Frost Dragon's power surged through his veins, coiling beneath his skin like a beast finally roused from its slumber.

This was the first time he had fought since his powers had awakened, and the difference was staggering. Energy crackled inside him, raw and untamed, filling every muscle with an intoxicating strength.

He felt reinvigorated. Stronger than ever.

His movements were sharper, faster—almost effortless, like the battle itself was bending to his will.

The weight of his blade felt lighter, and his reflexes heightened to an unnatural degree. He anticipated every strike before it came, dodging with precision and countering with devastating force. The demons fell before him, their attacks rendered useless against his newfound power.

He was no longer just a soldier in battle.

He was a force of destruction.

But through the chaos, his eyes remained locked on the maid.

She was the key.

Her frantic, erratic movements betrayed her lack of control—she had power, yes, but she couldn't control it. The demonic corruption inside her was tearing her apart, making her wild and reckless.

Simon cut through the battlefield, slashing through anything that stood between him and his target. The demons came at him, but it didn't matter. His sword became a blur, his enhanced reflexes letting him anticipate every move before it happened. He dodged with inhuman speed, struck with purpose—every kill was effortless, instinctual.

And finally, he cornered her.

The maid stood at the edge of the courtyard, her crimson eyes glowing with barely restrained madness. She bared her teeth, snarling like a caged animal.

Then she lunged, faster than any human should have been.

Claws aimed for his throat.

But Simon was faster.

He sidestepped smoothly, twisting at the last second. As she sailed past him, he brought the hilt of his sword crashing down against her temple.

A sickening crack.

The force sent her sprawling onto the bloodstained ground, dazed but alive.

Simon didn't hesitate.

Before she could recover, he pressed the flat of his blade against her throat.

She froze, her breath ragged, her body twitching with residual energy.

"Not today," Simon growled, then with the hilt of his sword he knocked her out.

Around them, the last of the demons fell, their bodies dissolving into black ash that scattered like cursed dust across the courtyard stones.

Izzy and Daxton stood over the remnants of their kills, heaving, their heavenly flames flickering like dying embers. But their eyes—their eyes still burned with fury.

The battlefield was silent now, except for the sound of their heavy breathing.

Simon took a deep breath, the power still thrumming through his veins.

Simon picked up the maid, she was still out cold "I've got her," he said, casting a sharp glance toward the prince's chamber where the faint, steady glow of the Heart's Flame Orchid still pulsed. His jaw was clenched, the adrenaline from the battle still surging through him.

"Take her to the dungeon," he ordered, as he tossed her to his men. "Make sure she's under the highest surveillance. I want two guards stationed at her cell around the clock—no one goes in or out without my permission."

The guards moved swiftly, gripping the maid's arms as she came through and began to hiss and thrashed, though her resistance was feeble now. Simon didn't miss the faint, dark aura that still clung to her, like shadows refusing to let go.

"I'll deal with her personally," Simon added, his eyes narrowing as he watched the guards drag her away. "Once Ayralina is done."

For three days, she labored tirelessly, oblivious to the battle outside, pouring every ounce of her strength into ensuring the orchid would take root within him. The task had been grueling, requiring control beyond anything she had ever attempted. Every pulse of energy, every careful movement, had been executed with the knowledge that even the slightest misstep could end his life.

Sweat dripped from her brow as she guided the orchid's essence into the prince's heart, coaxing it to bond with him, to become a part of him. His body, weak as it was, instinctively resisted at first. But the orchid, having absorbed his blood, recognized him—and accepted him. It had responded to his essence, sinking into his heart's core without force or rejection. The flower's glow pulsed one final time, then softened, fading as it fully fused with him.

And then, a miracle began.

The prince's frail, ice-kissed skin warmed, his tiny fingers curling with newfound strength. His once-labored breaths had evened into a steady, strong rhythm. Color returned to his cheeks, a healthy flush that had never been there before. His small chest, once barely rising, had lifted with ease, his breathing no longer a struggle but a natural, effortless motion.

Ayralina watched in awe, her exhaustion momentarily forgotten as the realization sank in—he was healing. The Fire Orchid had truly become a part of him, offering continuous protection and restoration. For the first time, he looked like a child full of life, not a fragile soul teetering on the edge of death. She had done it; she had finally succeeded.

The dungeon beneath the palace was cold and damp, the flickering torchlight casting jagged shadows across the stone walls. The air smelled of mildew, rusted iron, and the faint, lingering stench of old blood—a place designed to strip away pretense and dignity.

Simon descended the narrow stone steps, his boots echoing with each heavy step. His face was set in stone, jaw clenched, eyes sharp with the same determination that had carried him through countless battles. This was different, though. This wasn't a fight with blades—it was a battle of wills.

Two guards stood outside the reinforced cell door, their postures tense. They stiffened as Simon approached, stepping aside without a word. The door creaked open with a grating groan, revealing the prisoner inside—a woman hunched in the corner, her wrists bound in iron shackles etched with faint runes to suppress any lingering dark influence.

Another two guards were inside, one with a whip in his hand, panting and getting ready to strike again.

The concubine's maid no longer resembled the composed servant she had pretended to be. Her face was gaunt, her skin pale, and her crimson eyes burned with both defiance and something darker—something broken. She looked up as Simon entered, a twisted smile curling at the corners of her cracked lips.

"You've come out to play too?" she rasped, her voice raw and ragged.

Simon stepped into the dimly lit cell, closing the door behind him with a quiet click. The scent of damp stone and blood lingered in the air.

"That's enough. You can take a break for now," he dismissed the others without sparing them a glance.

As the guards left, he lowered himself onto the lone chair across from her, saying nothing. He simply watched.

The silence stretched between them, heavy, suffocating.

Then, without warning, he grabbed her jaw, his grip unyielding as he forced her to meet his gaze. His voice was low, dangerous.

"You're going to tell me everything—now. Or I'll make sure your suffering outlasts your usefulness."

She met his stare, her lips curling into a smirk, but the defiance didn't quite reach her eyes. It flickered—hesitation, doubt. She saw it in him. This wasn't a bluff. Simon would follow through on every unspoken threat.

For a moment, she held her silence. But exhaustion crept in, weaving through her bones, dragging her down. Fear gnawed at the edges of her mind. And somewhere beneath it all, maybe even a twisted kind of relief.

The truth had festered inside her for too long.

"What can you give me if I tell you?" she sneered, but her voice wavered.

Simon's expression remained unreadable. "A quick death," he said coldly. "That's the best you deserve. Otherwise, I'll let the whole kingdom hear your confession and hand you over to the demons. Then, you'll beg for that quick death."

He leaned in slightly. "What will it be?"

She swallowed hard. "They promised me power," she whispered, voice trembling. "The demons. They came to me when I was nothing—just a servant. Invisible. Forgotten."

Her eyes flickered to the cold stone floor, as if the weight of her past clawed at her throat.

"I was one of the captives who came into contact with the broken scroll. They call it the Phoenix Scroll."

Simon's grip on her jaw tightened before he finally let go, though his gaze never softened.

She shuddered, as if the memory itself was a wound still bleeding. "The power in that scroll—" her voice cracked, "—it tore me apart from the inside. It wasn't a gift. It was a curse. It burned me, twisted me, shattered my mind and body. I was never whole again."

Simon's jaw clenched. "And the demons saved you?"

A bitter laugh rasped from her throat. "Saved me?" She shook her head. "No. But they made the pain stop. For a price."

Her lips twisted into a ghost of a smile; one filled with something close to madness. "They promised more power. Freedom from the torment. All I had to do was serve."

Simon's fists curled, but his voice remained steady. "What did you do?"

A flicker of twisted pride glinted in her eyes. "Everything they asked."

She exhaled, slow and deliberate.

"I lured the Queen out, made sure she was vulnerable so the Frost Demon could find her. I opened the palace gates, let that creature roam freely in our kingdom." Her smile widened, her voice slipping into something unhinged. "All to draw her out—to lure Ayralina."

Simon's heart pounded, but his expression remained impassive.

"Why Ayralina?"

Her eyes darkened, her smirk fading into something colder. "You don't know, do you?" she whispered.

Then, a chuckle. "She is the Phoenix of royal blood."

The words sent a ripple of unease through the air.

"The demons fear her," she continued. "But it's more than fear. It's an obsession. Her power is tied to the scroll, to something bigger. A legacy. That's all I know."

A slow breath, then a whisper, barely audible—"Something about a golden child."

Simon's grip tightened on the arms of his chair, but he waited.

She hesitated, then her expression twisted, a mixture of agony and satisfaction. "There's more... forces gathering in the North. Armies of dark creatures—things worse than demons. The Frost Demon was just the beginning."

A violent cough tore from her chest, blood splattering onto the cold floor.

Simon leaned in, voice ice-cold. "What else? How many are working with you in the palace? Who else is involved?"

His voice turned razor-sharp. "Why the Orchid?"

For the first time, her expression faltered. Her voice dropped to a reverent whisper.

"The Heart's Flame Orchid... it's the key to unlocking the Phoenix Scroll."

She blinked slowly, as if caught in a trance. "But its power... it was too beautiful. I felt it. I needed it. It called to me, stronger than the demons' promises. That's why I came out of hiding. The Orchid's power is pure. Unlike the scroll. Unlike the demons. But I still wanted it all the same."

She lifted her gaze to Simon, something almost victorious in her smile.

"It doesn't matter. The North is rising. You can't stop what's coming."

Then—

A sharp whistle.

Before Simon could react, a dart shot through a narrow opening in the cell.

It buried deep in her throat.

A strangled gasp. Blood spilled from her lips. Her eyes, wide with shock, darted to Simon before her life drained from them entirely.

Simon whirled, drawing his blade. "Find the assassin—now!"

His men stormed the corridors, but he already knew.

It was too late.

As swiftly as the dart had come, the assassin had vanished—without a trace.

Chapter 22

AYRALINA CALLED FOR AN audience with the King. Gathering her people the group met up with King Cedrick and his royal advisors in the King's royal study. The study was a grand and intimate room. Lined with towering bookshelves stretching from floor to ceiling. The warm glow of candlelight flickering against the dark wooden walls. Casting shadows of what might seem to be images of stories of old, or possibly stories to come. She glanced from face to face as she prepared her thoughts. The air was thick with anticipation as she took a steady breath searching for the right words.

Over the past few days, they had all witnessed her tireless efforts—how she had fought relentlessly to save the Queen, pouring her energy into purging the cold poison, and how she had pushed herself beyond exhaustion to heal the prince, taking a risk no one else would dare to attempt. They witnessed her dedication first-hand. Her unwavering and willingness to sacrifice herself for the good of the kingdom, and for that, she had earned their respect—not just as a healer, but as a warrior and as a protector. They now looked at her as one of their own. That respect also extended to her friends, those who stood and fought alongside her.

"The Fire Orchid is now a part of him," she finally said, as she addressed all of those in the room. "It will continue to heal him from within, purging any remaining frost poison. It will continue to protect him for the remainder of his days, making him immune to all poisons and diseases."

"This must be kept a secret. If the demons find out, they will stop at nothing to reach him and extract the orchid. If it is removed before the prince is fully healed, his life will be in danger."

King Cedrick, visibly moved, clenched his fists at his sides, his expression a mixture of relief and overwhelming gratitude. His voice trembled as he spoke. "You've saved my son's life."

Ayralina nodded and continued. Her gaze swept across the gathered faces, her tone measured. "As the prince grows, the orchid's power will evolve with him. It will imbue him with a fire affinity, granting him the ability to wield fire as I do. But this gift is also a responsibility. His connection to the energy will make him stronger, more powerful, but it will also require guidance. I will leave a scroll for him to train with as he gets older. I will return someday—not just to retrieve the orchid, but also to help him understand and learn to control his abilities."

Simon stepped forward then, his expression resolute. "We'll ensure he's protected until that time comes. He'll be ready."

"Once the prince is of age to learn Simon, I want you to take him on as your apprentice." Ayralina met his gaze and offered a faint smile.

Simon shocked but nodded, he understood what Ayralina was asking of him.

"For now, his immediate danger has passed," she continued, her voice steady and confident. She exhaled slowly before continuing, "I've also developed a cure for everyone affected by the cold poison. It wasn't easy, but the method is now clear."

King Cedrick's eyes widened, his breath catching in his throat. "You mean to say... you can save the entire kingdom?"

Ayralina nodded solemnly. "Yes, but I can't do it alone. Please gather all your fire healers and those trained in energy work. Over the next few days, I will train them in the method to administer the antidote. Together, we can administer the cure to everyone who needs it."

"I'll see to it immediately," Simon said as he stood up. "We'll gather healers from every corner of the kingdom if we must."

"Pass this duty on to someone you trust who is capable," Ayralina replied firmly, her gaze locking with Simon's. "I need you here for the next phase of our planning. Aside from the cure, we must eliminate the root cause as well—we're going after the Frost Demon."

"Yes," Simon replied with a nod, his expression darkening. "Before we proceed, there's something you all need to know."

The room grew quiet as Simon stepped forward, his voice low and steady, though a sharp edge of tension lingered beneath his calm exterior. "During the interrogation of the concubine's maid, she confessed to everything. She was incited by demons, lured with promises of power and riches. But that wasn't the worst of it."

Ayralina and the King listened intently, their faces growing more grave with each word.

"She was one of the captives who had come into contact with the broken Phoenix scroll, of legend" Simon continued. "The power from the scroll had tortured her, twisted her mind and body. For years, she suffered under its influence until the demons found her. They offered her relief... in exchange for her loyalty. She's been a spy for them ever since."

Ayralina's jaw clenched slightly, but remained silent, letting Simon finish.

"She was the one who lured Queen Anaya out, making her vulnerable to the frost demon's attack. She also allowed the frost demon to roam freely within the kingdom's borders—all to lure you out, Ayralina."

The weight of his words settled heavily over the room, the implications clear. This wasn't just about the prince's illness. It was a calculated plan, part of something much larger.

Simon's eyes darkened further. "And there's more. She spoke of forces gathering in the North—armies and creatures even worse than the demons we've faced. The frost demon was just the beginning. Before I could get more from her, she was silenced, and the assassin vanished into thin air."

King Cedrick's face paled, his hand trembling as he reached out and clasped Ayralina's hands. His voice wavered with emotion, heavy with both gratitude and fear. "You've already done more than I could have hoped for. To repay this debt we will protect you."

Ayralina shook her head gently, her expression softening. "There is no need for that. If I have the power to help, it's my duty to do so."

She hesitated momentarily, then added, her tone growing serious, "But there is one thing I must ask."

"Anything," King Cedrick replied without hesitation.

"My identity and my connection to you must remain a secret," Ayralina said firmly. "The demons are searching for me. If word spreads, it will put everyone, including the prince and your kingdom, at greater risk."

The King nodded solemnly. "You have my word. Your secret will be protected." His gaze had hardened as he turned to his advisers, his voice carrying the weight of absolute authority. "Anyone in this room who exposes this secret will be executed, along with their entire family, without pardon." His tone firmed, leaving no room for doubt.

Before the gravity of his words could fully settle, Ayralina stepped forward, shaking her head slightly. "Thank you, Your Majesty, but death is too severe," she l said, her voice steady yet resolute. "A sworn oath of loyalty is more than enough. Let them vow their silence, and if anyone breaks that oath, let them face the consequences of their own dishonor."

The room fell into a tense silence as King Cedrick studied her, his expression unreadable. Then, after a moment, he gave a slow nod.

"Very well," he said. "Everyone here will swear an oath of secrecy. If that oath is broken, the betrayer will suffer eternal burning of their soul, never finding relief from the pain until death."

One by one, the gathered nobles and advisers placed their hands over their hearts, bowing their heads as they swore their silence. Ayralina watched them closely, searching for sincerity in their eyes. Only when the last vow had been spoken did she allow herself to breathe a little easier.

Over the next few hours, Ayralina worked tirelessly alongside Simon and the advisers, pouring over every piece of intelligence they had on the Frost Demons. Maps were spread across the massive war table, marked with sightings and past attacks, while reports from scouts and survivors were read and analyzed.

"We need to find their stronghold," Simon muttered, tracing a finger over a mountain range where the demons were last spotted. "They don't just appear out of nowhere—there must be a pattern to their movements."

Ayralina nodded, her mind racing. "It's not just about finding them. We need to flush them out, force them into a position where they have no choice but to face us on our terms."

While they awaited the gathering of the kingdom's healers, they couldn't afford to be idle. The Frost Demon had to be dealt with before more lives were lost, and before it could strike again. If they allowed it to fester in the shadows, no cure would be enough to stop the devastation it could bring.

Ayralina began instructing the healers in the intricate process of creating and administering the cure. She demonstrated how to combine their fire energy with the ingredients she had gathered, forming a restorative flame that could purge the frost poison from a person's body without harming them.

The healers, though initially hesitant, quickly gained confidence under her guidance. By the end of the day, the first wave of treatments had already begun, and the effects were undeniable. Those afflicted by the poison began to recover, their color returning, their strength slowly rebuilding.

As Ayralina watched the healers work, a sense of fulfillment washed over her. Though the road ahead was still uncertain, the kingdom was healing. She allowed herself a brief moment of rest, knowing that her work was far from over. The prince's future, the threat of the demons, and the search for the Ice Crystal Heart still loomed ahead. But for now, she had given the people a fighting chance.

Meanwhile, Simon and the three guards had been busy executing their plans. During one of their patrols, they were ambushed by a group of bandits. The guards, eager to prove themselves, rushed into the fight without coordination. Simon had to step in repeatedly, saving them from their own recklessness.

"Idiots," he muttered after the skirmish, shaking his head. "You're lucky you're alive."

Despite his gruff words, the guards began to respect Simon's leadership. After several more battles—and plenty of drinks—they finally accepted him as their leader. Their camaraderie deepened as they investigated the attack on the Queen, following a trail of clues that led them to the Frost Demon.

"We've fought this demon before," one guard admitted. "But he's slippery and has backups. Every time we corner him, he escapes."

Simon sighed, crossing his arms. "He escapes because you're too busy showing off instead of working together. If you want to catch him, you need to listen to me."

Their next encounter with the Frost Demon proved Simon right.

This time, they fought as a unit—coordinated and relentless. Their teamwork allowed them to wound the creature severely, its icy blood staining the ground.

But before they could deliver the final blow, it called for reinforcements. Again.

Only this time, its comrade was stronger, faster, and smarter, forcing them to retreat and let the demons escape.

But Simon refused to let it slip away.

Determined, he and the guards tracked the demon through treacherous terrain, navigating deep ravines and frozen cliffs until they reached its hidden lair.

There, concealed in the shadows, they listened.

The demon's rasping voice cut through the silence; its tone laced with desperation.

"Thank you for saving me, my lord. I wouldn't have escaped without you. To repay you, I bring news about Ayralina."

Simon's muscles tensed, his grip tightening around his sword.

A second voice—low and growling with frustration—responded.

"We're already behind schedule. You're fighting over Ayralina has cost us precious time. She is no longer your concern. If you don't make it to the assault in time, once this is over, there won't be a place in this world you can hide."

A third voice—cold, commanding, and final—cut through the conversation.

"Then stop wasting time. The others are gathering in the north. The attack against the Polar Bear Army cannot wait any longer."

Simon's jaw tightened as he exchanged a grim look with the guards.

The demons were leaving the kingdom.

They were regrouping in the north.

And their attack was imminent.

Simon turned to his men, his voice low but urgent. "The demons are pulling out. But Ayralina's got bigger problems—she needs to know they're on the move."

Without hesitation, they rode hard back to the city, reporting everything to Ayralina.

Her expression darkened, golden eyes burning with urgency as she processed the news.

"We need to finish this battle quickly," she said, her voice sharp with resolve. "The Polar Bear King will need reinforcements—and I intend to be there to provide them."

There was no time to waste.

Gathering their forces, Ayralina and Simon led the troops into the mountains, tracking the Frost Demons to their stronghold.

The journey was brutal—jagged cliffs, cutting winds, ambushes waiting at every turn. Their endurance was tested, their numbers threatened.

But they pressed on.

And with every victory, their forces grew stronger.

The final battle was coming—and they would be ready.

At last, under the cover of night, they launched their final assault. The battle was fierce, ice and fire clashing as magic and steel tore through the battlefield. Simon and the guards fought with precision, no longer reckless but a well-honed unit. Ayralina, wielding her Phoenix flame, faced the Frost Demon head-on, her power burning through its icy defenses.

After an intense struggle, they finally subdued the demons, capturing them before they could escape again. They secured the stronghold and Simon remained on guard. "This is only the beginning, we need to reinforce our allies in the north," he warned. "We need to find out who—if anyone—is pulling the strings behind this attack."

Ayralina nodded, her gaze sharp and resolute.

Simon and the guards approached King Cedrick, their resolve clear. "Your Majesty," Simon said, "we believe the threat is not fully eliminated. We'd like to follow Ayralina to the north and ensure the demon is dealt with permanently. She saved the prince, and we owe her our lives. Let us protect her."

The King considered their request carefully before nodding. "Very well. You have my permission to go. Do what you must and protect the kingdom."

With the King's blessing, Simon and the guards prepared to accompany Ayralina on her journey north.

Chapter 23

AYRALINA LEAPED FROM ROCK to rock, the cubs sprinting beside her, their movements fluid and precise as if they were one with the rugged terrain. She glanced over her shoulder and was surprised to see Simon and the three guards keeping up with her relentless pace. They moved with determination, their endurance far exceeding her expectations. Their focus was unwavering, and their steps were confident despite the brutal conditions.

Years of rigorous training showed in every step they took. No matter what challenges Ayralina threw at them, tackled each without complaint, completing every task with efficiency, not wasting time or resources.

Ahead, Daxton scouted for signs of danger, his white fur blending into the snow-dusted landscape as he moved with the grace of a predator. Izzy stayed behind, keeping a protective eye on the group to ensure no one was left vulnerable to ambush.

The terrain was merciless—steep hills, jagged rocks, and dense forests that seemed to stretch endlessly into the horizon. They had been running since dawn, taking only brief ten-minute breaks to catch their breath. Ayralina wanted to ensure they didn't lose the demon's trail, but her pace was grueling, deliberate.

They're tougher than I thought, Ayralina mused, casting a glance at them. She had purposely chosen the quickest but most treacherous path north, hoping they would fall behind or give up entirely. To her, they were unnecessary baggage—an escort forced upon her by King Cedrick's insistence to protect her. But they hadn't complained once, despite the sweat dripping from their brows and the exhaustion evident in their movements. Now, she was beginning to reassess her opinion. Perhaps they were more capable than she had assumed.

By nightfall, they reached a clearing near a small stream, its crystal clear waters reflecting the moonlight. The air was crisp, and the scent of pine lingered around them. Ayralina stopped abruptly and turned to face the group.

"We've covered a lot of ground today," she said, her voice commanding. "We'll camp here for the night. Use the stream to wash up and refill your flasks, but stay vigilant. We're getting closer to their territory, and I don't want any surprises."

The men nodded silently, their discipline evident even in their exhaustion. Ayralina, however, didn't miss the faint looks of relief that flickered across their faces as they began to set up camp. She smirked to herself. They're still human after all, she thought, a hint of amusement in her eyes.

As the campfires were lit and the group settled in, Ayralina found herself watching Simon. His movements were deliberate and efficient as he set up his tent, checked his weapons, and ensured his team was prepared for the night. There was something reassuring about his quiet competence, a steadiness that reminded her of the knights she had once fought beside.

Maybe the King hadn't been wrong to insist on their presence. Maybe, just maybe, they weren't the liability she had feared.

Izzy padded over to her, icy blue eyes glinting in the firelight. "They've earned your respect, haven't they?" she said quietly, a knowing look on her face.

Ayralina crossed her arms, leaning against a tree as she watched Simon and the guards work. "They're better than I gave them credit for," she admitted. "We'll see how they hold up tomorrow."

Izzy chuckled softly.

Ayralina rolled her eyes but couldn't suppress the small smile tugging at her lips. Tomorrow would bring new challenges, but for now, they had earned their rest.

That evening, a heavy silence hung over the camp, broken only by the occasional crackle of the fire and the howling wind that curled through the barren landscape. Snow shimmered under the moon's pale glow, casting a silver hue over the gathered tents and cloaked figures nestled against the biting cold.

Simon sat by the fire, staring into the flickering flames, his mind turning over thoughts he had kept to himself for some time. He had waited until everyone had settled in for the night, their soft breathing and shifting movements blending into the sounds of the wilderness. Now, with the fire's warmth between them and the night pressing close around them, he finally turned to Ayralina.

"I've been wondering something," he began, his voice quiet but firm. "I'm not sure if it's appropriate to ask... but it's about my teacher—Silvaris."

Ayralina, who had been gazing into the flames, turned her golden eyes to him, blinking in surprise.

"You said he was sleeping," Simon continued carefully. "Do you know when he will wake up?"

For a moment, Ayralina remained silent, caught off guard. Then her expression shifted—surprise melting into something softer, heavier. Sadness.

Simon immediately regretted asking. "I—I'm sorry," he said quickly. "You don't have to answer if I've crossed a line."

Ayralina's lips curved into a sad smile, her gaze distant. "No, you haven't crossed any lines," she assured him.

She let out a slow breath, watching how the cold carried it away like a ghost in the wind.

"When we fell to earth," she began, her voice laced with memories, "we were chased by demons. My husband, Silvaris, protected me, but in doing so, he was poisoned—infused with nether energy. It was designed to spread through him, to corrupt him from within."

She paused, eyes darkening as she relived the moment. "I had no choice but to put him into an enchanted sleep. It was the only way to stop the poison from invading him completely."

Simon remained still, listening intently, sensing the weight of her words.

"This," Ayralina gestured around them, "this journey to the Northern Realm... it is not just for the sake of the north. I also need to retrieve the Ice Crystal Heart. With it, Silvaris will finally be able to purge the poison from his body and wake once more."

Simon's breath was visible in the freezing air as he processed what she had just revealed.

"If he wakes without it," Ayralina continued, her voice quieter now, almost a whisper, "his life will be in danger."

A heavy silence settled between them. The fire crackled, sending embers drifting skyward. Simon looked down, his hands curling into fists over his knees.

"I see," he murmured. "Then we have no choice. We have to get the Ice Crystal Heart—no matter what."

Ayralina studied him for a moment before nodding. "Yes, I have to, this is my path after all. I am already grateful for all you have done, I can not take any unnecessary risk with your life"

A stubborn determination flickered in Simon's eyes as he met her gaze. "No, I will help you get it. Whatever it takes."

Ayralina smiled, and changed the subject. "Oh, did I mention? There are three others like you—Andre, Andrew, and Alex. They also carry a dragon scale within them."

Simon's eyes widened slightly in surprise. "Really?"

She nodded. "I'll introduce you to them soon. They are honorable, like you—driven and strong-willed. You'll find you have much in common."

They continued talking for a while, the conversation flowing easily as they shared thoughts and experiences. Eventually, Ayralina let out a soft sigh and rose to her feet.

"It's getting late," she said with a gentle smile. "Rest well, Simon. We have a long journey ahead."

Simon nodded. "Good night, Ayralina."

With that, she bid him good night and disappeared into the shadows of the camp, leaving Simon to ponder everything he had just learned.

Under the clear night sky, Ayralina sat on a boulder, staring up at the full moon. Its silvery glow bathed the forest in a soft light, and she felt its familiar pull, a bittersweet ache in her chest.

Izzy joined her, settling down quietly. The two were taking the first watch, allowing the others to rest after the grueling day.

"Do you think they'll last?" Ayralina asked, her gaze still fixed on the moon.

Izzy tilted her head, studying her friend. "Are you really asking about them, or is your mind elsewhere?"

Ayralina smiled faintly. "I miss him, Izzy. I always feel him closest to me when the moon is at its fullest."

Izzy nodded knowingly. "Of course, dear. He's a moon frost dragon after all. The full moon is when his power is strongest. He's probably reaching out to you right now."

"Do you really think so?" Ayralina's voice was tinged with uncertainty, hands reaching toward the moon.

"I know so," Izzy said confidently. "A love as powerful as yours can bridge even the greatest distances."

Ayralina sighed, her thoughts drifting to the past. "It's been so long, Izzy. Sometimes I feel scared I might not be able to make it. What if I fail?"

"You won't fail. You'll always find a way, because there is no other choice," Izzy reassured her firmly, her icy blue eyes steady and calm. "But first, you need to take care of yourself. I've noticed your powers fluctuating again. We should do another session tonight to stabilize you, just in case. How is the absorption process going?"

Ayralina sighed, the weight of her internal struggle etched on her face. "It's not," she admitted. "The Phoenix... She drained the entire volcano last time. She's stronger than me now. There isn't a single moment that I can let my guard down. If I do, she'll take over completely, and I'll be lost."

She paused, glancing down at her hands, faint embers sparking at her fingertips. "She's fueled me with incredible energy—I feel like I could fight for three days and nights without rest—but it's dangerous. If I burn out, I'm afraid she'll consume me entirely. She's not just powerful... she's relentless."

Izzy stepped closer and placed a comforting hand on Ayralina's shoulder. "Sweetie, don't apologize for relying on us. That's why we're here. You don't have to fight this alone. But you must finish absorbing her power. If you don't, she'll absorb you instead. And if that happens, we won't need the demons to destroy us—your Phoenix will do it herself."

Ayralina nodded slowly, her jaw tightening with resolve. "I know. I'll handle it. But right now, we have a battle to fight ."

Izzy shook her head gently. "No, Ayralina. You can't keep putting this off. If you let the Phoenix grow unchecked, catching the demon won't matter. Tonight, we'll do another session. You must let us help you keep her dormant."

That evening, as the group rested near their campfires, Ayralina retreated with Izzy and Daxton to a secluded spot away from the others. The moon hung low in the sky, casting a silvery glow over the clearing as Ayralina sat cross-legged on the cool grass. Izzy and Daxton positioned themselves around her in a protective circle, their heavenly tiger forms radiating calm, steady energy.

After what felt like an eternity, the last embers of the session flickered out. Ayralina slumped forward, exhausted but relieved. The Phoenix had been subdued—for now.

Izzy padded over to her, nuzzling her shoulder gently. "You did well," she said softly. "We've taken enough of the excess to keep her dormant for a while. But you'll need more sessions. This isn't over."

Ayralina nodded, her breathing still heavy. "Thank you," she whispered, her voice filled with gratitude. "I don't know what I'd do without you two."

"Don't thank us yet," Daxton said with a wry smile. "You've still got a demon to catch. And next time, let's hope we don't have to play babysitter to an overzealous Phoenix."

Ayralina managed a small laugh, the tension in her chest easing slightly. For now, she was stable, and for now, that was enough.

"Wake up," she said softly, rousing Simon. "Daxton got a whiff of something. It's time to move."

Daxton had already gone ahead to scout, and Ayralina wanted to ensure the group was ready to follow his lead. Despite the exhaustion from the previous day's relentless pace, Simon and the guards were quick to pack up, ready within minutes.

Impressive, Ayralina thought.

They moved cautiously, sticking to the shadows and hiding behind rocks and trees as Izzy picked up the fresh trail Daxton had left. The forest was eerily quiet, every sound amplified by the tension.

After an hour of tracking, the trail went cold. Ayralina frowned, her instincts prickling with unease. "We've lost him," she muttered, scanning the area.

Izzy stepped forward. "He's close, I can feel it. But something must've happened so he had to cover his tracks. Give me a moment to scout ahead."

Ayralina nodded and gestured for the others to stay hidden. Izzy moving silently into the forest, Ayralina's mind raced. The demons are cunning and they are led by humans, so she couldn't shake the feeling that they were walking into a trap.

As they waited for Izzy's return, Ayralina glanced at Simon and the guards. They were quietly observing their surroundings, their faces tense but determined.

"They have kept up better than I expected. You've done well training them," Ayralina admitted grudgingly.

Simon smirked. "We're not just palace decorations, you know. We're trained for situations like this."

One of the guards chuckled. "Speak for yourself, Simon. I feel like I'm about to collapse."

Ayralina allowed herself a small smile. "At least you're honest."

The camaraderie between Simon and the guards grew stronger with each passing day. Though they bickered and teased, their loyalty to one another—and to Ayralina—was undeniable.

Before long, Izzy returned, her expression grim. "He's doubled back and is heading toward the cliffs. If we move quickly, we can catch up to him before he reaches the caves."

Ayralina nodded, her resolve hardening. "Let's go."

Chapter 24

DAXTON LET OUT A guttural growl, straining against the chains binding his limbs. The fire suppression ring had drained his strength, reducing his powers to one-tenth of what it was. He hung upside down, strung from a tree like prey awaiting its demise. His once-pristine white fur was matted with blood, and the wounds across his body burned where the demons had struck him with enchanted ice blades.

This can't be how it ends, he thought bitterly, frustration and shame bubbling up inside him. I should have known it was a trap.

He replayed the events in his mind, the pieces falling together too late. While he was following the trail they had purposely left for him, the Demon Commander and its minions had feigned retreat, leaving just enough signs to stoke his suspicion and bait his pride. Broken branches, scattered tufts of fur, faint paw prints—all carefully staged to lead him deeper into the dense, shadow-choked forest.

They had used what appeared to be tiger cubs as bait, their pitiful cries echoing through the trees, tugging at his instincts. The scent had seemed real, the fear in their voices authentic. How could it not be? His heart had raced as he pursued the sounds, desperate to reach them before it was too late.

But it had been a lie.

The moment he stepped into the clearing, the trap was sprung. Hidden beneath the fallen leaves and dirt was a fire suppression ring—an enchanted boundary designed to suppress and neutralize any fire-based abilities. As soon as he crossed into its radius, a dull pulse rippled through the ground, severing his connection to his inner flame. The warmth that had always surged through his veins like a second heartbeat vanished in an instant, leaving him cold and vulnerable.

Panic flickered, but he fought through it, relying on brute strength. Illusions faded, revealing not cubs but grotesque demon minions cloaked in magic. Ice-tipped chains shot from the shadows, coiling around his limbs before he could react. He fought fiercely, claws slashing, muscles straining, but without his fire, his power had diminished. The enchanted bindings drained what little energy remained, sapping his resistance with every struggle.

Now, he was their captive, bound and dragged to their encampment, his body battered but his spirit burning with rage.

"Looks like the mighty tiger isn't so mighty after all," one of the demons sneered, jabbing him with the butt of a spear.

The Demon Commander approached, its towering figure casting a long, ominous shadow over him. A cruel smile twisted across its jagged features. "You fought well, but your heart betrayed you. You care too much."

The commander crouched beside him, its breath a venomous hiss in the cold air. "We've captured your precious cubs," it whispered mockingly. "Soon, they'll be taken far from here as hostages. Imagine that—your legacy, bound in chains, just like you."

His heart thundered in his chest, a mix of fury and fear. But even through the haze of pain, doubt flickered. Captured? No scent of his cubs lingered, no signs of struggle beyond the illusion. It was another trick—another layer to break him.

But he couldn't risk it being true.

Clenching his jaw, he glared up at the Demon, his eyes blazing with defiance despite the absence of his flame. This isn't how it ends. They may have him now, but he would find a way out—and when he did, he would make sure they would regret ever crossing his path.

As the demons turned to mockery and cruelty—hurling blades and arrows at him for sport—Daxton clenched his teeth. He forced himself to focus. I need to figure out how to warn others. Izzy will come looking for me. I just hope she doesn't walk into this trap as well.

Izzy prowled ahead; her movements as silent as the shadows around her. She scanned the forest floor, searching for signs of Daxton's trail. "This isn't right, Ayralina," she said, her voice tight with worry. "He's never taken this long to scout before. I can't find his markings anywhere. Something's wrong."

Ayralina placed a firm hand on her friend's shoulder. "Izzy, wait. You can't go alone. If Daxton's in trouble, it's dangerous for you to head into it unprepared. We'll all go together, but we need to be cautious. This could be an ambush."

Izzy hesitated, torn between her instincts and Ayralina's reasoning. Finally, she nodded. "Alright. Let's go."

After another hour of relentless searching, they entered a clearing, and the sight before them froze Izzy in her tracks.

Daxton hung upside down from a tree, his majestic white fur drenched in blood. Arrows and blades protruded from his body, and demons encircled him, laughing as they turned his suffering into a twisted game.

"Daxton!" Izzy screamed, rage and anguish overcoming her. She bolted toward him, flames bursting to life in her paws.

"No, Izzy, stop!" Ayralina shouted, but it was too late.

Izzy's fireballs roared through the air, but the demons dodged effortlessly. As she closed the distance, her body suddenly weakened, her movements sluggish. She felt her strength drain away and collapsed to the ground.

Realization struck too late. The demons surrounded her with cruel smiles, weapons drawn. Even as her energy ebbed, Izzy fought ferociously, killing several demons before finally reaching Daxton. She clawed through his restraints, cutting him down from the tree, but he was barely breathing. Blood pooled beneath him, and his chest rose and fell with agonizing slowness.

Ayralina held the cubs back, her heart breaking at the sight of Izzy and Daxton's battered forms. She tried to devise a plan, but before she could act, demons emerged from the shadows, encircling her group.

"Ayralina," Simon said, his voice taut with tension. "What's the plan?"

Ayralina's eyes darted to Izzy and Daxton. "Izzy's caught; she seems to be within a fire suppression ring. She won't be able to help us. Listen carefully: when the fight starts, I want you and the others to find a weak spot and escape. Ellie, Saber, stick with them and keep them safe. I'll rescue Izzy and Daxton and meet up with you when it's safe."

"No!" Simon protested. "We can't leave you to fight alone."

Ayralina's voice hardened. "You'll slow me down. If you want to help, get to safety. Trust me—I'll handle this."

Reluctantly, Simon nodded. "Fine. But you'd better survive."

The demon commander stepped forward, chanting under his breath. Ayralina's strength waned as the fire suppression field expanded, sapping her Phoenix fire.

"How do you like my trap?" He sneered. "It was made just for you."

"Charge! Capture her alive but kill the rest!"

Weakened by the suppression ring digging into her skin like a cursed shackle and outnumbered by the demons circling her like vultures sensing weakness, Ayralina struggled to hold her ground. Every breath felt like shards of glass scraping against her lungs. Her vision blurred, dark spots creeping at the edges. The ground beneath her trembled—not from the enemy's assault, but from the beast stirring inside her.

The Phoenix.

Its voice slithered through her mind, venomous and persistent, like wildfire licking at dry timber.

"Let me out," it hissed, its tone a seductive mix of mockery and hunger. "You're weak, fragile. You're going to die out here like the insignificant mortal you are. Only I can save you."

Ayralina gritted her teeth, blood trickling from the corner of her mouth as she forced herself upright. "No," she growled, her voice ragged but defiant. "If I let you out, you'll destroy everything—including the ones I'm trying to protect."

The Phoenix's laughter was a low, guttural rasp, echoing inside her skull like the cracking of embers.

"Fool," it spat, its rage simmering beneath every word. "You're clinging to an illusion of control. When you fail—and you will fail—I'll take over anyway. Why fight the inevitable?"

A demon's blade nicked her shoulder, snapping her attention back to the battlefield. The pain was sharp, but it paled compared to the inferno raging within. Blood soaked through her torn sleeve, warm against her cold skin. She was running out of time.

Demons surged toward Simon and the others—too many, too fast.

Panic clawed at her chest. She had no choice.

Summoning what little strength remained, she cast a protective force field around them, her voice raw as she shouted, "Izzy, help me toss them out!"

Izzy, bruised and bloodied but unbroken, met her gaze with fierce determination. Despite her injuries, she pushed herself beyond her limits, channeling her remaining power to hurl Simon and the others out of the clearing to safety. The moment they vanished; a crushing void filled the space they left behind—a vulnerable emptiness.

The Phoenix seized the opportunity.

Ayralina felt it like a dagger plunging into her heart.

"NO!" she screamed, but it was already too late.

Flames erupted from within, devouring her from the inside out. The suppression ring melted away like wax, its magic useless against the Phoenix's fury. Agony, unlike anything she'd ever known, wracked her body—bones snapping, muscles tearing, skin splitting as molten fire carved through her veins.

Memories flashed like dying embers: Simon's smile, Izzy's laughter, Daxton's steadiness... her children's faces, blurred by tears, screaming for help she couldn't give.

"Stop!" she cried out in the dark recesses of her mind, but the Phoenix roared over her pleas, drowning her in its wrath.

When the flames subsided, Ayralina was gone.

In her place stood the dark Phoenix—a towering, majestic monstrosity, 18 feet tall with wings that stretched 36 feet across the sky, casting shadows darker than night. Its feathers shimmered with hues of crimson and gold, beautiful and terrible all at once, like a sunset bleeding into an eternal abyss. Its eyes—Ayralina's eyes—were now molten gold, devoid of warmth, burning with nothing but rage.

Izzy, her breath shallow, staggered to her feet. Her gaze met the creature that had once been her friend. "Ayralina..." she whispered, her voice trembling with both awe and terror.

The Phoenix didn't even acknowledge her. Its blazing gaze fixed on the demons.

"Filthy creatures," it snarled, its voice a symphony of a thousand screams layered beneath a cold, regal timbre. "How dare you insult me with your presence?"

With a single sweep of its massive wings, it unleashed a torrent of fire, obliterating the demons in an instant—no ashes left, only the scorched earth where they once stood.

But the Phoenix wasn't finished.

It turned toward Izzy and Daxton, its flames coiling with murderous intent.

Desperation surged through Izzy. She grabbed Daxton's paw, their energies intertwining one last time. "We have to bring her back," she rasped.

They pooled the last remnants of their strength, their combined power a fragile thread against the Phoenix's inferno. They aimed for its core, a desperate plea wrapped in light.

The blast struck true—but it didn't save Ayralina.

It enraged the Phoenix.

"FOOLS!" it roared, its flames spiraling into the heavens. "You think your feeble magic can touch me? She's gone!"

Fire surged, engulfing them.

"NO!"

From somewhere deep inside, beneath layers of ash and fury, Ayralina screamed. The sound was raw, primal, filled with rage, grief, and the desperate refusal to lose herself completely.

She clawed through the darkness, fueled by Izzy and Daxton's final act of defiance. Their love, their sacrifice—it was the tether she needed. She fought, not with fists or magic, but with every shattered piece of her soul, wrestling the Phoenix for control.

But she was too late.

When the flames finally died down, the Phoenix was gone.

Ayralina collapsed to her knees, smoke rising from her trembling body. Her hands—her hands—were covered in soot and blood. She forced her eyes open, praying it had been a nightmare.

Izzy and Daxton lay motionless before her, their bodies broken, their eyes forever frozen in silent echoes of who they had been.

"No... no..." Ayralina's voice was a fragile whisper, carried away by the wind. She crawled to them, her fingers trembling as she reached out, hoping—praying—for any sign of life.

There was none.

Tears streamed down her face, mingling with the soot. The weight of their sacrifice pressed down on her chest, crushing her. She had saved no one. She had lost everything.

And the worst part?

It hadn't been the Phoenix who'd killed them.

It was her.

Review

HOLD, DEAR ADVENTURER—BEFORE YOU turn another enchanted page, allow me a brief moment. If the journey so far has awakened your imagination, stirred magic in your heart, or whisked you away to distant realms, your words of review on Amazon would be a treasured spell indeed.

Scan the QR Code or type the URL into a browser and scroll down the left side of the site to find the review section.

https://mybook.to/Phoenix1p

Your thoughts will guide fellow travelers toward this adventure, and your kindness means more to me than dragon gold.

Thank you deeply for your support!

Winter H. Rayne

Chapter 25

By the time Simon and the others returned to the clearing, the scene before them was staggering. The ground was scorched, the trees blackened, and the air hung heavy with the acrid smell of smoke. It was as if a forest fire had swept through the area, leaving destruction in its wake.

In the center of the devastation sat Ayralina, her body battered and seemingly fading. Her once-lustrous strawberry blonde hair had begun to darken, losing its vibrant bounce, now hanging in limp, lifeless strands. She trembled uncontrollably, cradling Izzy's fragile body in her lap, her fingers stained with ash and blood. Nearby, Daxton's lifeless form lay twisted and still, his once-pristine white fur now dull, matted with soot, and streaked with crimson.

"It's all my fault," Ayralina sobbed, her voice a fragile whisper, barely audible over the crackling remnants of the ruined landscape. Her tears carved clean lines down her dirt-streaked face. "It's all my fault. If only I'd been more disciplined... if I had better control... they wouldn't have died."

Her words were a broken mantra, each repetition slicing deeper than the last, echoing through the hollow emptiness around her. The weight of guilt was suffocating, pressing down on her chest, heavier than the wreckage that surrounded her.

Saber and Ellie ran over, tears streaming down their faces. Saber let out a roar of pain and agony while Ellie sobbed desperately for her mother.

Simon, frozen in shock, whispered, "No... What happened?"

The guards exchanged uneasy glances before one of them stepped forward. "Simon, what should we do?."

For a moment, Simon just stood there, his face a mixture of grief and determination. The weight of their situation pressed down on him, thick with sorrow and tension. He slowly stepped forward, his armor creaking softly with each measured movement. Above them, the sky burned crimson, casting long shadows that danced in the flickering glow of distant fires still raging in the aftermath of battle.

Ayralina was sitting in the dirt, her trembling hands clutching Izzy's lifeless body—a bond severed too soon. Her face was streaked with soot and tears, eyes glassy and distant, staring at a world that no longer made sense. The ground beneath her seemed to pulse with the lingering echoes of violence, but she was deaf to it all, lost in a sea of sorrow.

Simon approached carefully, his heart heavy. He knelt beside her, lowering his voice to a gentle murmur as if afraid to shatter the fragile thread of her composure. For a moment, he simply sat there, offering silent companionship in her grief. Finally, he placed a tentative hand on her shoulder, his grip firm yet comforting.

"Ayralina," he began softly, his voice steady despite the storm within him. "I know this pain feels unbearable, like it's carved a hole right through you. I've felt it too. Losing someone you love...it doesn't just hurt—it leaves you hollow. But we're not safe here. We're still in demon territory. The longer we stay, the more we risk all of us joining them."

His words hung in the air, sharp and undeniable. Ayralina didn't respond at first. She slowly turned her head, her hollow, grief-stricken eyes meeting his. For a fleeting moment, she looked like a shadow of herself—lost, broken, and unrecognizable even to her own reflection. It was as if she wasn't sure where—or even who—she was anymore.

But then, Simon's words began to break through the haze. Ayralina squeezed her eyes shut, a fresh wave of tears escaping before she drew in a ragged breath. She exhaled slowly, grounding herself in the reality she couldn't escape. The grief was still there, a raw and jagged wound.

She gently laid Izzy's body down, her fingers lingering for a heartbeat longer before she forced herself to let go. When she finally stood, her legs trembled, but her spine was straight. Her face, though streaked with tears, now held the faintest flicker of determination.

"You're right," Ayralina whispered hoarsely, her voice fragile but gaining strength with each word. "I can't... I can't lose anyone else. Not like this."

She wiped her face with the back of her hand, smearing dirt and tears into a warrior's mask.

Then, after a brief pause, her gaze hardened with a different kind of clarity—one born not from emotion, but from unyielding purpose. The flickering light from the dying flames cast sharp angles across her face, highlighting the steely determination etched into her features. She turned to Simon, her voice firm, cutting through the heavy silence like a blade.

"You need to return to the north kingdom," Ayralina said finally. The words seemed to cost her, as if each syllable weighed more than the last, but she didn't waver. Her posture remained steady, her expression unflinching. "Simon, we've missed something. You must flush out their allies. How did they know our whereabouts to set up this trap? We've been too hasty. We've committed a grave mistake."

The admission hung in the air, heavy and undeniable. She exhaled slowly, her eyes darkening with the realization of just how vulnerable they had become.

"We can't afford to let our guard down—not now," she continued. "Take the cubs back. It's too dangerous here. I will continue this journey alone." She paused, her jaw tightening slightly before she added, "Wait for me at the palace—I'll come back for you when I've finished in the north."

Simon's jaw clenched, the instinct to argue flickering behind his eyes. His fingers curled into fists at his sides, fighting the urge to reject her command outright. But when his gaze met hers, he saw the resolve there—etched into every line of her face, burning in the depths of her eyes. This wasn't just an order. It was a promise. A tether to hope in a world that felt like it was unraveling around them.

After a long moment, Simon gave a slow, reluctant nod, the weight of unspoken words pressing against his chest. "We'll be waiting," he said quietly, his voice low but steady, carrying the weight of both duty and something deeper. "Don't make us wait too long."

Ayralina managed the faintest ghost of a smile, a fragile ember of warmth amid the coldness of grief and uncertainty.

Ayralina then gently laid Izzy's body beside Daxton's and pulled a storage gem from her belongings. She activated the gem with a faint whisper, and a soft glow enveloped the two lifeless forms. Their bodies disappeared into the gem, which Ayralina then embedded into a simple necklace. Turning to Ellie and Saber, she placed the necklace around Ellie's neck, her hands trembling.

"Take them back with you," Ayralina said, her voice breaking. "Give them a proper burial. Honor them as the heroes they were."

Ellie's golden eyes shimmered with tears. She nodded silently, her small body trembling with emotion as the weight of her parents' loss settled on her. Saber stood stoic beside her, his head bowed in quiet grief.

Ayralina knelt before them, gathering both cubs into her arms. Her voice was gentle but firm. "I've avenged your parents' deaths. The demons who did this are gone. But don't let hatred consume your hearts. Your duty now is to protect our human friends. Stay strong, and keep Simon and the others safe. I promise—I'll return to you when my journey is complete."

Guilt gnawed at her heart. If they hadn't risked everything to save her, their parents might still be alive.

Ellie buried her face in Ayralina's shoulder, her silent sobs shaking them both. Saber pressed his head against Ayralina's side, offering his silent farewell. Ayralina held them tightly, her tears mingling with theirs.

Finally, she pulled back, her heart breaking anew as she met Ellie's tearful gaze. "Be brave," she whispered. "For your parents. For us all."

Ellie nodded, wiping her face with her paw. She straightened, her young face determined despite her grief. Ayralina smiled faintly, placing a hand on Saber's head before stepping back.

As Simon and the others began their return journey, Ayralina watched them until they disappeared into the forest. The clearing felt emptier than ever, the silence oppressive. She took a deep, shuddering breath and turned toward the north, her path now lonelier and heavier than before.

Each step felt like a battle against the weight in her chest, but she pushed forward. Izzy and Daxton gave their lives to protect me. I won't let their sacrifice be in vain.

The northern winds picked up, their icy chill biting at her skin. With a final glance over her shoulder, Ayralina whispered, "Goodbye," before vanishing into the shadows of the forest.

Chapter 26

WHEN AYRALINA WOKE UP, the person staring back at her in the mirror was a stranger. Her once vibrant, fiery blonde-red hair now hung in lifeless, jet-black strands, as if the color had been drained along with her spirit. The usual spark in her eyes—a reflection of the phoenix fire that had once burned within—was gone, replaced by a dull, hollow emptiness. Her skin, once glowing with warmth and life, had turned pale, almost translucent, as though the very essence of her being had been stripped away.

It had taken her days to traverse the frozen tundra of the north—days filled with exhaustion, hunger, and the relentless bite of the cold. She had barely survived. Halfway through her journey, a caravan of northern hunters found her collapsed in the snow. Though wary of her identity, they deemed her too weak to pose a threat and took her in, sending word of her arrival to the palace.

That was when she met King Tyrin. She delivered her report to him, but all she wanted afterward was a place to bury her sorrow. King Tyrin, showing unexpected kindness, offered her a room in the palace and extended his hospitality.

She was always cold now. Not the kind of cold that could be banished by fire or softened by sunlight, but a deep, soul-chilling frost that settled into her bones and refused to leave. Without the Phoenix fire, her body felt brittle, fragile—like thin glass on the verge of shattering. But she no longer cared. The fire was gone, and good riddance.

It was the Phoenix that had taken everything from her. It had burned away her past, her friends, her heart.

She tried to summon her powers—desperately grasping for even a flicker of warmth—but it was as if they had never existed. No ember of magic, no trace of the molten gold that once surged through her veins. Her hands trembled, not from the cold, but from the hollow ache of its absence.

Nights were the worst. They were filled with tears, memories, and the unbearable weight of loss. Her failure loomed over her like an unrelenting storm, pressing down until she could barely breathe.

She had come to the North to offer reinforcements to the King, only to bring shame to herself. Worse, she was powerless to retrieve the Ice Crystal to save her husband. That truth cut deeper than the cold ever could. She stared at her reflection, haunted by the knowledge that her strength had vanished when she needed it most. The fire had been her curse, but without it, she was nothing—a failure, a disgrace, a disaster waiting to happen.

Not only was she useless, but now she needed to be protected. A burden. The warrior who once inspired fear and respect had become fragile, reliant on the very people she had sworn to defend. The weight of her defeat settled over her like frost, seeping into the cracks of her spirit. She had crossed frozen lands and faced monstrous foes, yet none of it mattered. She had failed the one person who mattered most. And as her soul shivered in the darkness, Ayralina wondered if she'd ever feel warmth again—or if she even deserved to.

She had finally made it to the north. But what did it matter?

Without her powers, she was nothing but a shell—empty, fragile, and broken.

There was a soft knock at the heavy oak door, its sound barely audible over the crackling of the fire in the stone hearth.

"Enter," came a gruff voice from inside.

A commander in dark armor stepped in, bowing slightly before speaking. "Report, Your Majesty. Ayralina has slipped away from the guards. What are your orders?"

King Tyrin, seated behind an ornate desk cluttered with maps, scrolls, and half-empty goblets, didn't look up immediately. His rugged face was shadowed by the flickering light, his expression unreadable. After a brief pause, he answered, his voice firm and unyielding.

"Let her go. Only she can find her way back." He stood slowly, the chair scraping against the stone floor as he rose. His towering figure moved to the tall, narrow windows overlooking the darkened city beyond, the faint glow of torches lining the distant walls. "But keep tabs on her. Make sure she doesn't die."

The commander nodded, King Tyrin continued, his gaze still fixed on the horizon.

"Tell me—what's the latest with the demons?"

The commander straightened, his face tightening with concern. "The demons are gathering their forces, sire. They're waiting for reinforcements. As far as our intelligence reports, their armies from the northern human kingdoms have already arrived. Now, they await their allies from the North Sea."

King Tyrin's jaw clenched slightly.

"The North Sea?" he echoed.

"Yes, Your Majesty. It's said they have an uncountable number of cannon fodder—creatures bred for war. They won't cause us significant harm individually, but their purpose is clear. They'll overwhelm our lines, wear down our troops with relentless waves, and when we're exhausted, they'll strike with their true power. Their elites will fall upon us when we are weakest. What are your commands, sire?"

King Tyrin turned his gaze from the window, his piercing eyes filled with determination. "Send word to our allies in the North Sea. Tell them to create as many obstacles as possible—delay the enemy's reinforcements at all costs. The more time they can buy us, the better."

The commander hesitated, then asked quietly, "Do you believe Ayralina will return in time, Your Majesty? Can we truly depend on her?"

King Tyrin's gaze darkened, but his voice held unwavering conviction. "We need her. No matter the cost, she has to—and she will—rise to the occasion. She will become our strongest ally."

The room fell into heavy silence, broken only by the distant howl of wind beyond the stone walls.

"You are dismissed," the King finally said.

The commander bowed and exited swiftly, leaving King Tyrin alone with the growing shadows of war creeping ever closer.

King Tyrin stood at the tall, arched window of his study; his broad silhouette framed by the dim light of the setting sun. The sprawling kingdom stretched before him—flickering torches lining stone walls, distant banners fluttering in the wind, and shadows creeping across the land like silent whispers of the past. But his mind was far from the present. His gaze was distant, lost in memories etched deep into his heart.

"Old friend," he murmured softly, his voice barely more than a whisper, carried away by the cold evening breeze. "I will do my best to protect her... to shape her into the warrior that will make you proud."

His chest tightened with the weight of unspoken promises and lingering guilt. Ayralina wasn't just any girl—she was the daughter of the Phoenix King, his dearest friend, who had saved his life long ago when he'd been nothing more than a reckless, hot-headed young man. Back then, Tyrin's temper was like wildfire—untamed and uncontrollable—leading him into more battles than he could count, most of which he had no business fighting.

It was his fury that had nearly cost him his life that one fateful day. Surrounded, outnumbered, and beaten within an inch of death, Tyrin had thought his end was near. But fate had other plans. From the skies descended the Phoenix King— he was a young prince at the time, radiant and fierce, wielding fire and fury unlike anything Tyrin had ever seen. He had driven back Tyrin's attackers with unmatched strength, his flames leaving nothing but ashes in their wake.

From that moment, their bond had been forged in blood and fire. They fought side by side in countless battles, their friendship unbreakable. They were brothers in all but name, bound by loyalty and honor.

But fate is cruel.

When the Phoenix Realm was invaded, Tyrin received the news too late. The call for reinforcements never reached him in time. By the time he rallied his forces, the realm had already fallen, its proud cities reduced to ruins, and his best friend... gone.

The guilt gnawed at him, a wound that never healed. He had failed to be there when it mattered most.

When the news that Ayralina was sent to Earth reached him, Tyrin vowed to find her and watch over her. But tragedy struck again. His own kingdom was invaded, plunging him into war and chaos. He lost all contact with her, the girl who carried the legacy of his dearest friend. Years passed, and though he fought battles and wore his crown with pride, that void remained—a silent reminder of the promises left unfulfilled.

Until recently.

He had found her again. Ayralina. The daughter of the Phoenix King. Strong-willed, defiant, and filled with the same fire that had burned in her father's eyes. Now, she is battered and defeated. She was a reminder of everything he had lost—and everything he still had a chance to protect.

Tyrin clenched his fists, his jaw tightening with determination.

"I failed you once, my friend," he whispered to the fading light. "But I won't fail her."

He would raise Ayralina the only way he knew—through discipline, training, and hard-earned wisdom. He would shape her into a warrior worthy of her bloodline, worthy of the Phoenix legacy, not just for her sake, but for the memory of the friend he couldn't save.

With a final glance at the horizon, King Tyrin turned away from the window, his heart heavy but his resolve unshakable.

Simon made it back to the North Kingdom; his body travelworn but his mind sharper than ever. He wasted no time reporting his findings to King Cedrick, his voice steady despite the turmoil inside him. The King listened in silence, his expression unreadable, but the flicker of grief in his eyes told Simon all he needed to know—Daxton and Izzy's deaths were felt deeply.

But there was no time to mourn.

Demons still lurked within the palace walls, hiding in the shadows, waiting for the right moment to strike. Simon, along with Saber and Ellie—the fierce white tigers—moved swiftly, their blades and claws cutting through the darkness, flushing out every last remnant of the enemy. They fought with a vengeance, pouring their grief and frustration into each battle. The demons had taken too much from them. Now, they would take everything back in return.

When the last demon fell, silence filled the halls of the palace—a silence that felt both victorious and hollow.

Then came the burial.

The North gathered under the pale light of the twin moons, the air thick with sorrow as Daxton and Izzy's bodies were laid to rest. Simon stood at the front, gripping the hilt of his sword tightly, his knuckles white. He had fought beside them, bled beside them, and now he was forced to say goodbye.

Saber and Ellie stood side by side, their white fur clean and polished just for this occasion. Ellie, the younger of the two, let out a low, mournful growl, her golden eyes dim with sorrow. Saber remained silent, his massive frame tense with barely restrained rage. The cold wind carried whispered prayers as the pyres were lit, flames licking at the sky, carrying their fallen warrior's home.

The next morning, training began. Harder, harsher than before. Simon pushed his body to its limits, his sword an extension of his grief. Saber trained relentlessly, his powerful strikes leaving deep gashes in the training posts. Ellie, despite being younger, was just as fierce. Her movements fluid and precise as she honed her speed and agility.

They would not fail again.

And when the time came, when Ayralina finally called for them, they would be ready.

Chapter 27

"GET UP, YOU PIECE of trash!" The harsh voice snapped her back to the present, slicing through the jeers of the crowd like a blade.

Ayralina groaned, her face pressed against the cold, unforgiving dirt. Pain radiated through her battered body—bruises blooming across her ribs, cuts stinging on her arms, blood trickling from the corner of her mouth. But the worst pain wasn't physical. It was the grief. The crushing, suffocating grief of failure.

"Around here, you earn your worth," her opponent snarled, spitting near her head. "If you can't beat me, don't even think about leaving tonight."

Then he charged at her again, his intent clear—this time, he would finish her.

But just before the final blow landed, the referee stepped in. "That's enough, Fight's over," he announced.

Her opponent glared at him, fists still clenched, anger burning in his eyes. "She's still breathing."

"You've already won. Don't cause a scene. Get out," the referee snapped.

The words stung—not because they were cruel, but because they were true. At least here, in this grim, underground fight ring, there were no illusions. No false comforts. Just survival. And she was failing at it spectacularly.

She had nearly died a few times here, but every time, just as her opponent came close to finishing her off, the referee would step in, ending the fight before the killing blow could land. And then, she'd be tossed aside like a rag doll, discarded in the dirt. Yet, night after night, she kept coming back.

A week ago, Ayralina had wandered aimlessly, letting the streets swallow her, moving further and further from the palace's towering spires. She hadn't cared where she was going—only that she needed to get away.

That's when she found it.

The underground fight ring.

The muffled sounds of fists meeting flesh, the roar of a bloodthirsty crowd, and the thick, suffocating air, heavy with sweat, desperation, and pain.

She didn't know why she had stepped inside. Maybe to punish herself? Maybe to feel something—anything—other than the hollow ache carved into her soul.

And now, here she was. Battered. Broken. Crawling out of the ring with blurred vision and a heart even more bruised than her body. The crowd's laughter chased her like specters, each jeer a dagger twisting deeper into the fragile remnants of her pride.

She staggered through the darkened streets, her breath ragged, her steps unsteady. Hunger gnawed at her, sharp and unrelenting, but she ignored it. The cold bit into her skin, seeping through her tattered clothes, but she welcomed it. Maybe if she froze, if she starved, she'd finally pay the price for her failures.

What's the point? she thought bitterly, her knees buckling as she collapsed against a crumbling stone wall. I'm useless now. Everything I've done, everything I've tried—it's all led to nothing.

Her mind drifted back to King Tyrin—the fierce glint in his eyes, the quiet strength in his voice, the warmth in his actions even when words failed. He had given her shelter without question, protection without condition, hope without expectation. And she had repaid him with cowardice.

She didn't deserve his kindness. She didn't deserve anything.

Ayralina curled into herself, the weight of her mistakes pressing down like the darkness around her. She sat there in the silence of her despair, the faint sounds of the fight ring echoing in the distance. She thought about the opponent who had mocked her, the sting of his words cutting deeper than his blows. "Earn your worth," he had said. She clenched her fists, her nails digging into her palms. His voice haunted her, intertwining with the memories of her past failures.

Ayralina wiped the blood and tears from her face, her movements slow. Her body screamed for rest, but she forced herself to stand. She didn't know what to do or where to go from here. So just one foot in front of another she turned into a dark alleyway.

The underground fight ring had become more than just a place for Ayralina to punish herself—it had become a hunting ground. Demons had infiltrated its ranks, disguised as fighters, gamblers, and spectators. They had tried to kill her more than once, but each time, King Tyrin's men intervened, their blades cutting through the deception before it was too late.

But demons were nothing if not patient.

They learned her patterns, observed her weaknesses, and eventually followed her beyond the ring. It wasn't until she turned down a narrow alley, exhausted and alone, that they made their move.

A shadow loomed ahead. A man stepped forward, the dim light glinting off the steel in his hand. His crooked smile sent a chill through her spine.

"Money or your life," he sneered.

Ayralina barely reacted. She stood still, unflinching. "You've finally made your move," she said quietly. "No need for pretense, kill me if you want—it makes no difference."

The thug hesitated, thrown off by her insight. He reached for her anyway, rough hands groping for anything of value, but he found nothing. Frustrated, he struck her, sending her sprawling onto the cold stone.

"Just my luck," he grumbled. "You're already looking for death." Then his lips curled into something far more sinister. "But I can't let this golden opportunity go to waste. Since you want to die anyway, let's have some fun first."

Ayralina felt his dirty fingers claw at her clothing, the weight of him pressing down like a filthy cage. But beneath the fear, something else stirred. A spark—small and fragile, but still there.

Am I really this worthless? she thought. Is this what my life has come to?

The thug's cruel laughter echoed in her ears. His hands tore at the last piece of fabric—

And something inside her snapped.

No. I just want to die; Can't I even die with dignity? I won't let this happen. Even if I die, I will go down fighting. I will not give in!

A wave of fury rippled through her veins. Her eyes, once lifeless, flared golden. The thug froze mid-motion, his breath catching in his throat—but it was already too late for him.

The air around her ignited. A surge of fire erupted from her chest, a searing inferno that consumed him instantly. The alley filled with blistering heat, smoke curling against the walls. The man didn't even have time to scream—his body blackened, flesh disintegrating, his very existence reduced to nothing but ash.

Then, silence.

Ayralina gasped, clutching her chest. She could still feel the fire's remnants licking at her skin, but it did not burn her.

Panting, Ayralina sat in the ashes, her body trembling. Her powers had returned, albeit violently. The flames burned brightly in her eyes once more, but the realization of what had just happened left her shaken.

The sharp sound of clapping broke the silence, echoing through the alley like a roll of distant thunder. Ayralina turned her head, her fiery gaze meeting the source of the sound. A shadow emerged, stepping into the flickering light with an air of authority that was impossible to ignore.

"Well, well," King Tyrin said, his voice deep and commanding yet tinged with a calm confidence. He stood tall, easily six feet, his muscular frame evident even beneath the tailored layers of his northern attire. His white hair shimmered like freshly fallen snow, contrasting sharply with his rugged features—his strong jawline and sharp cheekbones spoke of a man forged in the harshest conditions. His piercing ice-blue eyes seemed to hold both wisdom and the weight of countless battles.

"She's back," he continued, a faint smirk tugging at the corner of his mouth. He reached up to remove his heavy outer coat—a dark, fur-lined garment that seemed as much a symbol of his strength as it was a shield against the northern cold. With a fluid motion, he stepped closer and draped the coat over Ayralina's trembling shoulders. The warmth of the fabric and the weight of his presence grounded her.

"I was about to step in," he added, his smirk fading into something more serious, "but it seems you didn't need my help after all." His voice carried a rare hint of pride.

Ayralina pulled the coat tighter around her, its warmth mingling with the lingering heat of her Phoenix fire. For a moment, she studied Tyrin, taking in the unshakable strength he exuded. He wasn't just a king by title; he was a ruler shaped by relentless challenges; a man who had earned every ounce of the respect he commanded.

"Thank you, for keeping me safe," she said softly, her voice steady despite the emotions swirling inside her. "And for letting me find my way back on my own."

Tyrin inclined his head slightly, his gaze unwavering. "You're welcome," he said, a faint glint of amusement returning to his eyes. His words struck a chord deep within her, a reminder of the balance she sought—not just within herself, but in those she chose to trust. For all his power and presence, Tyrin carried himself with a sense of responsibility, a protector's heart beneath the icy exterior.

Ayralina straightened under the weight of the coat, meeting his gaze with newfound determination. "I won't fall again," she said, her voice filled with quiet resolve.

Tyrin smiled, a rare and fleeting expression that softened his otherwise rugged features. "Good," he said. "Because the road ahead will demand everything you've got—and more."

Ayralina nodded weakly, just before the exhaustion overtook her, and she blacked out.

Chapter 28

AYRALINA WOKE UP IN a room with high, vaulted ceilings, its walls seemingly made of ice. Yet it didn't feel cold; instead, it exuded a warmth that reminded her of a mother's embrace.

She rolled over, every muscle in her body aching. Training with King Tyrin had been grueling. Days were spent as a punching bag for his warriors, and nights submerged in ice-cold baths meant to condition her body for the deep cold of the ice cave.

The polar bear cubs were her only solace. Mischievous and full of energy, they often sat with her, cheering her on or recounting their adventures. Their chatter was a welcome distraction as she endured the freezing water.

Despite her determination, her powers remained dormant unless her life was in danger. But Ayralina refused to give up. She couldn't let her friends' sacrifices be in vain.

"Tonight's training will take a different approach," King Tyrin announced.

He placed Ayralina in a subzero ice bucket and once again, began lowering the temperature further with his powers. "Now, focus on my voice and look within yourself. Tell me what you see."

"I see nothing," Ayralina replied, her voice trembling. "Only coldness and darkness."

"Then dig deeper," Tyrin instructed. "Find the flame inside you. Remember who you are and where you've come from."

"I can't," Ayralina said, panic rising. "I can't control her. I'm afraid."

"Don't worry about controlling her," Tyrin said calmly. "She's locked away, and I'm reinforcing that barrier. Right now, I want you to find the spark—the flame that is you. Think back to the first time you felt it."

Ayralina closed her eyes, letting the chaotic world around her fade into silence. The crackling wind, the distant voices, even the cold biting at her skin—all of it melted away as she turned inward.

She drifted through the corridors of her memories, past moments of light and shadow, seeking the pieces of herself she had lost along the way. Her mother's voice echoed first, soft yet unbreakable, weaving tales of their ancestors—phoenixes who had risen from despair to greatness, their flames burning brighter with every trial. Then came the laughter of her aunt, always steady, always reminding her that even fire must learn when to yield, when to smolder, and when to burn with purpose.

She thought of Izzy, her closest companion and fiercest protector. The tiger had been by her side through victories and failures alike, a constant in a world that often felt too heavy to bear. Ayralina had spent so long carrying the burdens alone, always looking ahead, always pressing forward, but now she felt herself being drawn back—to the very foundation of who she was.

The day she first conjured her flame flickered into view. She had been just a child, her hands trembling as the tiny spark danced in her palm. That moment had been one of pure wonder, untainted by fear or doubt. Back then, she had believed in herself without question.

Where had that belief gone?

A warmth began to stir in her chest, hesitant at first, like the flicker of a dying ember. But as the memories poured in, that ember caught, fed by the truths she had forgotten. It grew, stretching through her veins, igniting something deep within. The warmth turned to fire—unstoppable, consuming.

Ayralina gasped as the heat surged through her body, raw and wild. It burned, searing through every fiber of her being, forcing her to confront the power she had tried to contain for so long.

Tyrin, watching her carefully, stepped forward, his expression unreadable. He extended a hand, releasing a steady stream of ice energy. The frost curled around her, cooling but not suppressing, soothing but not smothering. The clash of fire and ice shimmered in the air, a delicate balance of opposing forces.

"Steady," Tyrin said, his voice calm and commanding. "You're stronger than this. Let it guide you, not control you."

His words tethered her, anchoring her to the present as the fire raged within. She focused, not on suppressing the heat, but on understanding it. The inferno wasn't her enemy. It was her. And if she feared it, she would only fear herself.

The energy within her began to shift, no longer spiraling toward chaos but instead merging, flowing in harmony with the icy energy wrapping around her. Her breathing steadied. Her pulse slowed.

Then in her vision she stood amidst an endless sea of glowing embers, the air thick with heat and the scent of burning. The space pulsed like a living thing, ancient and waiting, as if it had been calling her for eternity.

From the swirling inferno, a figure emerged—a shadow wreathed in fire, yet more than just an echo.

It was her.

Or rather, the version of her that had existed before the agony, before the weight of guilt and fear had crushed her spirit. This Ayralina stood unyielding, her presence radiant with untamed power. Her eyes burned like molten gold, fierce and unwavering. She was not a woman drowning in regret, not a warrior staggering beneath unseen burdens. She was the embodiment of fire itself.

The shadow Ayralina smiled. "I'm glad you found me again." Her voice echoed like a distant memory, both near and impossibly far. "I have never left you. You just forgot who you are."

Ayralina's breath caught. The words cut deep, stirring the long-buried wounds of hesitation, failure, and fear.

"I'm sorry," she whispered, her voice barely holding together. "I was too ashamed to face you. I lost myself... in the pain, in the guilt. But I see it now—we are one. I need you. Come back to me."

The shadow's expression softened, her fiery form flickering with warmth. "You've always been enough," she said. "You just needed to believe it."

She stepped forward, and the embers around them surged, flames twisting into a brilliant, living dance.

Then, suddenly, pain tore through Ayralina's very soul.

A jagged, searing force pierced through her spectral form, splitting her essence apart. Black flames erupted around her, choking, devouring—suffocating her light. A terrible smoke swallowed her whole.

When it cleared, another figure stood in her place. A reflection of her, but darker. Twisted.

A cruel laugh rang out from her lips, sharp and venomous.

The creature—her other self—smirked, eyes burning with malice. "You belong to me," she hissed. "Your power is mine."

Before Ayralina could move, the shadow surged forward, her clawed hand wrapping around her throat. Fire licked up her arms, black tendrils slithering over Ayralina's skin, seeping into her.

Pain. Cold and hot all at once. It burrowed into her bones.

"No...!" Ayralina gasped, struggling against the unrelenting grip. "You're the Demon Phoenix... Why are you doing this? Please, stop!"

The shadow's grip tightened. The flames grew.

"Because you are weak, Ayralina," the Demon Phoenix spat, disgust curling her lips. "And I am tired of being chained by a coward. You taint my very existence with your pathetic guilt."

Black fire surged over Ayralina's head, invading her eyes, her mind.

Visions of her past, and future struck her like daggers.

She saw Izzy and Daxton—dead. Lifeless, broken.

She saw Ellie and Saber, their eyes brimming with fury and betrayal.

She saw her family—gone. Burned to nothingness. She had failed them. She had failed them all.

She was drowning. Sinking beneath the weight of it.

Why am I even fighting? she thought bitterly. I'm so tired. She's right. I am a failure. I should just let go...

Somewhere beyond the darkness, a voice cut through the void.

"Ayralina! Ayralina, wake up!"

Distant, but insistent.

"We are here; you are strong. Don't give in—we need you!"

King Tyrin's voice.

She felt something—cold. Ice flooded her veins as Tyrin poured his energy into the water.

She shivered violently. Cold. So cold...

"Reach deep, Ayralina!"

"I... I can't. I'm so tired" Her voice was hollow, empty. "She's right. I'm a failure."

"No. She is you. And you are her."

The words struck something within her.

"No matter what, you must remember that."

Ayralina clenched her teeth, the fire inside her flickering weakly. She is me. I am her...

She gasped, eyes snapping open.

Her demonic reflection loomed before her, sneering.

"That's right," Ayralina whispered, her voice growing stronger. "You are me. And I am you. But we will not exist like this any longer."

A shift. A spark igniting.

Deep within her core, her phoenix fire roared back to life.

The Demon Phoenix recoiled, eyes widening. "What are you doing?!" she shrieked, panic seeping into her voice. "How dare you—Stop it!"

Ayralina's flames burned brighter, white-hot. "You wanted my power?" she said, her voice like thunder. "Then feel it in its truest form."

She lunged, gripping her demonic self. White flames erupted, devouring the black fire in a blinding inferno.

The Demon Phoenix screamed.

The darkness writhed, fought—but it was no match. The purifying flames burned it away, stripping the corruption, cleansing every shadowed part of her soul.

Then, in the last burst of fire, the dark figure was no more.

From the ashes, a magnificent white phoenix rose, its feathers gleaming like sunlight through the frost.

Ayralina stood breathless as the purified spirit circled above her, its energy familiar—hers.

It dove, merging into her, and for the first time in years, she felt whole.

A final eruption of light consumed everything, pushing away the last remnants of darkness.

Then—silence.

And warmth.

Not just power. Not just fire.

Something greater.

Ayralina exhaled, and for the first time in forever... She was complete.

When she opened her eyes, the world around her came back into focus. The wind still howled, the night was still cold, but inside her, the fire burned steady and strong.

Tyrin was watching her, his icy aura retreating as he sensed the transformation within her. He nodded, approval glinting in his gaze.

"You've succeeded. Congratulations, you are now whole," he said simply, but his voice had a rare hint of pride.

Ayralina exhaled slowly, feeling the truth of his words settle deep within her.

"Yes," she murmured. "I have."

Ayralina smiled, the fire in her eyes no longer flickering with uncertainty but blazing with purpose. "I remember now," she said, her voice steady. "I know who I am." She said with conviction in her eyes.

She looked at her reflection in the water, her fiery strawberry blonde hair and glowing skin were restored, and the flames in her eyes were back.

"I've succeeded," Ayralina whispered softly, her voice barely more than a breath. A small smile curved her lips, a flicker of hard-won pride shining in her weary eyes.

King Tyrin studied her for a moment, his stern expression softening slightly. Then, he gave a firm nod of approval. "Yes, you have."

Ayralina stepped out of the ice-cold bathtub, steam rising from her sun-kissed skin as her body naturally radiated warmth. A maid swiftly wrapped a thick towel around her, but before she could fully dry off, a sudden splash sent freezing water flying in all directions.

With delighted squeals, the polar bear cubs tumbled into the tub, their fluffy bodies sending waves sloshing over the rim. One of them, his fur dripping, let out an exaggerated whine.

"Aww, Ayralina! You made the water too hot!"

Ayralina laughed, golden embers flickering at her fingertips. "Oh, really?" She dipped her hands into the water, sending a gentle wave of warmth coursing through it. The surface shimmered like liquid gold before settling into a perfect, steamy temperature.

The cubs gasped in mock horror.

"She's cooking us alive!" one yelped dramatically.

"Save us, Father!" another cried, flailing his tiny paws.

King Tyrin stood there, arms crossed, his piercing blue eyes watching the chaos unfold. The great polar bear king, towering and regal, let out a slow exhale. Though his expression remained stern, there was a flicker of amusement in his gaze.

"Enough, you little troublemakers," he said in his deep, commanding voice. "It's time for bed."

The cubs groaned but obeyed, reluctantly climbing out of the tub before the maid could herd them off. But before leaving, they shook out their fur right in front of Ayralina, drenching her once again. With mischievous grins, they let out a chorus of giggles and bolted down the hall, their laughter echoing as they disappeared from sight.

With the doors shut behind them, the warmth of the moment dimmed, replaced by the quiet weight of unspoken words. The air between Ayralina and Tyrin shifted playfulness dissolving into something heavier.

Tyrin exhaled, turning fully to face her. "Rest tonight," he said, his tone steady but urgent. "You've done well, tomorrow, you face the Ice Cave."

Ayralina stilled. A slow, simmering energy stirred within her, an instinctive reaction to the gravity in his voice. She met his gaze, the firelight casting a golden hue across her skin.

"You really think I'm ready?"

Tyrin studied her for a long moment, the weight of centuries reflecting in his eyes. "Ready or not, we have no choice." His voice was grave. "The war rages on. Our allies in the North Sea are struggling to hold back the demons. Their forces are dwindling. In a matter of days, they won't be able to stand against the tide."

He took a step closer, his massive presence both protective and imposing. "My warriors are exhausted. They fight without rest, their spirits fraying under the relentless battle." His gaze sharpened. "And if you don't succeed in the Ice Cave, there may not be a kingdom left to save."

Ayralina swallowed hard. The warmth of her earlier magic—so effortless, so playful—now felt distant, swallowed by the cold, looming weight of duty.

Tyrin must have sensed her hesitation. His voice softened, though the steel in it remained.

"Remember who you are, Ayralina." His eyes held hers, unwavering. "You are the legacy of the Sunflame Phoenix reborn. You are fire and renewal. You are our last hope." He exhaled. "Have faith in yourself—because I do."

His words settled over her, burning away the last of her doubt like the first rays of dawn piercing the night.

Ayralina straightened, lifting her chin. Determination flared in her chest, a slow-building inferno.

"I won't let you down."

Tyrin held her gaze for a moment longer before nodding. His expression, though battle-worn, carried something rare—hope.

"You never have."

Chapter 29

KING TYRIN STOOD WITH Ayralina at the entrance of the Ice Cave, the jagged mouth of the cavern yawning before them like the maw of some ancient beast. Cold winds howled from within, carrying whispers of forgotten battles and long-lost souls. Frost clung to the rocky walls, shimmering faintly under the pale light of dawn, casting ghostly reflections that danced like phantoms across the ice.

Tyrin placed a firm hand on her shoulder, his grip strong and grounding, like an anchor against the storm that raged both outside and within. His eyes, sharp and weathered from years of war, held a rare softness—a flicker of something more personal than duty. Beneath the hardened exterior of a king was a man who cared deeply, more than his words could ever admit.

"This path is yours alone, Ayralina," he said, his voice low and steady, carrying the weight of both command and care. "No one can walk it for you. The Ice Crystal waits at the heart of this cave, but the true battle lies within yourself. Remember your training, trust your instincts, and never forget the fire that burns in your blood. You are stronger than you know."

Ayralina nodded, her heart pounding like a drum beneath her ribs. She swallowed the lump of fear and doubt lodged in her throat, forcing her breath to steady. She turned to face him fully, her eyes filled with determination, though a shadow of concern lingered.

"I've sent word to Simon, our ally in the northern human kingdom and to Andre in the Southern Lands. They are on their way to reinforce us. " she said, her voice firm despite the icy bite of the wind. "They'll set out to meet up with you. Try not to die before I make it out. Failure is not an option."

A brief, crooked smile tugged at the corner of Tyrin's mouth, a flash of warmth amidst the cold. But his expression quickly grew solemn, the weight of their uncertain future settling between them like the snow under their feet.

"Failure isn't what you should fear," he replied quietly, his gaze locking with hers. "It's giving up the belief in yourself. When the light is out remember to search for the light from within."

With one final nod, he turned and walked away, his figure growing smaller with each step, swallowed by the snowy horizon. He had a war to prepare for, troops to rally, and strategies to forge. Time was slipping through their fingers like grains of sand, but his faith in Ayralina remained steadfast.

The temperature grew colder with every step Ayralina took deeper into the cavern, the chill seeping through her clothes and gnawing at her skin like icy fangs. The walls glistened with jagged shards of frozen crystal, reflecting fractured glimpses of her determined face. Frost-coated stalactites hung like the teeth of a slumbering giant, and the ground beneath her boots grew slick and treacherous.

King Tyrin had told her that the legendary Ice Crystal lay at the heart of the cave, but he hadn't mentioned how far—or how merciless—the journey would be. It felt like she'd been walking for a century, though in reality, it had only been a day and a night. The cave seemed endless, a twisting maze of frozen tunnels and echoing silence, broken only by the sound of her ragged breathing.

Ayralina pulled out the Ice Crystal Compass King Tyrin had entrusted her with. It was a beautiful artifact, crafted in the delicate shape of an intricate snowflake, each crystal-like point carved with precision that seemed almost impossible. In the center of the snowflake was a slender, gleaming arrow suspended in place, floating as if by magic. The arrow glimmered faintly, its metallic surface catching the pale light that reflected off the icy walls.

The compass felt cool to the touch even through her gloves, and it pulsed softly with a faint, rhythmic glow—like a heartbeat frozen in time. Tyrin had explained that once she was close to the crystal, the compass would glow brightly, but until then, it could only sense the general path. The soft, ethereal light from the compass became her guide through the darkness, its faint pulse a reminder that she wasn't entirely alone.

The ice cave was a labyrinth of identical, twisting tunnels, each corner more disorienting than the last. Shadows danced on the glittering walls, playing tricks on her weary eyes. She could swear she saw figures moving just beyond the edges of her vision—phantoms woven from ice and light. Worse still, she knew dangerous creatures roamed these tunnels—beasts shaped by the bitter cold and endless isolation. Their faint growls echoed through the cavern, distant but never far enough to ignore.

Ayralina's pulse quickened as the compass grew warmer in her hand, its glow intensifying with each cautious step. Finally, after what felt like hours of navigating narrow passageways and slipping over icy ridges, the tunnel opened up into a vast cavern. She froze at the threshold, awestruck.

An immense underground lake stretched out before her, its glassy surface shimmering with an otherworldly blue light that seemed to pulse with a life of its own. The icy ceiling above reflected the glow like a frozen sky, casting ethereal ripples across the cavern walls. The cold here was sharper, almost suffocating, as if the very air had teeth.

Ayralina's heart skipped a beat when the compass lit up faintly, its glow shifting from soft white to a vibrant, pulsating blue. Then, to her astonishment, the compass began to hover just above her palm, trembling slightly as if drawn by an invisible force. It floated forward, the snowflake spinning gently, and the arrow within pointed straight toward the center of the lake—just as the Fire Orchid had once floated before her in another trial.

She stepped closer to the lake's edge, her breath misting in the frigid air. This was it—the final threshold between her and the Ice Crystal. "No way," she muttered to herself, groaning. "Do I really have to dive down there? Ugh, this really sucks."

She sighed, resigned to her fate. King Tyrin had warned her about this and ensured she was prepared. Taking a deep breath, she squared her shoulders, her reflection flickering on the frozen water like a ghost of the girl she used to be. Remember who you are, Tyrin's voice echoed in her mind.

The freezing cold hit Ayralina like a wall the moment she plunged into the underground lake, its icy grip seeping through her clothes and sinking into her bones. But she pressed on, her jaw clenched against the numbing chill, following the faint, pulsing glow of the Ice Crystal Compass as it guided her deeper into the dark waters. Each stroke felt heavier, the cold tugging at her limbs, but Tyrin's words echoed in her mind, steady and unyielding: "Remember who you are."

The water grew darker and colder the further she swam, the faint glow from the compass casting eerie, shifting patterns across the icy walls of the submerged cavern. Her breaths came in steady bursts, controlled and rhythmic, though her heart hammered with anticipation. Just as she was marveling at her resilience, proud of how far she'd come, a shadow shifted in the murky distance.

At first, it was just a ripple—barely noticeable. But then the water around her darkened as something massive emerged from the abyss below.

A kraken.

Its colossal, nightmarish form rose from the depths with terrifying grace, its slick, rubbery skin glistening faintly in the dim light. Dozens of massive tentacles coiled and uncoiled like serpents, covered in jagged, ice-crusted suction cups. Its glowing, yellow eyes locked onto Ayralina with a predatory intelligence, and it let out a guttural roar that echoed through the water, vibrating through her chest like a thunderclap.

Ayralina's instincts kicked in.

She twisted her body just as one of its massive tentacles lashed out, narrowly avoiding the crushing blow. The force of the attack sent a shockwave through the water, disorienting her. In the chaos, the Ice Crystal Compass was knocked from her grasp, spinning away into the murky depths like a falling star, its faint glow growing dimmer as it sank.

No! Panic surged through her, but she forced herself to focus. She needed that compass—it was her only guide to the Ice Crystal.

The kraken struck again, faster this time. Ayralina summoned a burst of her Phoenix fire, the magic flaring to life even in the freezing water. A trail of golden-red heat erupted around her, propelling her away from the beast's crushing grip. The sudden warmth seared through the icy depths, creating a protective barrier that forced the kraken to recoil momentarily, its thick skin blistering where the fire touched.

But the creature recovered quickly, enraged now, thrashing with renewed fury. Tentacles lashed out in every direction, turning the water into a violent vortex of churning currents and deadly limbs.

Ayralina darted between the beast's strikes, her mind racing. She couldn't fight it head-on—not here, not without draining herself completely. She needed to be smarter. Using the jagged ice formations that jutted from the cavern floor and ceiling, she twisted and maneuvered through narrow gaps the kraken's bulk form couldn't follow. The creature's frustration grew, and soon it tangled itself in the icy structures, thrashing wildly to break free.

But Ayralina had no time to celebrate. She still needed the compass.

Her eyes darted through the murky gloom, searching desperately. There—a faint flicker of blue light far below, sinking toward the dark abyss. She dove after it, her lungs burning from the lack of air, her muscles screaming in protest. The kraken roared again, ripping free from the ice with terrifying strength, its glowing eyes narrowing as it spotted her descent.

It surged after her like an avalanche, its tentacles slicing through the water.

Ayralina reached out, her fingers brushing the compass just as one of the kraken's limbs slammed into her side, sending her tumbling. Pain shot through her ribs, but she gritted her teeth and clenched the compass tightly in her fist. She couldn't lose it—not now.

Summoning every ounce of strength, she unleashed another burst of phoenix fire, a brilliant explosion of heat and light that carved through the darkness like a blade. The kraken shrieked in agony, recoiling from the searing blaze. Ayralina used the momentum to propel herself upward, kicking hard, her body a streak of fire and determination as she raced toward the surface.

The beast wasn't done. It lunged one final time, its tentacles stretching to drag her back down. But Ayralina twisted mid-stroke, channeling her magic into a concentrated burst.

A blazing spear of fire shot from her outstretched hand, piercing through the water and striking the kraken square in its massive, glowing eye.

The creature roared in pain, thrashing violently, but it didn't follow her.

Breaking the surface, Ayralina gasped for air, clutching the compass tightly against her chest. Her body trembled from exhaustion and the lingering cold, but she was alive. She had survived.

And she still had the compass.

A day later, after tending to her wounds and regaining her strength, Ayralina stood once more at the edge of the underground lake, her reflection flickering on the icy surface. Her body still ached, but the wounds were mostly healed. Only bruises dark and tender remain along her ribs, but her heart burned hotter than ever.

She stared into the dark waters, knowing the kraken was still down there—alive. She could feel it, lurking in the abyss, waiting. But this time, she wasn't here to survive.

She was here to end it.

Without hesitation, she dove back into the freezing depths, the cold biting at her like a thousand needles. But she welcomed the pain. It fueled her, sharpened her focus. She held the compass tightly, but this time, it wasn't her guide—it was her resolve.

The kraken didn't keep her waiting. It emerged from the darkness with a roar of fury, its wounds from their last encounter still fresh, its rage palpable. But Ayralina was ready.

She didn't dodge.

She attacked.

Summoning every ounce of her phoenix power, she ignited the water around her in bursts of searing light and heat. The icy lake hissed and boiled where her flames touched, steam rising in clouds of fury. The kraken's tentacles lashed out, but she was faster, dodging, weaving, and striking with precision. Her fire burned brighter, hotter with each strike, fueled by her determination to finish what she'd started.

The battle raged, a deadly dance of fire and shadow beneath the ice. The kraken roared in pain as Ayralina's flames seared its flesh, its tentacles thrashing wildly. But she didn't stop. She couldn't stop.

With a final, furious cry, Ayralina channeled all her power into one devastating burst of phoenix fire. A spear of blazing energy shot from her hands, piercing through the kraken's remaining eye and deep into its core. The creature let out one last, deafening shriek before its massive body convulsed—and then went still.

The kraken was dead.

Ayralina floated in the water, her chest heaving, her body trembling from exhaustion. But she'd done it. She hadn't just survived.

She'd won.

Clutching the Ice Crystal Compass, her heart pounded—not with fear, but with triumph. The battle with the kraken had tested her strength, her resolve, and her very will to survive. But she had faced the beast, not once, but twice, and emerged victorious. The taste of that victory was more than just relief—it was a spark, igniting a fire of conviction deep within her soul.

She had come here broken, haunted by doubts, but now she felt something she hadn't felt in a long time—certainty. She was no longer just searching for the Ice Crystal Heart. She was claiming it.

With the kraken's monstrous form sinking into the abyss behind her, its lifeless body disappearing into the darkness, she tightened her grip on the compass. Its brilliant, pulsing glow had intensified, now shining like a beacon, guiding her forward. The path was clear, unobstructed by fear or hesitation.

Finally, with the guardian of the lake out of the way, she continued her descent, diving deeper into the icy blackness toward the heart of the lake. The cold was sharper here, biting into her skin despite her phoenix blood, but she welcomed it. Every pulse of the compass was like the steady beat of her own heart, driving her onward.

The light grew dimmer the deeper she went, swallowed by the crushing darkness of the abyss. But Ayralina's resolve burned brighter than any flame. Her victory over the kraken had shown her what she was capable of. She wasn't the fragile girl who had fled from King Tyrin's palace, drowning in self-doubt. She was a warrior—a force forged in fire, tempered by ice, and hardened by battle.

The compass began to vibrate faintly in her hand, its glow intensifying with every stroke as she neared her destination. Then, through the murky gloom, she saw it—a faint, radiant light shimmering at the bottom of the lake like a star fallen from the heavens.

The Ice Crystal Heart loomed before her, encased in a massive block of solid ice that radiated an intense cold, a cold so piercing it seemed to reach beyond the physical and grip her very soul. Frost formed on her lashes as each step closer left her more immobilized. Her limbs refused to obey her commands, her breaths grew shallow, and her vision blurred. Panic clawed at the edges of her mind.

Silvaris.

His name was a desperate cry in the storm of her mind, a lifeline flung into the abyss. She reached for him, clawing through darkness, through the crushing weight of distance and silence. His face surfaced—serene, untouched by time. Too still. Too far.

She could almost feel him. The ghost of his breath, the echo of his heartbeat against her ear. But it was a memory, fragile as spun glass, threatening to shatter under the weight of her fear.

Then—contact.

Warmth surged through her, wrapping around her like a shield against the cold pressing in from all sides. It wasn't physical but something deeper, woven into the very marrow of her being. His presence anchored her, steadying her when exhaustion gnawed at her bones and fear whispered, she was already too late.

She would not let go.

The love she bore for him burned through her, a wildfire against the creeping ice. It consumed doubt, devoured fear, and left only purpose. His name became her pulse, her breath, her vow.

Hold on, Silvaris.

I'm coming for you.

Somewhere in the haze of her thoughts, a voice cut through the storm—steady, familiar.

"I'm here. You're never alone."

Silvaris.

The words snapped her back to the present. She clenched her fists, forcing slow, deliberate breaths. The air burned with cold, but within, she summoned the fire of her phoenix soul.

She recalled King Tyrin's lessons on balance—harness strength, but do not let it consume you. And Queen Izzy's unshakable words: The hardest battles are won with will, not power.

Ayralina exhaled, steady now. "This is just a test," she whispered. "Not of strength, but of will."

Far away, in the enchanted realm where time drifted like mist and the air thrummed with forgotten magic, Silvaris's eyes suddenly flew open. For the first time in a century, the spell binding him had faltered, its ancient threads unraveling with a whisper of lost power. He sat up abruptly, gasping, his chest heaving as the sudden rush of awareness flooded his mind like a tidal wave breaking against a fragile shore.

Then the pain hit.

It was as if every nerve in his body had been set ablaze, sharp and unrelenting, racking him with waves of agony. His muscles seized, his bones felt like they were splintering from the inside out, and a scream tore from his throat—raw, primal, and echoing through the hollow chamber where he'd slept for a hundred years. The magic that had cocooned him in timeless slumber now rebelled against his awakening, clawing at his very essence as if reluctant to let him go.

Memories danced at the edges of his consciousness—fragmented, distant, just out of reach—blurring with the searing torment that gripped him. His heart pounded, not from fear, but from something deeper, something primal. He couldn't explain it, but a feeling—a desperate, urgent pull—had dragged him back from the depths of his enchanted sleep. It was more than instinct; it was as if the very fabric of his soul had been tugged by an invisible thread woven across time and space.

A face appeared in his mind, fleeting and blurred, yet it gripped his heart with an intensity that rivaled the pain coursing through him. Golden eyes shimmered like starlight, a voice he couldn't quite hear but felt like a forgotten melody echoing in the hollow chambers of his heart. Who was she? The question echoed, unanswered, but the ache in his chest told him she mattered more than anything he had ever known.

His legs moved before reason could catch up, trembling under the strain. The once-dormant magic within him stirred, stretching like a beast long caged, awakening with a hunger that crackled through his veins, intensifying the agony until he could barely stand. Sparks of light danced across his skin, tracing ancient runes hidden beneath the surface, glowing with newfound life as if the magic itself was being torn from its roots.

Without warning, his form shimmered, edges blurring as the raw surge of magic overtook him. Pain and power collided in a blinding flash, and in an instant, he vanished—leaving behind nothing but an empty bed and a faint crackle of energy.

Back in the icy chamber, Ayralina steadied herself, her breaths forming clouds in the freezing air. She reached deep within, drawing on every lesson, every moment of struggle that had brought her here. The frost no longer seemed insurmountable. It was a challenge, yes, but one she could face.

Her steps grew surer as she moved closer to the Ice Crystal. The cold bit at her, but she refused to falter. The fire within her blazed brighter, stronger, until the ice beneath her feet began to crack and steam. She extended her hand toward the glowing crystal, the light so intense it illuminated the chamber in radiant blue hues.

The moment Ayralina's fingers brushed the surface of the ice encasing the crystal, a surge of energy shot through her like a bolt of lightning. It wasn't just a spark—it was an explosion, raw and untamed, coursing through her veins with a force that nearly knocked her off her feet. The phoenix flame within her roared to life, clashing violently with the ancient magic of the Ice Crystal. Fire met frost, two opposing forces locked in a fierce battle, their energies crackling and swirling around her in a chaotic dance of light and shadow.

Then, as if drawn by an invisible force, the Fire Crystals she had carried with her floated into the air, their vibrant glow pulsing with urgency. They drifted toward the Ice Crystal, their warmth colliding with the icy barrier that had stood untouched for centuries. The two forces spiraled together, fire and ice weaving in and out of each other like twin serpents, neither yielding, neither dominating.

Ayralina cried out—not in pain, but from the sheer effort of holding herself together, of staying connected to both forces. It felt as though she stood at the heart of a storm, her body the fragile bridge between flame and frost. But she refused to let go. Her will was iron, forged in the fires of countless battles within herself.

Driven by the flickering warmth of the Fire Crystal, now emboldened and radiant, Ayralina waded deeper into the freezing water. It bit at her skin, numbing her to the bone, but she welcomed it. She needed to feel both extremes—the scorching heat of the phoenix and the biting cold of the crystal—to find the balance within. She knelt, her breath ragged, and placed both crystals before her, their light reflecting in the dark water like twin suns rising.

Closing her eyes, she reached deep within herself, further than she ever had before. She sought the connection she had long struggled to control—the wild, untamed phoenix flame that had always threatened to consume her. But now, instead of fighting it, she embraced it, pulling it close like an old friend. She reached beyond fear, beyond doubt, to the very core of who she was.

In that fragile, powerful moment, the two crystals resonated with each other, humming in perfect harmony. Their energies intertwined like threads of destiny woven into the same tapestry. The fire's heat began to melt the ice, steam rising and curling around her like ethereal ribbons, while the Ice Crystal's radiant cold tempered the raging flame within her. It was no longer a battle. It was a dance—one of unity.

Ayralina felt the merging energies flow through her, filling every corner of her being with a profound sense of balance and clarity. The wildfire of the phoenix no longer burned uncontrollably; it pulsed steadily, guided by the cool, steady hand of the Ice Crystal's magic. She wasn't just containing her power—she was becoming one with it.

The Ice Crystal's power surged through her, unlocking a hidden potential she had never known existed. Memories flashed before her eyes—scenes from her training, moments of fear, of failure, of triumph. She saw her doubts laid bare, but also her growth, her resilience, her courage. It was as if the crystal had peeled back the layers of her soul, showing her not just who she was, but who she was meant to be.

She was harmonizing with them. The fire was not her enemy. The ice was not her cage. They were both parts of her—two halves of a whole.

When she finally opened her eyes, the Ice Crystal hovered before her, glowing softly with a light that was no longer cold but serene, like moonlight reflecting on snow. She reached out, her hand steady, and as her fingers brushed its smooth surface, she felt a profound calm wash over her. The ice had tamed the fire, and the fire had melted the ice.

She was now their master—a true Sunflame Phoenix, reborn from both flame and frost, her heart blazing with purpose, her soul tempered by wisdom.

Chapter 30

THE BITTER WINDS OF the North howled like restless spirits, carrying the scent of blood and ash across the snow-covered plains. The demons had come—not in scattered hordes, but in a wave of darkness, their twisted forms surging like shadows against the blinding white of the tundra. At the heart of this frozen battleground stood King Tyrin of the North, a towering figure clad in frost-forged armor, his crimson cloak billowing like a banner against the pale sky.

Tyrin's armor bore the scars of countless battles, etched with ancient runes that pulsed faintly with blue light, a gift from the old gods of the North. In his hands, he gripped the Frostfang, an ancient greatsword forged from the heart of a fallen glacier imbued with his essence, its blade gleaming with an icy hue, sharp enough to cleave through both flesh and shadow. His piercing gray eyes reflected the storm within him—a king who had bled for his people, who now stood as their final bulwark against oblivion.

The battle raged fiercely. Demons with molten eyes and jagged claws clashed against Tyrin's forces, their shrieks mingling with the cries of the wounded. His army, a fierce coalition of northern clans, hardened warriors from the FrostForest, shieldmaidens of the Ice Reaches, and the stalwart Guardians of the Glacier Hold, fought with grim determination. The snow was soon stained with blood, both red and black, as steel met claw in a brutal symphony of war.

But then, grim news arrived.

A battered scout stumbled through the chaos, his armor scorched, bearing a hastily sealed scroll marked with the crest of the North Sea Barrier—the first line of defense against the demonic tide. Tyrin tore it open, his gauntleted hands steady despite the chaos around him. The message was brief, smudged with soot and blood:

"The barrier has been breached. Their army is on the way. We cannot hold them off any longer. There were too many. We will regroup and repair the damage. Expect us to reinforce you in a few days. Hold the line, King Tyrin. We must not fail."

Tyrin's jaw clenched. The fall of the barrier meant the demons would flood the northern territories unchecked. His allies—warrior fleets from the Iceborn Coast, berserkers of the Frostfang Tribes, and the Sea Watch archers—were scattered, forced to retreat and regroup. But King Tyrin did not falter.

"We hold here, or we lose everything," he growled, his voice cutting through the roar of battle like a blade. His warriors, though bloodied and weary, roared in response, their spirits reignited by their king's unyielding courage.

The demons surged again, sensing weakness, but Tyrin met them head-on. He was a storm incarnate—his greatsword cleaving through armor and bone, his roars shaking the hearts of even the bravest foes. His armor, once gleaming silver, was now streaked with crimson, yet he fought with the fury of the North itself, refusing to yield even an inch of ground.

Days blurred together under crimson skies. Tyrin's forces dwindled, their lines thinning like breath on cold glass. But still, they held. The promise of Ayralina's return was their anchor, a distant beacon in the blizzard of blood and despair.

Just when hope seemed to flicker, when the demons launched what should have been the final crushing blow, a new sound rose above the chaos—the piercing cry of war horns, unlike any from the North.

The relentless clash of steel against claw echoed through the frozen plains as King Tyrin and his warriors fought with every ounce of strength left in their battered bodies. The night was thick with the stench of blood and ash, the ground slick with crimson and black, marking the cost of their defiance. The demons surged like a tidal wave, their twisted forms seemingly endless, their roars deafening amidst the blizzard's howl.

But just as their strength teetered on the edge of collapse, a sound cleaved through the chaos—a horn, distant yet unwavering, its call sharp as a blade and carried on the icy wind like a harbinger of salvation. A moment later, another answered, then another, until the night itself seemed to tremble with the arrival of vengeance. The reinforcements from the North Sea had come.

Across the horizon, banners emblazoned with the sigil of the Crested Wave rose like a defiant tide against the darkness. Armored legions advanced in disciplined ranks—stalwart shield-bearers forming an unbreakable wall, savage axemen from the Frostfang Tribes wielding weapons that had cleaved through giants, and cavalry mounted on frost-coated war beasts whose breath came in clouds of steam, eyes glowing like embers in the night. At their head, astride a warhorse draped in midnight-blue barding, rode General Brynn Icebane, Tyrin's most trusted commander. Her silver armor shone like a beacon beneath the pale moonlight, her frost-edged blade raised high, reflecting the carnage below as she signaled the charge.

Flanking them, marching in eerie, unbroken precision, came the northern elves—tall, ethereal warriors with eyes like shards of frozen starlight. Their banners bore the emblem of an ice-forged sword and shield, a symbol of a pact older than kingdoms. At their vanguard strode a legend—a general whose name was whispered across battlefields, whose exploits could fill libraries. His long, pale hair streamed behind him like winter's breath, his blade already unsheathed, humming with the promise of death.

Tyrin felt the surge before he even turned. Power, raw and unrelenting, flooded his veins. His war cry erupted into the night, a sound like thunder splitting the heavens, a god of war calling his warriors to arms. A second later, the defenders answered, their battle cries rising in a symphony of wrath and vengeance. With renewed ferocity, they surged forward, no longer fighting to survive——but to annihilate.

The storm had come, and the enemy would drown in it.

Steel met shadow. Flesh met fang.

The demons, once an unstoppable tide, faltered under the relentless assault. Frostfang cleaved through the twisted forms of the enemy, Tyrin cutting a path through the chaos, his armor drenched in blood, his eyes burning with unyielding fire. The demons were driven back, step by bloody step, beyond their first line of defense. But Tyrin was not satisfied with merely holding the line—they pushed further, reclaiming ground that had been previously swallowed by the demons.

The night stretched on, but the momentum was theirs.

By dawn's fragile light, the battlefield had grown eerily silent. Only the moans of the wounded and the crackling of dying fires remained. The snow, once pristine and white, was now a patchwork of ash and blood-soaked earth, littered with the bodies of the fallen—both demon and man.

King Tyrin stood amidst the wreckage, his greatsword Frostfang buried deep in the frozen earth, its icy runes dimly glowing with the remnants of battle's fury. His chest heaved with labored breaths, his body marked with countless wounds—slashes across his armor, blood trickling from beneath dented plates, bruises darkening beneath his skin. Yet his spirit remained unbroken, his gaze fierce as ever.

He turned to his weary warriors, their faces smeared with blood and sweat, eyes heavy with exhaustion but burning with victory.

Tyrin's voice carried across the field, strong despite the toll of battle.

"Rest now, my warriors. We have won this battle, but do not be deceived—this war is far from over. They will regroup. They will come back stronger. But so will we."

A solemn silence followed, broken only by the crackle of embers and the quiet sobs of those mourning the fallen. But within that silence grew a spark—a fierce, defiant flame that no darkness could extinguish. And as long as King Tyrin of the North stood, sword in hand, heart unyielding, the North would never fall.

The fires burned low in the great war hall, their flickering light casting long shadows across the faces of battle-hardened men and women seated around the massive stone table. Maps were sprawled across its surface, marked with blood-red ink and hastily drawn battle lines. The air was thick with the scent of smoke, steel, and the faint copper tang of dried blood.

At the head of the table sat King Tyrin of the North, his once-pristine armor battered from battle, a fresh scar etched across his cheek—a silent testament to the ferocity of the last fight. His piercing gray eyes scanned the faces of his council: commanders, strategists, and intelligence officers, each wearing the weariness of endless war.

The room fell silent as Tyrin's voice, low and steady, broke the tension.

"The demons are not retreating. They're waiting." He leaned forward, his gauntleted fingers tapping the cold stone. "Waiting for their general to arrive. This battle was never meant to defeat us—it was meant to exhaust us."

A murmur spread through the room, but Tyrin raised a hand, silencing them.

"Word has reached us," he continued, his voice growing graver, "that their general is not some monstrous fiend. He's a man—a human."

Gasps echoed around the table. Commander Brynn Icebane leaned forward, disbelief etched on her face. "A human? Leading the demon horde?"

Tyrin nodded solemnly. "He was once a decorated general, a hero who never lost a battle. His name has been lost to time, but his story remains. He sacrificed his entire life for his kingdom, fought with honor, and brought wealth and victory to his people. But his greatness bred jealousy and fear in the heart of his king. One night, after returning home from a glorious campaign, instead of banners and cheers, he was met with betrayal. Labeled a traitor, his wife and unborn child were taken... executed without trial."

The room grew colder, the flames seeming to dim as Tyrin's words hung in the air.

"In his grief and rage, he vowed vengeance. He traded his soul for power—to avenge his family. Since joining the demons, he has forged an army like none we've seen, built on fear and intelligence. They use humans as spies, infiltrating our ranks, turning brother against brother." Tyrin's fist slammed against the table. "He is smart, cunning, and ruthless."

Silence settled over the council, broken only by the crackle of the hearth.

General Kael, the youngest of Tyrin's commanders, spoke hesitantly. "How many are with him?"

Tyrin's eyes darkened. "He marches with 100,000 strong. They are one week out. Once they arrive, the enemy's numbers will double."

A heavy silence followed, and then Commander Brynn spoke. "We must hold the line until Ayralina returns."

But not all shared her conviction.

Across the room, Lord Varyn, commander of the Eastern Vanguard, stood abruptly, his face twisted with fear and frustration. "This is madness! We've already lost too many. Our soldiers in the North are exhausted, fighting day and night without rest. The reinforcements we've received—30,000 strong—are brave, but another 20,000 are still days away. They won't arrive in time."

His words grew louder, more desperate. "The Northern Human Kingdom sent us 10,000 soldiers, but how can humans stand against demons? Even with them, we have barely half the enemy's numbers. How are we supposed to win this battle? How can we gamble everything waiting for Ayralina? She's only one person! What can she possibly do against an army of darkness?"

A heavy silence fell over the room. Some commanders lowered their eyes, their faces shadowed by doubt. And then, the blow came—not from the demons, but from within.

"I refuse to throw my men into certain death," Varyn declared. "I will not watch them die for a fool's hope. I'm taking my 10,000 soldiers back to the Eastern Kingdom. We will defend our own borders."

Tyrin's jaw was clenched, his knuckles white as he gripped the table's edge. But he did not rise, nor did he shout. His voice, when he finally spoke, was cold and steady as the ice-covered plains outside.

"Cowardice wears many masks, Lord Varyn. I hope you find comfort in yours."

Varyn's face reddened with shame, but he turned and left without another word, his soldiers marching with him the following dawn. The loss of 10,000 warriors was a blow—a fracture in the fragile hope that had held the army together.

When the hall was quiet again, Tyrin stood, his shadow cast long and dark across the war table.

"Let the fearful flee," he said, his voice carrying the weight of kings and legends. "We do not need those who doubt. We stand with those who believe."

His gaze swept the room, locking eyes with each commander.

"Have faith in Ayralina, my council. She is not just 'one person.' She carries within her the power of the True Phoenix. I have seen it with my own eyes, and it is extraordinary. As long as we hold the line—no matter the cost—she will succeed. She will emerge from the Ice Cave, and when she does, she will burn the darkness from this world."

A renewed sense of determination settled over the council. Doubts remained, but they were now buried beneath the weight of Tyrin's conviction. They would hold the line—not because the odds were in their favor, but because hope was stronger than fear.

And hope's name was Ayralina.

Chapter 31

BENEATH THE ICE-CHOKED CLIFFS of Frostmourne Keep, deep in the frozen wastelands of the North, a war council convened. The air was thick with tension, the only sounds the crackling of black-flamed torches and the restless murmurs of lesser demons shifting uneasily under the weight of their masters' presence.

At the head of the long stone table sat Arian, the Demon Lord of Dominion—once a human warlord, now something far more terrifying. His crimson eyes burned with cold calculation, his sharp features cast in shadow. His mere presence demanded obedience.

To his right, Damien, his most ruthless captain, stood with arms crossed. He bore the sting of recent failure—the loss of Mayan de la Ruins had humiliated him—but war offered a chance for redemption, and he intended to seize it.

Across from them, seated upon a throne of twisted bone, was High Priestess Valthera, the Nether Witch. Swathed in tattered crimson silks, she exuded an aura of ancient horror. Her skeletal hands rested on a staff of cursed obsidian, its dangling charms pulsing with dark magic. It was whispered that her very breath could wither a man's soul, and the violet fire in her hollow eyes spoke of eternal hunger.

Around them, demon warlords and monstrous champions loomed, eager for conquest. The North would fall, and they would see it done.

Arian leaned forward, gauntleted fingers drumming against the stone.

"The time has come to claim the North." His voice was smooth, yet unyielding. "The Ice Crystal Heart holds the key to this wasteland. Once it is in my grasp, the North will break beneath my rule, and the balance of power will shift in our favor."

A slow, cruel smile curled his lips.

"King Tyrin will kneel."

A low growl of approval rippled through the council.

Arian's gaze shifted to Damien. "You will lead the first assault. I want Tyrin alive."

Damien smirked, inclining his head. "I will bring you the Polar Bear King, my lord."

Arian nodded. "Good. Take the Legion of Ash—they are brutal, efficient. Strike hard and drive Tyrin's forces toward the Frozen Wastes of Vareth. That is where we will ensnare him."

Damien's smirk turned lethal. "He will not escape."

Arian's attention flicked toward Valthera. "High Priestess, I trust your magic will prevent... unexpected interference?"

The Nether Witch chuckled, a dry rasp like dead leaves whispering in a tomb.

"Ayralina's flames are a nuisance," she admitted. "But fire bends before the abyss. My shadow bindings will suppress her phoenix fire—she will not burn what no longer exists."

She traced runes in the air, violet energy twisting between her fingers.

"Deliver Tyrin and his warriors to me, and I will do the rest."

Arian's smile darkened. "Then it is settled. Damien, you strike first. Valthera, prepare your rituals. Once Tyrin is ensnared, I will lead the second wave and wipe out the remnants of his army."

The heavy iron doors slammed open. A demon guard stumbled in, breathless, falling to one knee.

Arian's gaze snapped to him, his voice a quiet threat.

"What is so urgent that you would risk your life interrupting my council?"

The guard did not flinch. "My lord, forgive my disrespect, but there is someone outside you must meet."

Arian's fingers tightened on the table's edge. "Oh?" His smile was slow, predatory. "Let us see if he is worth your life."

The guard lowered his head, unshaken. "I assure you, my lord, it is. As for my life—it is yours to take whenever you see fit."

Arian tilted his head, amused. "Then bring him in."

The guard rose and turned. Heavy footsteps echoed through the chamber. A tall, cloaked figure entered, the air around him thick with unearthly energy.

Lord Varyn.

Arian's smile widened, wicked and knowing. "Well done, soldier. It seems your life is spared—for today." His crimson gaze flicked to Varyn. "Stay. Enjoy the show."

A hush fell over the war council. The room darkened, the weight of their collective malice pressing against the very walls.

The North would fall. Arian rose, his voice cold and final.

"We prepare for war."

Chapter 32

ANOTHER DAY HAD PASSED since Ayralina claimed the Ice Crystal, though time felt meaningless beneath the surface of the frozen lake. Encased in a cocoon of shimmering ice at the lake's dark bottom, she floated in suspended stillness, her body seemingly untouched by the cold. The world above was distant, muffled, and irrelevant compared to the transformation taking place within her.

She could feel the Ice Crystal's power growing stronger, resonating deeply within her core, its pulse synchronizing with the steady rhythm of her heart. The Fire Crystal, once volatile and wild, hovered close, its warmth seeping through the layers of ice like a heartbeat beneath frozen skin. Together, the two crystals began to orbit around her—at first, lazily drifting like leaves caught in a gentle current, then with deliberate, purposeful motion, drawn by an invisible force that connected them beyond the boundaries of fire and ice.

Ayralina watched in awe from within her icy prison as the energies started to merge.

At first, the combined form resembled a crystal orb, shimmering with hues that shifted from icy blue to fiery red. The colors flickered, wrestling for dominance. But as the moments passed, they stopped fighting. The red and blue intertwined, swirling together in graceful arcs until they bled into a vibrant, glowing purple—the perfect fusion of opposing forces.

The transformation wasn't over.

The crystal began to stretch and elongate, growing taller, its glow intensifying with every inch. It reached six feet in length, a pillar of radiant energy that pulsed with her heartbeat. Then, as if responding to her unspoken will, it started to curve at both ends, spiraling inward until the tips met and fused into a perfect circle—an unbroken loop of endless potential, symbolizing the harmony she'd long sought within herself.

The circular crystal began to spin gently, slow at first, then faster, until it became a blur of light and energy. Streams of violet luminescence danced around her, casting prismatic reflections against the walls of her icy cocoon. With just a thought, Ayralina realized she could control it. She willed the form to shift, and it obeyed. Fire surged, molten and fierce, bathing her in warmth. Then, with another thought, it cooled, transforming seamlessly into ice, sharp and pure. Each transition was smoother than the last, the energy responding with fluid with grace.

The duality of warmth and cold radiated around her, enveloping her in opposing sensations that no longer felt like contradictions. They were part of the same whole—her wholeness. She finally understood what Queen Izzy had meant when she'd said to trust her powers—to stop fighting, to let them flow freely, to guide her, to unlock strength greater than she could ever wield through force alone.

As the spinning energy wrapped around her like a protective shield, Ayralina closed her eyes, surrendering to the merging forces. She felt them settle within her, not as two separate entities, but as one unified essence. The crystal's resonance filled her soul with profound calm, an unshakable confidence blooming in her chest like a second heartbeat.

She was no longer just the girl who had struggled to control the flames or the one lost in the cold. She was both fire and ice, chaos and calm, destruction and creation.

A true Sunflame Phoenix, reborn at the bottom of the world, cocooned in ice but burning brighter than ever before.

When she opened her eyes, Ayralina gasped. She wasn't alone. Standing before her were Izzy and Daxton, their forms radiant and ethereal. Tears welled up in her eyes. "Are you really here?" she choked out, "Or have I finally lost it, did i die too?"

Izzy smiled warmly, stepping closer. "Yes, Ayralina, we're really here—but only in spirit form. We've been trapped within the Phoenix's energy ever since that last battle. Now that your powers have fully merged, you've released us."

Daxton placed his paws on Ayralina's shoulder, his voice steady and kind. "You've done it, Ayralina. You've accomplished what we always knew you could. We're so proud of you."

Ayralina dropped to her knees, tears streaming down her face. "I'm so sorry," she cried. "I'm sorry I couldn't save you. I'm sorry I couldn't control my powers back then and you had to sacrifice your life for mine...."

Izzy knelt beside her, gently lifting her chin. "Don't let this burden you, Ayralina. Daxton and I were already dying. Giving you our spirits was the only way we could ensure our legacy lived on. It was our choice, not your failure. By merging with the Phoenix, you've given us a chance to help you one last time."

Daxton nodded. "And you must carry our legacy forward, Ayralina. Ellie and Saber will be ready to inherit this power when the time comes. Until then, trust in yourself. You've already proven that you are worthy."

They spoke for a while longer, their voices filled with love and reassurance. Before fading, Izzy and Daxton shared their final teachings—how to pass on their powers when the time came, and how to wield her newfound strength with balance. As their forms dissolved into golden light, Izzy smiled one last time. "We'll always be with you, Ayralina. Now, go and protect the world."

Ayralina's heart ached as Izzy and Daxton vanished, but there was no time to dwell on her grief. A distant commotion reached her ears—shouts and the clash of metal. She closed her eyes, instinctively activating her newfound powers. A third eye in the shape of a flame opened on her forehead, projecting outward. Through this eye, she saw the battle unfolding beyond the cave.

The final battle had begun.

A horde of one hundred thousand strong demons surged across the frozen plains, their monstrous forms twisting and writhing as they thundered toward the northern stronghold. The ground trembled beneath their charge, an unholy roar filling the air as the sky darkened with the presence of their foul magic.

At the front lines stood King Tyrin, his armor gleaming despite the frost clinging to its edges. He gripped his sword tightly, his warriors gathered around him, shields locked, weapons raised. They were outnumbered, but not outmatched—not while he still drew breath. With a rallying cry, he led the charge, meeting the demon tide head-on, his blade carving through the darkness.

A thousand leagues away, another wave of one hundred thousand demons marched relentlessly forward, their glowing eyes burning like embers in the cold. They advanced with terrifying precision, an unstoppable force set on crushing the northern defenders.

The final war for the North had begun.

The flames within Ayralina's heart roared to life, an uncontainable surge of power and determination that burned brighter than ever before. Rising from the cold stone floor at the bottom of the lake in the ancient Ice Cave, she called forth the full force of her Phoenix essence. The flames that erupted around her were no longer the familiar hues of red and orange—they had evolved, transformed into a dazzling fusion of blue, purple, red, and white, each color representing the trials she had endured and the strength she had gained.

With a breathtaking burst of fire and ice, Ayralina propelled herself from the cave, streaking into the sky like a blazing comet. The very earth trembled beneath her ascent, shards of ice and rock scattering in her wake as if the mountain bowed to her newfound power.

Below her, the battlefield sprawled in a harrowing tapestry of chaos and bloodshed. Warriors clashed across the frozen plains, their cries of determination and despair echoing through the icy expanse. Broken banners fluttered in the frigid wind, stained with the blood of the brave and the fallen.

Then she finally appeared.

Ayralina's fiery ascent painted the heavens, a radiant beacon against the bleakness, her presence igniting hope where only fear had remained. Majestic phoenix wings, ablaze with her elemental fire, unfurled behind her—a glorious 24-foot wingspan that shimmered like woven strands of starlight and flame. The flames danced like living beings, trailing ribbons of light across the sky.

The battlefield grew still for a fleeting heartbeat as soldiers on both sides gazed skyward. The enemy's jeers faltered, and then a roar erupted—not from the demons, but from the hearts of the weary and battered warriors below.

"Ayralina is here!"

"The Phoenix has returned!"

"We are saved!"

Their cries surged through the ranks like a wildfire, drowning out the drumbeats of war. Ayralina's eyes blazed with golden flames, reflecting both fury and hope. She raised her hands, and from her heart burst the Flame of the Undying Phoenix—a radiant pulse of pure energy that cascaded down like a celestial wave.

Where the light touched, wounds knitted closed in an instant, torn flesh mended, and broken bones straightened with divine precision. Warriors who had collapsed moments before now rose to their feet, eyes wide with renewed strength. The fire did not burn them; instead, it empowered them. It was as though Ayralina had created an army of undying phoenixes, their spirits reborn in the heat of her flames.

Their war cries grew louder, fiercer, now echoing with a confidence that shook even the demon ranks. The tide of battle began to shift.

Hovering above the battlefield, Ayralina's gaze found King Tyrin, standing bloodied amid the wreckage. She smiled, the corners of her mouth tugging upward with both relief and mischief.

"Sorry I'm late," she called out, her voice carrying effortlessly over the roar of battle.

Tyrin grinned back, his Greatsword resting on his shoulder.

"Better late than never. Glad you could finally join the party."

With a nod of shared understanding, their bond sealed in both struggle and trust, Ayralina's expression hardened as she turned her gaze toward the heart of the enemy horde.

"Ellie! Saber!" Ayralina's voice rang out like a divine command, cutting through the clamor of war. "Come to me now!"

With a powerful sweep of her arm, she tore open a shimmering gateway, a rift through space and time itself. The portal pulsed with iridescent light, swirling like liquid stars.

From the radiant doorway emerged two majestic beings—Ellie and Saber, White Heavenly Flame Tigers, their forms as awe-inspiring as they were terrifying.

Ellie, the first to step through, was a vision of ethereal grace. Her sleek, muscular form shimmered with a pristine white coat, streaked with veins of glowing, celestial flame. Her sapphire eyes burned with wisdom beyond the ages, and with every graceful stride, the ground beneath her paws turned to glass, scorched by the divine heat she carried. The flames that trailed from her body danced like silk in the wind, elegant yet deadly.

Behind her came Saber, a colossal beast of unmatched ferocity. His frame was larger, his muscles rippling beneath fur as white as freshly fallen snow, streaked with jagged patterns of golden flame. His massive fangs gleamed like ivory swords, and his roar was a thunderclap that shook the heavens. Where Ellie was elegant, Saber was raw power—a force of nature wrapped in flame and fury.

The two tigers padded to Ayralina's side, their presence alone causing the demon horde to recoil in fear. Their unspoken bond with Ayralina radiated through the battlefield like an invisible thread, reinforcing the strength of their unity.

Ayralina reached out, placing one hand on Ellie's brow and the other on Saber's massive head. Her flames surged, growing so bright that the very sky seemed to pulse with their radiance. Through her phoenix essence, she channeled their inheritance entrusted to her, pouring it into the two tigers. As the sacred energy flowed into them, their bodies ignited with a newfound brilliance.

Ellie's white flames deepened, now laced with streaks of iridescent violet and azure, her eyes glowing like twin stars. She roared—a sound both pure and melodic, a song of battle and beauty intertwined. Her body shimmered with renewed grace, her speed doubling, her flames burning so intensely they left trails of stardust in her wake.

Saber's transformation was even more dramatic. His golden streaks blazed with hues of crimson and sapphire, his muscles swelling with raw power. His roar became a force of destruction—a shockwave that rippled across the battlefield, sending demons sprawling as if the air rejected their presence. His claws glowed like molten metal, searing through even the thickest of demonic armor with ease.

As the last remnants of their inheritance settled within them, Ellie and Saber felt something beyond just power—a warmth, a presence. It was their parents' joy, a deep and unshakable pride that resonated within their very souls. For the first time in their lives, they truly understood the legacy they carried. And as they turned their blazing eyes toward the battlefield, they knew they would make their parents—Izzy and Daxton proud.

Ayralina's eyes, ablaze with the undying flame, met theirs. "You are no longer just my companions. You are my wrath, my shield, my vengeance."

Not far from them, Simon, the steadfast strategist, rallied his elite unit with sharp efficiency. His voice carried authority born from countless battles.

"At your service, Ayralina," he declared, his tone steady and resolute, even amidst the chaos. His team assembled behind him; their loyalty etched into every line of their battle-worn faces.

Standing next to him are Andre, Andrew and Alex, long time no see, Ayralina they said excitedly.,

But there was no time to bask in reunions.

She nodded "Let's do this,", her voice filled with pride and vengeance.

Without hesitation, the group descended into the fray like falling stars, their arrival an explosion of light and purpose. Ayralina landed at the epicenter of the battlefield, her fiery wings folding behind her as she raised her hands to the sky. Fire and ice twisted together, spiraling into a breathtaking storm—a dance of creation and destruction. With a mighty cry, she unleashed it, the elemental storm tearing through the enemy lines with devastating force. The ground cracked beneath the sheer magnitude of her power, and demons were incinerated in bursts of blinding light.

Ellie moved like a phantom, her fluid, grace making her an untouchable wraith of heavenly fire. Her claws left trails of white-hot flame, slicing through demonic armor as though it were paper. She darted between enemy ranks, her movements a blur of elegance and precision, leaving nothing but ash and scorched earth in her wake.

Saber was the hammer to Ellie's blade. Where she danced, he crushed. His roars shook the ground, his massive form plowing through enemy lines like an avalanche of flame and fury. Every swipe of his claws sent demons flying, their bodies consumed by golden-white fire that devoured even their shadows.

Meanwhile, Simon with Andre and his elite unit fought with united brilliance, weaving through the battlefield with perfect coordination. Their strategies complemented the raw power of Ayralina and her celestial companions, a seamless blend of human ingenuity and divine might.

Together, they were more than warriors. They were legends in the making.

A beacon of defiance against the darkness.

And with Ayralina at the center, the Phoenix reborn, flanked by the White Heavenly Flame Tigers, the tide of war had truly begun to turn.

Chapter 33

THROUGH THE CHAOS OF battle, amidst the clash of steel and the guttural roars of demons, King Tyrin's voice cut through like a blade.

"Ayralina!" he bellowed, his greatsword dripping with black ichor, his warriors encircled by a relentless swarm of snarling demons. His forces fought valiantly, but exhaustion clung to them like a shadow, their numbers dwindling with every heartbeat.

As Ayralina soared above the battlefield, her radiant phoenix wings ablaze with hues of blue, purple, red, and white, her arrival ignited a surge of hope among her allies. But it did something else too—It enraged the demons.

The moment the enemy's dark commanders saw her descending like a falling star, their strategy shifted. The demonic horde doubled their effort to capture King Tyrin. They knew his fall would break the spirit of the North.

Demonic war horns blared across the frozen plains, their haunting echoes signaling death. From hidden trenches and shadowed crevices, fresh waves of demons surged forth. But they were not alone.

Jumping out from behind a jagged cliff, Lord Varyn led his troops—ten thousand strong—into the fray, their armor glinting beneath the cold, pale sun. Tyrin's heart clenched as he met the eyes of the man who had once been his ally, the friend who had abandoned him in his darkest hour. Now, that same friend stood against him, sword raised high, betrayal written across his face like a curse.

It was an ambush.

Tyrin and his warriors, already fatigued, suddenly found themselves completely surrounded. The demons struck first, monstrous beasts with jagged armor and molten eyes crashing into their defenses. Dark sorcerers emerged from the ranks, casting spells that tore through shields and sent warriors sprawling.

Then came Varyn with his army of 10,000 strong.

Human steel met with demon fangs in a blood-soaked melee, but Tyrin's forces had no chance to regroup. Varyn's knights cut through their flanks like a scythe through wheat, their disciplined strikes exploiting every gap in the defense.

Blades clashed. Screams filled the air. Blood splattered across the ice like crimson paint.

Tyrin fought like a force of nature, his greatsword Frostfang cleaving through demon after demon, soldier after soldier. His breaths came in ragged gasps, his muscles burning with exhaustion. He had fought beside Varyn in countless battles—he had never imagined he'd one day have to fight against him.

"Varyn, you coward!" Tyrin bellowed, his voice raw with rage. "Is this how you repay your King?"

Varyn's eyes were cold, devoid of regret. "I serve a new King now."

A monstrous demon, twice the size of any warrior, slammed into Tyrin with the force of a battering ram, knocking him to his knees. His vision blurred. His men were falling one by one. Their formation was crumbling.

"Ayralina!" he roared again, his voice filled with fury and desperation.

Above the battlefield, Ayralina's blazing eyes snapped to his position. Her heart seized at the sight of Tyrin's army being crushed beneath the demonic tide, of Lord Varyn leading the slaughter. She wasted no time.

With a fierce cry, she thrust her arms forward, summoning the full force of her Phoenix essence. Flames and shards of ice spiraled around her, a storm within her soul. A ring of fire erupted from her hands, spinning like a blazing vortex, and hurled it toward Tyrin's position with explosive force.

The flames struck the ground with a thunderous impact, encircling Tyrin and his warriors in a blazing barrier. The inferno towered above them, a living wall of flame that pulsed with Ayralina's heartbeat. The heat was intense but did not harm the warriors within—Ayralina's magic recognized her allies, shielding them even as it prepared to unleash devastation upon their foes.

For a heartbeat, the battlefield paused.

Both friend and foe turned their eyes skyward, captivated by the radiant figure descending like a comet. Ayralina's wings stretched wide, casting an otherworldly glow across the frozen plains. Flanking her were the White Heavenly Flame Tigers, Ellie and Saber, their celestial forms shimmering with divine light, flames licking at their fur as their piercing eyes locked onto the enemy.

But the demons had been prepared.

From the heart of the enemy ranks emerged Damien—a towering specter clad in black iron, his crimson eyes burning with fury. His greatsword, Bloodoath, pulsed with dark fire, its jagged edges licking the air with tendrils of malevolent energy.

A deathly silence settled over the battlefield.

"Tyrin," Damien growled, his voice like grinding stone. "Your time has come, when I am done with you, you will bow before me and beg for mercy."

Tyrin slowly pushed himself to his feet, breathing hard, but his grip on Frostfang never wavered. His piercing ice-blue gaze locked onto Damien's, his stance shifting to one of unyielding defiance.

"I yield to no traitor who gives up his humanity for corruption."

And with a thunderous roar, he charged.

The two warriors collided like storms, their blades meeting in a deafening clash that sent shockwaves rippling through the battlefield.

Bloodoath came down in a vicious arc, but Frostfang met it mid-swing, their impact shaking the ground beneath them.

Damien fought with ruthless aggression; his strikes were merciless and deliberate, and his strength was monstrous. His blade tore through the air in relentless sweeps, each blow meant to shatter Tyrin's defense and break him apart piece by piece.

But Tyrin did not yield.

He met every strike with unyielding force, countering it with the raw power of the North itself. His movements were fluid and calculated, and for every savage blow Damien delivered, Tyrin responded with crushing forces.

The battle raged in a whirlwind of steel and fury.

Damien feinted left, then struck right, but Tyrin was faster, dodging by a hair's breadth and slamming his gauntleted fist into Damien's ribs. The impact sent the warlord skidding backward, black blood dripping from his lips.

Damien snarled. "You're strong, Tyrin. But not strong enough."

He lunged forward, twisting mid-air as he brought Bloodoath down in a deadly arc.

Tyrin blocked—barely. The force drove him to one knee, but before Damien could capitalize, Tyrin surged upward, ramming his shoulder into Damien's chest.

The warlord stumbled, that moment of weakness cost him.

Tyrin moved like an avalanche. His greatsword swung in a mighty arc, cleaving through Damien's armor and slicing deep into his side.

Damien's eyes widened. He staggered, blood spilling onto the snow. His grip on Bloodoath faltered.

Tyrin towered over him, breathing hard, his own wounds bleeding, but his stance unshaken.

"You think war is about strength alone?" Tyrin's voice was like the rumbling of distant thunder. "You fight for power, Damien. I fight for my people. That is why you will fall."

With one final, merciless swing, Frostfang cleaved through Damien's neck.

The warlord's head hit the snow with a dull thud.

For a heartbeat, the battlefield fell silent.

Then, the Northern warriors roared in triumph.

The Legion of Ash faltered; their morale shattered as they watched their commander's lifeless body crumble.

The battlefield was drenched in blood, bodies strewn across the frozen plains like discarded dolls. The echoes of battle had begun to fade, replaced by the distant wails of the dying and the crackling embers of Ayralina's flames still licking at the remains of the fallen demons.

Tyrin stood amidst the carnage, his chest heaving, his greatsword heavy in his grip. His armor was battered, streaked with crimson, his muscles screaming for rest—but his battle was not yet over.

Out of the periphery of his vision, he saw a figure moving—slipping away through the chaos.

Varyn.

The traitor was fleeing, his once-pristine armor dulled with grime, his steps hurried and desperate. Tyrin's rage reignited, burning hotter than the flames that still smoldered around him.

Exhausted but driven by fury, he surged forward.

Varyn barely had time to react before Tyrin was upon him, slamming him to the ground with a force that sent his sword skittering across the ice. The former lord rolled onto his back, eyes wide with terror as Tyrin planted a boot on his chest, pinning him down.

"Please, Tyrin," Varyn gasped, struggling against the weight of the king's fury. "I... I had no choice. It was either this or death."

Tyrin's expression remained cold, his grip tightening on his blade. "And what of my men, Varyn? The ones you led to their slaughter? Did they have a choice?"

Varyn's breath hitched. "I—" He swallowed, his lips trembling. "I was afraid."

"Then let me put your fears to rest," Tyrin said, his voice devoid of mercy. "There is a price for betrayal, Varyn. I hope you'll be smarter in your next life."

Varyn's eyes widened in horror as Tyrin raised his greatsword high.

"No, please—!"

The blade came down in a single, clean stroke.

Varyn's head rolled across the ice, his expression frozen in terror. His body slumped lifelessly beneath Tyrin's boot.

Tyrin exhaled, his breath a ragged gust in the cold air. He wiped his blade clean on Varyn's cloak and turned away without another glance. There was no satisfaction in vengeance—only necessity.

Footsteps crunched over the frozen ground behind him. Ayralina approached, her presence a warmth against the cold that clung to his bones. Without a word, she placed a hand on his back, a surge of energy flowing from her fingertips into his battered body. His wounds knit together, the aches in his limbs dulled, and the exhaustion gripping his muscles eased.

Tyrin let out a slow breath and turned to her. "Thank you. That feels... better."

Ayralina smirked. "You'll need it." She turned her gaze toward the cliffside, where the wind howled through jagged rock. "It's not over yet." Her fiery eyes glinted with something between excitement and warning. "Are you ready for round two?"

Tyrin followed her gaze, his grip tightening on his sword. "Do I have a choice?"

She chuckled, a sound laced with both amusement and grim certainty. "Not really."

From the cliffs above, hidden in the veil of darkness, another pair of eyes watched.

Arian. The warlord stood motionless, his crimson gaze locked onto the corpse of his Captain Damien, and the pathetic fool Varyn, who had begged for his life. How sickening. Arian had no use for weak men who crumbled under pressure.

Ever so slowly, a smirk curled his lips.

The battlefield still trembled with the aftermath of Damien's fall, but there was no time for relief.

Tyrin barely had time to breathe before the air shifted. The temperature plummeted—not with the natural chill of the north, but something far worse.

A foul energy seeped through the battlefield, thick as poison, warping the very ground beneath them. Shadows slithered unnaturally, stretching where no light should allow them to.

Then, she appeared.

A figure drifted from the darkness, gliding over the ice as if untouched by the mortal world. Her obsidian robes, adorned with shimmering violet glyphs, billowed around her, though no wind touched them. Silver hair cascaded over her shoulders, unbound, moving as if it had a life of its own. But it was her eyes—endless voids swirling with abyssal power—that sent a chill through even the bravest of warriors.

High Priestess Valthera. The Nether Witch.

She clicked her tongue, amusement curling her lips as she surveyed the carnage. Her gaze landed on Varyn's severed head, then flicked back to Tyrin.

"You've made quite a mess, King Tyrin," she mused, her voice smooth as silk, yet dripping with malice. A smirk tugged at her lips. "I like it... Now, it's my turn to play."

Tyrin's grip tightened around his sword. Beside him, Ayralina stepped forward, flames flickering at her fingertips, her golden eyes locked on the witch.

"So be it," Tyrin muttered, setting his stance.

Valthera laughed, a sound that echoed across the battlefield like the cracking of bones. The air around her seemed to rot, the ground beneath her blackening as if life itself recoiled from her presence. The light dimmed, devoured by her power.

She stood tall, draped in tattered crimson silks that clung to her skeletal frame like funeral shrouds. In one bony hand, she clutched a staff of cursed obsidian, crowned with a pulsating blood-red crystal that oozed with dark energy.

Her violet-fire eyes locked onto Ayralina, a twisted smile curving her lips.

"Little Phoenix, come out and play with me," she taunted, her voice like dead leaves rustling in a forgotten graveyard. "You burn so brightly... but even the hottest flames flicker before they die."

Ayralina's fire flared in response, swirling hotter, brighter. She met Valthera's gaze without fear.

"Then let's see who will burn this day."

Ayralina's eyes blazed, her wings flaring as she stepped out on the battlefield with enough force to crack the ice beneath her feet. Ellie and Saber prowled beside her, their celestial flames burning hotter than ever.

"This one is mine," she said to them. "You guys can have the rest."

She met Valthera's gaze, unflinching.

"Then let's see which of us burns out first."

The Nether Witch struck first.

Dark tendrils lashed from her fingertips, writhing like serpents of the abyss, slamming into the ground where Ayralina had stood only moments before. The ice beneath them blackened, cracked, and then shattered into a void of endless darkness.

Ayralina moved like a streak of fire, flipping backward just in time as the abyssal tendrils erupted, seeking to drag her into the void.

Valthera laughed, the sound dry and hollow. "You cannot outrun the darkness, child. It is eternal."

Ayralina retaliated.

She thrust her hands forward, summoning a wave of pure phoenix fire—not just heat, but light. A torrent of blue, purple, and white flames surged toward the Nether Witch.

But Valthera did not move.

Instead, she raised her staff, and the flames died before they could reach her.

Ayralina's eyes widened. Impossible.

Valthera chuckled. "Fire bends before the abyss, little bird. Did you think I was not prepared for you?"

Then, with a flick of her wrist, she thrust her staff forward.

A shockwave of shadow magic erupted, slamming into Ayralina like a hurricane of darkness. The force sent her spiraling through the air, her wings struggling to keep her up. Seeing Ayralina in trouble, Ellie and Saber roared, lunging for Valthera, their divine fire trailing behind them in dazzling streaks.

But the Nether Witch merely smirked.

Valthera lifted her free hand and clenched her fist.

The air rippled.

Ellie and Saber froze mid-air, their flames snuffed out in an instant.

Ayralina's heart seized.

They weren't moving. They weren't breathing.

Black nether energy coiled around them like living chains, tightening with each passing second, draining them. Their celestial auras flickered, dimming, while Valthera's presence swelled, feeding off their strength.

They were trapped.

Valthera had bound them.

Ayralina's pulse pounded in her ears as she watched them struggle, their powerful forms weakening under the weight of the witch's sorcery. The tendrils shimmered with unnatural energy, pulsing in time with Valthera's breath.

The realization struck hard—the weaker the cubs became, the stronger the witch grew.

Valthera turned her gaze to Ayralina, her lips curling into a taunting smirk.

"You feel it, don't you?" she mused. "Their life slipping away, feeding me. Such precious creatures. I wonder how much longer they'll last."

Ayralina's fists clenched, heat surging beneath her skin. No.

With a cry of fury, she unleashed another wave of fire, pouring every ounce of her power into the attack. The battlefield roared with light and heat, divine flames tearing through the darkness.

Valthera's shadows hissed in protest, recoiling from the inferno. The witch's smirk faltered, her grip on the staff tightening.

The spell wavered.

Ayralina didn't hesitate.

She threw everything into the flames, driving them forward until they washed over Ellie and Saber. The nether tendrils cracked, then shattered under the force of her phoenix essence.

The inferno swept over Ellie and Saber, reigniting their celestial energy, breaking the shackles that bound them. Their eyes snapped open, now blazing with raw fury. With twin roars of unshackled wrath, they prepared to launch themselves at Valthera once more.

But Ayralina's voice cut through the chaos.

"Get out of here. Now!" she commanded, her tone like steel. "You are not her opponent. Do not interfere with my fight again."

Ellie hesitated, guilt flashing in her luminous gaze. Saber let out a frustrated snarl but obeyed, turning toward King Tyrin. Together, they leaped into the fray, leaving Ayralina to face the witch alone.

She wasted no time.

With a burst of speed, she launched herself forward, her wings unfurling in a fiery arc. The force of her charge sent embers spiraling into the air, the ground beneath her cracking from the sheer intensity of her power.

Her target—the staff.

Valthera's eyes widened. She wrenched back, shadows rising in desperation, but Ayralina was already there.

The flames around her surged, a living storm of heat and light, and her hands closed around the cursed weapon.

Valthera let out a snarl of pure rage.

But Ayralina only tightened her grip.

"Let's see how well you fight," she hissed, "without your crutch."

She grabbed the obsidian staff—and snapped it in half.

The effect was instantaneous.

A deafening wail erupted from the Nether Witch as her power unraveled. Her shadows vanished, the sky brightening as the abyss lost its hold. The ice beneath them ceased cracking. The battlefield was once again real.

Valthera stumbled back, her form flickering between corporeal and nothingness, her once-imposing presence now fading like smoke in the wind.

Ayralina hovered above her, flames burning in her hands, her eyes hard and merciless.

"You should never have come here."

With one final, searing blast of Phoenix fire, she engulfed Valthera completely.

The Nether Witch's scream echoed through the battlefield, "Arian, save me!" But it was already too late. Her screams, a sound that would haunt the ears of demons for centuries to come. Her form disintegrated, her very existence erased by the light.

The High Priestess of the Nether was no more.

The moment Valthera fell, the battlefield shifted. The demons hesitated, sensing the loss of their dark priestess. The Legion of Ash, already crippled by Damien's fall, now faltered completely.

King Tyrin, bloodied but unbowed, stepped forward, his voice booming across the frozen plains.

"The North stands tall! The demons will fall! SOLDIERS WITH ME, DRIVE THEM BACK!"

A new battle cry erupted from the warriors, their morale rekindled by the deaths of their greatest enemies. They surged forward, a wall of steel and fury.

Arian, stood unmoved, his red eyes cold and calculating. He had just witnessed the deaths of his two greatest subordinates, yet there was no anger on his face.

Only amusement. He knows they are now exhausted and has no other backups. They are now at his mercy.

Slowly, he turned, his black cloak billowing in the icy wind.

"Soldiers of the Dark Legion, Charge!"

A deep, guttural horn echoed through the valley, a sound like the death knell of gods.

The ground trembled. The sky darkened.

The final wave had arrived.

From beyond the horizon, legions of demons surged forth, their blackened banners fluttering like wings of carrion birds. The air around them pulsed with dark energy, and their footfalls shook the earth, a relentless tide of destruction led by the Demon Lord himself—Arian.

At the forefront, Arian rode atop a monstrous, abyssal beast, a creature formed from pure darkness, with glowing red eyes and jagged black armor fused into its flesh. He wielded a spear of obsidian, its edge shimmering with a sickly, malevolent light. His crimson eyes burned with cold calculation.

He raised his spear... and pointed at Ayralina.

The demon horde charged.

Ayralina barely had time to react. The northern warriors were exhausted, their bodies battered and broken from the previous waves of battle without rest. Even Tyrin, as powerful as he was, breathed heavily, his strength waning.

They wouldn't last.

She knew it. Arian knew it.

This was the killing blow.

But Ayralina wasn't done.

She closed her eyes.

She reached deeper than ever before, beyond fire, beyond ice, beyond even the power of the Phoenix itself. She dove into the wellspring of nature, into the energy that bound all life together—the ancient, untouched force that pulsed through every tree, every river, every gust of wind.

The ruby pendant around her neck ignited, with the very heartbeat of the earth itself.

She called.

And Mother Earth answered.

A shockwave of raw, untamed magic exploded from Ayralina, rushing across the battlefield like the first breath of a storm.

The ice cracked.

The mountains trembled.

From the frozen forests, towering ancient treants stirred from their slumber, their bark shifting as they rose to their full, towering heights. Their eyes, green as deep jade, glowed with newfound purpose.

The glacial river surge, water spirits and frost elementals came forth, their forms fluid and ever-shifting, their presence turning the battlefield into an ocean of moving ice.

From the buried ruins, stone guardians awakened, their massive bodies hewn from the bones of the North, their every step sending tremors across the tundra.

From the sky, the winds howled in answer to their Phoenix Warrior. The blizzard, once an unrelenting force of chaos, now bent to her will.

The North had come to fight.

A single snowflake drifted through the frozen air, landing gently on the foreheads of her allies. In an instant, warmth surged through their veins—not fire, but something deeper. The power of the land itself. The ice, the wind, the very breath of the North infused them, reigniting their will to stand, to fight, to win.

Ayralina's eyes snapped open.

Her body no longer blazed with fire. Instead, she pulsed with raw, untamed energy—nature's fury, ancient and unyielding. Her wings shimmered, no longer solid but translucent, woven from the light of the auroras above. The storm whirled around her in reverence.

When she spoke, her voice was not hers alone. It carried the weight of the earth, the whisper of the wind, the power of the sky.

"The North will not fall. Not today. Not ever."

For a heartbeat, the battlefield stood still.

Then, the world erupted.

The storm surged forward, a living force of ice and wind crashing into the darkness. Lightning crackled within the blizzard, striking down shadows where they stood. The frozen ground splintered, jagged spears of ice ripping upward to impale the soulless creatures that lurked in Valthera's wake.

Ayralina launched into the air, her form a streak of celestial fury.

But Arian moved first.

He threw his spear, the air screaming as it ripped through reality, aimed straight for Ayralina's heart.

But she did not flinch.

With a mere flick of her wrist, the wind shifted, and the spear slowed mid-air, caught in the swirling currents of the storm she had unleashed. With a crackling burst, lightning struck it from the sky, shattering the weapon before it could reach her.

Arian's eyes flickered with interest.

He leapt from his beast, landing with such force that the ice beneath him shattered, cracks racing outward like veins.

Ayralina met him mid-air.

Their first clash sent shockwaves through the battlefield, blasting demons and warriors alike off their feet.

Spear met flame. Shadow met light. Ice met abyss.

They fought across the battlefield, their battle tearing through the land, shaking the mountains, splitting glaciers.

Arian was not like Damien.

He was faster. Smarter. More deadly.

Where Damien had fought with brute force, Arian fought with mastery. His strikes flowed like water, his dark energy warping the space around them, making his movements impossible to predict.

But Ayralina had changed.

She was not just fire. Not just destruction.

She was the storm.

She was the land.

She was the North.

With a fierce cry, she unleashed her full power, summoning nature's fury.

The winds screamed.

The ice surged.

The earth cracked open, swallowing demons whole.

Arian braced himself, his dark magic swirling around him like a living void. He had planned for her fire. For her ice.

But he had not planned for the land itself to fight back.

With one final, all-consuming strike, Ayralina thrust her hands forward, sending a wave of fire, ice, lightning, and earth-shattering energy crashing into Arian.

The sky erupted.

The ground split.

And when the smoke cleared...

Arian was gone.

The battle had ended.

The northern warriors stood victorious, though bloodied and battered.

The demons had fallen, their forces shattered.

Ayralina descended slowly, her flames cooling, her wings folding as the world fell into silence.

Tyrin stood among his warriors, his massive frame weary but proud. He turned to Ayralina, shaking his head with a tired, crooked grin.

"You really can't just let us have a normal fight, can you?"

Ayralina laughed, breathless but triumphant. "Not when the entire world is watching."

Tyrin chuckled, but then his expression grew serious. He glanced toward the horizon—where Arian had vanished.

"Do you think it's over?" he asked.

Ayralina looked to the sky, to the winds that still carried whispers of power.

She felt it.

The war was not over.

Not yet.

But for today...

The North still stood.

And that was enough.

For now.

The underground fight ring was louder than ever, the air thick with the scent of sweat, blood, and desperation. The arena, hidden deep beneath the city, was a place of brutality—where only the strongest survived, and the weak were forgotten. The crowd roared, gamblers placed their bets, and fighters circled like predators, eager for blood.

And then, she walked in.

Ayralina.

The moment she stepped into the arena, a hush fell over the spectators. Many recognized her—the fallen warrior who had once fought here and lost, humiliated in front of the very crowd that now stared in disbelief. But tonight, she was different.

Her presence was commanding, her every step radiating confidence. Clad in form-fitting black battle gear, her golden eyes gleamed with purpose, and her flames flickered just beneath the surface of her skin, ready to be unleashed. The air around her crackled with raw energy.

The announcer hesitated before speaking. "Ladies and gentlemen... it seems we have a returning challenger." He smirked, his voice laced with amusement. "Ayralina has come back for redemption. But can she survive one hundred consecutive rounds?"

The crowd erupted in laughter and jeers. One hundred fights? Impossible. No one had ever lasted past fifty, let alone one hundred.

But Ayralina didn't care about their doubts.

She stepped into the center of the ring, raising her chin. "Bring them all at once" she said, her voice calm, unwavering. "One after another, is just too time consuming."

The first opponent lunged at her. She barely moved, sidestepping with effortless grace before delivering a brutal backhand that sent him flying into the wall. He crumpled, unconscious.

Then they all launch at her at the same time.

She danced through them like a storm—each strike decisive, each movement a lethal masterpiece. Her flames erupted, searing flesh, her kicks shattered bones, her punches left craters in the floor. The crowd's jeers turned into stunned silence as fighter after fighter fell before her.

Half of them were already out and she wasn't even breathing hard.

Two third of them were now out and her opponents began to hesitate.

With the last ten of them still standing, desperation began to fill the air. The organizers tried to throw all their best fighters at her, some were even switched out half-way for a more vicious opponent, more seasoned warriors, even mages infused with dark energy. It didn't matter. Ayralina tore through them all.

By the time the only one remained, he had already proven himself as the reigning champion of all the previous fights—a monstrous brute of a man, his body thick with scarred muscle and unnatural, enhanced with demonic strength.

He sneered at her. "You should have stayed down, girl."

Ayralina tilted her head. "You should have run when you had the chance."

He charged at her like a raging beast.

Ayralina didn't move—until the last second. With inhuman speed, she twisted, her flames igniting around her arm. She struck his chest with an open palm, and a burst of phoenix fire exploded outward, consuming him entirely. He let out a guttural scream before the flames devoured him from the inside out. His body disintegrated into ashes.

Silence.

And then, chaos.

The crowd erupted, gamblers screamed, and the announcer stumbled back in horror.

Ayralina turned to the organizers, her gaze burning. "It is over," she declared.

Before they could react, she raised her hand, and her phoenix flames surged outward. But this fire didn't burn everything—it targeted only the demons lurking in the shadows, the corrupt creatures who had been using the ring to fuel their dark business. The ones who had caused her harm.

Screams echoed as the demons inside the organization were purged, their bodies turning to nothingness under the cleansing light of her flames. The remaining humans watched in horror, realizing too late what had truly been lurking in their midst.

The underground ring—the place that had once been her humiliation—was no more.

Ayralina turned, walking away without another word. Ellie and Saber waited for her at the entrance, their glowing eyes filled with pride.

Tonight, she had done it, and she had finally redeemed herself.

The northern fortress was alive with celebration. Fires blazed high into the night sky, casting a golden glow over the snow-covered battlefield where so many had fought and fallen. The air was thick with the scent of roasted meat and spiced ale, as warriors raised their cups in victory. Laughter and cheers echoed through the great halls, a stark contrast to the brutal war they had endured just hours before.

Inside the grand hall, long tables were filled with food and drink, and soldiers—both human and beast—mingled freely, their differences forgotten in the wake of their hard-earned triumph. Minstrels played lively tunes, and even the wounded found themselves smiling, the weight of battle finally lifting from their shoulders.

At the center of it all sat King Tyrin, his massive form relaxed for the first time in days. He raised a goblet high, his deep voice cutting through the noise.

"To the warriors of the North!" he roared. "And to our allies who stood beside us!"

The hall erupted in cheers as Ayralina stepped forward, her long coat still dusted with ash, her golden eyes reflecting the firelight.

She lifted her own cup. "To those who fought, those who fell, and to the land we protect!"

The warriors roared in agreement, pounding their fists against the tables. The tension of war had lifted, if only for this night.

As the celebration carried on, Ayralina stepped out onto the fortress balcony, letting the cool northern air wash over her. The battlefield below was quiet now, covered in fresh snow, as if nature sought to cleanse the scars of war.

Footsteps approached, and she turned to see King Tyrin standing beside her, his expression thoughtful. He had traded his heavy battle armor for a thick fur-lined cloak, though the weight of responsibility still rested on his broad shoulders.

"You fought well today," Tyrin said, his voice gruff yet warm.

Ayralina gave a small smile. "I only did what had to be done. But I couldn't have done it without your men—or your support." She turned to face him fully. "Thank you, truly."

Tyrin let out a deep chuckle. "Don't thank me yet. There's still a war ahead of us. But if today proved anything, it's that the North is not so easily broken."

Ayralina nodded, her gaze returning to the battlefield. "You never hesitated to stand by me, even when others doubted. Why?"

The King was silent for a moment, then let out a sigh. "Because I made a promise. A long time ago."

Ayralina frowned. "A promise?"

Tyrin chuckled, a nostalgic look in his eyes. "Your father, the Phoenix King, and I were best friends when we were younger."

Ayralina's breath caught in her throat. "You knew my father?"

Tyrin nodded, his expression softening. "We grew up fighting side by side, pushing each other to become stronger. He was the most stubborn, reckless warrior I ever met—but he was also the most loyal. When we were just young fools dreaming of conquering the world, he saved my hide more times than I can count. So I made a vow—to always protect him and his families, no matter what."

Ayralina's heart clenched. Her father had rarely spoken about his past, and to hear that King Tyrin had been his closest friend—it shifted something deep within her. It made everything feel different, heavier, more personal.

"He'd be proud of you," Tyrin said, his voice steady yet warm. He turned to her, his sharp eyes softening. "I know I am."

The words shattered something inside her. A flood of emotion surged through her chest, and before she could stop herself, tears spilled down her face. Guilt clawed at her, suffocating, relentless. She didn't deserve praise. Not after what she had done.

"Ayralina?" Tyrin's voice was laced with concern. "What's wrong?"

She looked at him, her vision blurred with tears. For a moment, she couldn't speak, couldn't breathe. Then, with a shuddering sob, she finally let it out.

"I don't deserve your praise," she choked. "It was me—I killed Izzy and Daxton. They're my friends, your ally, and I killed them."

King Tyrin's expression shifted, shock flickering across his face before understanding settled in. His gaze darkened, with sorrow.

"Did that happen on your way here? When you were possessed by the demonic phoenix?"

Ayralina wiped at her tears with trembling hands. "Yes," she admitted. "And I need to tell them. I should have told them. But since it happened, one thing after another kept pulling me away, and now..." Her voice broke. "Now, I don't even know how to say it. I don't know how to face them."

Tyrin sighed, his expression solemn yet unwavering. "Some truths are hard to tell," he said. "But if you don't, it will haunt you. It will hang over your head, and worse—it will poison your friendships. Trust and loyalty are built on honesty, no matter how painful it is." He held her gaze. "I trust you'll do the right thing By them. Whether they forgive you or not... that's their decision. But they deserve to know the truth."

Ayralina swallowed hard, nodding slowly. She wasn't sure she had the strength, but she knew he was right.

For the first time in what felt like an eternity, she allowed herself to breathe. She sat with King Tyrin a little longer, speaking in hushed tones, grateful for the fatherly presence he provided.

And for the first time in a long while, she felt something beyond the weight of war.

She felt at home.

She smiled, turning to the King. "I will live up to that promise."

Tyrin grinned. "I'd expect nothing less from the daughter of a Phoenix King."

As the celebration carried on behind them, the two warriors stood side by side, knowing that while the war was far from over, they would face whatever came next—together.

Chapter 34

AYRALINA STREAKED ACROSS THE sky like a blazing comet, the dawn light painting her silhouette in fiery hues. She had been flying nonstop for nearly a day, driven by an unshakable restlessness that refused to let her stop. Ellie glided effortlessly beside her, matching her speed, while Saber trailed just slightly behind, his movements more measured but no less determined.

"Ayralina," Ellie called, her voice carrying easily over the rushing wind. "Why the rush? We just defeated the demons. You could take a moment to rest—you earned it."

Ayralina shook her head, her jaw tight. "I can't, Ellie. Ever since I came out of the ice cave, I've felt this... pull. At first, I thought it was just the urgency of battle, but even after the fight ended, it didn't stop. It's like an invisible thread is yanking me home." She exhaled sharply, her golden eyes flickering with unease. "I think it's the kids—or Silvaris. Something isn't right."

Ellie's expression darkened. "Do you think they're in danger?"

Ayralina hesitated. She had planned to come clean with Ellie and Saber, but the unease twisting in her gut left her too unsettled to explain everything now. She needed to get home first.

Her gaze remained locked on the horizon as she pushed forward. "If it's the kids, it just means they're hatching. It is about time. But Silvaris..." Her voice wavered for the first time. "If Silvaris is awakening—without the Ice Crystal to neutralize his poison—his life could be in grave danger."

Ellie and Saber exchanged a look, concern tightening their features.

No one said another word.

Ayralina just flew faster.

Saber, who had been quietly observing, finally broke his silence. His voice was steady, reassuring. "If that's the case, we'll deal with it. We've faced worse before, haven't we?"

Ayralina nodded, though her anxiety didn't abate. "We're almost there," she said as the familiar silhouette of her home came into view below. Her heart pounded as she descended swiftly, landing at the front door with Ellie and Saber close behind.

Ayralina burst through the door, her boots echoing on the wooden floors. She didn't pause to greet the house's familiar stillness; her instincts screamed for her to check the children first. She flew down the stairs, her breath catching in her throat as she rushed to the portal.

They were all safe, still snuggled in their flamed cocoon, still emitting a rhythmic, calm pulse.

"Thank the ancestors," Ayralina whispered, her heart slowing slightly. She turned to Ellie and Saber, who had followed silently. "The kids are fine."

Ayralina moved toward the next room, her anxiety mounting with every step. She pushed the door open—and froze. The bed was empty. The covers were thrown back, as if someone had left in a hurry. Silvaris was gone.

"No... no, no, no," Ayralina whispered, rushing into the room, her eyes scanning for any sign of him. His things untouched. But Silvaris himself was nowhere to be found.

Ellie stepped forward, her voice steady, concerned. "Ayralina, there's something else." She pointed to the far wall. Ayralina turned to see faint marks—marks she knew all too well. They radiated from a single point near the window as if something—or someone—had erupted with power.

"He's awakened," Ayralina murmured, dread filling her voice. She clenched her fists, her heart racing. "He's awakened, and without the Ice Crystal.. he ...he". She couldn't complete her sentence before she collapsed on the floor in tears

Saber growled low, his voice edged with urgency. "Ayralina, pull yourself together. We have to find him—now."

Somewhere out there, Silvaris was alone, battling the poison that coursed through him. Every passing moment pushed him closer to the brink of death. She didn't know how long she had before the poison fully activated and stole him away forever.

Ayralina turned to Ellie and Saber, her expression hardening with resolve. "Hurry we have to find him," she said, her tone firm and unwavering. "If we don't, there's no telling what will happen."

Ellie nodded without hesitation. "We're with you."

As they prepared to leave, Ayralina cast a lingering glance at the children's rooms. Her heart ached, torn between her duty as a mother and her desperate need to save Silvaris. She could only trust that the protections she had woven around them would hold strong in her absence. There was no time for second guessing—Silvaris needed her now.

Stepping into the night, the ruby necklace at her throat glowed faintly, pulsing as if in rhythm with her rising determination. It seemed to sense the storm ahead, its ancient energy stirring in anticipation.

With a final, lingering glance at her home, Ayralina unfurled her fiery wings and launched into the skies, her sharp eyes scanning for any trace of his path. The faint remnants of Silvaris's power shimmered in the air, leading her northward like a whisper on the wind. Ellie and Saber flew close beside her, their unwavering presence a source of strength.

Somewhere out there, Silvaris was struggling, fighting against the poison that threatened to consume him. The stars above flickered with an eerie uncertainty, their light dimmed by the heavy, foreboding air. Ayralina's heart clenched, but her resolve only hardened. This was no ordinary search—she could feel it in her very core. This was the beginning of something far greater and far more dangerous than she had ever faced.

Back in the kids' room, a cocoon quivered and began to pulse rapidly.

Review

Dear Reader,

You've reached the end of the first journey in the Legend of the Phoenix and the Dragon series, courageous reader, and I'm honored beyond words that you've ventured this far. If this tale has captured your imagination, brought magic into your heart, or filled you with wonder, would you please share your experience with an honest review on Amazon?

Scan the QR Code or type the URL into a browser and scroll down the left side of the site to find the review section:

https://mybook.to/Phoenix1p

It will help others find their way into this magical world.

Thank you from the depths of my heart—I'm forever grateful to have shared this adventure with you!

Winter H. Rayne

Epilogue

THE CHAMBER WAS SUFFOCATING in its silence—the weight of failure hanging heavy in the air. Torches of violet flame flickered along the stone walls, casting grotesque shadows across the rough cavern floor. The scent of sulfur and blood mixed with the faint tang of fear radiated from the kneeling warriors before him.

They had failed.

Arian stood at the center of the room, his towering form rigid, his hands curling into fists as he struggled to contain the rage thundering through his veins. His crimson eyes burned with barely restrained fury, twin embers of promised violence.

Damien was dead.

The Nether Witch, Valthera, had been erased from existence.

The Fire Orchid had slipped through their grasp.

The Ice Crystals were lost.

And worst of all—Ayralina still lived.

His jaw clenched so tightly that his fangs bit into the inside of his cheek, the taste of iron flooding his mouth. His chest rose and fell with slow, lethal control, but the storm inside him raged violently.

Before him, his warriors knelt, their heads bowed in abject shame, their bodies trembling under the weight of their failure.

Cowards. Weaklings. Disgraces.

They had made promises but they had delivered nothing but disgrace. Arian's voice, when it came, was a whisper of death—soft, but laced with venom enough to curdle blood.

"You assured me success."

No one dared move.

His voice dropped lower, the weight of it pressing upon them like a crushing vice.

"And yet... here you kneel. Empty-handed."

One of the demons, a captain, had the audacity to lift his head. His yellowed eyes flickered with desperation, his lips parting as he rasped, "General Arian, we—"

He didn't get to finish.

Arian moved like a phantom. One second he stood motionless. The next, his hand was around the demon's throat.

The warrior gasped, his claws scratching at Arian's unyielding grip, his feet kicking helplessly in the air as he was lifted off the ground like a ragdoll.

Arian tightened his grip.

The demon choked, his eyes bulging, his mouth forming silent pleas that would never be answered.

"Do not waste my time with excuses." Arian's voice was lethal, glacial, unforgiving. His nails dug into the warrior's throat, his strength casual, effortless.

"You failed. And failure demands consequence."

With a flick of his wrist, he hurled the demon across the chamber.

The warrior crashed against the stone wall with a sickening crack, his body crumpling to the ground in a boneless heap. The sound echoed through the cavern, followed only by the fearful silence of the others.

No one spoke. No one moved.

They knew better.

Arian turned away, exhaling through flared nostrils, the muscles in his arms still coiled with tension. He wanted to kill them all.

But that would serve nothing.

The mission had already cost them dearly.

King Tyrin remained free. Ayralina still stood. Their plans—meticulously crafted, painstakingly set in motion—were unraveling before his eyes.

He had wasted time.

And yet...

Something stirred in the back of his mind.

A memory.

A scent.

He could still feel the frozen winds biting against his skin, the way they howled like dying souls as he marched northward. He had sensed something in that bitter cold, something not of demon nor mortal.

Something ancient.

Something familiar.

Arian's lips curled.

Not in anger.

But in amusement.

The smirk that spread across his face was slow, dark, and knowing.

Perhaps the mission had not been a complete failure after all.

For in the desolate, frozen wilderness...

He had found Silvaris.

And Silvaris would change everything.

Lost in the Snow

Silvaris collapsed into a drift of snow, his body crumpling as if the very earth had pulled him down. The cold bit at his skin, sharp and unforgiving, but he barely registered it. The wind howled around him, whipping flecks of ice against his exposed flesh like tiny daggers.

He was dressed in nothing but a pair of thin blue silk pajamas, their fabric threadbare, offering no protection against the bitter cold. His bare feet burned against the frost, the skin already raw and reddened. Yet, he felt nothing. Not the pain. Not the chill. Not even the jagged shards of ice cutting into his palms as he struggled to push himself up.

His mind was a void.

A suffocating emptiness clawed at him, an overwhelming sense of displacement. Where am I? The thought formed, hollow and meaningless, echoing through his head like a whisper in the wind. He had no answer. No memory of how he had gotten here. No sense of who he was. Even his own name hovered just beyond reach, slipping through his fingers like water.

He clenched his eyes shut, desperation gripping him. He forced himself to remember—to grasp onto something, anything. But the darkness behind his eyelids only deepened, swallowing him whole.

His chest tightened. His pulse hammered. A gnawing fear coiled around his spine.

Why am I here?

The question tore through him, sharper than the cold. The snow blurred in his vision, the entire world tilting, unmoored from meaning. He clenched his fists, pressing them into the frozen ground, trying to anchor himself. But nothing came. No flicker of recognition. No fractured memory to cling to.

Nothing—

Except her.

Through the haze of confusion, a single image burned bright, vivid, and unshakable. A single thread woven through the tangled emptiness of his fractured mind.

A woman.

Her face was the only thing that felt real. It was etched into his consciousness with painful clarity—strawberry-blonde hair cascading in luminous waves, catching the light like molten gold. Her eyes—deep brown-black—held something more than mere warmth. There was power in them, quiet yet undeniable, like the pull of the ocean's tide.

She was small in stature, delicate in frame, but everything about her radiated strength. An unshakable force wrapped in grace.

And though Silvaris could remember nothing else—no past, no purpose, not even his own identity—he knew with every fiber of his being:

She was important.

An unbreakable bond tethered him to her, deeper than memory, deeper than thought. It was a connection that defied reason, an instinct carved into the marrow of his bones. He didn't know her name. He didn't know what she meant to him.

But he had to find her.

His heart pounded, each beat hammering the same undeniable truth into him:

I have to find her.

Shaking, disoriented, and barely holding onto consciousness, he forced himself onto his knees. The snow clung to his body, weighing him down, seeping into his clothes, his skin, his bones. But the cold no longer mattered. The fear no longer mattered.

Nothing mattered except her.

He would find her.

No matter what it took.

No matter how far he had to go.

And as the wind howled around him, unseen eyes watched from the darkness.

Arian's smirk deepened.

The prey had been found.

Acknowledgements

As I REFLECT ON this journey, it has been one of incredible growth. I never imagined I could become an author—what once felt like wishful thinking has now become my reality. I feel truly blessed to have embarked on this path.

From the bottom of my heart, thank you to everyone who has supported me. Without you, this miracle wouldn't have been possible, and I am deeply grateful.

The first person I want to acknowledge is my incredible partner, Todd. Without your encouragement, I wouldn't have had the courage to take the first step toward writing. So, Todd, this book exists because of you. Thank you for always believing in me—especially when I struggled to believe in myself. You are my partner in crime, my best friend, and an amazing father to our beautiful children.

Speaking of our kids, they are my greatest source of inspiration for writing these stories. Cruz, Morgan, Gemma, and Caleb—you are my pride, my joy, and my world. I may not say it enough, but you inspire me every day. You make every moment special, reminding me to live fully and love deeply. Through you, I've learned that nothing is more important than being present in this moment with the ones we love.

I also want to thank my wonderful sister, Nguyet, and my incredible sisters-in-law, Kim and Tammie. You have been a guiding light in my life, especially during my darkest moments. Your strength and kindness shine so brightly, inspiring me to step forward and bask in your warmth.

Kim, I want to thank you especially for always putting up with my endless requests and for being so willing to help and give unconditionally. You are truly amazing.

To my mom—though she may not fully understand these words, I still want her to know that she is an angel sent to me from above. She is an incredible woman with a story of her own, yet through it all, she has always given all of herself selflessly whenever there was a need.

To my second mom, Grandma Rosa. You have always been so supportive and encouraging, offering a helping hand whenever it's needed. Your kindness and generosity know no bounds—you give so selflessly, expecting nothing in return.

Thank you for everything you have done. You are truly an angel.

And of course I can't forget to mention my favorite niece Aileen, and my two favorite nephew Nicholas and Hunter. You guys always bring so much joy to my life. Keep being awesome!

To my coach, Cynthia—I can't say this enough: you are my rock. Thank you for your unwavering positivity and support, for teaching me, and for putting up with me. You always know exactly what to say to lift me up. Your gentle yet firm guidance has been invaluable on this soul-searching journey, and without you, I wouldn't have been able to bring this out of myself.

To my wonderful friends, Cha and Delveen—thank you for believing in me.

Cha, thank you for lighting this path for me. I still remember the day we sat down and talked about how we were both going to become famous authors. After five incredible years, I finally made it! I may not have many friends, but I like to believe that the ones I do have are the best of the best, and there's no one else I'd rather call my friends than the two of you.

I hope you both continue on your journey to becoming authors as well, you have my unwavering support and love—I know you can do it!

To my special friend Kellea, not much needs to be said between us, just you can't get rid of me so **EASILY**, in this life and I am so blessed to have you, thank you for keeping me so grounded, let's keep causing havoc together. (I made this a run-on sentence just for you!)

To my clients—your support and encouragement have meant the world to me. Thank you for reading this book, for believing in me, and for being part of this journey. Your enthusiasm has touched and inspired me in ways you may never know. Your kindness and appreciation push me to grow and strive to be a better person every day.

Special Thanks to:

Gerry W, Debbie S, Christine M, Janet the bus driver, Michelle R, Jeanine, Kelly, Amanda R., Danezra., Candice F and her beautiful mom Jen and nana Gillian.

Manufactured by Amazon.ca
Bolton, ON

45259493R00192